SIN CITY

HAROLD ROBINS

has also written

NEVER LOVE A STRANGER
THE DREAM MERCHANTS
A STONE FOR DANNY FISHER
NEVER LEAVE ME
THE CARPETBAGGERS
79 PARK AVENUE
NEVER ENOUGH

SIN CITY

Harold Robbins

ROBERT HALE · LONDON

© Jann Robbins 2002
First published in Great Britain 2003

ISBN 0 7090 7343 7

Robert Hale Limited
Clerkenwell House
Clerkenwell Green
London EC1R 0HT

2 4 6 8 10 9 7 5 3

Printed in Great Britain by
St Edmundsbury Press Limited, Bury St Edmunds, Suffolk.
Bound by Woolnough Bookbinding Limited.

*Harold Robbins left behind a rich heritage of novel ideas
and works in progress when he passed away in 1997.
Harold Robbins's estate and his editor worked with a
carefully selected writer to organize and complete Harold
Robbins's ideas to create this novel, inspired by his story-
telling brilliance, in a manner faithful to the Robbins style.*

For

Eugene H. Winick

*Also with gratitude to Tom Doherty,
Linda Quinton, Robert Gleason, Brian Callaghan,
and the other fine professionals at Forge.*

And to Junius Podrug and Jann Robbins.

Part 1

★ ★ ★ ★ ★

ZACK RIORDAN

1

IN THE BEGINNING, GOD SAID,
"LET THERE BE LIGHT."

The first time I saw the Strip I thought God lived there. I was twelve years old in 1966, when Betty and me came down on a Greyhound from northern Nevada. We'd left Mina that morning, a little alkali mudflat town with Highway 95 for a main street—the kind of dry-rotted little desert town that even rattlesnakes shied away from. When we got off the bus in Las Vegas, we put our bags in a dime locker and walked from the bus depot to the Strip. I hadn't had anything to eat except a Baby Ruth candy bar since Tonopah and my stomach was growling. Along the way Betty had dropped the three-day's pay she collected before we left Mina, plunking it into slots, a quarter at a time, whenever the bus made a stop. She only had a dollar left when we arrived in Vegas but she was sure she could get a job waitressing right away. Just walk in and go to work—Vegas was that kind of town. By the end of her shift, she'd have enough tips and maybe even an advance on her wages to get us a room and something to eat.

While Betty went into a restaurant to ask for work, I wandered up the Strip alone. It sounds corny, but I got stardust in my eyes the first time I saw the boulevard. It was Times Square, the Arabian Nights, a hundred carnivals, all thrown together and lit up at the same time—the Dunes, Aladdin, Sahara, Caesar's Palace. The lights struck me first, a brilliant neon collage, rocking on the Silver Slipper, blazing at the Stardust, beaming to the heavens from the giant searchlights atop the new Aladdin hotel.

And the people—holy mackerel, it was the first time I saw guys in those monkey suits they call tuxes and women in slinky dresses that sparkled. In Mina women smelled of talcum powder and wore loose-fitting flowery dresses Betty called flour sacks, and men had mud on their boots and sweat under their arms. These women in Vegas had dresses that molded to their bodies and exposed the luscious curves of their breasts. They smelled like expensive sex, Chanel No. 5, and Fleur de Rocaille. Even the men had an expensive smell, not like the Old Spice lotion that miners splashed on after showering.

Flesh and glitter, that was Vegas—flesh and glitter and the song of money. I had never heard the song before, not this loud at least. Nickels and dimes dropping in slot cups were the money sounds in places like Mina and Tonopah, but on the Strip the music was numbing, seductive, putting you in a dream state and robbing your senses, the forbidden tune played by Lorelei to lure Rhine sailors to their doom, the beckoning of the Sirens to tempt Odysseus. It filled your ears all the way down the boulevard—the rattle of dice and cries at the craps, cards being shuffled at the blackjack tables, the clatter of a roulette ball bouncing around the wheel, the hum of thousands of slot reels spinning, silver flushing from them.

Something spiritual entered my body and glowed inside me that night. I guess it was like the religious experiences that Holy Rollers in Mina talked about, when they woke up in the middle of the night and heard Jesus speaking to them. I only went to the Holy Roller church once and it scared the hell out of me, all that shouting and hysterical laughing, people talking in tongues. That's what it was like on the Strip, too, people shrieking and laughing and shouting mysterious utterances. "Bless these bones!" "Holy Mother, com'on six, gimme a six." "Jesus H. Christ, I hit the big one!" "Oh my God, my God, my God!"

Whenever I asked Betty about God, she always told me that God was a bright light that shined through the universe. I figured out that night, when I saw the Strip for the first time, that God lived on the Strip and lit it all up.

I also figured out something else that day. As soon as I was old enough, I knew I'd have to make something for Betty and me, otherwise we'd be migrants for the rest of our lives. I loved my mother, but as a neighbor once told me, Betty would always be hopping around on one foot, trying to keep her balance. If we were ever going to have something, I'd have to be the one to get it for us. Instead of pressing our noses against the plateglass windows separating the people with tuxes and slinky dresses from us streeters, someday we'd have the limos, the jewels, the fancy clothes.

I wanted *everything* for Betty and me.

She was a Utah Loletta, one of those wheat-blonde, blue-eyed, peachy-cream kids from St. George, the little town just across the state line. The Lolettas came in on busy weekends: towheads from Utah, tacos from East Los Angeles, dreadlocks from South Central, and Valley girls with tan freckles on their tits. They hung around the casino parking lots, giving head in cars for twenty dollars a blow and using their pen money for movies, fast food, and fast drugs.

The Mormons humped and grunted out the cute cookie-cutter Utah kids like rabbits. This one was about fifteen, just right for chaperoned barn-house dances, moonlight serenade hayrides, and of course, no lipstick on her naturally cherry-wet lips.

Right now those cherry-wet lips were locked onto Bic Halliday's cock in the casino's hotel elevator. Bic was the twenty-five-year-old loser son of the club's owner.

"Sonofabitch."

I stood in Halliday's security room staring at the monitor, feeling like Captain Smith when someone told him the good ship *Titanic* was nosing into an iceberg the size of Rhode Island. I was the hotshot, twenty-three-year-old, youngest casino security chief in Vegas. If I didn't get that lip lock off Bic's cock, I would quickly prove Newton's pet theory about gravity.

Bic wasn't just any kind of trouble, he was born trouble. His old man, Con Halliday, owned the casino lock, stock, and barrel. But Bic suffered the successful-man's-son syndrome: He had shit for brains and did all of his thinking with his gonads.

Bic had slipped the cunt past the guard at the elevators and pulled the emergency button in the elevator to stop the car between floors. Right now he was doing an Elvis hip gyration as he surfed her mouth with his erect member.

The bastard knew better than to pull a stunt like this. Prostitution was tolerated in Vegas, hell, it was the state's main industry after gambling and money laundering, but these Lolettas were trouble. The Lucky Star Casino down the street got a black mark on its gaming license after one of the girls screamed rape in its parking lot because a john stiffed her. Con Halliday already had more black spots on his gambling license than a seven-card spade flush. My job was to see to it that he didn't lose his license because somebody—besides himself— did something stupid. He hired me because I had a natural instinct for spotting a setup between a blackjack dealer and a player or a miscount at the roulette table—not as a damn baby-sitter for his twenty-five-year-old loser kid.

Bic grinned up at the camera, gave me the finger, and said something. There's no sound, just a surveillance camera, but he was talking to me. He knew I would be sweating in front of the monitor. He wanted the security-head job himself—yeah, like a guy with two drug busts and a statutory rape conviction is going to get by the gaming board in Carson City. This was his way of screwing me.

"You motherfucker," I told him, wishing I could stick my hand into the monitor and goose the kid so she'd bite off his dick.

"Bic pulled the emergency stop in the elevator," Bill, the watch commander of the security room, told me.

"Tell me something I don't know. Get the fuckin' engineer to drop the car directly down to the basement. You hear me, *directly* to the basement without stopping at Go. Have three guys, two to handle Bic and one for the girl, standing there when the doors open. You handle the kid. Put her in a cab and pay the driver to drop her off on the Strip." I thought for a moment. "Make it the parking lot at Caesar's. Tell her if she gets caught, to say she sucked off Hamel for permission to use the parking lot."

Hamel, a security boss at Caesar's, had pissed me off. When I asked him for information on a new dice switch that had been hitting the craps tables, he let me know that I was working a downtown grind shop while he worked for a Strip palace. That's what they called the downtown clubs on the Strip, "grind shops" that slowly grind pocket change from weekenders while the big bets were made on the Strip. "You people downtown let players buy in for twenty bucks and grind them down, a buck at a time." He was a shave-head former FBI agent who shit ice cubes. An accusation from the kid will give him diarrhea.

"Where's the guy who's supposed to watch the elevators?" I asked Bill.

"Bic slipped her in when he went to take a leak."

"Fire him."

"It's not his fau—"

"Fire him anyway. It'll look good if this gets to the Board."

"He might make a complaint to Carson City himself. Talk about some things Con doesn't want the Board to know."

He had a good point. I'd do it myself if I was in his shoes.

"Don't fire him. Promote him. Kick him up here to do monitoring. Fire him next month. Then if he goes to the Board he'll look stupid."

"Fire him for what?"

"Do I have to do all the fuckin' thinking around here?"

Bill shook his head. "I've always felt sorry for Bic and Morgan, growing up crawling on the casino floor. Bic got his first piece of ass when his old man took him out to the sheriff's chicken ranch when he was fifteen. I heard things didn't go too well. Bic's mother killed herself, you know, walked in front of train. Con said she 'greased the tracks.' Hell of a way to talk about the death of your wife, isn't it, greasing the tracks?"

Bic went slack-jawed, wide-eyed, tongue-drooping, and panted like a dog as he shot off in the girl's mouth. He thought he was being sexy cool but he looked like silent screen star Charlie Chaplin with his dick caught in the conveyer belt that's carrying a heroine to a rip saw.

Con claimed that if there was one pile of horse manure in the entire world, Bic would step in it. And now he was wiping his shoes on me.

I had to get away from the monitor. It was tempting me to be the guy standing in the basement when the elevator doors opened. I worked too hard to get the security chief's job to appreciate some crackhead trying to bust my chops. It wasn't every day a former thief got a chance at being head of security for a casino, even if it was in Glitter Gulch. I wanted Con's gamble on me to pay off. Besides, the skimming that was considered a perk of the job paid me more than that shave-head Hamel made at Caesar's.

Belle, one of my surveillance people, called me over to the screen displaying a blackjack table. Her name meant "pretty" in French, but we called her "Bell" because she was shaped like one. She was the best spotter we had.

"The pit boss thinks the guy's counting cards."

"How's he doing?"

"He's playing a hundred a hand, and kicking it up to a thousand when he needs a low card. Before the last shuffle, he wasn't taking regulation hits and letting the dealer bust drawing big cards. He loses a lot of small bets, but he's ahead eight thousand dollars in an hour."

There was nothing illegal about card counting, not on the law books, not as long as you counted in your head and didn't use electronics. But no club liked it, including the palaces or the grind joints, not in Vegas, Tahoe, Reno, or any place else. When you got caught, security took a mug shot of you and escorted you to the front door. Your picture got distributed to every casino in the state.

Most counters kept a running tally of the cards dealt, using a high-low count system, keeping track of the ratio of high cards left in the shoe to the number of low cards. Because dealers had to take a hit on hands up to a point count of sixteen, they were more likely to bust when the deck had a greater percentage of high cards.

Card counting was no easy matter because most casinos fought back by using a six-deck shoe rather than a single deck. That left the field open only to those few who could do it mentally or with hidden electronics.

"Have his shoes been checked?"

"Regulation," Belle said.

Counters sometimes hid electronics in their shoes, tapping with one foot to register a high card, with the other for a low card, feeding the information to a minicomputer strapped to their back or out to a van in the parking lot. Dingo cowboy boots and elevator shoes were automatically suspicious.

I was taught card counting by Paul Embers, the most notorious gambler in Nevada. Taught me a bit about cheating, too, and I picked up a lot more on my own. That gave me an advantage over shave-heads, who only studied how *others* cheat. The biggest tip-off to a scam was a sudden change in bets. If someone played a hundred dollars a hand and suddenly kicked it up to a thousand, and consistently won the big plays, it was a sure bet someone besides Lady Luck was setting the odds.

Belle was keeping a running tally of hands. Looking over the table play, I could see what got the pit boss suspicious. The guy was going against standard strategy at the times he was kicking up his bets—taking hits when he shouldn't, passing when he should take a hit—and was winning. As I watched, he took a hit on seventeen when the dealer was showing an eight. A typical player would not hit a seventeen, period, though there were some who took a hit if the dealer was showing a ten or ace. But to hit when the dealer was showing an eight was unusual—unless you were counting and knew the deck was loaded with low cards.

He was dealt a three, which gave him twenty.

The guy interested me more than the cards. He was definitely not card counting. He wasn't even looking at the cards other players were dealt. He spent half his time looking at his own cards and the other half trying to get a look-see down the low-cut blouse of the woman sitting next to him. She had big jugs and he was not making any bones about wanting to stick his head between them and let them slap his face. And she didn't hide the fact she thought the guy was a jerk.

"So why doesn't she move to another table?" I asked.

"Good question. She's losing and can't stand the guy. Two good reasons to change tables."

Ember always told me not to focus on the obvious, so I let my eye roam around the table and the vicinity. A mousy-looking guy with thick glasses who looked like a caricature of Woody Allen was seated to the winner's left.

Belle followed my gaze. "Woody's making five-dollar bets and digging a dry well."

"Maybe not. Look at how his eyes follow every card while the winner is distracting us by sticking his nose in the woman's blouse and the woman is letting everyone know how annoyed she is. They're a team. Woody's the counter, the winner's the shill he's signaling the count to. The winner and the woman are keeping us distracted so we can see the winner's not making a count. Page Con. Tell him to meet me in the pit."

I started out of the room but paused by a monitor where one of my people had directed a parabolic mike at a craps table. Most of our surveillance was done without sound, but we had long-range microphones available to key in on conversations. The Board didn't like mikes, but they looked the other way as long as we kept them strictly in the gaming area.

A big husky guy, maybe in his late fifties, with a high-school football-player physique turning to tapioca, was losing at a craps table and letting everyone around him get a taste of his bad mood. He was making bigger bets than the other players, but Halliday's was the only place in town where you'd find a craps player with five dollars' worth of twenty-five-cent chips standing next to a Texan with five-hundred-dollar chips.

"Fuckin' downtown joint, I get comped at the Tropicana and come downtown just to slum," came over the mike.

"Keep on losing you, bastard," the surveillant said, "when you're through we'll comp you a bus token back to the Strip."

My blood turned cold as I stared at the guy. I had seen him before, years ago.

He was the guy who killed my mother.

Part 2

★ ★ ★ ★ ★ ★

BETTY

Betty Riordan shifted in the backseat and hugged her baby tighter. She didn't need a rap sheet to tell her that the two guys with her in the big Caddie were thugs. It was 1954 and Vegas was a small town even though there were a bunch of new casinos on the Strip since Bugsy Siegel built the Flamingo: The Thunderbird, Desert Inn, Sands, and Sahara had risen in Siegel's wake. And the place attracted gangsters from Chicago and the East Coast like the faithful to mecca. A funny thing about the town, something no one ever said much about: Everything that was illegal everywhere else—gambling, whoring, quickie divorces—was legal here. Nevada was a poor state, about the poorest anywhere, a place where nothing grew, where the desert was so ugly no one wanted to come and see it. When the silver mines played out, the State had to make a Faustian bargain and sell its soul, although some would argue that when the mines closed even that was long gone—it had been shipped East in the form of silver bars to enrich generations of absentee mine owners.

Betty was being taken for a ride down to the Clark County Recorder's office. To change the name of her three-month-old baby.

She was twenty-two and had been on her own since she was sixteen. She knew how tough life was—and how much tougher it would get if you messed with guys like this; a couple of wops with short legs, thick necks, and big shoulders. She was just a lounge girl, a cocktail waitress in the bar at the Flamingo. Guys like these hurt people. Everyone knew who owned the town. The casinos each sent a messenger back East with a suitcase full of money every month. It all flowed through Meyer Lansky, and from him to the *capo di tutti capi*, the boss of bosses, Lucky Luciano, whom the feds had sent to prison and then deported to Italy but who still ruled the Syndicate.

"You know why they still obey Luciano?" a bartender at the Flamingo asked her, a guy from Jersey who knew all about the mob.

"Because he's tough. He's the only guy to ever survive a one-way ride. He was grabbed by four rodmen, taken out to a Staten Island beach, beaten, stomped, stabbed a dozen times with an ice pick, and had his throat slit ear to ear. They left him for dead on the sand. And he never fingered the guys for the job." He laughed. "By the time he got through with them, they wished they were in the hands of the cops."

Yeah, Vegas was a dirty town and you had to be careful, that was for sure.

Betty had no intention of giving the thugs any reason to hurt her. She accepted the fact that she had to change the baby's name. In a way, it was a relief. She really didn't like the name, Howard Hughes, Jr. Sure, he was a big shot and they said he was the richest man in the country, but she had discovered he wasn't a nice guy. Not that his character traits mattered to the men who ran the town. They applied muscle to anyone who annoyed a big player. Howard Hughes only played nickel machines, but he was Hollywood and the boys like to rub shoulders with him.

But she didn't like having to list the name of the baby's father as "Unknown." Benny, Hughes's man, told her she could make up a name for the father, but it didn't seem right. Besides, someday she would tell her son that his father was Howard Hughes and he wouldn't believe her if she put another name on the certificate of birth. She'd stick with "Unknown."

She was pretty much fatalistic about the whole thing. She never had really thought that Hughes would welcome her and her baby with open arms. Nothing ever went completely right for her, not for long at least, and she was used to moving on after life jerked the rug out from under her. Most of her income came from tips and she stuck most of those into the slots with the hope, but little conviction, that she'd be lucky enough to get a jackpot. When you fed the one-armed bandits your rent money, there was always the hope you'd double your money, but deep down she knew she'd walk away broke because she just wasn't lucky. And that was pretty much how life went for her. Jobs, men, nothing ever worked out for long. Men would stick around until they got into her pants, and jobs would turn sour because the other waitresses would get jealous that the boss was giving her the best tables or the customers would ask to be seated in her area.

The big man riding shotgun in the front passenger seat twisted around and looked back at her. "When we get through at the county, there are four roads leading out of town and a bus on each of them. You have to decide which one you'll be on."

"Can't I decide later?"

"Yeah, you can decide when Russian Louie hits town. If we have to decide for you, there'll be a piece of you on all four buses."

Betty pressed the baby closer to her chest and struggled to hold back tears. The joke about Russian Louie wasn't lost on her. Louie won a bundle at cards from some Sicilians. Some people said he had too many aces. After the game, they took him for a ride out in the desert and no one had seen him since. His disappearance became a standard joke in town: If you owed someone money, you'd say, "Yeah, okay, I'll pay you when Russian Louie hits town." *Bastards*. And Hughes was the biggest bastard of all. One thing was for certain, she wouldn't head back the way she had originally come to Vegas, by way of San Bernardino and L.A.

San Bernardino, a dusty little town where you taste dirt in your mouth even after you have a drink of water, had no good memories for her. The town was on the way to Las Vegas and Palm Springs, but it was nowhere, just a pit stop for gas and a piss. To her it was being a teenager trapped in an eight-by-forty travel trailer with her mother and younger sister, living at a rundown trailer court where dogs barked and seasonal farm workers with straw cowboy hats drank beer and played penny-ante poker under the shade of an oak tree, where men living lives of indifferent desperation got drunk on Saturday night in bars with dirt floors and came home to beat their wife and kids.

Her mother had been a waitress, too, but rather than gambling away her tips, she'd paved her way to hell with booze. Her mother had been pretty, at least until the liquor and hard living had wrinkled her face and deadened her eyes. But she had not been as pretty as Betty. Her mom claimed to be Irish and Italian, but an Indian woman told Betty her mother was a half-breed and she looked it, with her braised-copper skin and dark eyes. Betty had gotten her mother's shaded complexion, but gray eyes and dishwater blond hair from her father. She never met her old man, but her mother claimed that it hadn't been a one-night stand, but a loving relationship until the guy, a soldier stationed at Riverside Army Depot, got transferred and she never heard from him again. That happened right after Betty was born. Her mom claimed the guy took a walk because he was Jewish and wanted her to convert, but Betty never saw any religious leaning in her mother one way or another and figured her mother would have converted to Satanism if the devil had made the offer with a bottle of Johnny Walker Red in his hand. A lot of the kids Betty was raised with either never knew their fathers or wished they hadn't, and Betty never gave much thought about hers.

Her mom had been a waitress in greasy spoons and Betty had learned waitressing early. By thirteen, fully developed and looking older than her age, she was working weekends at a restaurant. Taking a taxi home one night, she had her first sexual experience at fourteen, when the cabby turned off onto a dirt road and stopped the car. He climbed into the backseat with her and raped her, giving her one hell of a beating when she tried to stop him. Her mom called the cops, but nothing much ever came out of it. The guy left town and a cop warned her she should be more careful and not lead a man on.

"You're attractive to men," her mother told her. "And once in a while they're going to get rough and take what they want. You have to get used to it because that's how life works."

When she was sixteen, she ran away from home after her mother brought a man home, a mechanic who had gotten her car started after it broke down. The guy moved in, making things even more crowded for Betty and her little sister, who was five years younger. Betty didn't care for the guy—he would sit and drink beer and just stare stupidly at her, like she was a piece of meat he wanted to squeeze. Sixteen was the right age, too, for leaving home. Almost all the girls around her by sixteen were pregnant, shacked up, or working. She got on a Greyhound bus for the hour-long drive to L.A. and roomed with two girls who were ushers at the Egyptian movie palace on Hollywood Boulevard. Waitressing paid more than ushering, so she lied about her age and easily got jobs because of her looks. Customers would always tell her that she should be in movies, but she didn't consider herself that pretty.

She didn't like L.A. It didn't seem like a real town, just endless streets and rows of houses. She also didn't like it because she never learned how to drive a car and public transportation was horrible. Everything was a bus ride or two away. After a couple of years, she moved on to Vegas because she heard waitresses got paid more there and the living was cheaper. She left nothing behind in L.A. The two girls she originally moved in with had long since left to shack up with men. One of them married, and she never bothered to make other female friends. She found she could relate better with men, for a while at least. But at some point, when she got tired of buying their cigarettes and beer and taking care of their food tab where she worked, there would be an argument, sometimes they'd knock her around a bit and then she'd quit her job and move on.

There were plenty of jobs in Vegas for waitresses, that's what everyone said. The Flamingo had opened the year before, quickly followed by Bugsy's violent demise, and more big clubs went up. And there were restaurants, bars, and half a dozen clubs downtown, and plenty of truck stops along the highway.

When her ID showed her at twenty-one and was no longer phony, she got jobs on the Strip. She was working the lounge at the Flamingo when she first heard about Howard Hughes staying at the hotel-casino. He was staying in a penthouse on the top floor and she saw him one day walking across the gaming room. He was a tall, slender man, with a thin mustache. Physically, he looked rather like the movie stereotype of a lounge lizard, one of those manicured gents who service rich women for a price. But his body language was more that of an absentminded scientist, looking at people and things as if he were staring at them from the other end of a microscope. And maybe poking them with a sterile instrument to see what makes them tick.

Benny, one of his assistants, a Mormon-type who ordered real ice tea, instead of the Long Island kind, would come into the lounge and jazz her about Hughes.

"Howie has seen you," Benny said. "He thinks you're a real fox."

"Yeah, like I'm going to believe that."

She wasn't born yesterday. But you could never tell, could you? It's happened before. A rich guy spots a girl and bingo!

Benny grinned. "He said that when he saw you, the earth shook under his feet, he heard Gypsy violins and time stood still."

She giggled. That was real Hollywood stuff, what they called a "cute meet."

"Oh, you're full of bull," she told Benny.

But what if . . .

A girl has to dream. That's why she hated San Bernardino so much. People didn't dream there. But Vegas was different. It was like a Hollywood set, a place where dreams came true. Not for everyone, but once in a while someone threw down a bet or pulled a slot handle and won a big jackpot.

"No, kidding, Betty. Howie really flipped when he saw you. Maybe he wants to put you in movies. He made Jane Russell and Jean Harlow into stars. He could do it for you."

"Sure. And maybe I'll pick a perfect fifteen spot in keno and end up owning the casino."

But what if . . .

She knew that they were putting her on. If you sat her down under one of those naked lightbulbs the cops used for third-degree questioning in Jimmy Cagney movies, she'd tell you that Benny was pulling her leg, that all "Howie" wanted from her or any other cocktail waitress was a piece of ass. But somewhere along the line, her own emotional needs bought into it. What girl hadn't dreamt of a rich guy like Howard Hughes sweeping her off her feet and riding off into the sunset with her in his arms? She had grown up during the Great Depression and its aftermath and had been nurtured on movies in which poor shopgirls like Diana Durbin meet rich playboys who fall in love with them.

"You got to meet Howie," Benny told her, "before he leaves."

"He's leaving?"

"Yeah, but he comes back every few months. He likes the place because it's more private than L.A. or New York. Vegas takes care of its own. He says that some day he's coming back to buy up the whole town. Can you imagine that? A guy owning a whole town."

The kidding went on for a couple of days and then Benny came into the lounge in the middle of her shift looking real serious.

"The boss wants you to join him upstairs."

"I don't get off until—"

"It's all arranged. You're off now. Come on, he doesn't like to be kept waiting."

She didn't know what to say and just followed along like a calf with a rope around its neck. Inside the hotel wing elevator, Benny pulled out a piece of paper and a fountain pen.

"Sign this."

"What is it?"

"A release from liability. The boss is a rich man, he doesn't want anyone claiming he made promises he never kept. It says you're seeing him just for social purposes and that you will never be paid anything for any reason."

"I wouldn't ask for any of his money."

"Then you won't have any problem signing the release."

Benny paused at the suite door.

"You ever been sick, Betty?"

"Sick? No, I never get sick. I haven't had a cold in years."

"How about personal stuff. You ever got anything from a guy?"

She turned red. "Of course not. What kind of girl do you think I am?"

He knocked and then opened the suite door with a key, and stood back and let her enter.

She walked in and stopped dead in her tracks. He was sitting in a stuffed chair, in his bathrobe, the richest man in the world, a guy who owned airlines, movie studios, defense plants, and tool factories.

He was reading a financial report and he looked up from it. He stared at her for a moment. His expression, as though peering through the microscope at a bug, never changed.

She didn't know what to say. She shifted on her feet and smiled but her lips trembled. It was so unreal. Just like in a movie.

He nodded at Benny who quickly backed out of the door and closed it behind him.

Hughes stood up and tossed the papers aside. He undid his robe and cupped his penis in his right hand. He began to massage it.

Twenty minutes later, Hughes walked her to the door as Benny opened it.

Betty was in a daze. She had walked in speechless and was walking out in the same state. She struggled to say something, something that would add some meaning to what had just occurred but nothing came out. She had had sex before, for an unmarried woman of her day she was quite experienced, but she had never experienced it in such a bloodless and robotic fashion. *Wam-bam, thank you, ma'am* was how the joke went.

She stopped at the door and turned to Hughes, feeling awkward, and finally said, "I—I really admire you, Howie." She leaned toward him to give him a kiss on the cheek but he stepped back and waved his hands as if she was a fly he was fending off.

"Get her out of here."

Out in the hall, Benny was all business. He took her by the arm and marched her to the elevator. Another aide was standing by, holding the empty elevator open.

"Don't forget what you signed."

"Signed?"

"The waiver, release, and confidentiality agreement. You are forbidden to mention to anyone what happened between you and Mr. Hughes. If one word of this ever appears in a tabloid, I guarantee you will be hunted down and punished. You are to forget what happened tonight. Period." He led her into the elevator. "Understand?"

She had never seen Benny so officious before. He had always acted like an all-right guy. "I'm not going to tell anyone."

Benny shoved a greenback down the front of her blouse, letting his hand slide over her breast as he did. "That's for being a good girl."

When the elevator door closed, she pulled the bill out—a hundred dollars. She suddenly felt dirty. She wasn't a whore. A couple of times she'd slept with a customer and let him tip her, but only when it was a guy she wanted to do it with and only when she was low on rent money. A hundred dollars was a lot of money. She made thirty dollars a week in wages and almost twice that in tips, but every spare cent went into the slots. But it still made her feel dirty. If Hughes had shown her one ounce of affection or interest, she wouldn't have minded. Instead he treated her like a bug.

But she soon shrugged off the feeling. My God, it was like sleeping with royalty.

Betty knew something was wrong when she missed her next period. The baby came right on schedule. Howard Hughes, Jr., was three months old when Hughes came back into town, again staying at the Flamingo.

She had been through bad times, getting sick a lot during the pregnancy and being unable to work. Early on, a coworker told her that there was a place down in Tijuana where you could get rid of a pregnancy, but she had been too scared and too broke to try it. Everyone she talked to had heard about a girl who bled to death after the Mexican doctor got through slicing her up.

Once the baby was born, she had added expenses and had to pay a neighbor woman to baby-sit. The situation was ironic: Here she was dead broke and the guy who caused the problem was as rich as Midas.

She wasn't going to the hotel-casino to blackmail Hughes. All she wanted was a little help, maybe a few thousand or even a little house for her and the baby, nothing much, nothing that he couldn't give without even missing it. Besides, how could he refuse to help a woman who had had his child?

At the hotel, she was stopped by security at the elevators. Benny came down and stared at her like she was someone from the NAACP crashing a KKK party. He looked real unhappy at the bundle of joy in her arms.

She explained what she wanted with trembling lips. And showed him the baby's birth certificate. "I just need a little help. Just a few dollars until I can get on my feet."

"Just a minute," he told her. He whispered to the security guard and the man made a call on the in-house phone. Within a minute two security people came into the area, a man and a woman.

"Come with us," the woman said.

"Where?"

"We're going to make you and the baby comfortable while arrangements are made."

That sounded all right. They would need time to take her request to Hughes. She followed them to a room that was empty except for a small table and two chairs. It instantly struck her that it was a security interrogation room. Not that Vegas security people did much talking with their mouths. Anyone who tried to rip off a casino—cheats or thieves—usually ended up in a shallow grave in the desert. The only guys who managed to rob a Strip casino pulled the stunt three years ago. They got thirty-five hundred dollars in cash from the Flamingo and a short lifeline when a mob enforcer caught up with them on Franklin Street in Hollywood and put four bullets into the back of their heads.

She was in the room for two hours, getting nervous all the time. After the first half an hour, she banged on the door. The security woman answered the door and Betty told her, "I have to go to my car and get a bottle of milk for my baby."

"I'll get it for you."

She gave the baby the bottle and rocked him to sleep. He cried a little, but he was pretty much a good kid.

After two hours, the door opened up and the two thugs came in. She knew who they were, she'd seen enough of them in her years as a lounge girl, gangster types that float around Vegas like scum sloshing in a tidal bay.

"Get up," the one who talked told her, "you're paying a visit to the county to change a birth certificate."

She stared out the window of the Cadillac, watching people, stores, and streets roll by. They rolled by Zackery Street and she had an inspiration.

"Zackery, Zack Riordan." She held the baby up and nuzzled her nose against his. "What do you think? Zack Riordan? Is that okay? I like Zackery Scott. Did you see him in *Flamingo Road* with Joan Crawford?"

"It's okay with me, girlie," the thug said.

After Howard Hughes, Jr., officially became Zackery Riordan, they drove her to the Greyhound bus depot.

"What'll it be, girlie?" The thug had gotten into the backseat with her.

"Reno," she said.

She'd never been to Reno. It was actually a bigger and more important city than Vegas. Compared to it, Vegas was a one-horse town. There'd be more casinos and more jobs than Vegas.

They pulled up near the bus station and the driver went in to buy her a ticket. The man next to her took her left hand. She started to pull it away but he kept a tight grip on her small finger.

"You're getting two C-notes and a one-way ticket. Make sure you never come back this way." He jerked back on her finger.

She screamed. *"You broke it!"*

"Your friend don't want to hear from you again, no how, capiche?"

She sobbed, dizzy, ready to pass out.

"Now when I say no how, he don't want to hear from any lawyer, either. You capiche that?"

Reno was 442 miles north of Vegas and the trip up Highway 95 took ten hours. There was little to see and few places to stop in between. The whole Nevada basin was one big sand box created by mountain ranges on each side that blocked out most rainfall. If you liked sunshine and dirt, Nevada was the place for you. But you had to share it with the lizards, snakes, and scorpions because they were the only other takers.

Two hours up the road she got off the bus at Beatty and found a medical doctor-veterinarian in a flat-top adobe near a weathered, bullet-holed sign that said GATEWAY TO DEATH VALLEY.

"I slammed a car door on my finger," Betty told him. Her hand was swollen. He gave her a curious look, but didn't ask questions as he set and bandaged her hand and gave her a couple of pain pills.

She caught the next bus heading for Reno. An old prospector, too old to work in the mines, too poor to live in a town, sat next to her all the way to Tonopah. Like everyone else in Nevada, he was looking for pay dirt.

"It's all free," he said, gesturing out the bus window at the endless sagebrush desert. "The federal government owns ninety percent of the state and they don't even want it, 'cept for a little piece to test their bombs on. The rest is up for grabs. You can fence in a thousand acres and nobody would notice."

He smelled like many old men who spent their last years walking across the desert to the mountains in search of a mother lode, the smell of Prince Albert pipe tobacco, dust, and dried sweat. His salt-and-pepper beard was nicotine stained around the lips and down one side from chewing tobacco. The old-timers smoked Prince Albert because the slender red tin can fit in their shirt pocket and could be used to stake out a mining claim. When a prospector was sure that the mother lode was under his feet, he'd fill out a claim form, stick it in the tobacco can, and bury it under a pile of rocks on the spot.

"What do you do with a thousand acres of dirt?" she asked, knowing the answer. "You can't grow nothing on it."

"When I hit it, I'm going to build me a house out here just like the Taj Mahal in India, close enough to the road so everyone can see it when they drive by. I'm going to build you and that little fella there a house, too."

She slipped him twenty dollars and told him her name when he left the bus at Goldfield. Who knows? Maybe he would find a vein of silver as big as a house. And then her and Zack would be on easy street. She'd heard about a waitress who had that exact thing happen.

Whenever the bus made a stop along the way—places like Goldfield, Tonopah, Mina, Hawthorne, each a dusty little desert town with Highway 95 as its main street—Betty slipped off the bus to try her luck at the three or four slot machines found in every bus waiting room. Her hand hurt like hell.

By the time the bus rolled down Reno's Virginia Street and under the big lighted sign that announced "The Biggest Little City in the World," the two hundred dollars the thug gave her was almost gone. She was down to twelve dollars. Leaving the bus depot, she hoofed it with Zack in arms to the most famous gambling casino in the world, Harold's Club. Not far away was the spot where new divorcees stood at a bridge over the Truckee River and threw their wedding rings into the river for good luck. With only twelve dollars in her pocket, she could use some of those rings and a pawnshop. She was hungry and hadn't eaten anything since morning in Las Vegas. But a dollar for food meant a dollar less to feed the slots and that much less chance of hitting a big one.

She couldn't take the baby in, so she sat him down against the wall next to an open door where he'd be in view while she played the nearby slot machines. It was common knowledge that the clubs liked to put their loosest slots near the entry doors so people walking by would be lured in by the sweet music of jackpots. She never had had any better luck with those machines than any other player but she believed in the rumor and always went to slots at entryways when she was getting low on money.

The quarter slot she started feeding had a two-hundred-and-fifty-dollar grand payoff for hitting three jokers, a pot so big it had to be paid by the house because there weren't enough coins in the machine. Most quarter machines only paid off twenty-five-dollar jackpots. When you hit a jackpot, you could see the coins gushing down on the other side of the glass plate that covered the coin holder. She bought a ten-dollar roll of quarters and busted the paper wrapping by knocking it against the payoff tray. She stuck the quarters in her side pocket and pulled them out one at a time. They lasted longer when she kept them in her pocket. When she pulled the handle, she tried different body English to make the tumblers hit pay dirt, jerking the handle real hard and fast at first, then moving it gently, pulling it down so slow the tumblers started moving one at a time. She could hear coins dropping in payoff trays all around her but all she got was two quarters several times for a cherry and ten for three yellow bells.

In twenty minutes she was down to her last two dollars.

A blackjack dealer playing a machine nearby said, "Not hitting it today?"

"Not hitting it any day."

"Cute kid you got there. You and your husband must be proud."

She hesitated. He was nice looking. Kind of cute really, with black curly hair that went with the black pants, white Western shirt, and black string tie of a dealer. She could tell he was sizing her up. She had had a wedding band, but had sold it for five dollars a month ago.

"My husband's, uh, dead." She wished the bastard was dead.

She left her seat and got eight quarters for her two dollars from a change girl. When she got back, the dealer was kneeling down, talking to Zack.

"How you doing there, young fellow?" He held out his hand for Zack to latch onto. "Hey, he's already got a grip."

She played the quarters with desperation. Every one knew you should never play when you're desperate because it killed your luck, but she couldn't help it. When she was down to her last quarter, she stopped and looked back to where the dealer was kneeling by Zack.

"He's a lucky kid to have such a pretty mom," he said.

On impulse, she went to them and rubbed the quarter against Zack's palm.

"Give me luck, baby."

She gave Zack a kiss on his forehead and went back to the one-armed bandit. She put the quarter in and carefully pulled down the handle, letting the tumblers engage one at a time. She stared as the tumblers spun and then came to a sudden halt, one by one. Joker, joker, joker—a two-hundred-fifty-dollar jackpot!

She let out a scream that might have been heard all the way to Vegas.

"You're my lucky baby," she told Zack. "Lucky, that's what I'm going to call you."

"New in town?" the dealer asked.

"Real new."

"I can help you get a job," he said. "I know the girls up in personnel. And a place to stay."

Her face began to flush as he gave her a good looking over. She had already gotten her figure back and it was a good one. Who knows? Maybe this was the right guy for her.

Maybe her luck had finally changed.

MINA, TWELVE YEARS LATER

Through the dirty classroom window, I watched a dust devil swirl across the playground. The only thing that made the Mina schoolyard different from the rest of the desert was a pile of dirt that marked the pitcher's mound and a gunny sack with dirt at each base. There were only three rooms in the school: first and second grades in one, third through fifth in another, sixth, seventh, and eighth in the last one. After the eighth grade, you were bussed forty-two miles to the high school in Hawthorne. The Mina school was constructed from three army surplus quonset huts set side by side. There were no hallways, no gym, no cafeteria, no air conditioning, and only an oil stove in the back of each classroom for heat.

Mina was called high desert, nearly a mile above sea level, but you couldn't tell that by looking. Every direction out of town was flat, sagebrush and alkali flats. Mina itself was a dusty little kindling-wood town with about a hundred houses and a block of scattered businesses stretched along Highway 95. It wasn't noted for anything except a whorehouse.

The class burst into laughter as Nancy Barr broke into tears and ran out. Mrs. Wormly, she pronounced it *Vermly*, glared at us and banged her yardstick on her teacher's desk. I got the same yardstick on my butt so many times I wouldn't be surprised if my rear had inch marks on it.

"Be quiet. You should be ashamed of yourselves."

Mrs. Wormly had a round tummy, protruding rear, big, heavy breasts, thick arms and legs, puffy red cheeks, and a double chin that bounced when she got excited and talked fast. She wore flowered dresses and always had her hair pulled back into a bun. Her husband, who taught the third through fifth grades next door, was short and stumpy, with a round tummy like his wife's. He had a bald pate with a ring of red hair and so many freckles he looked like he was rusting.

"Not another word. You should be ashamed."

She was right, but when you're twelve years old like I was, some things are funnier because you just don't know any better. Nancy Barr, who was in the eighth grade, a year ahead of me, had gone up to the front of the class to put the nine times multiplication table on the blackboard. It was Gibbs who saw the small dark stain on the back of Nancy's dress and said, "Poo-poo." Janey Hopper called him dumb and said the stain was from Nancy's first period, but by then us boys were laughing and shouting "caw-caw."

"The next person who laughs goes to the office."

The "office" was a small room that had a desk, phone, bookshelves for extra books, a closet where brooms and mops were stacked, and a bathroom with a toilet and sink. All three teachers used it, although Mr. Wormly, who was also school principal, called it his office. He used to teach us older kids, but he developed hives and itched all over and the doctor in Hawthorne warned him he would have a nervous breakdown if he dealt with us anymore.

The Wormlys belonged to the Holy Roller church, which was in a quonset hut even uglier and smaller than the school's. I went there once with Gibbs and his mother and it scared the crap out of me. People yelling, clapping, and stamping their feet, a woman foaming at the mouth and mumbling some kind of gibberish they called speaking in tongues.

Mrs. Wormly gave me her "you-little-bastard" glare. She always focused on me as the school troublemaker, maybe because I saw her playing with herself. At the beginning of the school year, I had to pee real bad and the other boys were holding the boy's bathroom door closed so I couldn't get in. I ran into the office and burst into the bathroom. Mrs. Wormly was on the toilet. Her hand was down between her legs and her mouth was open, her tongue hanging out the corner of her mouth. She screamed when she saw me. I screamed, too, and ran. I never saw a woman's twat, though I knew it had hair like a man's, and I didn't know why she'd have her hand down there, but Gibbs told me his sister, who went to Hawthorne high school, jerks off by rubbing a button down there, that he had once rubbed it for her for a quarter, and that was probably what Mrs. Wormly had been doing. I ended up peeing behind the school.

Mrs. Wormly called Roberta Potter up to the board and I went back to watching for dust devils. We liked to chase them down on our bikes and run into them. At three o'clock we ran out of the classroom and I headed for Main Street with my buddies, Gibbs and Gleason.

Mina didn't have any street named "main"; it's just what we called the line of businesses along Highway 95, the two-lane road that ran hundreds of miles down the middle of the state. There wasn't much in the way of businesses along the main drag: a motel with most of the fourteen one-room units rented out to locals, a general store, two gas stations, three bars, and two restaurants. The only institutes of significance in the town were the three-room school and the whorehouse.

An old-timer had left property to build a better school, but it was across the tracks, near the whorehouse. The choice was between the whorehouse or the new school and the locals decided on the whorehouse because it paid a good chunk of the taxes in Mineral County, which says a lot about Nevada. Mineral County covered nearly four thousand square miles, three times the size of Rhode Island, and had only about six thousand people, about a third of whom lived in Hawthorne, the county seat.

"When a girl has a period," Gibbs told me and Gleason as we walked toward the main drag, "that means she's ready to get pregnant."

"Nancy Barr's gonna have a baby?" Gleason asked.

Gleason was also in the seventh grade, but he was a puny, four-eyed runt with skin so pale we called him "polar bear." Unlike Gibbs, who was an authority on sex, and me, who knew just about everything else, Gleason only knew book stuff, which meant he didn't know shit from Shinola.

"No, numb nuts, she's not pregnant. But the bleeding comes when a girl's old enough to get married and have kids. Now she's ready any time a guy sticks his boner in her."

"Nancy's getting married?"

Gibbs lifted his eyebrows and I swatted Gleason on the back of the head. "Don't think about it, okay? Your dad say it's okay we ride on the train?" Gleason's father worked for the railroad.

"Yeah," Gleason said. "My dad's letting us ride in the caboose."

Gleason headed up the street to Wilson's Motor Court, where he lived with his mom and dad in a one-room cabin, and I huddled with Gibbs for a moment.

"Did you get the pamphlets?" he asked.

"I'm getting them. MaryJane said she'd have them."

MaryJane was the madam who ran the Pink Lady, the town's whorehouse, across the highway and the rail tracks that paralleled the road. I also lived across the tracks, in a three-room shack with my mother, Betty, and her boyfriend. We hadn't discussed the pamphlets in front of Gleason because he wasn't as tough as me and Gibbs. The little yellow belly would get scared and tell his mom and spoil it for us to make some money in Hawthorne. MaryJane was giving me sheets advertising the Pink Lady because I told her a man who worked on the train was going to pass them out in Hawthorne. But Gibbs and I were going to do it.

"A hundred sheets at ten cents a sheet means ten dollars; seven for me and three for you."

"Wow, that's cool," Gibbs said.

Three dollars was more money than Gibbs ever had in his pocket at one time. I got the bigger cut because the Pink Lady was my personal contact.

Gibbs and I split at the corner. I headed down the main street, passing the barbershop. The old guy waved at me from where he was reading the paper in his barber chair and I waved back. I didn't like the guy much. He liked to talk about the size of a boy's dick as he cut your hair.

At the café, Betty was standing at the end of the counter in her white blouse, black skirt, and white nurse's shoes. A coffee cup with red lipstick smeared on the rim and a cigarette burning in an ashtray were in front of her.

Betty always looked the same to me, even though she was pretty old, about thirty-four. All the kids at school said she was the prettiest woman in town, though some of the mothers didn't like her. Women were jealous of her because their men liked to go into the café and talk to her.

"Hi, there, Lucky. Want a roast beef sandwich?"

"Sure." That was my favorite—thin slices of roast beef on top of white bread and covered with brown gravy. It always came with mashed potatoes and green beans in every restaurant I ate at, and I ate in a lot of restaurants. Betty didn't do much cooking. About the only things in our icebox, which was what Betty always called a refrigerator and I picked up the habit, were a pack of baloney, bottles of Pepsi, chocolate cupcakes, and usually a box of Cream of Wheat and milk. Plus her boyfriend's beer. We kept any foods that rats could get at, like bread and Cream of Wheat, in the icebox.

"Hey, Zack, come'er and rub my coins. I'll split the jackpot with you," yelled a guy playing a nickel machine.

"No thank you, sir," I yelled back. I crunched down in my seat and ate fast. This rubbing coins stuff was Betty's fault. She would tell the story about the big jackpot to anyone who'd listen. I was always being asked to rub coins and was really embarrassed because no one ever won anything.

You could tell customers liked Betty, just by the way they laughed and talked with her. And she knew how to take care of them. If eggs were runny, she told the cook to do them right. It made her good tips, but didn't make her popular with the other waitresses or the cook, who was often also the café owner. After a few months working a place, the other waitresses would start ganging up on her, get her transferred to the breakfast shift, where tips were half as much, or even get her fired.

I gobbled up everything on the plate not because I was that hungry, but from habit. Betty had been working in Mina for nearly six months, almost a record for her, but you never knew when she'd quit her job and we would climb aboard a Greyhound for another town. I'd come home from school or she'd come and get me at school and we'd throw together our things and go down to the bus depot and wait for the next bus. Betty never did get a driver's license. She told me she was too nervous to drive, but maybe it was because all the towns we lived in were small enough to get around on foot. And when we moved, we didn't take much. She always rented furnished places and all I had to throw into a small cloth bag was a pair of pants, a cut-off, two shirts, socks, underwear, my portable radio with an eight-track cassette, and my collection of Superman comic books. The only shoes I had were the black high-top Keds I wore every day. When they wore out, I'd grab enough change from her tip jar to get another pair. That didn't mean we were poor. Most people didn't have much more than us, although some of them owned their own home and car.

Besides Mina, we'd lived in Reno, Carson City, Winnemucca, Tahoe, Elko, and Virginia City. Reno and Carson City we ended up at more than once. When we left town, there was never much left of Betty's paycheck after buying bus tickets, so there wasn't always enough to eat until Betty got working and bringing home tips. I made and lost friends quickly and never had a dog or cat. Betty was my only real friend. Kids like Gibbs and Gleason flew by like the Burma Shave road signs you see on long stretches of road.

"Gotta go," I told Betty.

We lived across the highway and tracks just a few houses away from the Pink Lady. There was Hop, Betty, and me. Hop's real name was Paul Hopkins, but everyone called him Hop. He was tall and what they called raw boned, with big hands, shoulders, and knees on a medium-frame body. He worked at the alkali lake mine about ten miles out of town, coming home caked with dry mud. After he came in from work and showered, he'd put on his cowboy hat, pointed toe boots, pearl button shirt, and Old Spice aftershave. He claimed to be a cowboy from west Texas, but Gibbs's dad said he was an Okie from Arkie. He was okay when he didn't have a belly full of beer, but he got loud and argued with Betty when he had a few too many.

I tried to take care of Betty, but it wasn't easy. A neighbor once told me that some people don't land on both feet when they jump from the cradle. Betty was one of those who was still hopping around.

When I reached the house, I tossed my schoolbook on my couch and grabbed a soda from the icebox. The place was a wood shack with a rusty corrugated tin roof. The outside walls had black tar paper and tacked-on chicken wire to hold a coat of cement stucco but the stucco was never put on. There was one bedroom, a bathroom that stunk because the septic tank in the backyard was backing up, and a combined kitchen-living room. The furnished place came with a yellow countertop, refrigerator, a square kitchen table with chrome legs and red plastic top, four chrome chairs with red plastic pads, a stuffed sofa, which I slept on, a stuffed chair, and a bed and dresser in the bedroom. Hop owned the black-and-white TV, but its rabbit ears only brought in one station, from Reno, and it was real fuzzy.

Mrs. Wormly gave us homework to turn in on Monday morning and I got right to it. It always amazed Betty when I did that. Betty always ate the frosting on a cupcake first and let the rest dry up. I ate the cake part first and saved the frosting to savor.

I heard the screen door open and Patty yell, "Anyone home?" as she came in.

"I'm here."

"Hi, Zack. I need to use my iron and board. I'm late for work."

Patty was a prostitute who worked at the Pink Lady. Some of the women lived in trailers in back of the house of prostitution, but Patty lived next door with her husband, who worked at the same mine as Hop. She was Indian, but not full blood. Betty was the only woman in town who was friendly toward her.

Patty was the reason I had an "in" with MaryJane, the madam at the Pink Lady. I had never been inside the Pink Lady, but I'd stood at the door while the girls gave me money and told me what to pick up at the general store and got a peek inside at men and women standing at the bar. I know some of the girls by name—Dixie the Pixie and Barely Legal Holly were names I liked best.

All the kids liked the Pink Lady because at Halloween they gave a big bag of candy to each of us instead of the apple or home-baked cookie most people handed out, but I was the only one who ran errands for the girls.

The ironing board was already set up by the kitchen table and Patty turned on the iron. "I don't know where time goes. I just got up and now it's time to go to work."

I wasn't exactly sure what Patty did at the Pink Lady. Gibbs said that she laid on her back and guys paid to stick their boners in her pee hole, but being told about it and actually being able to imagine it were two different things.

She slipped off her red dress and stood in black bra, panties, garter belt, dark hose, and black patent shoes with the highest heels I had ever seen. As I watched her from the couch, I got a boner. I didn't know why I got the hard-on. I would get them once in a while, even at school, and once in a while I woke up with one or with my underpants wet.

Sometimes Patty would sit on my couch smoking a cigarette and talking to Betty with her legs spread apart enough so I could see a dark place between her legs. I dreamed of what it would be like to stick a boner in her hole. I had money, over twenty dollars hidden in the couch and another five dollars in Betty's tip money I was going to use tomorrow in Hawthorne. Gibbs said she'd do it with me for five dollars, but I wasn't exactly sure what "doing it" involved. Besides, I was afraid of her husband, even though Gibbs said he wouldn't care, that his father said Patty's husband "rented her out."

"Patty, how much does a fuck cost?" My mouth was dry and I could barely got out the words. When I heard them, I was shocked.

"What did you say, honey?" She stared at me in surprise as she struggled into her dress.

"Nothin'." I bowed my head and put my book across my lap so she couldn't see that my pants were bulging from my throbbing boner.

She turned off the iron and came over to the couch and grinned down at my book. "You're becoming a little man, aren't you, sweetie." She sat down on the couch beside me and I smelled the lilac talcum powder she wore. It made the throbbing in my boner race faster. She moved the book and undid the buttons to my fly and slipped her hand inside and squeezed. "Pretty soon you're going to be old enough to give girls a real ride."

I was paralyzed with fear and wonderment at the feel of her hand, but my hard-on was going wild. She put her arm around my neck. Her breath hit me with a warm smell of whiskey.

"Do you want some relief, honey?"

She leaned down and slipped my erection through the fly hole. Her hot lips went on it and I almost screamed. Her wets lips made a sucking sound and I immediately exploded in her mouth. My hips jerked and I instinctively pumped back and forth, trying to shove it further into her mouth. She took her mouth off my boner and spat into a tissue she pulled from her dress pocket.

She put the book back on top of my erection and gave me a kiss on the cheek.

"You never forget the first time, sweetie. That's why I did it. So I'll always be remembered."

She was right.

The next morning I met Gibbs and Gleason at the turntable where the train swung around and headed back toward Hawthorne. When the hard rock mines in the mountain had been operating full blast, Mina had been an important rail spur. Now the train only worked part-time and Gleason's dad always said that pretty soon they'd shut it down entirely and the family would have to move to a town where he could find work. Gibbs and Gleason didn't move as much as Betty and me, but Mina was the third school each had attended, and that was true about many kids. People moved to where the work was and little desert towns thrived when there were jobs. When a mine closed, so did the grocery store, barbershop, and clothing store. The restaurants, gas stations, and motels sometimes survived on the highway trade, but the rest of the town moved on.

I told Betty that Gleason's dad was taking us to the carnival in Hawthorne. We were going to the carnival after we handed out the pamphlets, but would hitchhike home because the train would have already made its last trip to Mina. I learned that it was better to lie to her so she didn't worry.

I had a hundred sheets of paper hidden under my shirt, ads for "pleasure services" at the Pink Lady, a "fully licensed and doctor-certified establishment." I read one of the pamphlets and was surprised that it didn't say anything about the place being a whorehouse. MaryJane wanted me to be sure and tell the man she thought would be passing them out not to worry about sheriff's deputies, "they're my best customers," but to watch out for the shore patrol. Hawthorne was in the middle of the Nevada desert, but had a navy base. For miles coming into Hawthorne we rolled by giant dirt mounds, extending out into the desert as far as the eye could see, looking like enormous burial mounds.

"My dad says there are dinosaur bones buried under those mounds,"

Gibbs said, "and the army and navy's keeping 'em secret."

Gleason scoffed. "There's ammunition in them, bullets and artillery shells for the army and stuff for big navy guns."

Gibbs slapped him on the back of the head, nearly knocking his glasses off. "Yeah, well maybe you don't know so much. Everyone knows there's a sea monster in Walker Lake. Could be the dinosaurs are its cousins."

Walker Lake was the thirty-odd-mile-long lake on the north side of Hawthorne. It was said the lake was bottomless. Occasionally a fisherman disappeared and they'd be a lot of talk about the sea monster. The navy had a big research and bombing range at the lake.

"The navy keeps the monster a secret because it's using it for research," Gleason said. "The monster is left over from the time when Nevada was at the bottom of a primeval sea, even before Lake Lahontan covered most of the state a couple million years ago. Back in those days dinosaurs swam in it, but they all died when the sea dried up, all except this one."

"Naw," Gibbs said, "The navy created the monster by feeding it radiation, like those giant ants created by the atomic bomb."

The two argued about sea monsters and giant insects the rest of the way into Hawthorne.

We staked out the El Capitan Club, the only casino of any size in town. Even at that, it was a small fry compared to a place like the Harold's Club in Reno. I sent Gibbs around to one entrance and I took the other, with Gleason hanging out with me. We each carried a shoebox with black and brown wax polish, a brush, and a shine rag, and offered a quarter shine to every man who came by, along with a Pink Lady pamphlet. Most of the passersby were sailors and marines and they were more interested in the pamphlet than a shine.

"Spit shine, just two bits," I told two marines, handing them each a pamphlet.

"Okay, kid, but if I can't see my face in it, you don't get paid."

The two looked over the pamphlets as I got down on my hands and knees. Gibbs's old man had been in the army and he'd taught us how to spit shine. You put on polish, and get a shine going, then spit on the toe and keep applying more spit, polish, and elbow grease.

"Hey, kid, you get a bonus for every trick turned by guys who go there?" the one I was shining asked.

I spit on his shoe and looked up. "Naw, just a dime for each pamphlet I hand out."

"You ought to ask for a bonus. Or offer extras. Sell rubbers."

"He can take it out in trade," his buddy laughed. "Hey, kid, you ever fuck any of them yourself?"

I flushed. "Yeah, all the time. Try Patty, she's the best lay."

After his buddy left, I thought about his comments. I knew what rubbers were. I heard Hop and Patty's husband joking about them: Hop said it was like taking a shower with a raincoat. I was sure I could make more money selling rubbers to guys than handing out pamphlets and polishing shoes, but they were only sold behind the counter in drugstores and you had to be a grownup to buy them.

I passed out all fifty of my pamphlets and had made two dollars on shines by the time it was to hit the carnival. Gibbs had passed out only half of his.

"I threw the rest in a trash can."

"You only get paid half," I told him.

"Hell, no, just tell MaryJane you passed them all out."

"You don't cheat the customers," I sneered, repeating what Betty had said many times. "You get half."

"Up yours."

"Up yours, too, you queer."

"Asshole."

"Dip shit."

We kept it up until I ran out of insults and had to pay Gibbs a quarter. Gleason then took on Gibbs in cussing and lost. Gibbs had the dirtiest mouth in school. He even knew a Mexican word for a woman's twat. You had to admire that kind of knowledge.

A carnival was my favorite of all things. Bright lights all over, with a rainbow of colors in red, blue, green, yellow, on everything, flashing and pulsating, the fun music that made you want to pick up your feet and open your wallet, the breathtaking Ferris wheel taking you up higher and higher, the big disk that spun while you sat in a compartment, the midway with its gyp games and hustlers urging you to "win a goldfish, just toss a dime so it stays on a plate, it's easy, watch—"

Yeah, sure, the carnie's dime stayed on a plate, but mine skidded off. Over where you threw baseballs at metal milk bottles to knock them off a stool, a woman no bigger than me was working the booth and could easily knock them off, but I swear I saw a guy who threw like Sy Young and couldn't get all three to fall off no matter what.

I bought cotton candy and wandered down the midway alone as Gibbs and Gleason went up together in the Ferris wheel. I wanted to check out the freak show.

"Boy, come here," a voice beckoned.

A Gypsy woman dressed in silks and scarves and gold chains, her dark face wrinkled, gray eyes faded, stood in front of a small canvas booth not much bigger than a telephone booth and gestured for me to step inside.

"I'll tell your fortune for a dollar."

"I don't have a dollar." I kept on walking.

"You're a lucky young man."

That made me stop. My mother called me Lucky every day of my life. It hung around my neck like Mrs. Wormly's double chin.

"I'm not lucky," I said defiantly.

"You're lucky, boy, and you can have what you want."

"I want everything," I snapped back.

"You're going to get it. But you're going to lose something, too." The old Gypsy woman gave a shrill laugh that got its claws into the skin of my back and clung there as I hurried away.

I didn't know what she meant, but she put me into a foul mood.

"Let's go," I told Gibbs and Gleason after I saw the Alligator Man and a two-headed calf at the freak show. On the way to the highway to thumb a ride, I told them what the crazy old woman said.

"You're going to lose your dick," Gibbs said, "that's what."

7

The desert in late November had turned cold and the wind was mean. High desert was like that—hot as a bitch in the summer, cold and dismal in the winter. I left school at lunchtime to run down to the restaurant and get money from Betty for lunch. Her tip jar next to the bed was empty when I crept in to get a handful of coins before leaving for school.

The lunch crowd was slow and Betty was in a bad temper.

"The customer says the gravy's too greasy," she told the cook, sending back a plate of biscuits and gravy. The cook gave her a dirty look and Betty turned her back to him. "The bastard takes bacon left on breakfast plates and uses it for his gravy," she whispered to me.

"There was no money in the jar."

"Hop took it all for his beer. Now that he's laid off at the mine, he has nothing to do but drink and eat, with me doing the buying."

She gave me a dollar in change and grabbed the coffeepot to refill a customer's cup. I left the café with an uneasy feeling. Betty was even tempered most of the time. When she started getting mad at people, things would go to hell pretty damn quick.

That night I sat on my couch and watched a fuzzy version of *I Love Lucy* on TV. Gibbs claimed there were places where people got a whole bunch of TV channels, but that didn't happen in Mina. Hop sat on the other end of the couch drinking beer. Every once in a while he'd fart. That's why Betty hated beer—it made men fart. His face was red and he didn't look like a happy camper. Neither did Betty. She sat at the kitchen table doing her nails as she read *True Romance* magazine. She had come home from work early, saying she felt ill. Betty never got sick and would crawl to work if she had to carry her sickbed on her back. The only time she missed work was when she was down or mad.

The pan of water on the stove was boiling and I got up to get the Cream of Wheat out of the icebox.

"You eighty-sixed me at Emerson's." Hop spoke quietly but I felt the anger in his words.

"I didn't do anything to you," Betty said. "I told Emerson I wasn't paying any more of your bills."

"You're a fucking bitch."

"Don't you talk that way in front of Zack! I don't make enough money to keep you in beer."

"You could join your friend Patty at the Pink Lady spreading your legs. That's all a fucking cunt like you is good for."

"Get out of my house, you bastard." She grabbed the sugar bowl off the table and threw it at him. "Get out! Get out! Get out!" she screamed.

He came off the couch and started for her. I stepped in front of him. "Keep away from my—"

He hit me hard, slamming me with his open hand across the side of the head. I saw stars and flew backward, slamming into the wall. Betty grabbed the pan of boiling water off of the stove and threw it in his face.

We ran next door to Patty and Joe's with Hop screaming he was going to kill us.

The next morning we waited for the Greyhound in front of Emerson's bar. We didn't say much. We never do at these times. I had my small duffel bag and Betty had her hard-shell suitcase. Anything else we owned—plates, dishes, my bike, things like that—was left for the landlord. Betty hadn't paid last month's rent, so the landlord could have the stuff.

When the bus was getting ready to pull out, Gibbs and Gleason rode up on their bikes and scanned the windows, looking for me. In a town where a shout carries almost from one end to another, it didn't take much time for everyone to know we were leaving. I crouched down so they couldn't see me. I didn't want to say anything to them. I liked Gibbs, and Gleason, too, though he was a little turd, and I even liked Mina. But I had to be tough and not care.

We were an hour down the road before I realized the bus was heading in the opposite direction from Reno. Reno had always been our hub, the center of a wheel with the little towns of northern Nevada spread out from it like spokes. This time we were heading south.

"Where we going?" I asked Betty.

She took a deep breath. "Vegas, baby, we're going back to my old stomping grounds."

Las Vegas. The name didn't mean a whole lot to me. Reno was the biggest town I ever saw and I assumed Vegas was bigger than Mina and smaller than Reno, maybe something like Hawthorne.

"It's been twelve years. They won't remember me there."

She leaned closer and showed me a story in a day-old Reno newspaper. "See this guy, that's Howard Hughes, your father."

Betty told me many times that my father was a big shot named Howard Hughes, but when your old man was someone you'd never seen or spoken to, it was like telling you about the tooth fairy. The article was about some big financial deal the Hughes guy was pulling off.

"How come he never comes around to see us?"

"Honey, he's busy and important. And he really doesn't know about you. He comes to Vegas sometimes. Maybe you'll meet him there."

Part 3

★ ★ ★ ★ ★ ★

THE MAN WHO
BOUGHT LAS
VEGAS

In the wee hours of the morning, late in 1966, Thanksgiving weekend, a representative of the Desert Inn hotel-casino stood beside the tracks at the deserted North Las Vegas train station. In the distance, the rotating front light of a locomotive was visible coming down the track. A cold wind blew off the Spring Mountains. He shivered and pulled the parka that he wore over his business suit tighter. Behind him, two limos and a van were waiting.

His orders had been very specific: A man would be getting off the train. He was not to attempt to speak to the man or even make eye contact. He was to ask no questions. He was to obey all instructions from the man's bodyguards and aides. All he had to do was simply stand by with the vehicles and guide the convoy to the hotel. Entrance at the hotel would be made through the back and up a service elevator. The entire top floor of the hotel, the penthouse wing, had been set aside for the unnamed visitor. The elevator had been programmed so a key was necessary before it would assent to the penthouse level. The doors to the two stairwells were locked from within, a violation of the fire code. Two armed guards were posted in the hallway. Two more guards were waiting at the rear of the hotel.

Even more bizarre requirements had been made. Workers from a medical supply company had sterilized the top floor, including all furnishings. Other workers had sealed holes and cracks that could let in any dust or pests. Heavy black curtains had been put up at all the windows.

Who the hell is on that train? he wondered. He had some ideas, guesses. He thought nowadays no one but the president had a private train. It wasn't the president because the hotel would be swarming with Secret Service agents, but it had to be someone just as big. He had a name in mind, a guy who in his own way ran an organization that was not as big as the government, but was a government in and of itself. Vegas was a mob town: Most of the casinos were indirectly owned or controlled by the Syndicate, and the guy who pulled the financial strings of all the mob "families" was a Palm Beach Jew named Meyer Lansky.

He wondered if Lansky was on the train. A few years ago he would have guessed that it was Lansky's boss, Lucky Luciano, the boss of bosses. But after a roller-coaster ride in which Luciano was sent to prison, released for putting a stop to enemy sabotage on the New York docks during World War II after the *Normandie* was blown up—he was that powerful, running the Syndicate from his prison cell—and deported to Italy, Luciano had died of a heart attack in '62. Lansky and Luciano had been the financial spiders behind the Vegas casino boom, financing Bugsy Siegel and then having him murdered when his fingers got sticky after he had sent his girlfriend to Switzerland to stash Flamingo construction "overrun" money in a Swiss bank account.

Lansky was still pulling the mob purse strings, overseeing the finances of not just the usual mob rackets—extortion, dope, prostitution—but controlling a worldwide gambling network built by mob money that included "legal" venues like Vegas, London, and the Carribbean. With Luciano dead, the boss of bosses shifted to Vito Genovese, but he was no more likely to be the man on the train than Luciano—Vito was serving a fifteen-year term in Leavenworth and ran the mob from there.

As the train's light got brighter, he thought about the last time he had stood by these same train tracks. It had been about seven years ago, back when Jack Kennedy was on the campaign trail for the presidency. Kennedy rolled into Vegas on a train, made a short speech from the back of the caboose, then stepped down and worked the crowd, shaking hands and kissing babies. He shook hands with Kennedy, sort of, although it was more a brushing of hands than a real grip, but the story grew in the telling. Too bad about Jack, though. That prick Oswald killed him and Ruby gunned Oswald down. Christ, it was like a movie the way things went down. Later Vegas swarmed with feds checking out Ruby's movements because he'd been in Vegas before the shooting and had a connection with Meyer Lansky and the whole fiasco over the Castro assassination that led to Kennedy getting knocked off.

They say Robert Kennedy was going to run for president in '68, but he wouldn't vote for him despite the fact the guy had balls. Robert Kennedy went after corruption like a retriever to a duck. He'd be bad for business, mob business, and he was too friendly with that Negro leader, Martin Luther King, who was causing so much turmoil in the country.

The train stopped and three well-dressed men stepped down. They were all clean shaven, clean cut, and the hotel representative suddenly realized they probably were Secret Service agents and that the train did carry the president.

One of the men approached him and the rep said, "I'm from the Desert Inn."

"Fine. Just stay out of the way."

The men fanned out, checking the perimeters. Once the "all clear" was yelled a van backed up near the Pullman train car. The back doors of the van opened and he saw oxygen tanks, medical apparatus, and a white uniformed attendant. A moment later a stretcher was carried down from the train. The stretcher had a back on it so the occupant could sit up and be carried like an Oriental potentate on a litter.

He had been told not to speak or even make eye contact with the man, but no one said he couldn't stare. The man was fragile-looking, thin and gaunt, almost emaciated. His expression was self-possessed with an edge of grimness.

He was a living legend. If not the richest man in the world, probably the richest in America. He had been orphaned at seventeen and immediately took control of his deceased's father's tool company, which made a drill bit that the petroleum-hungry world lusted after. During his career of the past thirty years, he had started an airplane manufacturing company; set the coast-to-coast air speed record; had a ticker-tape parade down Broadway when he set an around-the-world record; built the world's largest airplane (which flew only once and then for just a mile); founded TWA; owned two movie studios; launched the career of stars like Robert Mitchum, Jane Russell, and Jean Harlow; had romantic interludes with Ava Gardner, Katharine Hepburn, and Yvonne De Carlo; married beautiful Jean Peters; and worked hand in glove with the CIA on international intrigue.

Now a month short of his sixty-first birthday, he was becoming a different kind of legend. His nervous system was polluted with codeine and Valium. His mind was torn by obsessive-compulsive fears and paranoia.

Over the next four years, he would set out to buy up the poorest state in the nation, owning seven casinos and vast land holdings, accounting for nearly one out of every five tax dollars collected by the state. He singlehandedly did what the federal and state government could not do: drive much of the mob from Vegas. He did it not with a stick, but a checkbook. He simply bought them out.

He did all of this while sitting in a leather chair in a black-curtained penthouse, naked, refusing to see anyone but a few Mormon aides, paranoid, drugged, sick, and wasted. He peed into bottles he stored in the closet, kept a diary of his bowel movements and enemas, and had such a morbid fear of germs that he would not touch anything without handling it with a piece of tissue paper.

Howard Hughes had arrived in Las Vegas.

Part 4

★ ★ ★ ★ ★ ★

THE HUSTLER

"Hey, Lucky, am I working today?"

The kid asking me the question was my age, sixteen, a kid from the same high school class I was in, but I didn't know him well because I didn't go to school much. I ran a rag delivery service, hiring kids to pass out advertisements on the Strip and in Glitter Gulch, the downtown gambling area. Everything from jewelry stores advertising wedding rings to escort services wanted handouts distributed to people on the streets, mostly to men. ("It's legal in Nevada," the escort service handout said, but didn't define *what* was legal.)

Because I needed people over eighteen for the more racy stuff, I tried to use the winos who hung around the downtown soup kitchens, but they were unreliable, so I was always on the lookout for older-looking kids. Besides, even the massage parlors—aka whorehouses—didn't like seedy-looking characters handing out their stuff.

The truant officer used to bug Betty about me hooking, but since I had turned sixteen, there was no more flack. I would just quit school and no one could make me go back. But I kept up my school contacts for my business. I came by the school to pick up my crew and drop them off in their designated territories.

"I can't use you today, Frankie, hit me up on Friday. And, guy, my name is Zack." I got real close to him and smiled when I said it. I've been told that when I'm annoyed I grin like a Doberman.

Kids who would come by the apartment picked up on Betty calling me "Lucky" and pretty soon they were doing it, but I didn't like it. I was superstitious about luck. I figured you only get so much luck in a lifetime. Sometimes I wondered whether I had used up all of mine that day when Betty rubbed a coin in my palm. A lifetime of luck for a quarter jackpot. Since then, life had been an uphill battle, but things weren't all that bad. Betty was working. She still changed jobs every six months, but Vegas was growing. I handled all of the bills and made her hand over her whole weekly paycheck. Her check was minimum wage with the usual deductions but the real money was in tips. She still flushed every loose dime she got down the toilet—slot machines weren't called one-armed bandits for their generosity. But with what I earned and my handling her check, the rent and utilities got paid. Sometimes I even let her coach me out of a few bucks when she was out of money. "I'm a sucker for a good-looking dame," I'd tell her.

Yeah, me and Betty were doing all right, and I had a couple hundred put away for a rainy day, but we still had our noses pressed up against that window.

I leaned against the fender of my '57 Olds Rocket 98 and shot the shit with Frankie while I waited for my crew to arrive. It was Friday night and I had one kid for downtown and three for the Strip. On Saturday nights, the crew was doubled. They got paid one-third of what the businesses paid me to distribute the fliers, but I didn't get to pocket the rest of it. I paid one-third of my cut to Tony Lardino, a dumb sonofabitch everyone called Tony the Bat—behind his back. Tony was eighteen, had hands the size of baseball gloves, a beer belly, and a big butt. He carried around a baseball bat as though always on his way to a game. His idea of fun was seeing who could fart the loudest and kicking ass on someone smaller than himself, maybe cracking one of the guy's kneecaps with the bat just for the fun of it. I would've liked nothing better than to put some tire marks from my Olds across the bastard's back, but his uncle was Morty Lardino. Morty controlled Vegas street crime, prostitution and drugs mostly, and reported to a guy in L.A. who reported to someone else, probably Giancana, in Chicago. There was always a pecking order. My scam was small-time stuff, but not too small for Tony to learn the ropes of the protection racket by shaking me down.

I couldn't keep change in my pockets and my Olds in gas and tires with everyone getting a cut, so I skimmed a little here and there.

I loaded my crew into the Olds and headed out to make the Strip drop-offs first. The transmission on the Olds banged into gear as I pulled from the curb. I liked the Olds because it was a lean, mean street machine and made me feel like I was one of the hardasses. I called it a salmon color, though Betty said it looked pink to her, not faggot-pink of course, but a masculine pink—like salmon. A two-door hardtop without the center post, it had chrome spinners, fender skirts, white leather seat covers, a three-carb V8 with a 371-cubic-inch Rocket engine, automatic transmission, power windows, power steering, a rear end lowered by heating the springs and letting them flatten, and a Smithy muffler that rattled windows for a block when you let up on the gas. A kid's car, for sure, but that's what I was.

The problem with it was the power steering made a loud whinny noise when you turned and the transmission slammed into gear and bled. The guy who sold it to me said it just needed adjustment, but it hemorrhaged red fluid and a friend's old man told me I had gotten taken. I needed to figure out a way to dump the lemon on someone else before the transmission fell out. The problem with not having an old man and a mother who knew zilch about cars was that I didn't know a straight eight from a four banger. This was my first car and I didn't want to be taken on another one. I always figured I was entitled to one mistake. But just one.

I had made sure Naomi sat up front with me and put the three dudes in the backseat. She lived with her mother in the apartment below us. Naomi was Korean and Negro, her old man had knocked up her mother when he was stationed in Seoul and brought her home as a Korean War bride. She was the prettiest girl I ever saw, with curly black hair, golden tan skin, and big, dark, curious eyes. Her eyes reminded me of the pictures of European children after World War II, sad kids with big round eyes. You saw the pictures in department stores and casino gift shops. Naomi's eyes looked like that, big and intense. I got an erection just looking at her. I don't think God made any more beautiful creatures than the black-and-tans that came out of black GIs screwing Japanese and Korean girls.

I had a real crush on Naomi, but she was going with a guy on the school's football team. Everyone knew he was diddling her, but the closest I got was making out with her while watching Clint Eastwood and Shirley MacLaine in *Two Mules for Sister Sara* at a drive-in. She let me feel her up and finger-fuck her. Next day I heard the jock was going to kick my ass. I backed off because Naomi said she wanted to go with him, which was a relief for me. I saw the guy naked showering after phys ed. He had muscles in his hair. A real intellectual who liked slapping guys on the ass with a wet towel. I didn't hang around school much and I started avoiding it even more when I found out a guy who could scare the peas out of the Jolly Green Giant wanted to kick my ass. But I still wanted to dick Naomi. If the moron caught up with me, it wouldn't be the first time I got my ass kicked, but it would sure as hell be for the best reason.

"Listen up, we have a special this weekend," I told the crew. "I got some rubbers that glow in the dark and have bumpy ribs on them. They're two bucks apiece. Tell the guys that not only will they protect them from the clap and syphilis, but even the most hardened whore will be begging for more."

Everyone groaned. Hernández, a Mex kid whose family moved here from Tucson, was the first to give me some lip. "You're always pushing condoms or some other screwy thing, Zack. Last week it was porno comic books. None of this stuff sells worth shit."

"They're shit to you, but I work off of volume," I told him, my voice displaying the contempt we entrepreneurs feel toward the little people. "These extras add up in the long run, increasing the bottom line." That was actually a lie. I had a closet full of junk that didn't sell, but I was waiting for the big one, the item that would take off and make me big bucks. It was just a matter of trying different things until something connected. Like pulling the handle of a slot machine—one day all three bullion bars line up and you hit the big one. Only difference was I used my brain. When you were pulling slots, the brains were all in the machine.

I let Naomi out last, leaning toward her and placing my hand on her thigh as I asked, "Elvis and Mary Tyler Moore are in *Change of Habit*. Want to see it with me tomorrow night?" God had invented drive-in theaters to give kids a place to make out. I heard half the babies in this country were conceived during dusk-to-dawn movie nights.

"Can't. Bobby's taking me to a team party. Besides, he would stomp you if I went out with you."

"Let me take care of muscle head." I gave her thigh a squeeze. "I just want to show you a good time."

She leaned closer to me. "Tell me something."

"Yeah."

"How come you get a bulge in your pants every time we're alone for thirty seconds?"

She jumped out of the car, laughing.

I pulled away from the curb, transmission slamming into gear, and hadn't gotten a hundred feet before Tony waved me over with his baseball bat. Shit.

He waited on the sidewalk with a couple of his buddies, little pricks hoping to grow up and pack a gun someday so they could be big pricks.

"I hear you been welshing on me, Riordan."

Tony had his baseball cap pulled down low and hit the bat against the side of his shoe like he was wearing cleats and knocking dirt off of them. The accusation that I was skimming and not giving him his full cut had scared the crap out of me the first time I heard it, but it was Tony's favorite line and he pulled it on me at least once a week. Now it only pissed me off.

"Aw, Tony, I wouldn't do that to you, man, you know that, not after everything you do for me. Hey, man, look what I've got. These rubbers are from France, they glow in the dark."

He squinted at me like it's the first time he ever saw me. "How come you ain't in the war? You're not one of those fucking peaceniks, are you?"

Tony was like that lately, asking everyone he bumped into why they weren't in uniform. He'd been real patriotic ever since the draft board gave him a 4F for high blood pressure.

"Man, I'm too young to be in the army. And if I wasn't, I wouldn't go anyway. Let the gooks fight it out themselves."

"Yeah, sure, and when the Commies rule the world, guys like you will suck the dick of Ho Chi Hitler."

I parked the Olds in front of our apartment house and climbed out. I usually spent my time checking the crew but I wanted to come home and check my closet of goodies. Not even Lardino liked the glow-in-the-dark rubbers and I wanted to see if I had anything else to try on the street—again.

Our place was on the second floor. It had only one bedroom and Betty insisted I take it. She sacked out on the couch in the living room. It worked out better that way because I actually used the apartment, even ate there once in a while, but I rarely saw Betty. Vegas was good for her—it was a twenty-four-hour town and she was a twenty-four-hour girl. She worked nights at a lounge in the Dunes and only came home to sleep during the day. She never brought a man home. I knew she dated, but she had too much class to let a man stay the night at our apartment, not to mention the lack of privacy. A guy like Hop was different—she lived with him and considered him her husband. Once in a while she'd come home with a bruise on her face because some guy had hit her. I didn't go for hitting a woman. I carried a two-foot plumber's wrench in the Olds. Rather than a piece of lead pipe that would get me arrested, I could always claim that it was just a tool. If I ever caught some geek knocking around Betty, I'd lay that wrench across his teeth.

I started up the stairs when Naomi's mother, Suke, sounds like *Sue-key*, came out from her apartment. She dealt blackjack at the Horseshoe. Naomi never mentioned what happened to her old man. Most of the kids I hung out with were like me—their father was a name or a memory.

"Lo-key, please come help me. I need strong man."

Nothing got a man—or a boy's—adrenaline pumping like a woman talking about his strength. Even if she pronounced his name a little pidgin. And it wasn't just any woman—Suke was just as attractive to me as Naomi. She wasn't as pretty as her daughter, was a little fuller of figure, but she had a cute little china-doll figure with small breasts, a slim figure, and tight buns. And again, the irresistible eyes. Unlike her daughter's, they were small and secretive, her eyelids like temple doors. I had to admit I went for women from the mysterious East.

I followed her into the apartment, toward the cubbyhole-hallway at the intersection of the living room and the doors to the bathroom and bedroom.

"What ya need, Suke?"

"No light." She showed me a new lightbulb. A glass light cover would have to be removed to change the bulb. She had a flimsy wooden stool beneath the light.

"No problem." I started to get on the stool and she stopped me.

"Stool too weak for you. You hold stool, I screw."

"Okay . . ."

I knelt by the stool and held it with both hands. She put her hand on my head to steady herself as she climbed onto the stool. My blood instantly heated from the smell of jasmine and the warmth that radiated from her.

She stood upright on the stool. Her short, thin-strapped black dress only came halfway down her thighs, exposing her copper-toned bare legs, which were firm and smooth and shined as if she had nylons on. When she reached up to fiddle with the little screws that held on the glass cover, her short dress went up and I saw her black panties covering her crotch. I didn't know if it was my shaking hands or the shaky stool, but she lost her balance and started teetering.

I stood up, grabbing her bare legs. She fell against me and slid down. I kept my hands around her and she slipped through them, my hands going up her bare legs and into her dress until I had a handful of bun in each hand by the time her feet hit the floor. She looked up at me, her mysterious eyes barely open. Her little breasts were pressed against my chest. She said something, I wasn't sure what. My hands were burning, brain frying. The smell of her jasmine perfume stole my mind. I squeezed her buns. She stood on tiptoes and pulled my head down with her hands. Her lips were hot and wet and tasted like sex as she pushed her tongue into my mouth.

When she pulled back, I was almost breathless and just stared at her, my throbbing penis ready to burst. A shoulder strap had slipped down and her breast was exposed. I felt its sexual message down to my toes. She smiled and kissed me again with her wet lips as she pulled down the other shoulder strap. I put my hand on the exposed breast but she pulled it away and led my head down to it. I kissed her breast and tasted her nipple with my tongue. The guys at school were all breast men, the bigger the better they said, but I always thought that anything more than a mouthful was a waste.

I was shaky and scared and needed to release. My dick pressed against my pants so hard it hurt.

Suddenly her hand went down inside my pants and she grabbed my penis. "Nooo!" I cried. I leaned against her as the volcano in my pants erupted.

"It's okay," she whispered. "Boys can have many times."

She led me into the bedroom and to her bed. She quickly pulled her dress over her head and stood before me, breasts naked, wearing only bikini panties. I fumbled off my clothes, all except my underwear. I was a cherry, nervous as hell, and had already pre-ejaculated.

She came and put her arms around me and rubbed her naked breasts against my chest, then pulled down my shorts. I stepped out of them and tried to steer her onto the bed, but she slipped from my grasp and pushed me down on the bed, on my back. Working at the top of my head, she started kissing me, licking my neck, going down to each of my nipples. I thought breast-fucking was only what guys did to girls, but I was wrong. When her erotic tongue teased my nipples, I felt it down to my toes.

Her tongue continued down my stomach, then to my penis, still limp. She held it up and kissed under it, running her tongue over my testicles and sucking my balls, then coming up and putting my whole penis in her mouth. As she sucked on my penis, it started to stiffen and get bigger. It grew in her mouth until she couldn't hold it all. Her mouth slipped off my erection and she grinned at me. "Boys good for many times."

She slipped off her panties. I tried to pull her down and mount her like I had once seen a guy do with a girl in the backseat of a car at a drive-in, but she pushed me back down and straddled me, kissing me as she rubbed her cunt against my hard-on. She was soft and wet and I slipped in easy and started pumping and I gasped as her strong legs tightened their grip on my penis.

"You want to fuck daughter, but mother better."

I loved Las Vegas. Not just the Strip but even Glitter Gulch downtown, which was a whole lot seedier than the Strip. Vegas really had stolen the title of the biggest little city in the world from Reno, which had become a poor cousin. To me, Vegas was like Hollywood, bigger than life, but even better because Betty told me that there really wasn't any place called Hollywood, that it was just a cheap and dirty street in Los Angeles and "Hollywood" was really movie studios and thousands of people scattered all over the L.A. basin. I guess the thing I liked most about Vegas was the vibration—you felt it everywhere you went, driving down the Strip or Fremont Street, walking through the casinos, in restaurants, hell, even getting gas at a self-service convenience store. The vibration came from the sound of money. There was no place else in the world where money made a louder noise than in Vegas. Some of that noise came from a guy Betty said was my father.

During the first couple of years Betty and I were in Vegas, Howard Hughes was always in the news because he was buying up the town. He even bought Harold's Club in Reno. People called him "the man who owned Las Vegas." But they also said things about him that weren't as flattering. He stayed at the top of the Desert Inn like some kind of spider spinning webs with his money. Everyone had a Hughes story, and all of the stories were about how weird and crazy he was. It made me wonder whether being crazy could be passed from father to son.

Betty had finally broken down and told me how he ran us out of Vegas when I was only a few months old. She made me promise never to say anything about him being my father. I would have gone up and told the guy off for what he did, but I kept my mouth shut because Betty was scared of him and she was doing good in Vegas. She was in her late thirties now, still pretty but a little worn. She still went twenty-four/seven, but there were a few lines on her face and some-times her feet hurt from being on them all night.

But no matter how much I told myself I didn't care, the fact I passed by the Desert Inn almost every day and knew a guy who was my father and who owned the place lived there, sometimes stuck in my craw. I told Naomi about it, after swearing her to secrecy. "No father's better than a crazy one," she told me. She had only a hazy memory of her own father, who cut out when she was three, and it was more a feeling than an image of the man. "Violence, yelling, my mother crying, that's what I remember about him and I don't want him back in my life."

Yeah, well, at least she had that.

Like I said, I loved the Strip. I was too young to gamble, but kids could walk through the clubs to get to restaurants, shows, and hotel rooms, and I'd do that just to hear the music of the casinos, the spin of the roulette wheels and wheels of fortune, the shuffle of cards, and the jingles and jangles of the slots. So much money, so many people, and everyone having a good time—except for the sore losers.

And the celebrities—all the ones you'd want to see, guys like Elvis and Wayne Newton, Jimmy Durante, Sammy Davis, Jr., but the King of the Strip was Frank Sinatra, though you either worshipped the guy or hated him. My favorite Sinatra story was the one about a casino manager who knocked out Sinatra's two front caps. After Howard Hughes bought the Sands, Frank, who had been the top bill at the place, got pissed because he wasn't getting the respect he thought he deserved and Hughes wouldn't return his phone calls. Frank wasn't the kind of guy who controlled his temper.

Angry when the Sands casino boss cut off his credit line, he went across the street and signed to perform at Caesar's Palace, then he came back and had a confrontation with the casino manager to rub it in. Frank called the guy a few names and got popped in the mouth. Hey, maybe the tourists loved Sinatra, but the little people on the Strip had had it with him. Pretty soon the posters went up that said that the guy who popped Sinatra ought to be mayor.

11

I used to hang around the parking lot in back of the Desert Inn in between checking on my crew, sometimes sacking out in the Olds to get some shut-eye. I woke up in the dark one night, it was just before Thanksgiving, not that the holiday meant anything to me—Betty worked holidays because people were more generous with their tipping. I had gotten out of the car to take a piss near a Dumpster when a security guard opened a service entrance door. Headlights and engines went on and three vehicles, an ambulance and two limos, lined up at the door. Other men came out and then a man came out on a stretcher. The guy on the stretcher was naked except for a hotel towel thrown across his midsection. He was skinny, no, more than that, he was wasted, emaciated, a dried mummy almost, skin stretched taunt from bone to bone. His skin was so pale, he glowed in the dark. He had long unkempt hair and a scraggly beard. I couldn't help but stare at his sunken cheekbones and eyes that were dark sockets, his fingernails and toenails so grotesquely long and curled.

No one noticed me standing by the Dumpster except the dude himself. When the attendants paused before lifting the stretcher into the back of the ambulance, the guy's eye caught me and he turned to stare. For a moment I was jolted by recognition, not that I knew the guy, but a feeling that I should know him.

Then he was gone, hustled into the ambulance, a flock of other guys jumping into limos, and the motorcade took off like it was carrying the president or somebody.

I hailed the security guard as he was closing the service door. "Who's the roadkill?"

"You just saw Howard Hughes, kid, the richest man in the world. He's leaving Vegas. He's been here for four years, almost to the day, and damn near owns the whole state."

"Where's he going?"

"With that guy, who knows. Probably to hell."

Suke taught me more about sex in a month than the regulars at the Pink Lady had learned over a lifetime. People related in different ways and Suke was a sexual animal.

"Lo-key, all men too impatient," she told me, as I eagerly jumped on her naked bones. She pushed me to the side. She was small built, but every ounce was muscle. "You have to talk to woman with hands and lips before you pump like dog fucking leg."

She had me start at the top of her head, coming down the side of her cheeks, my lips caressing the soft skin of her neck and under her ear, down the lush valley between her breasts, running my tongue over her nipples, slipping down to tease her bellybutton with my tongue, working my way down the insides of her thighs and to the soles of her feet before my head disappeared in the pink between her legs. She taught me to lick her vulva and go back to her lips so she could taste her own femininity, going back slowly to the pink and the sweet little button there.

"Work it slow," she told me, moaning with pleasure as I wet-kissed her neck while my penis spoke to her womanhood.

After a month, I considered myself quite a stud.

"You very good," Suke said. "Your cock not as big as Naomi's Bobby but you know how to use better."

"You fucked Naomi's boyfriend?" I was shocked.

"Only once. He love himself too much to give a woman good pleasure. But he hung like horse."

12

"The big spender wants your personal attention," the bar service manager told Betty. He jerked his head toward a guy sitting alone at a cocktail table.

The guy was big, with hulking arms and legs, a big round face, bald pate, and thick neck. Still solid, some of his pumped-up chest had slipped down to hang around the belly and hips as fat. He wore a thick gold chain around his neck, flashy gold Rolex, and a big gold ring with a ruby on his pinkie. His powder-blue shark-skin leisure suit was the kind of thing guys wore who wanted to imitate the Rat Pack. It matched the yellow silk shirt open at the neck, showing a puff of black hair like a furry cravat.

She recognized him. He had been in the lounge the night before, demanding to be comped for drinks because he dropped a wad at the craps table. He was loud and a little obnoxious, the owner of one of the big Chicago-area used-car dealerships, but he had given her a twenty-dollar tip.

She went over to him. "Hi. Matt, isn't it? A ball and a beer, Old Thompson's?"

"You got it, babe."

When she brought the drinks, he tossed a twenty-dollar chip on her tray.

"It's comped—"

"For you, pretty lady. You know, you're the best-looking doll I've seen in Vegas."

"Oh, com'on, this is a showgirl town." But Betty blushed anyway. She had a vain streak in her that ate up compliments from a man. The only approval she got in life was for her looks.

When she got off her shift at midnight, he was waiting for her with a bottle in a bag. "Thought we'd have a drink in my room."

He looked like he had already put away several drinks. Betty hesitated but he grabbed her arm and guided her toward the hotel elevators.

"The first time I saw you, I flipped, and that's no bull. I have so damn much money I can't spend it all and I've never found a woman to really enjoy spending it on until I laid eyes on you."

Yeah, it was bullshit, Betty knew it, but the guy had money and liked her, so why not show him a good time? Who knows? she thought, maybe they'd really click. He was probably lonely despite his money and business. Lots of guys she ran into in Vegas were like that. They spent all their time getting rich and then didn't know how to spend the money. Once in a while a girl got lucky and hit the marriage jackpot with one. And when they didn't, the guy usually gave them a nice tip for their time.

She wasn't a whore, even prided herself that she wasn't into the soft prostitution that many of the lounge girls practiced by going up to a room with a guy and picking up fifty bucks for half an hour's work. She believed that she had true affection for all of the guys she slept with. She never asked for money and was always a little shy when it was offered. She would push it back and make the guy offer it again before she'd keep it, then give him a peck on the lips.

Once they got inside his room, Matt was all over her like a wild animal in heat. His big sprawling hands started pawing at her breasts, then he ripped open the thin cotton blouse.

She pushed him back. "Hey, dammit, that cost me money!"

"I'll buy you a dozen blouses, babe."

He managed to get her skirt and blouse off and pulled her slip up over her head. Standing in her pink panties and bra he forced her roughly down on the bed and sprawled on top of her.

"Jesus, slow down a little."

"I know what you want, babe." She felt the throbbing bulge against her skin. As he unzipped his pants, he hungrily devoured her thin lips and forced his tongue in her mouth. He tasted like whiskey.

He jerked off her panties and with one violent motion thrust his phallus deep inside her and started pumping. The intensity of his passion increased and she was about to scream for him to stop when he finally exploded inside her. He felt heavy on her and she pushed him off her body as he lay gasping beside her. She felt used, dirty, and her body ached. She never dreamed it would be like this. He was dozing off when she quietly slipped off the bed and got dressed.

"Bastard," she muttered under her breath as she examined her torn blouse.

He had thrown his fat money clip onto the end table and she picked it up, peeling off a ten, a five, and two ones—the blouse had cost seventeen dollars. She put the money clip back on the table.

As she turned around, he came off the bed yelling, "Thieving bitch!" He moved fast for a big guy. His big fist caught her in an uppercut, slamming her gaping mouth shut, breaking her jaw, and driving her teeth into her gums. The punch lifted her from her feet and sent her flying backward against a wall. She bounced off and he hit her again, this time the punch landed on the side of her head. She fell to the floor, her brain bleeding inside her skull.

I woke up from the sound of pounding on the door. Two cops were standing outside when I opened it.

"You know Betty Riordan?"

"She's my mother."

"She's been hurt. We'll take you to the hospital."

They didn't say much to him about what happened, just that a guy hit her. When I asked why, they just shrugged their shoulders.

They let me off at the emergency entrance and I ran in. The reception nurse avoided meeting my eyes when I asked for Betty. A minute later a doctor came out of a room down the corridor and his eyes found mine. I ran down to him.

"I'm sorry, son, your mother is dead."

I didn't believe him. I flew past him and into the room. She lay naked on a gurney. Her head had been shaved and her face was black and bloody. I gasped and lost my breath for a moment. When the doctor came in behind me, I pushed by him and staggered out of the room. It hadn't registered in my brain yet.

I didn't know how long I'd been sitting outside on a brick wall when I saw a plainclothes cop come out of the hospital and walk toward me. I hadn't cried. I was cold and stiff and it all seemed unreal.

The cop blew his nose noisily onto a handkerchief before he pulled out a pad and pencil and began asking me questions. Stupid stuff, like name and address and Betty's date of birth. I was answering them like a robot when he threw me a curve.

"How long's your mother been hooking?"

"My mother's not a whore!" I came off the wall with my fists ready.

"Hey, take it easy, kid, I'm just doing my job. The guy who hit her says she turned a trick and tried to rob him."

"That's a lie! You fucking asshole!"

I came at him swinging and then I was on the ground with my arm in a hammerlock and the cop's knee in my back. I started crying my eyes out.

I stood in the hallway at the Clark County Courthouse when the case was called.

The guy's name was Matt Kupka. I had seen him earlier in the hallway with his lawyer, Jack Stein. I didn't understand much about the legal stuff. I knew that he'd been charged with murder and I wanted to be there to see his face when he was sentenced to fry. I came to court for each of his court dates, but nothing ever seemed to happen in the courtroom. Kupka would sit at the counsel table and shoot-the-shit with the bailiff while his lawyer and the deputy district attorney went into the back room with the judge. This was the third time I'd been to court since Betty was killed and I was anxious to see the guy get punished.

Naomi had heard that Stein was the best lawyer in Vegas, and Charlie Ricketts, the prosecutor, was a dump truck who worked up cases and dumped them just before trial, but that didn't mean shit to me—it was an open-and-shut case. The jerk beat a woman half his size to death, he had a prior incident of assault on a woman—it didn't take a rocket scientist to get a conviction.

Kupka and his lawyer came down the hallway laughing and talking like they were on their way to see Milton Berle at the Flamingo rather than Kupka getting ready to have his ass tossed in the slammer.

They never looked at me. I made sure to glare at Kupka every time I saw them and he avoided eye contact like the plague. I followed them into the courtroom and took a seat at the back. It was one-thirty, after the noon recess, and the usual hangers-on who had nothing to do with their lives but watch courtroom drama were gone.

Stein and the deputy DA greeted each other like old school chums and sauntered back to the judge's chamber. I sat and drilled holes with my eyes in the back of Kupka's shiny head, fantasizing what it would be like to crack his skull with the two-foot plumber's wrench I kept in my car.

The lawyers came out and the judge took the bench. "I understand the district attorney's office has a motion to make in this matter."

"Yes, your honor. At this time, we would move to dismiss all counts in the interest of justice."

"Very good. This matter is dismissed in its entirety."

"*No!*" My scream ricocheted off the courtroom walls. Everyone froze in midmotion. "Wha—what are you doing? He has to go to jail."

"It's the woman's son," the prosecutor said.

"Bailiff, take the boy into the jury room."

Charlie Ricketts came in a few minutes later. The bailiff came in behind him and stood at the door. He sat down beside me and put his legal file on the jury table, some of the contents spilling out. I hated to be around the guy. He had bad yellow teeth, smelled of b.o., and wore polyester suits that looked like he rolled around a lot when he slept in them.

"Son, it was a very tough case."

"I'm not your son." I spoke quietly. I wanted to punch his lights out. The dirt bag was probably no more than thirty and I hoped he didn't live to see thirty-one.

Ricketts shook his head. "Zack, there are some really bad things about this case that no one can talk to you about. You're not—"

"My mother wasn't a whore."

"I'm sure you loved your mother, Zack, and she was a good mother, but we have to deal with something called evidence. The evidence in this case is that when the police examined your mother, she was still clutching money taken from Mr. Kupka's bankroll, money we know was his because his fingerprints were on it, too."

"The newspapers said it was a lousy seventeen dollars."

"It could have been a single dollar. He caught her robbing him and in a moment of anger, lost his cool and—"

"Is that how you describe a two-hundred-and-fifty-pound gorilla beating to death a woman with his fists? Losing his *cool*?"

I grabbed one of the pictures that had slipped out of the legal file.

"You don't know my mother. If she found a dollar on the street and was hungry, she'd look around for the owner of the money. You see her blouse." I tapped on the picture. "That blouse cost her seventeen dollars. He ripped her blouse and she was just taking back what he owed her."

"Zack, it's hard on you, son—"

"I said I'm not your son, you fucking dump truck. You dumped the case because you're a piece of shit instead of a lawyer. See my face, shithead, remember it, because someday I'm gonna burn your ass."

Ricketts sighed and looked over to the bailiff.

"Take the little bastard to Juvie. Maybe they'll find a nice home for him where the foster father will fuck him in the ass each time he mouths off."

15

I thought I knew all about Juvenile Hall. Hell, half my friends had done time there, but what I didn't know was that kids who lost their parents, even orphaned babies, were tucked in with the incorrigibles. I was there for a week when Suke came to visit me. They wouldn't let Naomi in because she was under eighteen.

"I try to get you out, to stay with me." She shook her head. "I have conviction for shoplifting, five years ago, but they act like I kill some-one."

"It's okay, I'm going to San Bernardino to stay with my mother's sister."

She brightened up immediately. "Thank God, you have family."

"They're not family. I only met my aunt and her husband once. They're white trash. Betty couldn't stand them and neither could I."

Betty's sister, Marcy, had acquired none of Betty's good looks or good qualities. She and her husband had picked me up in my own '57 Olds. "Our car broke down and we took the bus to Vegas," Marcy confessed. I sat in the backseat with their twelve-year-old son and ten-year-old daughter. A guy once told me that the way you get the best out of a litter of puppies is to throw the whole batch into a river and see which ones swim out. These two snot-nosed, whiny little twerps would have sunk to the bottom. After a hot ride across the desert with no air conditioning, if we'd been near a river, I swear I'd have thrown them all in and held their heads under.

"We're not rich people, Zack. We can hardly feed our own, isn't that right, Honey?" Marcy said.

Honey was another real piece of work. He had a day-old beard, watery bloodshot eyes, needed a haircut, and looked like he robbed Salvation Army Dumpsters for his clothes.

"Not rich at all. We'll need every cent the county pays to keep you.

But we love you, boy, because you're family, don't we, Marcy?"

That was it in a nutshell. I came with a government check. Which was why my "loving" family wanted me. The only thing that made the trip worthwhile was that the Olds dropped its transmission three miles from Barstow and we abandoned it. I was glad the car died. I didn't want it abused.

Home was a three-room shack in San Bernardino that didn't even have the dignity of having a whorehouse nearby. Someone had made a half-assed attempt to stucco the walls, but the chicken wire showed through. The place was a pigsty. Betty was no shakes as a housekeeper, but she hadn't been a slob, either. These people were disgusting. My "room" was a rusty army cot with a dirty mattress on a screened-in porch.

"Honey will put in windows this winter," Marcy told me. "He's handy with tools."

I looked back to where Honey was hugging a beer in front of the TV. "Yeah, he's real good with a bottle opener."

"You'll register at San Bernardino High, that's what the county people require, that you be in high school in order for us to get a check. You'll like the young people here. They're much more down to earth than those Vegas types."

She wasn't kidding about them being down to earth—some of the country farm boys I saw looked like their knuckles hit the ground as they walked. The girls wore Levis and had wide hips. Only the Mex girls turned me on.

I lasted two weeks with my loving family. The first time Honey had too much to drink and got mean to the kids, I hit him in the nose with my fist loaded with a roll of nickels. The nickels splattered all over and so did his nose.

I left with the clothes on my back and seven dollars in my pocket. I hitched a ride at a truck stop with a long-distance driver who dropped me at the bottom of an off-ramp only a few blocks from Suke and Naomi's door.

The girls were happy to see me and I choked up because I knew their reaction was genuine. Naomi had to baby-sit at a neighbor's and she gave me a hug before she left.

"What if aunt has police come?" Suke asked when we were alone.

"Never happen. Their only interest in me is the monthly check. They'll collect that until someone figures out I'm not around and then they'll be too afraid to let the cops find me. They'll say I ran off the day before and I'll be back."

They had their apartment almost packed up.

"We move to uncle in Koreatown," Suke said, referring to the mid-Wilshire area of Los Angeles. "After what happen to your mother, I no like Vegas. And Naomi's boyfriend, he knock her up. Mother say, Bobby no marry nigger-chink."

"Nice lady. Maybe she'll rot in hell."

Suke made me take a shower and shave—"You stink. Go shower and I make you feel good." When I came out of the bathroom with a towel wrapped around me, she was waiting in bed.

I climbed into bed and the excitement in my loins began to rise as I looked at her glistening naked body. I still had my towel on and she slowly took it off and started moving her featherlike hands over my body in a hypnotic motion, the tingling sensations giving me goose bumps. She did an around-the-world number, touching every erogenous zone on my body from my head to my toes. My throbbing organ was fully erect when she took my penis in her mouth and ran her warm tongue around it, circling it like she was licking an ice cream cone, before she took all of me in her mouth and starting sucking on it. My juices came spurting out crazily all over her mouth, as I shot off.

We snuggled under the covers with Suke resting on my arm and I shut my eyes. I must have dozed off immediately. Next thing I knew it was dark in the room and someone was climbing into bed. Suke stirred at my other side as Naomi spread herself against me, hooking her leg over my leg. Her body was lithe and hard and hot. She kissed me on the mouth as she found my penis with her hand and massaged it. It jumped up at command. She rubbed against me, running her pubis up and down my leg, her cunt warm and lush. Then she was on top, taking my erect penis and guiding it inside her wet opening. As she straddled me, Suke spread herself over my face, rubbing her hairy pubic mound against my lips. I licked her and found her clitoris, and pressed the hot button with my tongue. "Mother-daughter, best of all," Suke gloated. A beginning tremble was signaling my coming orgasm and a few moments later my body shuddered and exploded.

17

I wasn't going to be a state kid, stuck in some foster home. I had turned seventeen the day I left my "loving family" in San Bernardino and I looked even older. I was tall, an inch over six feet, and my beard was heavy. I had what Naomi called a movie tough-guy look. "Like Lee Marvin in *The Professionals*. It's your eyes. Like you're not sure whether to kill someone or not."

Suke offered to take me along with them to Koreatown, but Vegas was my home. Also Betty was here, buried without a headstone. I needed to figure out a way to stay. And I needed money. There was two hundred dollars stuffed in the couch in our place upstairs. The couch belonged to the landlord, but the money was mine. He hadn't rented the place yet, and I still had a key. I slipped in and retrieved my wad. I thought about the fact my mother had slept on the couch, and I sat down on it and talked to her for a minute as if she was sitting right next to me.

"Hey, Betty, things are going pretty good. And you were sure right about your sister, Marcy. What a dumb bitch. But I'm doing okay, so you don't have to worry."

I wiped the tears from my eyes before I left to hit the streets, trying to figure out what I could do to survive. Not having a car in Vegas wasn't as bad as other places because everything that was anything was concentrated in two areas, Glitter Gulch and the Strip.

The first thing I did was use eighty dollars to buy a headstone for Betty. It wasn't dignified, being the only one out there without her name on a stone. Coming back from the granite place, I thought about my options. Living in the desert wasn't as hard as most other places. Sure, it got cold in the winter, but it was survivable most of the year. There were bums who lived outside of town in caves dug into the soft sandstone sides of dried riverbeds. We had the same thing in Mina and Hawthorne, men who had nowhere to go when the mines closed and lived Stone Age, coming into town to pick up a day's labor now and again and more often to hit the soup kitchens in North Las Vegas. The Salvation Army had a mission downtown that I heard served beans that weren't too bad. And they let you stay a while in their bunkhouse as long as you were willing to listen to a sermon about God and salvation.

I couldn't run my handout business, not without a car. Besides, Tony Lardino had taken it over after Betty was killed and I dropped it. That left picking up odd jobs like yard work and washing cars.

Fuck that! I'd sooner bust into parked cars of tourists and grab their cameras and rip out their radios before I'd get calluses raking someone's yard for peanuts.

An idea was germinating in my mind as I walked past a house where an old guy sat on the porch playing cards by himself. I had seen him before, camped out on the porch, dealing out poker hands like there were other players at the table. His hands were kind of messed up, like he'd broken them. He had the look of a casino dealer, lean and wiry, intense and quick even when he was playing alone, but his hands were too screwed up for casino dealing. I figured the guy had once been a dealer and hurt his hands; now he lived poor on a little Social Security.

His house was little more than a tarpaper shack, but what really interested me was an old travel trailer in the backyard. It wasn't much of a trailer, one of those things that looked like a camel's hump on two wheels. Not more than ten or twelve feet long, you couldn't stand up in it. You got into it on your knees through a small door on the side and had to crawl around inside. Little windows in the front and rear gave enough light so you didn't think you were in a coffin. An old station wagon with a hitch was parked in the driveway, so I guess he pulled it at some time, but from the look of the dried, cracked rubber on the half-flat tires and the weeds growing around them, the trailer hadn't seen a road in a long time.

I went through the picket fence gate, lifting it up to push it aside because it was hanging on only one hinge.

"Hi."

The old man looked me over. "Howdy. What can I do for you?"

"I was looking at your trailer."

"You interested in buying it?"

"No, more like renting it. I need someplace to stay."

"Where do you live now?"

"Down the street, but I have to move."

"It isn't a live-in trailer. You can't even stand in it. You working?"

"No, but I'm gonna be. I've got money." Betty and I had been paying one-fifty a month for the one-bedroom dump we rented. If the old man was on Social Security, he probably wasn't getting more than a few hundred a month, maybe no more than two-fifty. "I can pay you fifty a month, if I can use your icebox for a couple things, and your stove." I figured I could live on Cream of Wheat if nothing else.

"Haven't I seen you driving by here sometimes with your mother? Where's your folks?"

"I don't have any. Look, you want to make a deal or not?"

He chuckled. "Don't be such a hard-ass, kid. I need to know whether you're gonna knock an old man over the head for the jar of pennies I keep under my bed. But you look okay to me, just a little snarly. I'll tell you what, we'll draw for the first month's rent, double or nothing."

He shuffled the cards. His hands were twisted and gnarled from the old injury or arthritis, but he was still quick.

"They call you Lucky, don't they?"

"How'd you know that?"

The old man shrugged and gave a small, secretive smile. "I hear lots of things."

He spread the cards in a fan.

"Pull your card, kid."

I looked over the fan of cards and drew a card. Ten of hearts. Not bad. It beat eight of the twelve other cards in the deck.

He pursed his lips, started for the center of the fan, changed his mind and flipped over a card off to the left.

Ace of spades.

I pulled my wad out of my pocket and peeled off five twenties. It left me with just twenty bucks.

"I guess they were wrong," he said.

" 'Bout what?"

"Calling you Lucky."

I said an emotional good-bye to Suke and Naomi after helping load their car. I refused the money Suke tried to stuff in my pocket, telling her that I had plenty. "Save it for Naomi's baby," I told her.

My next stop was Morty Lardino. He held court at the back of a pool hall on a side street downtown. Morty was a small-time racketeer in a town that still had the shadow of the mob. People said Howard Hughes bought the mob out of Vegas with his checkbook, but they laughed all the way to the bank because they only got themselves out of the limelight. Vegas was a sea of loose money and it had an irresistible appeal to crooks. Besides, bottom feeders like Morty were always around. Morty was strictly a street-crime guy, collecting a commission from pimps, getting a cut from the drug pushers, importing girls and renting them to the whorehouses outside the county limits where prostitution was legal. But there were too many *legal* rackets in Nevada for a small-time hood to get rich quick. And the type of protection rackets that flourished on the East Coast, like laundries or garbage collectors, didn't go well in a society where everyone owned guns and a lot of sheriffs still wore cowboy hats.

"Mr. Lardino," I said, respectfully stopping five feet from his table. He was alone at the table. Another man had gotten up and gone to the john as I came in.

Morty was not quite as big as Tony, but he had a cold mean look, a junkyard dog with a small brain and big teeth. I heard his old man was a wop and his old lady a Jew. I was Heinz ketchup, but Betty said I had some Jewish and Italian blood, so I planned to play that card with him when I had a chance.

Taking a cigar out of his mouth, a diamond the size of Mount Rushmore flashed on his ring finger. He wore a black jacket heavily coated with dandruff and a dark-blue shirt with white polka dots, gray slacks, and white shoes. A gold chain was on his wrist and around his neck.

I hated the gold chain look—it reminded me of that creep Kupka, who was weighed down with the stuff.

"What'd ya want?"

I came up to the table. My throat was dry. I heard Morty was a real ball breaker. A drug pusher had four fingers missing from his right hand and the word on the street was that Morty had stuck the guy's hand under the blade of a paper cutter and pulled the handle himself after the dealer had shorted him on a payoff.

"I'm looking for a job?"

He flicked ashes off of his cigar as he squinted at me. "This look like the unemployment office, kid?"

"No, sir, but I heard you need someone to run errands." What he needed was a bagman. The morning paper said a man was arrested last night trying to shake down a cop posing as a prostitute. I knew the dude, he hung around with Tony Lardino. His job was to collect money from the pimps and pushers in a bag and bring the bag to Morty. Every dime. The job paid well, but acting as a go-between for crooks and a mobster wasn't exactly considered an opportunity assignment.

"You a wise guy?"

"No, sir, you can ask Tony about me, I ran the rag pushers for six months and paid him a cut. I was with him once when you drove up, but you probably didn't notice me."

"What's your name?"

"Zack Riordan, sir."

"Riordan. Yeah, I know who you are. Your old lady got popped by that car salesman."

I felt my blood rising. "Can I have the job?"

"How old are you?"

"Twenty-one."

His squint deepened. "You're shitting me, kid. You ain't a day pass nineteen."

I grinned. "I'm almost twenty-one. Besides, if I get busted, I'll be a first-time youth offender. I won't do any time."

"You got an old man?"

"No. But I don't need anyone."

"Yeah, that's right, you were a big-time rag pusher." He threw back his big head and laughed.

The man who had been at the table with him came back from the john. Morty pointed his cigar at him.

"This is Sam. He'll show you how to work the route. You know how to count, kid?"

"Count? Sure, I'm good with arithmetic."

"Make sure you count real accurate, kid. You won't have any fingers or toes to help you add with if I catch you skimming."

"Working the route" meant hanging around the streets, watching the action. After you got to know the players—the pimps, prostitutes, and drug pushers—it was pretty easy to estimate what they were taking in. Once each night I took a collection from the players, stuffing the money in my jacket pockets. Sometimes it was nickel-and-dime stuff from a pusher, but a pimp was usually good for a couple hundred. Sam and Morty knew from past history exactly what each player should pay. I got grilled when it wasn't exactly what they expected. I kept track of the take using a code scribbled on a piece of paper small enough to swallow it if I got busted.

Most of the action took place downtown in Glitter Gulch. Street-walkers and overt pushers were a no-no on the Strip. Most whores got sent over to the Strip by a call from a hotel bellman. A few hung around the cocktail lounges after slipping a bartender a twenty, but the lounges in the big clubs had service managers who, following the universal policy, tolerated prostitution only if it was done subtly.

Once a night I made a run up to the Strip and hit the bellmen and barmen on the route. I needed a car for that; it didn't look good for a mob bagman to ride a city bus, and I asked the old guy I rented the trailer from if I could use his station wagon for a few bucks when I needed it. He let me use the car as long as I kept gas in it, accompanying me several times just to get out of the house. His name was Paul Embers and I was right about his prior occupation. He was an old-time dealer and gambler, now living poor.

"I worked all the old clubs," Paul told me, "from Cal-Neva on the California-Nevada border in South Tahoe, to Harold's Club and Harrah's in Reno, down to Binion's Horseshoe on Glitter Gulch and the Dunes on the Strip. I dealt blackjack the night the Flamingo opened. Bugsy stood right next to me watching me deal to George Raft, who came in to help his pal Bugsy. I've seen mushroom clouds from the atomic blasts at the testing grounds. In 'fifty-six I saw Elvis when he opened at the Frontier. He sang 'Heartbreak Hotel' and 'Blue Suede Shoes.' He flopped and they fired him after a week. I've seen so many Helldorado Day parades I should be the grand master."

Embers hadn't been just a casino dealer, but a professional poker player, the kind of guy you would call a card sharp. Despite his hands being deformed, he could still shuffle and deal better than me.

I asked him what happened to his hands.

"Jack slipped and a car dropped on my hands when I was fixing a tire," he explained.

Cards were his life—his sex life, his children, his filet mignon. And poker was his game.

"Poker's the only real game of skill in a casino," he said. "All the rest are just pits where you throw your money because the odds are always with the house. With six decks, blackjack's become a game of chance to all but a few freaks who can count that many cards. You can have runs of luck with poker, good and bad, but you have the same odds as everyone else at the table. With the odds neutral, it comes down to who's the best poker player."

Embers knew everything about poker—including how to cheat. He started teaching me to play and to watch for cheating.

"You can't play poker timidly, you have to be completely fearless. A poker table is a battlefield in which no quarter is asked or given. I've played poker all my life. Played my first game in Helena, Montana, in the back of a saloon when I was sixteen. I've seen men lose their homes, jobs, families, and their lives at the turn of a card. Poker is my poison and my aphrodisiac. The only hand I won't bet on is aces and eights. It's the bad-luck hand Wild Bill Hickok was holding when he got shot in the back by Dirty Jack McCall."

He showed me how to cheat.

"With a false shuffle and cut, the cards look like they're being mixed, but they don't change order," Embers told me. "You then deal out the cards in a prearranged order from a cold deck. Slipping aces to the bottom and dealing them to yourself is another easy scam. Dealers will peek at the top card, see it's something they want, and deal the next cards or off the bottom until they can drop the good card on themselves or their buddy. When playing blackjack with a single deck, one of the swiftest moves is to gather up the cards on the table and slip some back on the top where you want them rather than on the bottom where they belong.

"Marking the back of cards with your fingernail so you can identify them later is the easiest cheat. Another trick is to hold back a couple of aces, hide them up your sleeve, and pull them out when you need them. A trick used by some small-time grind joints is to use decks with fewer ten-count cards than smaller cards, that way the dealer doesn't go bust as often when he's forced to hit a sixteen. But the easiest way to cheat is simply to use a marked deck." He spread a deck out on the table we were sitting at and pointed at a card. "What's that card?"

"I dunno."

"Ace of diamonds, queen of hearts, jack of spades—in this deck, the aces and face cards are marked. Watch." He bent the end of the deck and let them flow by his thumb at high speed so I could see the pattern on the back in motion. "You can tell the deck is marked because there are interruptions in the pattern on the back of the cards as I fan them."

I picked up one of the cards and examined the familiar design on the back.

"Paul, this is the deck you pulled the ace from to beat me out of an extra month's rent. You cheated me."

He stared at me like I'd just accused the pope of bigamy. "Of course. This is Las Vegas."

I met Janelle at a lap-dance club. I had just turned twenty-one, my phony license said I was twenty-three, and I could pass for twenty-five. Sometimes even I forgot how old I really was.

The last several years had gone by as if I was operating at jetsetter speed. My bagman job with Morty Lardino lasted until a drug dealer high on his own supply pulled a Saturday night special on me when I asked for Morty's cut. I was out of the North Las Vegas alley and halfway to the Strip before he got it cocked and locked. I don't know what happened to the guy—the word on the street was that Morty cut off his balls, stuffed them in his mouth, then buried him up to his neck in an ant hill out in the desert.

Facing a gun in the hands of a crazy was bad enough—Vegas and the mob had taken a backslide that made it unhealthy to be associated with guys like Morty. Since the mob discovered Vegas back in the forties, the town had been neutral territory, like seeking sanctuary in a church back in the days of the king's men. There were hits, but never in town. The designated target was taken far out into the desert and simply disappeared, or followed home to Chicago or Jersey and hit. But after the boss of bosses, Vito Genovese, died in prison in '69, and guys like Tony Spilotro, the mob's Chicago enforcer who took out Sam Giancana, came to Vegas to fill the void created when Howard Hughes left with his billion-dollar checkbook, mob disputes—some of them acted out in Vegas, even one in the parking lot of a big club on the Strip—erupted. The War of the Godfathers was no place for a kid who was getting paid chump change to do Morty Lardino's dirty work.

Soon after I left Morty's employment, the fat man died scarfing down a plate of spaghetti. I heard that he suffered a café coronary from gulping down a sausage too fast. I also heard he choked to death when a couple of Jersey thugs stuffed his cloth napkin down his throat. Tony disappeared from the streets, too, DOA. He caught a college student flirting with his girlfriend and scattered the guy's brains with his baseball bat. While he was in the state slammer, another con—a guy who had to eat his shit on the streets of Vegas when Uncle Morty was alive—gutted him in the prison yard with a homemade shank.

Windell Palmer, a nerdy jerk I did some street deals with, picked me and George Leroy Smith up at Embers's house. Leroy was a pimp from L.A. Windell was a world-class twerp, the prototype of the skinny kid with Coke-bottle eyeglasses who got sand kicked in his face at the beach but still never redeemed himself by eating Wheaties. Next to him, Woody Allen was Dirty Harry.

I met Windell when I spotted him using quarter-size metal slugs to get a free Coke at a gas station. Turns out he stamped out the slugs with a machine he put together with scarps and a sewing machine motor. I had him stamp them out by the thousands and put them into the paper rolls that held ten dollars worth of quarters and sold them for five dollars a pop. They worked fine in quarter slots, but the casinos were on to it real fast and we stopped selling them. Most casinos considered it a capital offense to rip them off. Thugs who earned their living in every kind of known racket reacted with the violent indignation of a religious fanatic if someone took them for a buck.

Leroy brought me into another racket—pimping—but I never considered myself a contender for a shot at the title. There are some things you need to be born to do well. Kids who learn how to stand up on skis at three years old become good skiers, but they have to be born with the knack to ski good enough for the Olympics. I learned that lesson first when Embers tried to make me into a world-class card shark—I learned all the moves, I could spot a false shuffle, a bottom deal, a marked deck, the whole nine yards, but no matter how many hours I spent in front of a mirror watching my own hands, I didn't have the speed and finesse that Embers had before his accident. Pimping was something else I only had amateur standing at.

"You're a thug," Embers said, disgusted at my assertive approach to playing poker and my lack of finesse in handling a deck. "You have no patience, no timing, you're always risking everything for the big pot. Poker is an introspective game, like chess, but you treat it like a fist fight. It's a game of strategy and math, but you refuse to deal with the science of the game. You make blind bets, relying on luck. You draw on inside straights no matter how many times I tell you no poker player does. You chase Lady Luck, but she's a prick teaser who flashes her snatch but crosses her legs when you try to stick it in."

"I take chances because I want to be somebody, Embers, and I don't have the rest of my life to wait."

He taught me to spend as much time watching a player's eyes as his hands. "Persian rug dealers know you expose your desires with your eyes. When they lay out the carpets, they watch your eyes and know the carpet you want by the way your pupils dilate. Once they know you want it, they have you by the balls."

He was wrong about one thing—I did catch the math about casinos. No matter who's playing, the casinos ultimately win because they play strictly by the odds. "The stars may lie," Embers said, "but the numbers never do."

After Morty Lardino choked to death eating his napkin, and Tony ran into an old friend's homemade shiv in the state pen, I had gone back into the rag business, working the streets distributing pamphlets for massage parlors and escort services. The cops had gotten wise to the racket and required a license, forbidding minors from passing out racy stuff, so I got the license in Embers's name and hired guys from a revolving pool of mission puppies—derelicts who didn't smell and look so bad that they scared off the customers. Advancing from passing out pamphlets to soliciting business was a natural step, and pretty soon I was ferrying guys to the parlors and making "dates" for the escort services. The next step was having my own stable of girls and that's where Leroy came in. He was a bona fide pimp from L.A. who ran girls on Sunset Boulevard. He came to Vegas to open a "branch office" but ran into trouble with the guy who controlled most of the street action and who had a lock on the best spots.

With my tourist contacts generated by the handouts, I was a natural for teaming up with Leroy—I provided the johns and he provided the whores. The girls turned the tricks in hotel rooms rented downtown and in North Las Vegas, but they never walked the streets.

"Consider yourself part of a franchise like Kentucky Fried Chicken—we even serve white and dark meat," Leroy said.

I was paid twenty-five bucks for every john my guys brought in.

From that amount, I had to give the guy who copped the deal five and the driver five, and Nike Monte, Morty Lardino's replacement as street boss, too five plus a piece of Leroy's action. That left me with ten bucks. I wasn't getting rich, but with my other action, it helped keep me from having to do honest work. I could have cut Leroy from the deal and run girls myself, but I didn't have the balls to be a true pimp. It took a real prick to manage whores.

"The greatest pimp in the world was Iceberg Slim," Leroy told me. "He said a pimp is the loneliest bastard on earth, a guy who's gotta know his whores but who can never let them know him. He's gotta be God to the bitches. Is that shit profound or what?"

When Windell picked us up at Embers's, he was driving a brand-new Plymouth Fury.

"Where the hell's that tin can you drive?" I asked the nerd. His usual transportation was one of those minicars that Honda put out, hardly bigger than motorcycles and looked like they were built from recycled pea cans.

"This is a loaner," he told us as we cruised toward the Strip. The car had a new-car smell and the dealer's price sticker was still on the side window.

"They give you a loaner when they repair that piece of junk you drive? Bullshit."

"Naw, it's not that kind of loaner. I did a favor for a guy and he loaned me the car. He borrowed it from the dealer."

I looked back at Leroy just as a cop car drove by and both of us froze.

"Windell," I said, keeping the murderous rage out of my voice, "is this car hot?"

"Call it borrowed."

"Bullshit."

"Would I lie to you, man?"

"Do chickens have lips?"

"Okay, it was borrowed but the dealership don't know it."

"Stop this car, you little fucker, and let us out!"

The three of us made the ride to the Strip in Embers's station wagon. On the way, Windell explained to us how his friend copped the cars.

"He goes into a dealership and test drives the car. When they park it back on the lot after the drive, he does a key switch, slipping a dummy key for the brand of car onto the ring and takes the real key off. Then he comes back during the night and drives it away."

Leroy and me debated investing in the scheme all the way to the Pussy Kat Dance Club.

The Pussy Kat was a takeoff on the old taxi dance places of the twenties and thirties where you paid a dime to dance with a girl. Only in this case, the girl stripped in front of you for a hell of a lot more than a dime.

Sure, I could've gotten a girl to strip for me without paying, but somehow paying a woman to take off her clothes appealed to me. And of course not just any woman could get my juices flowing—like Philip Marlowe said in *Farewell, My Lovely*: "I like smooth shiny girls, hard-boiled and loaded with sin."

He would have loved Janelle.

With all the free pussy Leroy and I could get, we still ended up at the Pussy Kat with Windell when we were carousing the Strip area. We paid the ten-dollar admission fee and got the usual entrance admonishment.

"Dances are twenty dollars, plus gratuity. Drinks are five. You have to order two drinks. Don't touch the girls, their hair, their ass, their little toe, nada. You touch and he will escort you out."

The bouncer was a guy with cannonball biceps, pects like hubcaps, and no neck.

These lap joints weren't kidding when they said hands off. Not that they gave a damn about what customers did with the girls later—most of the girls could be "dated" on the side. But to appease the city's self-appointed moral busybodies who were down on anything sexual because they weren't getting any themselves, the clubs strictly followed the rules to keep their licenses.

We took a table and ordered the mandatory watered-down drinks. There were mostly young guys in the club, a bunch of frats from USC, a rich kid's school in a L.A. slum. There were several lap dancers doing their thing when a carrot-top with freckles came over. She sized us up to see who was the big spender and made a beeline for Leroy. Smart girl. I had just paid him the five hundred I owed him, which left me with fifty bucks. Windell probably had a pocketful of the quarter slugs he stamped out.

"May I dance for you?" she asked Leroy.

"Give me the treatment, Red. I've been stranded on a desert island for ten years and you're the first woman I've seen."

"Well, honey, you've just been rescued."

She started gyrating to the beat of the music, slowly twisting, teasing. It didn't interest me much even though she was only a couple feet from my table. Lap dancing was personal. The guy who paid for the dance got the heat.

A girl entered the room and my eye caught hers and she came to the table. She was platinum blonde, so silvery that her hair looked like freshly minted silver. Her pale hair and pale skin made her hot red lips stand out even more. It was love at first sight for me. Well, if not love, then at least lust.

She smiled. "I'm Janelle. May I dance for you?"

"Please," I said, a little too eagerly.

When she started moving her body to the beat of the music, everything faded around me in the club, except her. I felt like someone had turned off the lights and shut down the noise, leaving only a bright spotlight on her. The redhead taking it off for Leroy moved in jerky movements with the disco music. But Ms. Platinum moved fluidly, seductively, like a queen cobra slithering to the subtle tone of a flute. She stripped down to her scarlet brassiere and panties. Her nipples were ready to jut out of the thin silk bra. She removed the brassiere slowly to reveal a cornucopia of succulent flesh, firm but lush, not too big but more than a mouthful. Her green eyes teased me as she got closer and closer. I felt the heat surging in my loins. Then she stepped out of her sheer silk panties to reveal the soft, fleshy mound that had been shaved. There was something wetly erotic about a shaved pubis. I always wondered why statues of men and women never showed pubic hair. I figured it was because bodies were so much more sensual when the groin was naked.

I looked into those laughing green eyes and wanted to taste those red lips so bad—both sets—I was ready to spread her onto the hard knob throbbing between my legs.

You know, I could have gone over and got it off with one of Leroy's girls, or gone to one of the legit houses beyond the county line, even just hung around one of the clubs and picked up a female tourist hoping to get laid at least once during her three days in town, but it wasn't the same. This girl, Janelle, didn't just get my testosterone pumping, she got under my skin and into my head.

She took it all off, naked, down to red nail polish and unusual jewelry—rings on every finger, including one on her middle finger with a chain that looped back to a bracelet.

When she finished dancing, I pulled the fifty bucks out of my pocket and handed them to her.

"Over here, Janelle." The call came from a frat jock.

She raised her eyebrows at me. "Current customers have the option for another dance."

"Yeah, I—shit!" I realized I had given her my last money. Leroy and the redhead were gone, probably out to my car, where Leroy was getting his tires rotated. I leaned across and whispered to Windell. "You got any money?"

"Twenty slug quarters."

I turned around to her, oozing with charm. "My buddy went someplace with the redhead. He's holding my money, he'll be back in a minute."

She smiled like a loan officer who just discovered that the applicant had neither job nor collateral. "Enjoy your drink."

Her voice sent shivers up my spine. I went after her, grabbing her arm. "Hey, I'm not kidding, my buddy's got the money."

"Hey, beat it, she's going to dance for me," the frat said.

"Piss off—"

Someone behind me clamped a hand on my arm and I turned to look up at the bouncer. I swear the ape's hand circumnavigated my arm.

"You were told no touching."

I got one backward glance at Janelle as the bouncer escorted me out. Contempt, that's what she had for me, contempt because I didn't have the price of a dance. Which only served to turn me on. I'd be hemorrhaging lust until I had this ruthless bitch. The next night I went back with money in my pocket but was told she was on "sabbatical" for a week.

Windell was always coming up with harebrained schemes and I got busy trying to figure out a way to make his latest one work. He had an idea about bribing an engraver at the Mexican company that manufactured most of the playing cards for Vegas to mark aces and ten-point cards.

"We'd only need it one night," he said, "and we could rack up millions."

Yeah, and spend it on new arms and legs after the casino bosses amputated ours and left us lying out in the desert as coyote bait. But the idea was intriguing. Everyone was always trying to beat blackjack using a count system or by positioning someone to see what the dealers dealt themselves. In Vegas, they called it "going for the money." Every few months a scheme by players or players-and-dealers hit the papers. Then people like Windell and me who dreamt of breaking the bank at a casino—illegally, of course—would get their adrenaline up and lie awake nights trying to figure out the perfect way to pull it off.

A couple of weeks after being put down by Janelle, I was cruising down Fremont Street in Glitter Gulch, rolling around my head a going-for-the-money idea, when I saw Janelle walk into the Golden Gate. I parked and found her inside the club, methodically losing money at a quarter machine. She reminded me of the way Betty used to play the slots, as if she was there to make a contribution rather than having any real hope of winning. I slipped onto the stool next to her.

"Long time no see."

She glanced at me. Not a real look, just a sideways glance. She wore a tank top that displayed her nipples.

"It's the big spender."

I grinned. "You're making a mistake. You don't know who you're talking to. I'm Big Zack Riordan, the guy who runs this town. If you're real nice to me, I'll buy you a fur coat to warm up that cold personality of yours."

She made a little sound deep in her throat like she was going to be sick. "What'd you buy it with, sport, those slugs your friend had? Go jack off, will ya?"

I always carried a handful of Windell's metal babies with me and I pulled one out and flipped it up and caught it. I dropped it in a slot and pulled the handle.

"Women usually come crawling to me after—"

I looked as the tumblers stopped on a jackpot emblem, then a second one, and a third. A light flashed above the machine and a fog horn went off. I stared stupidly at the three medallions on the pay line and the list of winning combinations.

I had just won my first jackpot since I was three months old—five hundred dollars. From a quarter slug.

Janelle leaned over and her hot, wet tongue licked my ear. "Wanna fuck?"

22

We went to her place. I still lived with Embers. The little humpback trailer flipped over in a high wind and I replaced it with one that was slightly bigger but still as ratty. Janelle's place was the usual one-bedroom, one-bath, drywall, low-income Vegas apartment. They grew like cabbage patches as casinos opened and workers poured into the town.

She poured into my arms the moment we stepped into her apartment. I kicked the door shut as I was kissing her. Her body was hot and solid, firmer than any woman I'd ever been with. She yanked her tank top over her head and pushed her skin-tight blue jeans down, leaving her standing in white silky bra and panties. We moved our way to the couch in between our kissing and my stripping.

I undid her bra and buried my face against the lush melons, Chanel No. 5 robbing me of my senses. Her nipples were distended with excitement. I took one in my mouth while my hands pulled off the white panties and I moaned with delight. I had never felt a naked pussy before. "Eat me," she cried. My lips found her clit and I worked into a frenzy of passion, as she grabbed the back of my head and pulled me in deeper and deeper as she spread her legs, grinding her hips and arching her back. As soon as she exploded, she was ready again, pushing me back onto the couch and mounting me. I stood up, holding her buttocks in both hands, letting her ride my erection, pulling her back so my cock rubbed against her clit. She grabbed me by the side of my head and bit my mouth as she came again.

23

"Trying to take a casino is too risky," Embers said. "You're not looking at jail time if you get caught, but a bullet in the back of the head."

Janelle, Windell, and me were at the New Frontier scarfing up the cheap buffet. That was one good thing about Vegas—the town was full of ninety-nine-cent breakfasts and three-ninety-nine buffet dinners. All the casinos wanted you to do was lose your shirt when you came for the cheap eats.

"No one's ever gotten away with making a big hit on Vegas. This isn't just a town and gambling isn't just an industry. The underworld tentacles reach from one end of the country to the other."

"Nobody's been smart enough to do it yet," Windell said.

Embers's opinion of Windell's smarts was evident by the way the old man chewed the tough roast beef as he looked at Windell, as if wondering what mud hole it had been dragged out of.

I said, "Windell's idea about hitting a bunch of clubs with marked cards and all of us running around pulling in thousands every hour at blackjack tables is impractical. I was thinking more in terms of one club, one deck, one table, one hit. If we can get a dealer to substitute marked decks for regular ones, we could easily earn six or eight thousand at a table before anyone started taking a closer look. The secret is not to get greedy. When we reach a set amount, say five thousand, we cash in. If each of us pulls that stunt once or twice a week, by the end of the month we'd have a hundred grand or more."

Embers snorted. "By the end of the first week, you'll be in a shallow grave with coyotes digging you up."

Janelle and I had been knocking around together for three months when I made reservations at the restaurant in the Sands for Janelle's birthday. I didn't have a suit and one birthday wasn't worth laying out the bread for one, so I rented a tux. It wasn't a wedding, but I wanted to wear a tux because I never had one on before. Janelle wore a blue sequined dress that fit her as if it was painted on and displayed her valleys, peaks, and dangerous curves. We really thought we were hot stuff. Here I was with a real tux on and going to a fancy restaurant, like we were rich people, not just a lap dancer and a guy with a pocket full of slugs.

When we came up to the maître d's desk, the guy looked at me like the Acme rental tag was hanging from my monkey suit. He had a glass of clouded liquid on the desk, the kind of stuff you feed an ulcer. There was a whispered conversation between him and a cold, pale broad wearing black lipstick who was holding menus.

"I'm sorry, Mr. Riordan, but it became necessary to rebook your reservation for tomorrow night. We have an opening at ten-thirty then."

"Tomorrow night? I'm from New York, pal. I'll be returning tomorrow night. I made this reservation three days ago."

"I'm sorry, but we don't have a table tonight."

"I can see empty tables." I was getting hot under the collar.

"Those are reserved," the cold broad said.

"You got in high rollers and you're giving them our table," Janelle said angrily.

"Why don't you take your business elsewhere."

Janelle leaned across the desk. "Up yours." She grabbed the front of the woman's dress, jerked it open and poured the iced drink down it.

I had tickets for a show, but we split with the bitch screaming hot and loud. Two security dudes came out after us onto the sidewalk and I whipped around and gave them my best sneer.

"You're off the reservation, assholes."

"Leav'em alone, Rocco," Janelle said. "I'll have my old man send around some of his boys to teach them manners."

That stopped them. I didn't know if I could pass for a tough guy, but Janelle definitely had gangland written all over her.

We ended up eating hamburgers and milk shakes at a drive-in. I was still burning from the put-down. "Those dirty bastards, I'll show them someday, you wait and see, I'll shove the Strip right up their asses."

"Don't hold your breath, Zack. They've got one thing that we'll never have.

"What?"

"Money."

"I'll have money."

"Not in this town you won't—the people who have it, keep it." She took her purse and a straw and went to the restroom. When she came back, I could see white powder on her nostrils.

I hated when she did that, taking a hit. I tried cocaine once at a party and was dizzy for three days, so I knew I had to use it carefully. Janelle claimed she wasn't hooked on the stuff, but she was always wired or crashing. She worked two jobs, lap dancing at the Pussy Kat and dealing blackjack part-time at Halliday's, the biggest of the grind joints downtown. On the side she did private lap dances for a guy who gave her tickets for shows along the Strip. The guy was nothing more than a lightbulb distributor, but Vegas was one hell of a lit-up city. Janelle swore to me that she had never turned tricks and I didn't push it or believe her. Her background was similar to Betty's—junkyard trailer-park life in Modesto until she was old enough to push out on her own. She'd been in Vegas for two years, after dumping a guy she had shacked up with in Frisco, getting rid of a pregnancy with an abortion, and deciding to head for Vegas where she could earn some real money.

"One of my friends is a schoolteacher in L.A. She flies to Vegas every Friday night and returns on Sunday. Even after expenses, in two nights she earns more from dating than she does a week teaching."

There was no question about it, sin paid more than schools. But for all of Janelle's hard work, she had nothing but some hot clothes because the money went up her nose.

I knew Janelle was hurt by the rejection at the restaurant, but she had something of the same fatalism of the poor that Betty had, the inner belief that no matter how much she tried, nothing would ever go right for her. But I was still sweltering inside. Some bastard got away with killing my mother because he had money. It was my turn to have the dough, to get a piece of Vegas besides the six-by-six pauper's plot Betty was in.

"I'm pulling a big one with Windell," I said. "You can be part of it."

"Part of what?"

"Windell's got a gimmick."

"Windell's a perverted twit who probably jacks off in his sister's panties."

"He's a genius, screwy for sure, but a real whiz at gimmicks."

"You know your little friend is banned from every casino in town? He's tried everything from triggering the payoff mechanism in the coin drop of slots to manipulating the reels with a magnet. That crazy bastard went into the Thunderbird with an enormous electromagnet and battery in a backpack and tried to control the reels. The battery started leaking and he ran screaming out of the place with acid burning him."

"That's why I'm the boss. You know what marked cards are?"

"Yeah, they got stripes on them, prison stripes. Unless you try to use them in Vegas, then they got a skull and bones on them."

"Cards are all personalized with a casino's logo. Windell had an idea to get to the Mexicans who manufacture the cards and get a whole shipment of cards to a casino marked."

"Windell needs electroconvulsive therapy."

"The idea stinks, I know. You'd need to have special dies engraved, bribe a million people, the whole nine yards. But Windell finally came up with a horse that's in the money."

She sighed theatrically. "What's the play?"

"We know the dealer's hole card in blackjack."

"Christ, Zack, don't you think that and every other card scam has been tried in every casino in town? Look at Embers's hands."

"What do you mean? What about Embers's hands?"

"You don't know?" She stared at me. "You really don't know? Embers got caught cheating in a high-stakes poker game. He got his hands smashed to teach him a lesson. The grind joints keep a piece of lead pipe around to break knuckles with. That's the kind of lesson cheaters get in Vegas."

"Jesus." That explained a lot. Including Embers's aversion to getting involved in any schemes. Poor bastard. He loved cards. He must have wanted to win so bad that he stepped over the line.

"Look, you don't have to be part of it. I'll find someone else. I just thought you'd like to have a piece of the action. Enough money to go back and buy that crummy restaurant we got thrown out of tonight."

"Zack, players come up with schemes to get a peek at the dealer's hole card everyday—and get dragged into the back room by security just as fast. Didn't you read just yesterday about that dealer at the Frontier who was looking away for a moment whenever she had a high card buried? It was a signal to a player. I guarantee you they left the casino for jail or intensive care, and probably both."

"Shut up and listen." I stuck a French fry in her mouth. "Windell has brains. He could build an A-bomb with a kid's chemistry set. This time he didn't come up with an idea to mark cards, but to read the markings already on them."

"Come again?"

"Cards are marked on their face, right: The painted cards—jack, queen, king—all have pictures, the two of diamonds has twos and a couple diamonds, ten of clubs, ten clubs on it."

"Okay, that's what a deck of cards looks like. How's it marked?"

"It's marked by the amount of ink used."

"What—"

"Listen to me. The cards with the most ink are the painted face cards, right? Right. The cards with the least ink are the numbered cards, especially the smaller ones. There's less ink on a two than on a ten or a jack, right?

"What Windell has concocted is an *ink reader*. It doesn't read the value or type of card, but the *amount of ink* on the face of card. When you pass a card by it, a light glows if there's a lot of ink. Aces, face cards, tens, have a lot of ink. Twos, threes, fours, so forth, have less ink."

"You think you can sit there and pass the cards over an ink reader as they're being dealt?" Janelle laughed so hard she choked on a French fry.

"Don't laugh yet. I'm not stupid, I know the casinos have two-way mirrors with cat walks, surveillance cameras, pit bosses, and floor-men."

"They see everything that goes on at the tables, every move, every motion."

"That's where you're wrong. There's a hole in their system, a blind spot."

"Where?"

"The palm of your right hand."

"Excuse me?"

"There's a deck of cards in the glove compartment."

She took out the deck and broke the seal.

"Now, imagine you're dealing from a card shoe at Halliday's. Do it on the seat. Show me exactly what you do."

"I'm given six decks of cards and an empty shoe. I do the same thing with each deck, opening the box, fanning them onto the table so the players can see the deck is true, and removing the jokers." She slipped the cards out of the box and fanned them to lay them on the seat.

"Show me how you deal from a shoe." As she dealt, I said, "Stop. What are you holding in your right hand?"

"A card."

"Facedown, lying across your finger. If you had something attached to those fingers that could read the amount of ink on the card—"

"How could I have that? The security people—"

"Won't see it because it's part of your jewelry."

"Excuse me?"

I laid it out for her. She wore very distinctive jewelry, a ring on each finger and a chain going back to a bracelet. Windell could make jewelry, taught by his old man who was a jeweler. Windell duplicated the rings she wore on her right hand and the chain that ran from the middle ring to her bracelet.

"The chain to the bracelet hides an electrical connection that goes up your arm and to a battery pack in the small of your back. The palm side of the middle ring is sensitive to ink. When a high card with a lot of ink passes over it, the top of the ring glows."

"Security will see the glow."

"No, they won't; Windell thought of that. You can't see the glow under normal lighting. You have to wear special dark glasses, like watching a 3D movie. It's really simple. You deal just as you normally do, drag a card out of the shoe for each payer, and then you drag out your hole card. When you deal from a shoe, you push the card out of the shoe with your right hand and then lift it with your fingers and put it down in front of you. When you lift the card with your fingers and put it down, the face of the card will be exposed to the palm side of your rings. That's the part of your rings Windell has cooked up to be sensitive to the ink used on the face of the cards. I'm not going to be counting cards, I'm only going to be interested in whether you have a high or low card in the hole. If it's a high card, the ruby ring will glow a little. I won't know exactly what your hole card is, but most of the time I will know whether it's a high card or not. After you deal yourself the face-up card to go with your hole card, I will have a pretty good idea as to whether I should take a hit or not."

"You won't win all the time."

"That's the beauty of it: We'll lose a lot, but over time, we'll make a killing."

"I don't know . . ."

"Don't you see? No camera, no pit boss, no sky walker can see your palm when you're dealing. And everyone knows you wear that strange jewelry. It's your trademark; it won't trigger any suspicion. It's a sure thing."

"How did you duplicate my jewelry?"

"Remember I took a picture of it so I could show it to a friend?"

"You bastard, you planned this without telling me."

"I'm telling you now."

"It won't work."

"Why?"

"Because it just never does."

"It doesn't work because people screw up and do stupid things. And the most stupid thing they do is get greedy. I'm not planning to break the bank. We do it in shifts, me for a couple hours, Windell the next day, we cut it for a couple of days, I figure we could take in a hundred grand from Halliday's before—"

"Halliday's! No way José. Con Halliday is old school. Maybe you better look at Embers's hands again."

"He got it at Halliday's?"

"He got it from Con. The story is that Con used the butt end of that six-gun he packs to bust Embers's knuckles when he caught him cheating. A few years ago some mob-punk from Chicago walked into Halliday's and offered to sell Con 'protection.' The skinny is that the guy was shipped back to the Windy City in a body bag with a slot machine handle up his ass. I swear, it's true—I used to ball the ambulance driver who took the punk to emergency."

"It has to be Halliday's."

"Get another dealer. Everyone in this town wants to go for the money."

"You're the only one with the right jewelry. If someone comes in with strange new jewelry, security would be on to it. It has to be you and it has to be Halliday's."

"Fuck you."

"Fuck them, those two who treated us like trash tonight and everyone else in this town who thinks they're better than us because they have money. I'm going someplace, Janelle, and you can be in or out, up or down. How do you think a guy like Con Halliday got his own casino? He robbed, cheated, or made a deal with the devil. He did it with a gun, a pen, or a lie. Halliday, Rockefeller, the Wall Streeters— they're grifters like the rest of us. They're just bigger crooks than us, that's all."

Part 5

★ ★ ★ ★ ★ ★

CON HALLIDAY, THE KING OF GLITTER GULCH

"Why'd you leave Hot Springs?"

"Had a spot of trouble." Con looked away from the owner of the club and stared at the neon sign behind the bar across the room. It advertised Halliday's Smooth Irish Whiskey. A leprechaun in green drunkenly rocked sideways every second or two. There was an expression of dazed satisfaction on the little guy's face, like he just belted down a quart of the Irish whiskey. The name of the saloon-casino in downtown Las Vegas was the Lucky Irishman Gambling Hall and the man he was talking to ran it. Con thought it was kind of funny that a Jew would be running a poker and red-eye whiskey joint. Howard Mintz was the first Jew he had met in his life. Where he came from, people thought Jews had horns.

"Got in a little hassle workin' for Arbe." Jack Arbuckle ran the biggest gambling establishment in Hot Springs. The Arkansas town was wide open and illegal as hell. When the drought turned the middle part of the country into a dust bowl and the stock crash brought on the Great Depression, people got hungry enough in places like Hot Springs to become real tolerant about sin that created jobs and money.

Mintz picked his teeth with a gold toothpick. Con had never seen a gold toothpick before. He was twenty-two years old, born and raised in the Panhandle of Texas; the only part of the world he had any personal experience with was the parched Panhandle and the stretch of road from Hot Springs to Vegas.

"You know, Arbe and I go back a long time," Mintz said. "We ran booze together, good Scotch and Irish whiskey from French Canucks in Quebec and ran it down through Hampshire to Boston. I came out West after Prohibition died and gambling got legal. That was in 'thirty-one. Arbe ended up running a joint in Hot Springs that Capone used to own. How's Arbe doing? Hear he's got a regular rug joint."

The Lucky Irishman was on Fremont Street, the center of gambling in Vegas. The clientele was mostly long-distance truck drivers, military personnel, women in town for a quickie divorce, and weekend gamblers from Los Angeles. The place was not a "gambling palace." Like the other casinos in town, it was a sawdust joint. There were no rug joints, fancy places with carpeting, in Vegas. The rug joints were all back East and on the gambling ships that operated out of L.A., Jersey, and Miami.

"Yeah, it's got real carpeting made back East and glass chandeliers. Arbe said to say hello. He said you might be able to fix me up with a job."

"What kind of work did you do for Arbe?"

"Different things. Made sure there was no trouble in the club. Watched the games for cheating."

"You got a name?"

"Conway, but my friends call me Con."

"What's your surname?"

"My what?"

"Your last name, family name."

Con's eye went to the Irish whiskey sign. "Halliday, Con Halliday."

Mintz didn't bother looking at the neon whiskey sign; he hadn't expected the truth from a man who left Arkansas in a race with the sheriff for the state line. He picked his teeth as he studied the young man in front of him. Con looked like dirt cowboy, boots worn at the heels, straw cowboy hat frayed along the brim, faded shirt and pants— the kind of poor Westerner created by the Dust Bowl and the Great Depression. The war was supposed to fix the economy for everyone, but the little Arkie and Texas towns that had their asses kicked by the dry years were still down for the count.

Mintz decided Con could handle himself. Along with his big six-one, six-two frame, packing maybe 210 or 220 pounds, he noticed the widespread hands, scarred and knuckle-split, and palms that were rope burned. His hair was bleached blond from the sun and his face a healthy red even before he took a drink. He could have played a man-to-ride-the-river-with in a John Ford western.

"What kind of trouble did you have?"

"Caught a man cheatin'." Con spread his big hands. "There was an argument, a knife . . ."

Mintz raised his eyebrows and shrugged. "Doesn't sound like that much trouble for Hot Springs. The sheriff declares it self-defense and Arbe sweetens the sheriff's envelope for the month and pays for the deceased's pine box."

"It was the sheriff's cousin."

"Ahhh." Mintz worked his tongue and the gold toothpick back to a socket left over from his yanked wisdom teeth. "You ever kill anyone else?"

Con shook his head. "A nigger once."

"How come you're not in the army? We got a war going, you know."

"Punctured an eardrum when I was a kid." Con wished he *was* in the army. Stories about Japs throwing American babies up in the air and catching them on their bayonets inflamed him.

"You from Arkansas?"

"Texas Panhandle."

"Why'd you leave?"

"Nothing left for me there. My ma died when I was little. Lived with my pa and worked our little ranch until the wind and dust came and the cattle started dying 'cause they couldn't eat dirt."

"Where's your father?"

"Dead. Killed himself after we lost the ranch."

"Too bad, but I hear there's a lot of that happening. The banks are bastards."

"The town, too. No one helped, they didn't like my pa 'cause he enjoyed a little gamblin' and drinkin'. Bunch of holier-than-thou barn Baptists treated us lower than dirt."

"Well, I guess you aren't going back there."

"Can't. I burned it before I left."

"The ranch?"

"The town."

25

THREE YEARS LATER

Con came down the stairs of the Lucky Irishman. He had been standing at the railing on the second-floor landing watching the action at one of the poker tables. He was the unofficial casino manager. Mintz was involved in offshore gambling out of San Pedro, L.A.'s port, and spent half his time keeping the ship afloat out beyond the twelve-mile limit and the Coast Guard off his back. That left Con running the Lucky Irishman. Cheating was the biggest problem—by the customers, by the hired help. A casino was a bank with loose money lying everywhere in sight and reach and there was always someone who couldn't resist the temptation.

At the bottom of the stairs, he nodded at the ladderman who was sitting on a tall stool smoking a cigar as he kept an eye on the tables. "The punk wearing the zoot suit at table three."

A punk to Con was a guy who thought he was tough but wasn't. Guys like the one wearing the zoot suit ran small-time rackets, backroom dice or cards in places like L.A. or Kansas City. When they came to Vegas they thought the odds casinos used to relieve suckers of their money weren't meant to apply to them and they expected to walk away with a killing. Sometimes they cheated.

To Con, a zoot suit, with its wide-shouldered, six-button, double-breasted jacket and high-waisted pants was the mark of a city guy who didn't know what tough really was. Three years in Vegas had rubbed some of the corn off of Con, but he wasn't that far from the days when he roped cattle and wrestled them to the ground to cut their balls off. He still wore a cowboy hat and boots, but the hat was now a Stetson and the boots handmade in Mexico. They complemented his Mississippi riverboat gambler's pinstriped suit and fancy red-silk vest. He packed a long-barreled Colt .44 with the holster tied down to his right leg and a long-handled boot knife.

"What's the gaff?" The ladderman snicked cigar ash onto the sawdust floor. His job was to sit on the elevated stand and spot cheats and skimming, but he had learned long ago that Con could smell them when they walked through the door.

"Lap cards."

An old technique, tried and true: A player drops a high card or two, an ace or king in his lap, and switches when he needs to improve a hand. The zoot suit, with its oversized, bulky jacket and pants, was perfect for hiding cards.

"I'm going to take him out back," Con said. "I'll have Benny make sure no one follows us out. Let me have your cigar."

Benny was the relief bartender, floor sweeper, and bouncer. He was at the row of nickel grinders playing his favorite slot machine, screen stars. The machine had only one reel and it paid off on some stars, nothing on others. Humphery Bogart, Cary Grant, Ingrid Bergman, and Ronald Coleman paid off. Marlene Dietrich, Orson Welles, Sidney Greenstreet, Peter Lorre, and Zachery Scott were losers. The big pay-off was twenty nickels for Betty Grable, the actress who had her legs insured for a million bucks and was the GIs' most popular pinup girl. It was the only honest slot in the house. Mintz kept it honest because Betty Grable was his favorite star.

"He loves white bread," Mintz's accountant, Sol, told him many times.

Con had long ago figured out that the reason Mintz made so many trips to L.A. wasn't only for business. Sol confirmed his suspicion that Mintz had a girl stashed away in a pad off of Sunset Boulevard.

"A bottle blonde with big cans. I met her when I dropped off some folding money when Mintz was back East."

"How's he handle his marriage?" Con asked.

"He married a woman for her money. To him, that's all she has, money. At first he took an extra drink at night to handle it. Now he porks any babe that will stand still long enough."

"I'm taking someone outside," Con told the husky bartender. "Watch the door."

Nickels were dropping into the coin tray of the slot. "Hey, I just won ten on Gary Cooper. He's my favorite actor, you know, the strong silent type, doesn't say much. Did you see him in *Along Came Jones*? Laughed my ass off when he got mistaken for outlaw Dan Duryea. I heard he can take John Wayne with his dukes."

"Don't bet on it. The Duke would wipe the shit off his boots with that skinny drink of water."

Con casually moseyed over to the poker table where zoot suit had the biggest pile of cards. As he went across the room, the gritty throaty voice of Fran, one of the two B-girls Mintz kept at the joint, could be heard singing from the bar, where she was entertaining a couple of soldiers from Camp Roberts sent out to practice desert maneuvers during the atomic blasts in the desert. *"You're in the army now / you're not behind a plow / you're digging a ditch / you son-of-a-bitch / you're in the army now!"*

The last few years had been good for the club and Vegas. The war had brought the army–air force and the atomic bomb to the desert, along with soldiers with money in their pockets. Mintz was pleased to help the war effort by relieving soldiers of their money at the gambling tables and providing an even more intimate form of relief—two rooms upstairs were used by house girls for "entertaining" when they weren't hustling the customers for drinks.

The club had six poker and two blackjack tables, a layout for New York craps, and a dense pall of tobacco smoke. Only the poker tables and smoke went full time. The club also took bets on national sporting events and got the scores in from telephone calls from the East and Chicago. A single row of four nickel machines and one quarter slot machine were against the wall that led down the hallway to the bathrooms. Mintz made little money off the slots and only kept them to amuse the wives waiting for their husbands to finish playing cards or craps, but increased his take by using ten-stop machines—slots that had only ten symbols that could appear on the pay line on each of the three reels that spun, instead of the standard twenty. There were still twenty symbols on each reel—cherries, oranges, yellow bells, black jackpot bars—but half of them never made it to the pay line because the spinning wheels had a gearwheel that only allowed them to stop at every other symbol.

Cheating was frowned upon by the casinos only when they lost money at it.

Four other players were at the poker table when Con approached. He recognized three of them as regulars, one a local, and quickly eliminated the fourth as a possible backup to the punk. Some of the punks brought a buddy along packing heat in case things went to hell. He deliberately avoided looking at the punk as he came up to the table.

"Throw me some luck, Con. I've lost my shirt and I'm down to my short hairs," the local player said.

"Sometimes luck isn't a lady but a real bitch," Con said. As he spoke, he "accidentally" dropped the cigar into the punk's lap.

The guy shot up from his chair, brushing his expensive suit. "Fuck!" The cigar flew out of his lap. So did an ace of diamonds.

The local stared at the card on the floor like it was a snake. "Holy shit."

Con took the punk's arm and led him away from the table. He had four inches and fifty pounds on the guy. The fingers of his big hand completely engulfed the punk's arm.

"We need to have a little talk," Con said.

He led the guy into an alley at the back of the club. When they got outside, the punk jerked his arm loose and faced Con.

"Listen, pal, I've got friends in town—"

"Not in my place you don't."

"Let's make a deal. You keep the chips on the table and I'll give you a hundred-dollar watch—" His hand went in under his coat where the long gold chain of a pocket watch hung down the front of his baggy pants.

Con moved with the speed of a striking rattler. He clamped his big hand over the man's gunhand, and twisted his arm into a hammerlock. He took away the gun, shoved the punk's face up against the building, and held him there while he shook the bullets from the five-shot .38 onto the pavement.

"I admire a good card mechanic," Con said, "a guy who's so smooth with his hands that you can't see him ripping off a card from the bottom, or a good number-two man who can deal seconds. If I think he's really good, I even invite 'em to sit down and show me his stuff."

"You're in deep shit, pal, I'm going to—"

Con hit him in the small of the back, then the kidneys. He slammed the guy's head against the brick wall. The punk dropped to his knees.

"But you're not a mechanic, *pal*, you're just a chippy," Con said.

The ladderman came out of the back of the club. "Benny's watching the door. I didn't spot a backup."

"Let him know he's not welcome back here," Con said.

As he went back inside, the ladderman pulled a sap from his coat pocket and brought it down on the man's jaw as he looked up.

Mintz came back to the club from a trip to L.A. with news that they were going to have visitors. "Bugsy Siegel and the Little Man are coming. You know who they are?"

"I read the papers. Siegel's some kind of gangster, New York or someplace."

"You're in the stone age, Con. Lucky Luciano's the boss of bosses for the whole country, not just New York. The Little Man is his right hand and Bugsy's the Little Man's number one."

"Who's the Little Man?"

"Meyer Lansky, that's who."

"The guy who owns a piece of this place?"

Mintz glared at him. "Who told you that? That asshole Sol? He's got diarrhea of the mouth."

"Naw, hell, I heard you talking to him on the phone." That was true, but Con didn't know who Mintz had been talking to until Sol told him. It didn't take long for him to figure out that Mintz skimmed a cut off the top each month and sent it to Lansky, and put another cut away for himself, before he figured Uncle Sam's take.

"Keep your mouth shut about it—it ain't nobody's business."

"These guys, they're all with the Syndicate?"

"That's what the papers call the boys, but Unione Siciliane, that's what Luciano likes to call it, like Frankie Yale used to call the rackets before Capone had him bumped off for hijacking his liquor. It's only for guineas—Jews can't join—but the Italians all have muscles for brains, so Lansky runs the business end."

"What about Bugsy Siegel? He got muscles for brains, too?"

"Don't you believe it. Ben's almost as smart as the Little Man and neither one needs outside muscle to handle their beefs. It's the other way around. All these boys were all tough Lower East Side kids, got to know each other running rackets on the streets. When Luciano

went into bootlegging, Bugsy and the Little Man formed the Bug and
Meyer Gang and sold him protection, riding shotgun to fight off hi-
jackers and hijacking when the money flowed that way. Now check
that out, cowboy. A couple Jews, one not much taller than a bar stool,
providing protection to Sicilian gunsels. That tell you how tough these
guys are?

"You know how they met? The Jews on the Lower East Side had
the Irish on one side and the Italians on the other—and the guineas
and the micks were both bigger than us. We had bigger brains and
smaller muscles. The Irish toughs hung around waiting for us to get
out of school and would make us drop our pants to show our circum-
cisions. But the Italians were more mercenary. When Luciano was a
teenager, he ran a gang of toughs who sold protection to Jewish kids
on their way to school and back. It was penny-ante stuff, but hey, in
those days a nickel bought a beer. Luciano told this pint-sized runt to
fork over his pennies for protection and the runt told him he didn't
need protection: He put up his dukes and told Luciano to fuck himself.
Now imagine that, here's this big guinea son-of-a-bitch backed up with
his punks talking to this little kid, and you know something, Luciano
took one look at the kid and said, shit, he don't need no protection.
That little guy was Meyer Lansky."

"Little guys are the toughest," Con said.

"They have to be. Lansky's only about five-three, five-four. Bugsy's
bigger, but he's not big like you dumb-ass cowboys."

"Bugsy's a funny name for a guy."

"He's *chaye*, it's Yiddish, it means he's crazy wild. Usually, the guy's
pretty straight—hell, he can be a good joe, pick up the tab after a
meal, be real polite to the ladies—but piss him off and hey, watch out,
your ass is grass and he's a lawnmower."

"How'd you get to know these guys?"

"I ran a carpet joint out on the Jersey shore for Meyer, a real sweet
roadhouse, carpeting you could bury your toes in and a real cut-glass
chandelier right in the middle of the place. Our sheriff lost the election
and the new one came in with axes and busted up the place so the
bum that paid for his election didn't have no competition. After that,
I floated out west to Little Rock and Hot Springs before settling down
here."

Mintz poked his finger in Con's chest. "You watch yourself when you're helping them out. It's *Mister* Siegel, you understand, and *Mister* Lansky, no Bugsy or Little Man stuff. Luciano is the only one who can call them by their street names. To the rest of us, they're Ben and Meyer. To punks like you, they're *Mister*. You got it?"

"Yeah, *Mister* Mintz, all except the part about helping them out."

"Sam Pollack at the Silver Horseshoe owes Meyer start-up money from when he was opening the club and he's missed a couple of payments. Bugsy was coming out to Vegas to look-see a club and Meyer came along to collect. Meyer asked me to accommodate him with some local muscle."

Con grinned. "Is that what I am? Local muscle? Muscles between the ears like the Sicilians?"

"You're whatever these boys want you to be—and you'll shut up and like it. Don't let their hundred-dollar suits fool you; these guys would just as soon kill you as look at you."

"I'm not rubbing out anyone—"

"Now don't be stupid, they only kill when it's absolutely necessary and then only each other. Luciano laid down the rules: Killing's bad for business. Killing civilians gets bad press and the boys hate bad press."

That evening Bugsy and Meyer ate dinner at the club with Mintz and Sol. Kosher delicacies were brought in from L.A.'s Fairfax district. "They're meat and potato guys, but I don't want them to think they can't get good kosher food in Vegas," Mintz said.

He also didn't want them to be lonely—his B-girls joined them for dinner.

Con played the "Bones" dice slot machine as he listened with one ear to the table conversation. The machine used standard dice combos—seven, eleven, snake-eyes, and so forth—instead of fruit, bells, and bars. From his eavesdropping he learned that Siegel had an itch to build a casino out on Highway 91, the ribbon of blacktop that left downtown and snaked across the desert to California.

Mintz bad-mouthed the idea. "Ben, you're talking a mile out of town. There's nothing out there but a couple fancy motels that pretend to be resorts, the Last Frontier and the El Rancho. No one wants to go out to that strip of sagebrush and rattlesnake nests to gamble when they can come downtown where all of the action is. For the size of place you're talking about, people hav'ta come out from L.A. just to gamble. No one's gonna do that. If it weren't for the dog faces out at the army camp, we'd be a ghost town."

"No one comes out from L.A. because all you've got here is a bunch of nickel-dime sawdust joints," Siegel said. "They got more action at Woolworth's counter than how you grind nickels from truck drivers and soldiers. Look what they got in Palm Springs? Indians own the town but Hollywood money has gone out there and turned it into an oasis. And there ain't a damn thing to do there except play golf and tennis. The Hollywood crowd likes excitement and they don't mind spending money. Give them a place to gamble with some class and they'll come out here. When they do, the rest of the suckers will follow."

Sol had told Con earlier that he didn't like the gangsters. "Some people think these morons are glamorous, but they're just crooks who steal more than other crooks. Bugsy and Meyer started Murder, Inc., before Lepke Buchalter and Anastasia took over the action. Lepke had a reputation for hurting people, but he's no more. They fried him at Sing Sing and the warden lowered the juice so he'd cook slower. My cousin got mixed up in the rackets, was talking to the cops because the mob tried to kill him. They poisoned him when he was in the hospital."

Sol warmed to the subject and went on with his harangue. "Back in the old days, the twenties and early thirties, the mob was divided between two Mustache Petes, two old-time Sicilians who had spaghetti bellies, thick lip hair, and made people call them 'Don this' and 'Don that' like they was manor born. One of the black mustachios had a handle of Masseria and the other was Maranzano. When Luciano and the boys were coming up in the rackets, these guys both squeezed Lucky to have him kill the other.

"Luciano knew he was being used and he had to play it clever to keep from getting rubbed out himself. He pretended to team up with Masseria and lured him to a restaurant without his body guards. When Lucky got up to take a piss, four of his boys came in and loaded the mustachio with lead. That made Maranzano head of the American mob with Luciano his number two. But Marazano ain't no dummy and he immediately puts a hit out on Lucky and gives the contract to Mad Dog Coll.

"Lucky got Bugsy and Meyer and the boys together to figure out how to hit Maranzano before Lucky got it. Once Lucky went down, so would all his boys, Jews first. Maranzano didn't want no Jews in the organization. It was Meyer who spotted Maranzano's weakness. Maranzano had a thing about the IRS. He was worried more about them than the FBI because he couldn't account for all the dough that came his way. So Meyer brought in four Jewish gunsels who could pass for IRS auditors and spent weeks training them to walk and talk like accountants. Then he sent them over to Maranzano's offices.

"A gunsel couldn't just walk into the offices because there was an army of thugs guarding the mustachio. But these four 'accountants' came in flashing phony government IDs, and Maranzano let them into his private office to check out books that had been cooked. They loaded him up with lead and gutted him like a slaughterhouse pig, and next thing you know Luciano was boss of bosses. Gave both of the Mustache Petes a big going away: Must have been a hundred black limos, bumper to bumper; goddamn flowers came in by the trainload. It was something to see, really something to see."

The mob protected Vegas. "It's off-limits to hit any of the joints. One time two guys came in with shotguns and took the day's take. Mintz just shook his head and handed over the money. Then he made a phone call to a hotel down the street. When the bad guys hustled out of town, two of Albert Anastasia's boys were in a car behind them. Anastasia's boys waited until they crossed the state line and then pulled up beside them and sprayed 'em with a machine gun." Sol shook his head. "You don't mess with these guys no how."

"It's funny, you say the Jew mobsters and Italian mobsters are pals, but I hear Mintz calling Italians names every time he talks about them."

"Yeah, I never said they were pals, they're business associates. And there's no name-calling face to face. We call them wops, guineas, or dagos behind their backs. They call us Hebes, mockies, or geese. But the Italians and Jews all eat from the pie, so they don't kill each other. Unless it's necessary."

"What do they call guys like me?" Con asked.

"Schnooks."

———

Business must be good in the rackets, Con thought, looking over Bugsy's clothes when he was introduced to him. Bugsy dressed sharp in his snap-brimmed hat, pinstriped suit with high-waisted trousers, suspenders and narrow pegged cuffs, a rakishly tailored overcoat with fur-lined collar, handcrafted shoes with pointed toes that shined so you could comb your hair in the reflection, and a handmade silk shirt with six-inch collar points. Everything was monogrammed, Sol told Con.

That evening after dinner, Con dropped Bugsy and Meyer off and waited in an alley behind the Silver Horseshoe. He drove them in Mintz's 1942 Packard touring sedan, the most luxurious automobile Con had been in, and he loved to drive it. Black with dark red sides, it was a seven-passenger model with a running board, duel spare tires on side mounts, a jump seat behind the driver, and a minibar that pulled out from the back of the front passenger seat. Mintz had told him it was one of the last cars produced in America in late '41 and bought it the day the Japs bombed Pearl Harbor. After that, American car factories started turning out tanks and airplane engines.

"The best American car made, better than a Cad," Mintz had told him. "FDR rode in one to the inaugural the day he was sworn in. Hell, it's even Stalin's favorite car. That Ruskie liked a Packard so much FDR had the tooling sent to Moscow so the Ruskies could make them."

Mintz claimed he once loaned the car to Warner Bros. for Bogart to ride in for the opening of *Casablanca* but Mintz made a lot of claims and Con sometimes wasn't sure what side of the line they fell on.

Bugsy and Meyer came out a few minutes later with a very frightened Sam Pollack. "Drive," Bugsy said, after they hustled Pollack into the backseat. "Find a place where the sand is soft and the digging is easy."

They put a shovel on the floor of the backseat so Pollack would feel it under his feet during the ride.

Con was uncomfortable taking orders from the gangster, especially an order like that, but he knew he had to wait to see how the hand played out.

When he had driven a few miles outside of town, Con turned off onto a dirt road that he knew went to an old abandoned mine.

"Bugsy, I—" Pollack said.

"What'd you call me?"

Bugsy hit Pollack. Then again. And again. "All right, that's enough," Meyer said. "Pull over here," he told Con.

Con pulled the car over and brought it to a stop. The two men yanked Pollack out of the backseat. Bugsy knocked the casino owner to the ground. Meyer got the shovel and threw it down on the ground by Pollack.

"Start digging," Bugsy told him.

Con felt the long-barreled .44 he kept tucked in his belt. He wasn't sure what to do. He was more concerned about being mixed up in a murder than Pollack's life.

"I didn't mean to cheat you!" Pollack said. "It'll never happen again." He was shaking.

Bugsy pulled out a gun from a shoulder holster. "Dig, you bastard." He fired the gun at Pollack's feet, kicking up dirt on the man.

Meyer looked on impassively. Con watched with an increasing sense of apprehension. If they killed Pollack, they would not want a witness around to pin it on them. There was also something unreal about the situation. A gangland hit was not something he had experienced and he watched the scene unfold as if he was watching a movie.

When Pollack had dug out a foot-deep hole about man-length, Bugsy and Meyer climbed back into the car. "Once around the park, James," Bugsy said, grinning.

On the way back, the two in the backseat talked about how Bugsy and George Raft, the gangster-playing movie star, had become pals. They never mentioned Pollack, whom they left standing knee-deep in the empty grave. The casino owner would have to hoof it back to town. Con had no doubt in his mind that every time Pollack counted out the cut he sent the boys back East, he'd remember the grave waiting for him.

27

The next day, Mintz handed Con a yard. Con looked at the hundred-dollar bill and raised his eyebrows.

"From the Little Man. He says you did real good last night. But he had a question. He saw your hand itching to pull your heat out. What did you plan to do with that cannon—rub out Pollack . . . or the boys?"

Con grinned. "Hell, wouldn't you know it, I saw a coyote out in the bushes and was going to blast it if it came any closer."

Con drove the two gangsters down Highway 91 for about a mile out of town. There wasn't much out there: the couple joints that weren't much more than fancy motels—the El Rancho and the Last Frontier—along with a lot of dry, ugly desert. Bugsy wanted to show Meyer where he envisioned someday putting a carpet joint. Mintz didn't come along. He was noticeably nervous around Bugsy. Smart man, Con thought. Bugsy walked around with a stick of dynamite on a short fuse between his ears.

Con leaned against the car and rolled a cigarette as Bugsy laid it on the Little Man. "We're wasting our time with illegal clubs and gambling ships. We pay the cops and politicians through the nose and we still get shut down every time some news rag runs a story about civic corruption." He swept his hand at the desert. "Look at this. We could build a real casino, not a sawdust joint, but a gambling palace bigger and better than anyone's ever seen. And we won't have to pay a dime to anyone for the privilege to operate."

"I don't know; it's a long way from L.A. In the summertime, the tires on a car can melt just coming down the highway."

"Naw, the weather here's not that bad, it's resort stuff—a few bad days a year and months of sunshine and light breezes. I'm telling you, Meyer, I've gotten in tight with that Hollywood crowd. If I build a fancy playground for them, they'll come. They'll fly, drive, any way they can to drop a bundle at the tables."

"You're too damn much of a gambler," Meyer said. "Running a casino is a business, not a gamble. Gamblers can win and lose, but a businessman has to win every time. Especially if you're going to be borrowing the money from Lucky and the boys. They don't want to see their bread stuffed down a toilet hole."

Listening to the two talk, Con wasn't so sure people would drive all the way from L.A. to drop money in the Nevada desert, but there was no doubt that the town had a lot of appeal to the racketeers in Chicago and the East. Elliot Ness had done a good job for Vegas when he went after Capone for tax evasion. Was it a coincidence that in 1931 Capone was convicted of tax evasion—and Nevada legalized gambling? The mob soon learned that they could run money through the sawdust joints in Vegas and get it back clean. Not that Vegas was that important to the mob—it was small potatoes compared to the return from illegal gambling, prostitution, protection, and hijacking rackets.

Mintz never complained about the cut he gave Meyer for the Lucky Luciano gang each month. "It's a cost of doing business," Mintz told him, after Con revealed he knew about the action, "like taxes. Only if you don't pay these guys, they cut your nuts off."

Mintz himself had a small-time racketeering background before settling in Vegas. He boasted that he met Meyer Lansky at a bar mitzvah in Brooklyn and hit him up for a loan to start the Lucky Irishman after he had dumped a card room in Jersey when a gang war broke out.

"Meyer has finesse. He knows the business end of the rackets: what the percentage should be, the cuts, what the politicians and cops should rake in."

Siegel got his way and the desert oasis he wanted alongside the narrow strip of blacktop leading to L.A. went up in the desert. When he was in town during the construction, Siegel often asked Mintz for Con and the car. Con wasn't sure if he liked him or the car better.

Con watched the Flamingo being built and heard the rumors about the overruns on construction and suspicions from the mob that Siegel was skimming. Skimming *their* money. "That ain't healthy," Mintz told Con.

Bugsy wanted all men in black tie for the grand opening the day after Christmas 1946, but relented and let Con attend in his riverboat gambling outfit since Con couldn't find a tux in his large size. Even the janitors had to wear tuxedos.

Con drove Mintz to the gambling palace, going by the fabulous pink neon Flamingo sign.

It was raining like hell.

"Jimmy Durante, Rose Marie, and Xavier Cugat are opening," Mintz said. "Bugsy's arranged for planeloads of stars to fly in, but half the flights are grounded in L.A. because of the weather."

As he and Mintz raced across the half-empty parking lot to the door, Mintz said, "Not a good sign, not good at all. The boys aren't going to be happy."

Mintz said only a few of the Hollywood crowd showed up, but to Con, it was like getting his own movie studio tour—George Raft, Sonny Tufts, Charles Coburn, George Sanders, Vivian Blaine, Lon McAllister, with shows featuring Tommy Wonder, the Tunetoppers, Eddie Jackson, Jimmy Durante, and Xavier Cugat.

"There's more stars here than a Texas night."

Mintz shook his head. "You don't see Coop, the Duke, Lana, Ginger; they all got grounded in L.A. Bugsy hasn't even got the hotel finished. People are staying at the El Rancho and motels. Siegel opened it early because the place is hemorrhaging dough."

Con came with Mintz to watch the gambling action as an accommodation to Bugsy, to make sure there was no skimming by the help. They came back the next night. Half the crowd had gone home. The following night they sat in the lounge and watched Jimmy Durante.

"There's twelve of us in here," Mintz whispered. "Holy shit, an audience of twelve watching Jimmy Durante. The boys aren't going to like this."

Mintz never identified exactly who "the boys" were, but it wasn't hard to figure. Lucky Luciano was out of prison and deported, but still ran the mob. Meyer, Siegel, Anastasia, Vito Genovese, Frank Costello, Joe Adonis—they all still reported to Lucky. It was those "boys" and others like them who bought into Siegel's desert dream, which was now looking like a nightmare.

The Flamingo closed after the first of the year.

Bugsy had paid a visit to Mintz that left Mintz sweating. "He needs to raise money. I told him I can't put any more into it. I thought the bastard was going to blast me on the spot." He bit the end off a cigar and spit out the piece. "I need you to take a trip for me."

"L.A. again?" Con asked.

"A little farther. Havana."

"Havana? You mean Cuba?"

"That's the only Havana I know."

"What do you want me to do?"

"Lucky is coming in from Sicily to talk to the boys. The joints in town have taken up a collection to help make things more comfortable for Lucky in his exile. We need someone with muscle and a rod to deliver it."

"You want me to take a bag of money to Havana?"

"Yeah, I want you take a bag of money."

"Why not go yourself?"

"Because I've got you to do my dirty work." He tapped his own chest, spilling cigar ash on his coat. "My ticker has been acting up. I can't stand any excitement, you know what I mean?"

"Think someone might go for the dough?"

"Sure, and if they get it, you can throw yourself under a train. There ain't gonna be no place to run if you fuck Luciano."

It would have been faster flying to Miami, but Con, who could have faced stampeding cattle, took the train because he was sissy-scared of boarding an airplane. He hung onto the bag of money and kept his .44 handy, but the rail ride to Miami turned out to be uneventful. Once there, he caught a boat for Havana. He was still a couple miles out to sea when he got a whiff of something sweet and pungent.

"It's Havana," a sailor said. "Coffee roasting, rum and sugar boiling, tobacco drying. And the perfume of the *putas* in the city. Cowboy, there are more whores in Havana than cows in Texas."

The town vibrated under Con's feet. The action was like rodeo day, only the excited animals were cars, busses, and people. Noise from the sidewalk cafés, casinos and bars, ships in the harbor, whores and hustlers on the street hammered and pounded him. The town was one big bordello. Everyone was whoring, from the customs official who held out his hand for *mordida* to the cab driver who overcharged and the kid who banged on the taxi window and shouted that he could get you a cold drink or a hot woman.

Con checked into the hotel Mintz instructed him to and immediately left a message for Meyer at the front desk. He wanted to get rid of the bag of money before it grew wings and flew away.

"Mr. Lansky will meet you in the lobby in twenty minutes," a clerk told him over the phone.

Con took a seat in the lobby near the entrance to the hotel casino. He smoked two hand-rolled cigarettes before he saw Meyer and Bugsy come out of the casino with a third man. He recognized Lucky Luciano from his pictures but was surprised how handsome the mobster looked, even though he had a drooping eye, part of the damage caused when he was taken for a ride. The eye added extra malice.

Con started to get up, but sat back down. None of the three looked happy. Luciano and Meyer stared across the lobby empty-eyed while Bugsy's expression was murderous. Con had seen Bugsy loose his cool twice: when they took Pollack for a ride in the desert and opening night at the Flamingo, when a man naively called him "Bugsy" and he kicked the man in the pants. He was sure he was about to witness number three. Luciano paused by his chair.

"I'm telling you to get back to Vegas and straighten things out," Luciano said in a subdued voice.

"Nobody tells me what to do. Anybody who tries to push me around is going to get his ass burned."

"You're out of—"

"Fuck you, I'm tired of taking heat over the Flamingo. If you cheap bastards had given me the backing I needed, I wouldn't have gotten holes in my knees begging from outsiders."

Bugsy stomped away, his face a mask of fury. Luciano still had the deadpan expression on his face but his eyes followed Bugsy's exit. Meyer's expressionless face cracked a little and for just the briefest moment Con thought he saw a look of remorse on Meyer's face, but it went blank again.

He turned to Con and took the bag. The two mobsters walked away without saying a word.

That night, as Con was standing at a craps table watching the action, he felt Meyer's presence beside him.

"Tell Mintz to let the boys in Vegas know that Lucky was pleased with their gift."

"Sure thing."

They watched the throw of the dice. "You know," Meyer said, "people have been throwing bones across the table for thousands of years. Did you know Palamedes, a hero of the Trojan War, invented the game and taught it to his fellow Greeks during the siege of Troy?"

"I never knew that, but Mintz claimed some Greek invented the slot machine way back when." Mintz had also told him that Meyer loved knowledge and was almost pedantic about demonstrating it.

"Sort of. A guy named Hero of Alexandria made a vending machine for holy water two thousand years ago."

Con moved aside a little to give Meyer room at the table. "You want to place a bet?"

Meyer shook his head and moved away from the table and Con followed him. "I got a good lesson about gambling a long time ago," Meyer said. "When I was a kid, my mother sent me to the bakery with a nickel. Being a wise guy, I dropped the nickel at a curbside craps game. I went home busted and my mother cried because it was her last nickel. But, you know, Con, it was a good lesson because I figured something was wrong with that game. I kept watching and finally figured out it was all a dance. The guy running it would have a shill play and let him win, with loaded dice, of course, and when everyone got excited and threw down bets, he'd switch the dice and rake in the suckers' dough.

"Even when the dice aren't loaded, there's no such thing as a lucky gambler. There are just winners and losers. The winners control the game."

They paused to watch the action at a roulette wheel. "Luck depends on how you use it," Con said. He threw a hundred-dollar bill on 00.

"You sure you want to do that?" Meyer asked.

"Positive." Con used his big frame to subtly push back a croupier. His hand disappeared below the table as he leaned over the table as if he was really interested in the action. The ball spun, flipped and flopped, and came to rest in the 00 canoe.

After collecting thirty-five hundred dollars from an unhappy croupier, Con sauntered away from the table with Meyer.

"How did you know the wheel was gaffed?"

"The sound of the ball rolling. It's got a metal core that makes it a little heavier than an ivory ball. And it falls a little unnatural when the electromagnet that draws it to a canoe gets turned on by that switch."

"Aren't you worried that upstaging their gimmick is gonna annoy the people who own this place?"

"Naw, I had the boss with me. This is another little donation for Mr. Luciano's vacation in Italy." Con handed over his winnings.

Meyer's face lit up several watts. He tried to keep from laughing. "How did you pin the club on me?"

"Hell, every croupier in the place looks at you like Jesus H. Christ is paying a visit."

"Walk me to my car," Meyer said.

They came out the front entrance and walked down a line of cars parked down the circular driveway.

"What do you think of the Flamingo?" Meyer asked.

Con knew it was a loaded question. It wasn't just a question of money between Meyer and Bugsy—the two were old pals. He answered cautiously. "I think the Flamingo will make money eventually. It's still being finished and people in L.A. aren't in the habit yet of driving three hundred miles."

"I agree with you, Bugsy's no fool. Unfortunately, he's more of an idea man than a businessman. If he'd step aside and let us put businessmen in the club to run it, I think it would be a gold mine. Bugsy's too much of a gambler." He seemed to be talking more out loud to himself than to Con.

A Cuban suddenly stepped out of the bushes and drunkenly waved a gun at them, jabbering in Spanish, of which Con caught the words *reloj de pulsera*.

"He wants your watch," Con said.

Meyer was wearing a short-sleeve shirt that exposed the diamond-studded gold watch on his wrist. Con was between Meyer and the robber. "Give it to me." He held out his hand to Meyer, who took it off his wrist.

"Here you go, partner."

As Con was about to give the watch to the man, it slipped from his hand. The thief made a grab for it and Con's big fist caught him on the side of the head. The Cuban went down like a hammered steer.

Con took the gun. "So damn rusted, it probably wouldn't shoot any-way." He unloaded it and tossed it in the bushes. He picked up the gold watch and brushed it off before handing it back to Meyer. "Sorry, Mr. Lansky. Didn't mean to get your watch dirty."

The next morning as Con was packing, a small package was delivered to him by the bellboy. Inside was Meyer's diamond studded watch—and thirty-five hundred dollars. The note read: *A token of my appreciation.* No signature.

The day Con left Havana, Meyer Lansky, Lucky Luciano, Vito Genovese, Albert Anastasia, and a host of other big and small members of the New York families met in a banquet room at the Alhambra hotel. The hotel, with its reddish covered bricks made of fine gravel and clay, was modeled after the Alhambra palace in Spain. In the middle of the hotel casino was a replica of the Fountain of Linos, an alabaster basin supported by the figures of twelve white marble lions, symbols of strength and courage. Built like a fortress on a cliff above the Malecón, overlooking Havana harbor, the hotel had been financed with mob money. Lansky himself had suggested the design of the hotel. The little man knew history and selected a model from Spain.

The meeting took place in the *sala de los abencerrages*—the name of a palace room derived from a legend in which Boabdil, the last king of Granada, invited the Abencerrages chiefs to a banquet in the room, then had them massacred. Some people thought Lansky used the name because he admired Baobdil's cleverness.

At the meeting, a grave Meyer Lansky rose from his seat to bring the "Siegel problem" before the group.

"The Flamingo was projected to cost a million and a half," Meyer said. "It's up to nearly six million and still counting, but that's not the problem we have to discuss. Lucky got suspicious about possible skimming when he got word from a friend who saw Virginia Hill in Switzerland."

Virginia Hill was Siegel's girl and was as crazy tempered as Bugsy. She was known throughout the mob world as the lover of gangsters. Bugsy was her latest.

"I did some checking through sources." Meyer's voice grew quieter. "Virginia has a Swiss bank account. In her name and Bugsy's."

———

On June 20, 1947, less than six months after the Flamingo's grand opening, Bugsy was sitting in his Beverly Hills mansion when a member of Murder, Inc., fired a .30-caliber army carbine from outside the house and put four slugs in him. The first bullet entered Bugsy's left eye.

In Las Vegas, minutes after the echo of the fourth shot that hit Bugsy had faded, three men walked into the Flamingo hotel and announced they were the new management.

A week after Bugsy's death, Con picked up Meyer at McCarran Air-field with the big Packard. Meyer rode in the front seat with Con.

"Sorry to hear about Mintz," Meyer said.

Con shrugged. "Guys with bad tickers shouldn't try to pork the young stuff."

Mintz had been humping a new B-girl upstairs at the club when he clutched at his ticker and yelled he was dying. He was right.

"Mintz's widow wants to sell the Lucky Irishman," Con said. "I want to buy it. I've been running it for years while Mintz has been hopping in bed in L.A. and here in Vegas. I can turn more money than he ever did."

"You have the money?"

"I have some of it. I've been saving." He didn't mention that he'd been skimming from the club for years or that he had increased his stake playing poker. Meyer wouldn't appreciate either avenue.

He handed Meyer a sheet of figures. "This is the breakdown for the club. And what I'll need." Sol had fixed it for him, explaining that Meyer would be impressed if he laid black and white numbers on him.

"I met Ben when we were both just kids," Meyer said. Con glanced at Meyer in surprise. The Little Man went on reminiscing. "I first saw him when a fight broke out at a curbside craps game. Someone yelled that the dice were loaded and fists started swinging. Ben was just a wet-nosed kid, and I was three and a half years older, but in those days the streets were mean and anyone over the age of ten had to take care of themselves. During the fight, a gun dropped and Ben ran over and picked it up. The guy who dropped it came at him and Ben held the gun in both hands and smiled as he pointed it at the guy. The guy just stopped cold in his tracks and looked at the business end of his own gun. We heard the police sirens scream as a squad car came around the corner. I ran over and grabbed the gun and threw it down an open storm sewer.

"And you know what Ben said to me? Not thank you. Not mind your own business or even screw you. He just looked at me and said, 'I needed that rod.' "

Meyer shook his head. "Can you beat that? 'I needed that rod.' I'll never forget it."

He stared down at the paper Con had given him. "You've been around long enough to know the rules. Don't forget 'em. Someday you'll pay us back but you'll always owe us for the accommodation."

"You're working for me now," Con told Sol when he returned to the club. "Call a sign company, we're changing the name of the club. I want a big sign, a thousand bulbs flashing the name Halliday's. And no goddamn leprechaun. Tell 'em I want a bull, a snorting, bucking, kicking, piss-and-vinegar Texas longhorn."

Part 6

★ ★ ★ ★ ★ ★

"I HAD
THREE QUEENS."

The day came when we were to put Windell's magic card-reading gimmick into play and get a chance to have some real money in our pockets instead of pennies and lint. I was sleeping in Janelle's bed, soft and comfortable, and having one hell of a dream as a beautiful woman was sucking my dick. I didn't know who the hell she was, but she looked like one of those hot Asian chicks with succulent breasts and pretty, pouty lips like those dames you see on ads for massage parlors. She thought I had the greatest egg roll in town.

I awoke and realized that Janelle was under the blankets. I felt her hot hand around my still-asleep cock and then a pressure slowly began to build up in my abdomen. Her fingers squeezed my balls while her wet tongue began to run up and down my cock, now coming awake and responding to her licking. The heat was rushing to my loins. I grabbed her head and moved her mouth over my throbbing organ. It was hard now. "Suck it. Harder." A rush of heat and fire swept through me and I came, feeling the electric shock down to my toes, pumping my cum into her hot juicy mouth. Then she was on top of me, rubbing her nakedness on my body, my cock between her thighs, rubbing her wet cunt over my cock until it grew stiff again and I plunged into her. She was tight between her legs and she squeezed my dick inside her. Her tongue flicked my ear and her teeth nibbled on the lob for just a second before her teeth sank into it and I yelped.

"Fucking bastard," she said.

Janelle worked a mid-shift at Halliday's, noon to eight, and afterward would go home and get ready for her night job at the Pussy Kat. Hitting the casino in daylight worked perfectly for our scam because Windell and I had to wear special tinted glasses to see the glow of the ring. The glasses made me real uneasy. It was no big deal to see someone wearing sunglasses while playing craps or blackjack: Vegas was that kind of town, a place of dark glasses for cool dudes and red-eyed hangovers, but these glasses had a little reddish tint to them, although the red was more noticeable out in the sunlight than under casino lights.

I'd been in Halliday's a couple of times over a period of months when Janelle was getting off her shift, but not so much that anyone would recognize me. Just in case, I grew a goatee and wore a baseball cap. I called Windell about three o'clock before I left the house to head for the casino.

"Did it work?" he asked about the test run that Janelle tried at home.

"Like a charm. She wore the phony jewelry and I could see a glow when she pulled a high card with her fingers. It's not perfect, sometimes the card doesn't get drawn across your gimmick, but it's like an eighty-percent deal."

"I still think we need to hit it together, double the take—"

"No, I told you, I'm going in alone today."

I signed off with him and left the house wondering how brains like Windell's get miswired. All high-grade ore between his ears and not a speck of good sense. It wasn't a question of him not coming in out of the rain—he wouldn't even know it was raining.

I was nervous walking into the club and hid it behind a little bravado, getting a beer and jeering at a prostitute hanging out at the bar whom I recognized as being one of Leroy's former girls. I guess she figured the early bird gets the worm.

I dumped a roll of quarters in a bandit and then moseyed over to the pit to check out the table games. It was Wednesday afternoon, the place wasn't packed, but business was good, five of the eight blackjack tables were open. I paused by the first table, checking out the action, then casually drifted to the next one, Janelle's table. Bingo! As she drew cards from the shoe and touched them with her fingers, her ruby ring sometimes glowed. I took off my glasses and pretended to clean them. I watched a dozen cards get pulled and couldn't see the ring glow.

I kept going, like I was sizing up each table. I spotted something at another table. I didn't know what it was about me, but as old Embers said, I was a disaster at poker but I could spot a cheat every time. He said he knew a woman who could walk the aisle in an antiques store, hardly look at the items, and some alarm bell went off inside her that told her when there was a counterfeit. "Human Geiger counters," he called me and the woman, but that was because he and every old guy in town had bought themselves a Geiger counter so they could go prospecting for uranium. The stuff was more valuable than gold and easier to find.

I knew the dealer, a woman, was skimming. I spotted it and casually hung around the table for a couple minutes and made a few dollar bets when it happened again. Once in a while, after raking in chips, she'd put her hand up to her neck as if she was scratching it. She was palming a chip and dropping it down her bra. Not too shabby. Pick up an occasional twenty-five-dollar chip and she could rake in several times more than her salary each month. And it wasn't like handling a cash register, where they could count out the drawer and see if the dealer had pocketed chips; they had to catch her in the act because there were no tracks made by the chips and money that flowed across the table.

After dropping a few bets, I went over to Janelle's table and sat down, trying to keep a lid on my excitement and nervous energy. Grinning like a winner or appearing jittery before the first hand is dealt would look suspicious to the spy in the sky. Halliday's had two-way mirrors in the ceiling and catwalks that security personnel used to spy on people.

Halliday's tables had minimum bets of one to five dollars, but he prided himself on no-limit bets. According to Janelle, if the betting got too rich, she signaled the pit boss, who kept an eye on the play and sent over a floorman to belly up to the table and keep both eyes open.

I had ten yards on me and shoved the whole thousand across the table. "Hundred-dollar chips." To insiders, they weren't "chips" but "checks," and I wanted to sound like a tourist. My game plan was to walk out with forty-nine hundred dollars in my pocket after an hour's play: Get in, win fast, and get out before they decided to check me too close.

Knowing most of the ten cards that ended up as Janelle's hole card turned Lady Luck on her head. After twenty minutes and doubling my money, the pit boss passed a signal to Janelle to shuffle more frequently. Janelle had forewarned me that it was their way of terminating a run of luck by a player—if a random shuffle had accidentally stacked the cards in a player's favor, they just shuffled again.

I couldn't keep the grin off my face as the chips started piling up in front of me. Maybe if I'd been robbing the poor box at church I would've had a little conscience, but hey, this was just one grifter pissing on another.

It was so damn easy . . .

"A counter?" Con Halliday asked, as he looked down at the blackjack table from the catwalk and two-way mirror above.

"No, he hasn't been here long enough. Thirty, forty minutes maybe, but he's having a hell of a run of luck."

Aaron Bous had been Con's security manager for a year and that made him an old-timer as a Halliday security chief. The old man was death on security because cheating was money straight off the top. Runs of luck were no problem, because no matter how lucky a gambler got, the odds were always with the house and either the gambler would be grinded down or others would lose, but a dollar stolen was a dollar out of Con's pocket. There was always some wise guy coming up with a new way to cheat and Bous figured no one could keep up with it. Con's attitude was that you could spot any gimmick if you looked hard enough.

"Reshuffle?"

"Yeah. After every ten hands. It looks real clean to me, Con. The guy's just having a run of luck."

"He's a grifter. I don't know what the gaff is, but it's there."

Bous looked to the security woman that was on the catwalk on the other side of the two-way ceiling mirror. "You see anything?"

She shook her head. "Only that he's too damn lucky."

"He play any other tables?" Con asked.

"He dumped a few bucks at table five. Dollar bets."

"What'd he start with at this table?"

"Hundred-dollar checks."

"The guy plays a buck at one table and increases his bet a hundred times at the next table? You'd have to have shit for brains to think he's not going for the money."

I flipped a hundred-dollar chip onto the cocktail tray of the cutie who brought me a 7-high and caught a look from Janelle that would have made a Doberman turn tail and run. I was four big ones ahead, four thousand in chips on top of my own grand, and was right on schedule: Another ten or fifteen minutes and I could say sayonara. The nervousness I'd felt when I first sat down was gone and I was surging with confidence.

Then a shadow fell across the table.

A Mack truck wearing a cowboy hat sat down at the empty seat to my right. I didn't need an introduction to know that the infamous Con Halliday was dealing himself in. He put down a dollar bet.

"Is that okay, honey?" he asked Janelle.

"It's a five-dollar table, Mr. Halliday." Janelle smiled bravely, but her lips gave a little quiver.

"Well, we'll waive that limit, honey, I wouldn't want those busybodies in Carson City to claim I was making big-money bets in my own casino." He grinned at me. "How ya doing, son? Looks like you got a piece of my retirement there."

"Not really." I think that's what came out. I had the 7-high glass to my lips and almost spit a mouthful of the stuff onto the table.

People started crowding around. Con Halliday was a celebrity in Glitter Gulch and attracted a crowd wherever he went. And it wasn't hard to spot him, with that big body, big hat, and Mississippi gambler's suit.

"I thought I knew all there was to know about blackjack, son, but watching you play, I realized that I had missed something because you handle those cards the way Conway Twitty plays his guitar."

His words were pure corn, his grin glittered, but his eyes were snake-mean.

"I been lucky."

Janelle dealt me two cards and I hardly looked at them. The people who crowded around the table made me claustrophobic. I knew Janelle's ring flashed when she took her hole card, but nothing was registering. Halliday took a hit on twelve and Janelle turned up a six, giving him eighteen that he stood on. The palms of my hands were sweaty and I wiped them on my pants.

Just when I thought things were bad, they suddenly went to hell.

Someone sat down to my left and I turned to look into another pair of sunglasses. Betty always said that when you get goose bumps, it's because a goose had walked over your grave. I felt a whole flock of them walking up and down my spine.

"Hey-hey, this must be a lucky table," Windell said.

No fuckin' brains. Not one ounce.

Windell noticed Con Halliday on my other side. Con looked at him. Then he looked at me. And it struck me like Krakatoa blowing under my chair: *we were both wearing the same red-tinted sunglasses.*

I didn't know what the odds of that were, but I'm sure Halliday could have told me. The dismay on Windell's face said he had connected with Halliday's thought, too.

"Gotta hit the head," Windell said. He got up from the table and pushed into the crowd.

Windell left for the bathroom, but I was shitting my pants. "Hit the head" ricocheted around my head. Mindlessly, I scratched the table for a hit. A buzz went around the crowd.

Con Halliday leaned over to me and spoke very quietly. "You have a real interesting way of playing, son."

"Yeah?"

"You just took a hit on twenty."

I looked down at the table. I had three queens.

I took a seat in the security manager's office. There had been no rough stuff. Con had taken me by the arm and led me through the crowd as if I was his date for dinner.

When I sat down and looked up at Halliday, he looked like a Sequoia ready to come down on me.

"When you go for the money, boy, you have to think about whose money it is. If I let a punk come in here and rip me off, why, punks would be on me like a pack of dogs after a coon."

I was sweating blood, but I knew better than to show fear to Con Halliday.

"Mr. Halliday, I've heard a lot about you. I know you're a straight shooter. And I'm going to accept your apology when this is all over. And I'm even going to let you buy me a drink."

He started a chuckle that grew into a guffaw. "Why you fuckin' little turd, when this is over, a glass of water'll leak out your belly."

Oh shit.

The door opened and Aaron Bous, the security manager, came in. He was red-faced and breathing heavy. Two of his men were behind him. "The other one got away. He was faster than he looked, ran like a goddamn jackrabbit."

"Fuck 'em, we've got this one. Bring in the girl and the cards."

"The girl . . . ?"

"The dealer."

Bous's red face went green. He turned to the two security officers. "Find the girl."

"Find the girl? What'd you mean, find the girl?"

"I thought you wanted me to—"

"All three of you went after the squirrel?"

"We know where she lives—"

"You fuckin' idiot, you think she'll be sitting on her porch with six decks of marked cards in her lap? Those cards are flushed down a toilet by now, along with whatever other gimmick they had going."

"Con—I—"

"Shut the door," Con said. He was suddenly calm.

The two security men threw their chief a frantic look and quickly backed out, shutting the door. Bous stared at the big man, his mouth agape. He moved his jaw and finally got motor control to spit out some words.

"We've got this one—"

"We have no evidence. Nothing." Con turned to me, his eyes registering snake eyes, and that flock of geese crawled back up my spine. Ember's crippled hands flew through my mind.

I suddenly got calm. "I imagine cheating costs you a bundle every year."

He didn't say anything, just stared at me as if he was sizing up which of my arms to rip off first.

"What'd it be worth it to you if I told you one of your dealers was skimming?"

"You little punk—"

Bous started for me and I flew up, kicking back my chair. If they were going to take me down, I was going down swinging, but Con's arm shot out and blocked his security manager.

"You got a few seconds before I cripple you. Make 'em good," Con said.

"I spotted a dealer skimming as I sized up the action."

"He's talking about that bitch he was teamed up with."

"Talk," Con said.

I shrugged. "You've lost nothing from me. You got your money back and an extra thousand. I tell you which dealer is ripping you off, and I walk out of that door." I grinned. "On my own feet."

"Well, you know, you ain't told me shit. I spotted you immediately and if anyone else was ripping me off, I'd know it."

I took a deep breath. "You're a betting man, aren't you? I'll bet you the five grand I won against the name of the dealer who's skimming."

"How do I know you're not in with the dealer?"

"You'll know the moment I tell you how it's being done. I've been told I have a nose for telling this sort of thing. I spotted the grif immediately."

"He's just bullshitting you, Con. Let me have him for a couple minutes and I'll teach him a lesson he'll never forget."

"He does have a point," Con told me. "You're betting me with my own money."

"Forget the money. I'll up the ante. If I'm right, give me this dipshit's job."

Bous's red-green face went a dark shade of purple and something akin to foam gathered on his lips. I had already cased out the security manager as being just part of the furniture and that Con prided himself on being able to sniff out grifters.

Con grinned. "You remind me of someone, kid. Me. I'm going to be real disappointed if you lose the bet and I'm going to have to geld you like a steer."

"Your dealer's dropping chips into her bra. Want me to search her?"

"Who do I have to kill?"

I had been on the job over a year, as security manager for the past couple months. Seeing the guy who killed my mother playing craps caused my past to rear up and kick me in the face.

I left the security room, my head buzzing. It was Matt Kupka I had spotted on the security monitor, for sure. The guy who killed my mother wasn't someone I would forget. It had been seven years since that bastard walked out of the courthouse and I was thrown into juvie. I knew what I had to do and my mind was wrestling with how to do it. I had thought about the guy a thousand times, had even toyed with the idea of asking Con for the name of an East Coast mobster who could put out a hit on the guy, but it had all been a fantasy. Now it was real. He was in the casino.

As I headed down the hallway to my office, Morgan Halliday, Con's daughter, came out of his office. Morgan was seventeen, rather pretty in a freckle-faced, California girl way, and hated my guts. Last year when she had been seriously into boys and had put the make on me, I told her to turn it on to someone else. Not only the boss's daughter, she was jailbait because of her age. On top of that, since she was a little light in the boob department and she had caught me making a crack about her using Band-Aids instead of a bra, she called me "street trash" and that was usually how our conversations went after that.

Con sent her off to Switzerland to something called "finishing school," whatever the hell that was, and she was back now before she shipped off to some snooty Eastern college for poor little rich girls. I knew about what happened to her mother after Morgan was born. Her mother, Con's second wife, had been a showgirl, heading East with a Broadway producer when their plane crashed, killing everyone on board. Morgan, like her half brother, Bic, grew up crawling under the feet of gamblers on the casino floor.

I barely looked at her as I hurried by.

"Screw you," followed me down the hallway.

I didn't bother to look back and went into my office. Finishing school hadn't done anything for that mouth of hers. I paged Con but he was nowhere around; he'd gone to a private poker game. Someday he would lose the club at a game—if his jerky son Bic didn't lose it for him first.

Using a couch as a hiding place had been my thing as a kid and I figured it was the last place anyone would look searching my office, so I kept my stash and a few odds and ends there. I had over twenty grand in cash. All of Con's "favorite" employees got "tax-free" bonuses off the top—he'd just grab some bills and hand them to you when you'd done something that particularly pleased him. I picked up maybe five, six thousand in a year that way, and had doubled that at craps. Not that I was any hotshot player. My system was simple: I would wander around one of the big clubs and check out the games. I never put down a bet until I found someone running hot, then I bet on them. The odds are with the house, but when you're lucky, the gods change the odds.

Besides the money, I'd collected a few other things during my short tenure as security manager: the snub-nosed .38 that belonged to Bous, the previous security manager, and a bottle of knockout drops I took from a woman who lured men to their rooms and slipped them a Mickey Finn to knock them out so she could rob them. She chose married men because few of them ever filed police reports the next morning. I tucked the piece in one pocket and the drops in another.

When I got down to the casino floor, Kupka had left the craps game and was talking to a woman playing a slot, trying to put the make on her. I hoped to hell she iced him. The guy had been slugging down drinks and I figured he would take a piss before he left the casino, so I posted myself at the hallway to the johns. I had everything on my mind but a plan.

The door to the men's room opened and out came Sally, putting on her lipstick. Sally was a prostitute. We tolerated the girls as long as they were discreet because it was good for business, but she knew a quickie in a toilet stall was a no-no. She saw me and did a double take, then tried to walk by me. I shot a look at Kupka, who was still talking to the woman, but I could see that she wasn't buying his act. A plan started to germinate in my mind.

"Come 'ere."

When the men's room door opened again and a little man with a big belly came out, he took one look at me talking to Sally and hurried by.

She grinned. "His wife's playing keno. With that belly, she'll never see the lipstick ring around his dick when they go to bed tonight. Hey, don't bust me, I was just picking up some change."

"I've got a job for you and it pays two hundred."

"Who do I have to kill?"

"I'm doing the killing. You see that big slob coming our way?" The woman playing the slot had definitely iced him and he was heading for the can. "He's going to take a piss. When he comes out, tell him the casino's providing a limo to take him to the Strip and you bring him out back."

"That's all?"

"During the ride, feed him whiskey that'll be already set out. Don't drink it yourself."

I didn't think Kupka would recognize me—I was a kid when he killed Betty—but I didn't want to take the chance. I went out the back and got the club's limo where it was parked down the alley. It was a '42 Packard, a long black-and-red dinosaur from a golden age when cars had more curves than a dame. Con had said he made sure the car was part of the deal when he opened Halliday's over thirty years ago. "I'm sentimental about it," he told me. "I used it one night when I helped Bugsy Siegel and the Little Man rub out a guy." Con drove the car when he went anywhere and once in a while we used it to give a big spender a ride to his hotel.

A storage cabinet behind the front seat had a bottle of Scotch and a supply of glasses. I dumped the whole vial of knockout drops into the Scotch and brought the car up to the back door. I was behind the wheel as Sally came out with Kupka and they got into the back.

When they were seated, I started driving.

"Offer the gentleman a drink, Sally. That's twenty-five-year-old Scotch."

He grabbed the bottle as she clumsily tried to pour Scotch into a glass while the car was moving. He drank from the bottle, sucking down enough to stupefy a stud mule. He sat back and burped—a real class act.

He put his big hand on her knee and worked his way up her inner thigh, pushing her short dress up, then grabbed her hand and rubbed it against his growing shaft. "Take it out. Suck me," he commanded.

"Sure, sweetie, lay back and close your eyes. I'll take real good care of you."

She unzipped his pants. He wore no underpants and his phallus sprang straight up out of his pants. We were ten minutes out of Vegas and Sally had blown him when he noticed that the bright lights were gone.

"Where the fuck are we?"

A better question was, Why the hell wasn't he asleep? The guy had the constitution of an ox.

"Going to the United Nations," I said, "a private club where there are women of every color and creed." I grinned at him in the rearview mirror. "It's a special event arranged by the casino because of the trouble we gave you."

"Don't worry, honey, by the time we're there I'll have Tom standing at attention again and saluting."

Kupka relaxed. By the time we pulled into a parking area above Hoover Dam, he was snoring. I parked the car and met Sally outside the car.

"I have to pee," she said.

"Don't come back until I call you."

She looked at the gun in my hand and scooted off. As she disappeared into the bushes, I stepped over to the edge of the parking area. A stone wall about three feet high separated the area from a hundred-foot drop into the water. If you survived a body flop into the water, you'd get sucked into the dam. I didn't know what happened when someone got sucked into the dam, but I had a pretty good idea that they got torn to pieces before they were spit out the other end. I wasn't sure why I had brought Kupka out here, but I knew if I killed him, the dam was better than the desert to dispose of the body. He'd always be in a desert grave, ready to be found, but maybe he'd be fish food once he got ripped apart by the water pressure in the dam.

I looked down at the dark water and thought about what my next move should be. I couldn't shoot the guy while he was asleep. Besides the cowardice of it, I wanted him to know why he was dying. It struck me that there were worse things than dying. The bastard hurt women. Maybe I should cut off his balls instead of killing him. I liked the idea.

Con was always threatening to turn me into a steer. Why not turn Kupka into one? Footsteps crunched behind me and I swung around.

"Where we at?" He was a little rummy. He had not only the body of an ox but the single-mindedness of one.

"Sally needed to drop a load."

He stared at my features in the moonlight. "Don't I know you? Your voice . . ." He got closer, squinting.

"Yeah, you know me. Remember the woman you beat to death in your hotel room? She forgot to give you something."

"Her fuckin' kid!"

I swung at him, bringing the gun in a roundhouse punch to the side of his head. It bounced off his temple like it hit a brick wall. He punched me, his big fist catching me in the chest, and I staggered backward. My chest felt like someone had laid a tire iron across it. I brought up the gun but a hand the size of a baseball glove grabbed it and twisted it out of my grip. The gun went flying. I hit him with a left to the face, his nose crunching under my fist. I waded in with a right and then two more lefts. He caught the blows on the back of his forearms and head-slammed me, almost knocking out my eyeballs as my head flew backward. I staggered back, hitting the short wall at the edge of the cliff and started over it. I rolled to the side, feeling nothing but empty space at my back for a second before I got up, still dazed, but my feet under me.

Affected by the knockout drops, his movements weren't fast, but he still had the single-minded instinct of a gored water buffalo. He staggered into me and got his big hands around my throat. I couldn't gag or breathe; he was too strong for me. I heard a *thump*. Kupka grunted and released the pressure around my neck. A big rock fell to the ground and Sally stumbled backward. Kupka went down to his knees and I used the side wall for support to get my wobbly feet up from under me.

I had to finish him before he got me. I saw the gun in his fist, my oxygen-starved mind slowing down the frames. The gun came up and went off. The bullet knocked Sally backward, and she disappeared over the side of the cliff. I kicked him in the side of the head. He rolled over sideways and I dropped on his back with both of my knees and heard the breath swoosh out of him. But he rolled back at me and I went stumbling over him and to the ground. As I started up, he grabbed me by the throat again and forced me down to my knees. My right knee hit something hard.

The gun.

"I'm going to kill you like I did your mother, you stupid shit."

My hand closed over the gun butt. I brought it up into his crotch and fired. He screamed and staggered back, holding on to his bloody crotch.

I stood up. "That was for Betty. This is for Sally."

I shot him in the stomach. He fell to his knees and I put one between his eyes.

I dumped his body over the cliffside and hoped the hell he'd be ripped into fish food by the action of the dam.

Tears burned my eyes as I drove back to Halliday's, not for what I'd done, but for my mother and Sally. Most people would have fled before taking on a mean bastard like Kupka, but Sally had picked up a rock and gone after him. She owed me nothing and I don't know why she did it. Maybe she was tired of being used and abused by all the Kupkas of the world and wanted to strike back.

Windell Palmer II was a schmuck, a rock-solid nerd, and he knew it. His father, Windell I, owned a big jewelry store located near a freeway exit off-ramp to the Strip. You could buy a wedding ring set and get a discount certificate for a marriage ceremony good at a wedding "chapel." Their best gimmick, though, was an offer to buy the "used" wedding rings from a previous marriage. With the country in the throes of a sexual revolution and a war between the sexes, the divorce rate was the highest ever and business was good.

But Windell was never part of the business. When he was ten, he got busted for shoplifting. It wasn't the first time he had lifted stuff, just the first time he got caught. His mother had spotted the bulge in Windell's shirt when they got into the car and found a small steel toy car with real rubber wheels. She marched Windell back into the store to teach him a lesson and stood by helplessly sputtering as the store manager called the police and had her ten-year-old son busted. It cost five hundred dollars for a lawyer, two trips to juvenile court for his parents, and a lot of anger from Windell I because he had to leave his jewelry store to go to court. After that, they sent Windell to an aunt in L.A. who lived near Silver Lake so he could attend a private school in the hopes it would reform him. Windell stopped stealing but learned another vice, masturbating. Had Windell kept it a private sport it would've been okay, but he spanked his monkey in class and the aunt shipped him back to Vegas.

Windell moved from public-display masturbation to other vices, the most distinguishable of which was grifting. He always had a con, whether it was making keys to steal cars or making devices to open the payoff gate inside a slot machine. For every way to make a buck, Windell had criminal intent. As Zack had suspected, when God made Windell he left a few of the operating parts out of his brain, the ones that provided common sense, along with a sense of loyalty and discretion. He suffered from the delusion of infallibility, that he was smarter than anyone else and would never be caught. Windell I, who banned him from the jewelry store after he caught Windell peddling gold bracelets to young girls for sex, had long given up on his son.

Windell answered the door to find Janelle standing outside his room.

"I need to talk to you."

Windell lived in a boarding house in West Las Vegas. His father told him that he'd be better off with the people on the wrong side of the freeway than near his own family. What he meant was that it was cheaper rent, and since he was still supporting his twenty-something son, he had a right to complain. Windell hated the meat-and-potato grub the old widow running the rooming house served, so he lived on fast-food hamburgers and the cheap buffets casinos offered.

Janelle sniffed the air in the room as he closed the door behind her.

"Jesus H. Christ, this place stinks. You ever clean it? Or does that only happen when you take your annual bath?"

"Hey, I didn't invite you."

She sat on the unmade bed, her back to the headboard, her four-inch platform shoes on his sheet. Janelle looked good to Windell, even though he knew Zack complained that she was a cokehead who looked like shit. Her lap-dancing days were over and she was blackballed as a dealer in the entire state even though Con never brought charges. Janelle and Zack were splitsville now, had been for over six months, and he'd heard that her habit had gotten so hungry she was turning tricks. Before Zack moved into a room at Halliday's hotel wing, he tried to get her into rehab but the argument had exploded into a knockdown, drag-out fight that earned Zack an inch-long scar on his temple from a broken beer bottle.

Maybe Zack turned up his nose at needle tracks, but to Windell she was a prime snatch. No one had ever accused him of being a romantic.

She lit a joint and took a deep drag. "I need money, Windell."

"Don't we all."

"Real money. I've been around this old town too long," she crooned.

"I haven't got any bread."

"I don't want a loan. If I did I sure as hell wouldn't ask a dirtbag like you." She handed him the joint and he took a deep drag and held it.

"Then haul your whore ass back out onto the street."

"Don't get upset, Little Man." She knew Windell liked the reference to Meyer Lansky's nickname. "Look at this dump. Zack's living at the casino and eating steak and we're one step from pushing a shopping cart full of trash down the street." She got the joint back and snicked ashes onto the floor.

"Zack's my friend."

"What's your *friend* done for you lately?"

"No shit."

Zack had been security manager at Halliday's for over three years. He modernized the security system, replacing the skywalks with visual monitoring equipment. He had slowly slipped Windell back into operations at the club, letting him help design the security system and acting as a part-time handyman for electronic problems around the club, but it didn't pay Windell enough to get laid once a week.

She kicked off her shoes and pulled her knees back. Her legs were bare and tanned and he could see white panties glowing between her thighs.

"You're a smart guy. Zack says that all the time. I know you have a way to go for the money."

His mouth was dry. She was right. Windell had gone from one vice to another, but the one that stuck in his head like a fly buzzing around was going for the money. Like guys who can't resist the impulse to wave their weenies in public, it was an irresistible impulse. Everyone who came to Vegas, whether to gamble or live and work here, had been brought by the same lure—money. When he wasn't pulling petty grifts, Windell was thinking about the "Big One." Even the preacher down at the local bible church surreptitiously dropped nickels and dimes from the collection box into slots.

She spread her legs apart a little, hiking her dress up her copper tanned thighs. He knew she cared zilch about him. She just barely tolerated him because Zack let him hang around. A rubber tire around the middle, thick glasses, fat lips, and a chronic acne problem weren't the best attributes to attract a woman like Janelle, but he didn't care. He was used to paying for it.

"I've been thinking about knocking over my old man's jewelry store. I know the alarm code."

"And what, make a run for Mexico with a pocketful of wedding rings? We'd be busted before we made it. No, we need a plan, Little Man, one that's foolproof and no one will ever catch on to, something no one has done before. I know you have one burning inside of you."

He unconsciously rubbed the hard bulge straining in the crotch of his pants. "I got one, but it means busting Halliday's."

A smile appeared on her face. He could see she was real pleased at the idea. He felt the heat spreading through his loins.

"This time Con won't let us walk away if we get caught," he said.

"Then we won't get caught. You're a smart guy."

"It means fucking over Zack."

"Still have to pay for pussy?" she crooned, slowly spreading her legs apart all the way, exposing her white lacy panties and rubbing her fingers over her mound. "Come and get it. This hot cunt is waitin' for you."

The Old Man wanted to see me in his office. Con Halliday was only in his early sixties, but prematurely gray hair and high living made him look older. A quart of whiskey a day lined his nose with blue veins and reddened sagging cheeks.

He built Halliday's into a prime downtown casino, but in terms of the big clubs on the Strip, it was small time. The Strip dominated everything. My eyes were always on the Strip; Con was satisfied downtown. It wasn't just being the big frog in the little pond, but downtown he was a bona fide character. His string tie, Stetson hat, and big .44 hog tied down to his right thigh were part of the lore of Glitter Gulch. He was reputed to have killed three men in gunfights and no one doubted the rumor or cared if it was really true—when you were a character, you were expected to be bigger than real life.

Over the years, he'd turned Halliday's into an Old West museum, with Western memorabilia scattered around the place—Wild Bill Hickok's navy Colts, the scattergun used by Doc Holiday at the gunfight at the O.K. Corral, Annie Oakley's sweat-stained buffalo hunter's outfit, a plainsman's hat with three bullet holes (the window sign claimed it was the hat worn by Butch Cassidy when he and the Sundance Kid shot it out with the whole damn Bolivian army). If you looked a little too close, you might see the "Made in Japan" imprint on Cochise's scalping knife. Everyone in Vegas was a grifter and the more Con bullshitted people, the more he was admired—and believed.

I'd been with Con three years, and while I wouldn't say he was like a father to me, by not having a father, I picked up what Embers and Con had to offer. But Con and I were heading for a crisis. I was still the youngest security manager in Vegas, and now I was being offered a job that didn't pay any better than Con paid me, but it was on the Strip—security manager for the Sands. I felt loyal to Con, so I told him I'd been offered the job.

I wanted to move up in life and security manager at Halliday's was a dead end no matter what I got paid. I had another job in mind and it meant Halliday had to give up some of his authority and part with a piece of his ego—I wanted to be casino manager.

Since its inception, Halliday's had only had one casino manager and that was Con. I didn't think Con would have shared the top job with Bic, even if his son had been less of a loser. Running the casino, being a great character, was Con's life. But he was running the casino into the ground. He bought himself a load of trouble by allowing in men named in the state's black book of undesirables. His license was on probation and could be jerked the next time he got into trouble. He needed a backup on the license or he'd have to close the doors. Bic couldn't be trusted and had been busted for drugs. Morgan was away at school and wasn't even old enough. That made me a perfect candidate. Con knew how I operated.

The club was going downhill because Con wasn't keeping up with the times. Glitter Gulch was becoming a ghost town. The Strip was the place and the only way for a grind joint to operate was to offer comps to the small-time gamblers who came in on the weekends. These people spent maybe four, five hundred bucks over a two- or three-day junket, coming in on a chartered bus from San Diego or L.A. and staying in discount rooms and eating cheap food. They were no-frills gamblers, steady and reliable, and just like people who read horoscopes, they only remembered when everything went right—the fifteen-hundred-dollar jackpot they won last year and not the several grand they lost since.

To get these mama-papa gamblers, Con needed to steer more and more away from the professional gamblers, the poker pros, and serious blackjack and craps players. There were less of those each year as women began to spend almost as much money on gambling as men. "Pretty soon you're going to want me to put in a merry-go-round for the damn kids," Con grumbled, when I told him we should offer a comp of a hot dog and drink when anyone cashed a hundred dollars worth of chips.

"Why not?" I sneered back. "Circus Circus is raking in millions with kiddie treats."

So that's where it stood between us. I wanted to run Halliday's day-to-day operation. Con would still be the boss, it was his place, but he had his head in the "old days" and if someone like me didn't come in with new ideas, the place would get crummier every year. I was tired of Con's "bonus" money dribbled out to me like I was a kid. I wanted a piece of the action. I had ideas and if they worked and he made money, I wanted to make real money, too. Bottom line, Con needed new blood, new ideas, and someone with the twenty-four/seven energy to make Halliday's shine and I was the kid who knew how to spit-polish.

When I walked into Con's office, there was a surprise waiting for me. She was about five-foot-six, maybe a hundred and twenty pounds, a blonde showgirl wearing a white suit and a lot of sex appeal.

"Zack, say hello to Chenza Berlin."

Chenza was high-class sex. Don't get me wrong, Janelle had sex appeal or at least she did before whatever in her life that she was running from caught up with her and she began looking for help with a nose full of cocaine. Janelle had street sex appeal, the stark sexuality of a cocktail waitress exposing some tits and ass as she bends over to serve your drink. But this dame was a class act, a woman wrapped in pearls and sable getting out of a Rolls Royce. My first impression of her was of a cheetah with a diamond choker, a long, slender blonde cat with black spots that hunts alone. My second impression hit me right in my libido. I almost looked down at my crotch to see if my cock had come out of my pants.

After a proper handshake—her hand was sensual and cool—I sat down, wondering who the hell she was and what she was doing here.

"Chenza used to be a Follies lead," Con said. "She retired a few years ago on her ill-gotten gains."

"In other words, I got dumped when some of my body parts started going south. But I'm not here to write my life story. I have a friend who comes in from Hong Kong to play shimmy at the Dunes. He's being cheated."

That was information enough for me to write her biography. Ex-showgirl, too old for the ramp but still has class and sensuality, ends up as an "escort" for whales. Whales were big players, the kind of gamblers who came into town and could drop a couple of million in a weekend without batting an eye. None of them came downtown because the action for that kind of money was all on the Strip. A woman like Chenza could pick up fifty grand or more in gifts and cash for a weekend with a whale. Two or three weekends a year would support a big house, a red convertible Mercedes SL, and a maid. A high-class form of prostitution, even though no one called it that.

"Why do you think the Dunes is cheating him?"

"I don't. The Dunes is not the problem. It's a private game between my friend, Mr. Wan, and Tommy Chow. It's taking place at the Dunes."

I recognized the name of both men as legendary whales. Both were Chinese. Wan was from Hong Kong and Chow from somewhere back East. I had never seen either of them in action. Chemin de fer, referred to as "shimmy" by pro gamblers, was a form of baccarat popular in Europe, but I didn't know the chicken from the egg. It was the big-money card game in Vegas back in the fifties before it got replaced by baccarat. I knew basically that in baccarat the house was the banker who players played against whereas in chemin de fer one of the players acted as the bank. The casino provided the setting and croupiers for the game and took five percent from each pot as a commission.

I'd seen the games played, but didn't have much experience with them. No baccarat table ever existed at Halliday's. Con said it was a snooty rich man's game. He was right, but more money could pass over a baccarat table during a night of play than Halliday's saw in all the slots, roulette, card tables, and keno combined. The big Strip casinos fought over whales like Wan and Chow, bringing them in from around the world in private jets, putting them into royal suites, comping everything from the finest foods and wines to diamond-studded cheetahs as bedmates.

"Chow is cheating," she said.

"How do you know?"

"He's winning too consistently. Mr. Wan has played Vegas for many years and has never lost consistently."

"Just because he's losing you think he's being cheated?"

"He isn't just losing, he's being taken for millions. If it keeps up, Mr. Wan will not come back to Vegas."

And I figured that would make her a big loser, too. "There's a real simple solution. Your friend doesn't have to play with Chow."

"That won't work. Mr. Wan will lose face if he refuses the challenge."

"Are the Chinese really that much into—"

"When you are in Mr. Wan's position, they are. He has extensive interests in gambling in the Far East. If he lets himself be cheated, he would open himself up for more cheating."

Chenza took out a cigarette and Con almost fell over his desk to light it. She blew smoke in my direction. She could have blown dirt in my face and walked over my naked back in spike heels and I would have sucked it up. Yeah, I was thinking with my dick again.

"How much is he losing?"

"Maybe a million a match."

I whistled. "And he keeps on playing."

"Let's just say Mr. Wan enjoys the challenge. Once he uncovers the method . . ."

Oh, he was *that* kind of Hong Kong businessman, the kind that words like *triad* and *tong* were whispered about, but never to his face. The Asian mob had not hit Vegas, but that was only because Howard Hughes left behind a city up for grabs and the Chicago, New York, and Jersey boys all ripped off a piece of it. I looked to Con with a question on my face.

"Chenza came to me because she knows my reputation for sniffing out cheating. Wan's arriving in town this coming week and, unfortunately, as you know, I'll be tied up with the planning commission on that expansion we're working on."

I quickly translated Con's b.s. There was no planning commission meeting, no expansion plans, and he would have cut off the fingers on both hands for a chance to get in Chenza's pants. It took me a second, but I knew Con well enough to know why he was dodging the bullet— vanity. The bastard was half-blind and wore a secret pair of bifocals only in private. He'd have to wear the glasses in order to see the table action, but he was too vain.

"Con tells me that you're also very well versed in cheating," she smiled.

"Ms., uh, Berlin, may I call you Chenza?"

She smiled noncommittally. What a bitch. But I loved it.

"I'm not in Con's class in nosing out grifters. What exactly did you have in mind?"

"I'll pick Mr. Wan up at the airport next Tuesday and accompany him to the Dunes for the game. Chow will be flying in from New York and they'll start the game about ten o'clock that night. They'll play for a few hours, with minimum bets of ten thousand dollars, and then retire and start again the next day. In three days, if things go as usual, Mr. Wan will be poorer by a million or two. By then, he'll want to know what the gaff is."

"What about Dunes security?"

"They know nothing. We'll have to have an excuse for your presence in case you're recognized."

"Why don't you just put a leash around my neck and I can pant by your side." I couldn't resist the sarcasm. She was implying that the security manager from a Glitter Gulch joint wouldn't be recognized on the Strip.

"Why don't you be my escort?" she purred suggestively.

I had the cheetah image down right. She had claws and teeth that could rip a man apart, but first she snuggled and rubbed up against them.

"Won't people be a little suspicious why I'm with you when you are considered Wan's escort?"

"They'll just assume Mr. Wan is doubling his pleasure."

I was to get five thousand dollars for watching the games, whether it was one night or three, and an additional five if I spotted the trick. I held out for an extra ten thou if I spotted it. The surprise was that she would be paying me herself. She was hiring me, not Wan. Apparently he'd be more satisfied catching Chow himself. I guess the money she paid me was chicken feed compared to what she got for "escorting" Wan, not to mention his gratitude if she exposed Chow.

"Well, what do you think of her?" Con asked as soon as she was out the door.

"I wouldn't kick her out of bed."

"I'd get down on my old hands and knees and howl like a prairie dog if she dropped her pants in front of me."

"Con, we have to talk."

He checked his watch. "I've got to run—"

"You've been avoiding me for a week. You know I've been offered the security job at the Sands."

He heaved a great sigh. "Well, you know, son, I took you in when you were down, out, and stealing me blind. I knew you'd leave one day. My health is . . ."

"The only thing wrong with your health is fast women, slow horses, and that you confuse a bottle of Scotch for a wet nurse. Let's cut the bull, Con. Your glass runneth over because you have to spend half your time just being Con Halliday. You need someone to run the day-to-day operations of the club, a real casino manager, not some flunky who has to run to you every time a decision has to be made."

"Zack, you know I love you like a son."

He hated his son, but that was beside the point.

"Con, it's come down to this. I'm bored. I've got security down to running itself. I need more action. I can either get it with you, or I can take my chances on the Strip."

"Son, at Halliday's you're somebody. On the Strip, you'd be just another rent-a-cop, someone they replace when the next FBI agent retires."

"The decision is up to you. I can run this place, you know that. You made Halliday's the star of Glitter Gulch and I can keep up that reputation, but I also have some fresh ideas on how to increase business." I knew Con didn't give a damn about increasing business unless it increased his prestige, so I hit him with the big one I had thought out. "You don't understand your importance. It's time you started thinking about the Con Halliday heritage you're going to leave behind and not the day-to-day crap that a manager should take care of."

He nodded, looking up at the ceiling as if he expected divine intervention. "You're right, son." He slapped the desk with his big hand. It sounded like a gun firing. "You're damn right. I'll tell you what I'll do. We'll cut for it."

He grabbed a new deck and broke the seal. "High card and you get the casino manager's job; low card and you stay in your security manager's job for another year. If we have equal cards, you stay at the job for another year with a good raise. It's a win-win-win scenario for you."

He fanned the cards out. "Draw."

I shook my head. "You first."

He hesitated and then pulled a king. "Damn, I was hoping for an ace."

There were fifty-one cards left in the deck and only four aces, which meant I had one chance in about twelve in pulling an ace to beat his king.

I pulled a card and flipped it over. Ace of spades. I grinned at him. "Goddamn, Con, second time in my life I've been lucky."

He flipped over the entire deck. There were no aces and the only king was the one he drew.

"You sack of cow shit, you cheated me," he shouted. "You palmed that ace." He drew his .44 Colt and pulled back the hammer. He pointed it at my chest. "I ought to plug you and tell the cops I caught you skimming."

I shrugged. "You'll get blood on this Texas longhorn chair cover. Of course I palmed the ace. You've been cheating employees with that cold deck for years." I didn't bother telling him that I hadn't lost at cutting cards since Embers took me for my rent money. I came in with an ace up my sleeve because I knew he'd pull out that crooked deck.

"My first act as casino manager is to eighty-six Bic. Put away your gun. You know it has to be done or he'll cost you your license. Better coming from me than you."

Con stroked his chin and looked back up to cowboy heaven before replying. "Okay, son, the ranch is all yours, you're the ramrod."

His head came down and he stared at me with those snake-eyed dice he had for eyes. "But you make one goddamn mistake and I'll be on your ass like a rattler on a desert mouse. I'll chew your goddamn head off and swallow you whole."

I loved Vegas. It allowed people to be themselves.

35

The day before I was to check out Chenza's whale and the game, I drove over to Windell's place to talk to him about ways to cheat at chemin de fer. I first went over every possible scam with Embers, but the card sharp was from the old school, the smoke-and-mirror type of cheating using cold decks, bottom dealing, and the other tricks of card mechanics. The world was fast going to electronics and the one person who knew electronic cheating best was my old friend Windell. I kept him employed part-time in Halliday security for no other reason, I figured, than to neutralize him, sort of like paying a mobster protection so he doesn't firebomb your store.

A surprise was coming down the stairs of the rooming house when I was approaching in my car—Janelle. I hadn't seen her in months and didn't like the stories I heard about her from people who knew her. I never loved Janelle, not the kind of love that romance books claimed moves mountains, but I hated to see her waste her life with drugs. I pulled over before I reached the house and waited for her to get in her car and drive away. If there was anything I knew about Janelle, it was that she wouldn't go near Windell even if she was down to her last fix. Something was up. Money. I could smell it.

There was something else strange. She wore a heavy canvas backpack. Janelle wasn't the backpack type. Years ago Windell had nearly burned himself toting a battery in a backpack because he was trying to use a powerful battery to control the reel spins on a slot machine. I wondered if he was back to his old schemes and whether he had recruited Janelle to help him.

I followed Janelle down to a bank on Eastern Avenue. She went in and waited in line. I had to walk by the bank a couple of times before it was her turn with a clerk. She opened the backpack and pulled out ten-dollar rolls of quarters, a load of them. What kind of penny-ante nonsense was that? Quarters? Was Windell back making slugs, only this time minting real-looking-quarters? After she left, I hurried up to the teller who was still putting Janelle's quarter rolls into a box. She had put up a closed sign on her window.

"Excuse me. My friend thought she left her sunglasses here—did you just help her, Janelle . . . ?" I raised my eyebrows and gestured toward the door.

"With Riordan Vending Machines? No, she didn't leave her glasses here. You might look on the check-writing counter?"

I muttered my thanks, briefly checked the counter, and left the bank barely able to keep from kicking the first person who crossed my path. Riordan Vending Machines? Here I was busting my butt to make something of myself and these two losers were involved in a two-bit scam. And using my name. But what the hell money could there be in quarters? Janelle wasn't stupid. And neither was Windell, even if he lacked good sense. They wouldn't go to all the trouble of setting up a phony bank account just to cash in quarters. Not unless there were so many quarters to make it worth their while.

When I got back to Halliday's, I went into the accounting office and collared Clarke, the accounting manager. "Give me the coin sheets for the last six months."

After looking them over, I had him give me the same six-month period for the previous three years, and I found an inconsistency. We were down in one sector for about thirty thousand dollars a month for the last three months from the same time period in the previous years. "Does Con know anything about this?" I asked.

Clarke shrugged. "He gets the results, but it's no big deal. Business is off a little from prior years. It's not that much."

"Thirty thousand a month can get lost in the shuffle, but this isn't money off the top. The loss is entirely in *quarters*."

I went to my office and did some thinking and calculating. It didn't take a rocket scientist to realize that Windell and Janelle had come up with a scheme that was hauling about a thousand dollars a day in quarters out of the casino. We didn't add up change in the count room; we weighed it to determine its value. A thousand dollars in quarters weighed about fifty pounds. Divided in half, about twenty-five pounds each into a couple backpacks, they could make two deposits a day and thirty thousand dollars a month. Into the "Riordan Vending" account.

I wondered how many other accounts in Vegas banks had my name on it.

I shook my head at the sheer audacity of it. Only Windell would think of a two-bit way to steal a bundle. They were taking enough money to eventually get rich, but not enough to have alarm bells go off, especially the way Con ran the casino.

There was no way I could cover this for Janelle and Windell, it was too much money. And I didn't want to. Ripping off the casino under my nose was as good as ripping me off, and by putting the bank accounts in my name they were framing me. The latter part had to be Janelle's idea. Windell wasn't that clever when it came to screwing people.

I called in Mike Elliot, my assistant, who I was promoting to security manager. I told him what was going on. "Bring in Windell Palmer, get him in on the pretext that we need something electronic repaired immediately. And get me the count-room surveillance tapes. The hallway tapes outside, too, for the past three months. The only place with that much change at one time is the count room. Someone in there has to be an accomplice."

"That's twenty-four hours a day, seven days a week of videotapes. It'll take days just to fast forward through the tapes."

"Do it. And get me Windell's work sheets. He's only around here ten or twelve hours a week. Windell's sloppy—and greedy. I'll lay you five to one that he made up a service call to bill each time he came to make a haul. We'll identify the phony service calls and look at the tapes for those times."

"You must know this guy pretty well."

I grinned. "You don't know the half of it."

Windell sweated bullets in the conference room, which was set up with a TV, VCR, the surveillance tapes, and his billing sheets. It was easy to see how he could haul out tons of quarters. His "tool case" was mounted on a dolly. The case was three feet tall, but he only used a few inches for tools; the rest was all storage space.

"We have to talk, Zack," Windell said.

"We will, old buddy, but first you have to sing."

Coordinating the tapes to the service orders, I realized how Windell had pulled it off. He had repeated service calls on the coin scale that change was weighed on. Clever as hell, but only a nerd like Windell would spotlight his crime by billing twenty bucks for a service call on the scales.

"You're a sly little bastard. You rigged the scale to give false weights. One of the count people skims off the excess and you stuff it in the tool case."

"Can I talk to you in private?"

"Sure." I sent my security people out of the room.

"Janelle put me up to it, Zack, no kidding. She even spread her legs for me."

I put pen and paper in front of him. "I'm going to cut you a deal you don't deserve. Put down a full confession, tell me exactly how it came down, naming Janelle and your buddy in the count room."

"What'll I get out of it?"

"You walk out free and clear. But you can never enter Halliday's again."

"That's it?"

"Roll on the other two and you get to walk." I squeezed Windell's shoulder with my hand. "We're like blood brothers. Wouldn't you do the same for me?"

Surprisingly, Windell had nice, neat handwriting. And a real knack for details. He laid it all out like an accountant would, incriminating himself, Janelle, and an employee on the graveyard shift in the count room.

When he was done and signed his name, I handed the confession to Mike Elliot. "Take Windell and his confession and dump him at LVPD."

"Zack! You promised me. You made a deal."

I shook my head. "Windell, I'm not trustworthy. You should know my word's no good."

I hit him in the mouth, knocking out his two front teeth. "Tell the cops he resisted arrest."

When the day came for the whales to battle at shimmy, I drove out to Chenza's place to pick her up. At the Dunes we'd take a limo to the airport to pick up her Hong Kong friend. She lived in a sprawling hacienda-style adobe on a bluff outside of town. I parked my car, then went through a wrought-iron gate into a courtyard surrounded by lush foliage. To my left was parked a silver Aston-Martin with license plate number 007.

A middle-aged Chicano woman answered the door and led me into a living room that provided a view of Vegas from its floor-to-ceiling windows.

Chenza came out a few minutes later and went directly to the bar. "Jack Coke?"

The woman does her homework. I saluted her with my drink. "Did you have a game plan?"

"You're the security manager."

"Casino manager."

"Really. Congratulations."

She kissed me full on the mouth. I fumbled to set my glass down. She stepped back. "Don't get too excited. All you get for being manager of a grind joint is a kiss."

"What would I get if I ran the Strip?"

"More than you could handle."

She had a way of getting to the point. I could be just as blunt. "I want to fuck you."

"Who doesn't?"

I followed her out the door, imagining in my mind her firm buttocks on top of my rock-hard dick.

"I like your car," I said. "It looks like something James Bond would drive."

"It's the car he drove in *Goldfinger*."

"That must have cost a few bucks."

She rolled her eyes. It was a dumb remark. A woman like Chenza didn't pay for anything. She took one look at my Ford Maverick and stopped short.

"We're taking my car," she said.

"Embarrassed to be seen in mine?"

"Yes."

She threw me the keys of the Aston-Martin and I climbed in, hoping I could handle driving on the right side. I got it out of the driveway without denting the fenders and drove in silence for a minute, but I wasn't someone who let dead dogs lie, or whatever the expression. I hated cars. When I started driving, I only had money for junkers and no old man to take me into a garage and show me how to change a set of spark plugs.

"Listen, I'm not a car person. I bought the Maverick because it was cheap and a no-brainer in terms of maintenance—when the ashtray gets full, I buy another."

"You also don't know anything about clothes."

"Look, lady—"

"No, you look. Vegas is as phony as Hollywood. If you want to be big time in this town, you have to act the part. We're stopping at Syd Devore's."

"What's wrong with the way I'm dressed?" It was my best suit.

"You're dressed like a pit boss, a medium-quality ready-made suit. Tonight you're mingling with the rich and famous. Do you want to look like one of them or an employee?"

I was ready to tell her to take her sweet ass out onto the street where she belonged, when she leaned over and put her hand on my thigh. Testosterone flooded my brain.

"Zack, I know what you want—respect, money, being a somebody. But you'll never get it by just working hard. In this town, you only get it if you look like you have money. Money breeds money. If you want me around, you're going to have to look like you're somebody."

I gave her a sideways glance. "Does this mean I get some pussy?"

"Zack, a real man doesn't say it that way."

"How does a real man say it?"

"With money."

We picked up Hong Kong Wan in a stretch limo. He walked off the chartered plane with bodyguards who looked like sumo wrestlers in three-piece suits. They could have scared the sushi out of a samurai. One of them was carrying a suitcase attached to a wrist chain. A *suit-case*, for crissake, not a briefcase.

Wan could have been sixty or eighty, I couldn't tell. He was small built, thin to the point of almost being emaciated, with dark eyebrows so thin they looked sketched on and raven black hair without a speck of gray. You might mistake him for a schoolteacher if you missed his eyes—fathomless in their blackness, eyes that could suck you in.

Chenza gave Wan a cheek peck and introduced me. The airport was just around the corner from the Strip, and I told the limo driver to take a longer route to give us time to talk.

"Chenza thinks Chow is cheating," I said. "What do you think?"

"I suspect she is right. At first I was not pleased when she suggested bringing in someone to uncover the trick. I would prefer to do so my-self, but since she wishes to help . . ."

"You have any clue as to how he's doing it?"

Wan spread his hands on his knees. "I have some small experience with cheating, having an interest in gambling establishments, how-ever, I now fear Chow has devised a scheme that I cannot penetrate."

"How's he aroused your suspicions?"

"We have had three private games and each time I lost a million dollars, exactly."

"No matter how you varied the bets?"

"No matter what I bet. It is as if he is toying with me, challenging me."

As I stared into Wan's swirling black holes, I had an image of Chow drowning in a whirlpool.

"Anything unusual in his style of play?"

"He insists upon using his own chemin de fer table. He takes it with him no matter where he plays."

"His rabbit foot?"

"Precisely."

"He must be really attached to that table."

"More than you can imagine. Mr. Chow ran a gambling establishment in Saigon before the city fell to the Communists. When he fled the country, there was room on the plane for only one item, the table or his wife." Wan giggled like a little girl. "We Chinese are superstitious."

Wan wanted to go to his suite to rest up for the match that was to start at ten. Of course, Chenza went with him to tuck him in bed. She took a suitcase with her with the explanation she was staying in the suite next to his. I wandered around the casino while I waited for Chenza to return. What she said to me in the car really got to me. She said I was *common*. Street trash, I could take. Low class, maybe. But common was poison. One thing about Con, he might be from *common* stock as me, but he played his country-fried character to the hilt. I decided I was going to stop being common. The new Armani suit set me back eight hundred, with another four hundred for the hand-stitched silk shirt, tie, belt, and Gucci shoes. I stuck my old suit and shoes in a Salvation Army Dumpster. I was going to do the same with every item of clothing I owned. From now on, it was to be nothing but the best.

A kidney-shaped table was being set up by maintenance people in the area roped off for high-roller baccarat games. Jeff Holland, the assistant security manager, was standing nearby.

"Hey, hey, what's up, Zack."

"Just hanging loose. A friend of mine is playing tonight and I'm here to observe the game. I've always been on the other side of the rope when high-stakes baccarat is played."

Holland shook his head. "My wife and I have saved for three years toward the down payment on a house. These guys throw enough money on the table at every hand to *buy* a house."

"Too rich for my blood."

"You don't look like you're hurting. Nice suit. I hear you're the manager now at Halliday's. When Con the con fires you, drop by and I'll get you up in here, working security."

"Is it a sure thing Con's going to can me?"

"Do bears shit in the woods? You're the only security manager Con didn't fire after six months and the only casino manager he's ever had. You must have something going, but if Con doesn't get you, his kid will. He's been eighty-sixed from here, did you know that?"

"I've eighty-sixed him, too."

Holland laughed. "Kid, you've got balls, but the Hallidays will cut them off one day. Didn't your pappy ever tell you that blood is thicker than water?"

I walked around the kidney-shaped table. The wood was old and venerable, the chemin de fer layout done in ivory.

"Nice table."

"Yeah, it's that Chow dude's personal table—he won't play on any other."

I bent over to take a closer look at it, squatting down to check underneath.

"I checked it over, just for the hell of it," he said. "I didn't see anything unusual. If that table's gaffed, it must be with the ghost in the machine."

I went to dinner with Chenza that evening. We looked like a million dollars walking into the restaurant, grabbing the best table in the place. Everything was comped.

"You pack a lot of weight in here," I said.

"Only because I'm tied to Wan. If it wasn't for his money, they wouldn't let me in the door."

I told her about the time a restaurant ran out Janelle and me because they wanted to make room for high rollers.

"Keep reminding yourself that only money counts in this town," she said, "Vegas has no art, no science, no culture, no soul. No one in the whole state has a pedigree any longer than the great-grandfather who worked the mines or robbed banks. Money is the measure of everything. You either have it or you don't. You're in or you're out. It's as simple as that."

She toasted me with her wineglass. "To the youngest casino manager in Vegas—who'll be the youngest casino *owner* someday."

"I'm going to have it."

"I know you will. You're smart enough, tough enough, fast enough . . . you're even enough of a bastard."

Chairs were set back from the table for myself, Chenza, and the rest of the players' entourages, but I preferred to stand and watch the action. I had an intuitive feeling that Mr. Wan would be important in my life. I wanted to impress him, big time.

Tommy Chow's features were not what I had expected. I assumed that with a name like that he would be young and flippant, but he turned out to be a beach ball with a bald head and short, jerky movements. His wrinkled business suit looked cheaper than the one I gave to charity and made Wan's short red Chinese robe with fanning sleeves, white shirt, black tie, and black pants look even more impressive.

Chow made me nervous just watching him, and watch him I did, him and everyone else who touched the cards. The croupier who sat in the indentation of the kidney-shaped table laid out six decks, one at a time, showing they were true, then shuffled them. After Wan made the cut, the indicator card was put near the bottom of the deck, the decks put in the card shoe—in shimmy known as a *sabot*—and the shoe passed to Chow, who was on the croupier's right, to deal.

Because of the large size of the table, the cards Chow dealt to Wan were placed on a paddle and given to Wan by the croupier. The action was watched by a ladderman on a tall stool back from the table. Another casino croupier handled the banker's money and took the house's cut. Both Wan and Chow had stacks of thousand-dollar chips.

The game was played a little like blackjack, with two cards dealt, then a possible hit with a third card, but the point count was different. The objective was to have cards totaling nine or be closest to nine. Chow took the first turn as dealer-banker, dealing Wan and himself each two cards. Unlike Vegas-style baccarat, shimmy allowed a small amount of discretion in taking hits. After checking his cards, Wan would have to decide whether to take a hit or not. The rules were so complicated, players usually needed a chart to tell them when a hit was required or an option, but these two were old pros at the game. Aces counted as one point; other cards had their normal face value, with the ten and painted card—jack, queen, king—counting as zero.

In the first game, Wan was dealt a ten and a three. The ten didn't count, so he only had a total of three. He took a hit and got a five, which now gave him a total of eight. Chow had two queens, both of which had no face value, thus he had zero. He drew a seven, which was beaten by Wan's eight.

After the first win, everything went downhill for Wan. It wasn't so much that Chow's hands were good—he rarely had a natural nine—but that Wan's were so bad. If luck was a lady, she was a real bitch to Wan.

When the game broke up several hours later, Wan was down beaucoup bucks. I didn't know exactly how much, but enough to buy a whole damn tract of houses. I went over to the table and examined the back of the cards and the shoe.

"What do you think?" Chenza asked.

"It has to be the deck, the shuffle, the shoe, or Chow is a card mechanic."

"Card mechanic?"

"A card sharp who's so smooth you don't spot him dealing from the bottom or taking cards out of play."

"That can't be done with a shoe."

"It can, especially if the shoe is bugged. There are clip joints that use shoes with a false compartment where cards are stored. As the dealer pulls out cards with his right hand, he holds the shoe with his left to release cards from the compartment. But there's nothing wrong with the shoe."

"You think Chow's a card mechanic?"

"If he is, he's the best I've ever seen."

"Find the gimmick. Wan's only going to be here one more night. He's already dropped half a million."

She left me in her dust and I went back and examined the table again. It had to be something electronic. I wished Windell wasn't cooling his heels in jail. My limit with electronics was turning light switches on and off.

The table looked solid to me. I even looked over the paddle used to distribute cards. Nada. I examined the shoe again. No secret compartment. The deck could have been marked with a Windell-type invisible substance, but that would require special glasses. I had the cold feeling that I wouldn't be seeing Chenza again, or the enigmatic Mr. Wan, if I didn't solve her mystery.

I left the casino, certain that something was rotten not only in Denmark and just as sure that I was somehow going to be a fall guy. Chenza had made it clear: If I wasn't sharp enough to bust a grifter, I wasn't in her class. Yeah, I was thinking with my dick again, but I had never made love to a cheetah before either.

The next night I showed up at the Dunes decked out in another new suit with all the trimmings. I took a seat next to Chenza. She gave me a sucker token smile, the kind a waiter who refills your glass of water gets.

"Bitch," I said, through clenched teeth.

"Amateur."

That set the tone for the rest of the evening. As I watched, hour after hour, Wan's money moved across the table that Chow sacrificed his wife for. I just didn't get it. I didn't take my eyes off of Chow and he exposed nothing. I watched the three croupiers and they exposed nothing. The ladderman was clean. I even looked out into the casino and found no one waving flags to tip Chow. Whatever Chow's scheme was, it was too good for me. I just knew it had to be electronic. There was no way I could miss his hand movements even if he was the best card mechanic in the country.

Wan was down almost another half a mil when I went over to the food table set up for the players and guests and poured myself a glass of cold water. I thought I was the best and this pint-sized Chinese, Vietnamese, whatever the hell he was, was making a fool out of me. And Chenza was colder toward me than the ice water.

I leaned my head back and looked up at the gold-veined, mirrored ceiling above the playing area, reflecting the play between Wan and Chow. It suddenly hit me between the eyes, a bolt from the gods. I almost laughed out loud. It was so damn simple, so damn clever, I wouldn't have tumbled to it in a million years if I hadn't spent so much time card sharping before Embers's mirror.

I stepped over to the table and whispered in Wan's ear. I left the roped area with Chenza staring at me open-mouthed and Wan still at the table, his body shaking as he tried to keep from exploding with laughter.

A joke, it really was. Funnier than hell.

––––––––

I answered the door to my Halliday room at three in the morning. I already knew who it would be before I opened the door. Chenza stormed in, not at all a happy camper. The scent of her perfume overwhelmed my nostrils—and my gonads.

"Wan kept on playing and losing. He lost a million, all together. He sent you this," she said coldly.

Twenty chips were in the envelope, each worth a thousand dollars.

"Tell me what you whispered to him, what was so funny? Why's he paying you off?"—the edge in her voice building.

"So many questions, so little time."

She slapped me hard. "Listen to me, you prick, I hired you for the job. Something came down tonight and I want to know."

The slap stung my face but it also turned me on. The desire in my loins had already ignited when she walked in the door.

"I'll tell you. But first you owe me for that sting." I seized her arm and forced her toward me and kissed her hard on the lips. I thought for a moment I could feel the response rising in her body, but then she angrily tore away from me.

"Stop it," she hissed and gave me another slap on the face.

"That makes two now you owe me," I smiled. My adrenaline was up and running. I grabbed the top of her thin dress and ripped it from her body. She stood naked except for her stockings and garter belt. Her breasts were hard and strong and definitely had not gone south. There was no fear in her face, only defiance.

"This dress cost me a thousand," she said, looking straight in my eyes.

I grabbed a handful of chips and pushed them into her hand. "Keep an accounting." I grabbed her arm and held it behind her back while my other hand cupped her pubis. I kissed her hard on the lips again but this time she responded back, eagerly pushing her body against mine.

"You want me, don't you."

She didn't answer. Her eyes were closed, her heart pounding.

"Say it." I squeezed my hands on her buttocks.

"Yes," she moaned. "I want you."

––––––––

I was feeling warm and cozy and still sleepy when Chenza suddenly bit my ear.

"Ouch! Do you like raw meat, is that your thing?"

"I don't like being left out in the cold. What did you tell Wan?"

"You hired me to find out who was cheating. I did."

"And?"

"Wan was cheating."

"What do you mean? He lost a fortune."

"That was the idea. He was cheating so he would lose."

She sat up in bed and shook her head. "What are you talking about?"

"Wan's the grifter, not Chow. Everyone in the place was watching Chow, looking for the trick, and no one, including me, was watching Wan's play. When I looked up at the ceiling mirror, I saw a hand motion that I used to practice in front of a mirror. It was so damn funny because it was Wan, not Chow, who was the card mechanic. He was switching good cards for bad ones. He could have hid a six-deck shoe up those big sleeves."

"This makes no sense at all."

"Why Wan was losing on purpose? That I can't tell you, but I can give you a pretty good guess. Vegas is the biggest and loosest bank in the world, the place of choice for mobsters and drug lords to wash their money. Wan obviously is making a payoff to Chow for something. If he gives Chow cash, Chow has to account for it, show the IRS it came from a legit source. The casino is inadvertently washing it for them. Wan brings in a suitcase of cash, buys chips, loses them to Chow, and the casino writes Chow a check when he cashes in his winnings."

"That's bizarre."

"That's business," I said, as I kissed her on the mouth, then pushed her head down on my hard phallus.

Part 7

★ ★ ★ ★ ★ ★

SHOWGIRL

Hollywood is a place where they buy a kiss for fifty thousand dollars
and a soul for fifty cents.

—Marilyn Monroe

Chenza looked at May Epstein, the casting director, and two words came to her mind—*very musculine*. She often wondered why some women seemed a bit masculine, had that certain hardness in their features, even the facial hair. She was told it was because they had too many male hormones, but as a twenty-year-old who'd learned nothing in high school and hadn't attended college, she thought hormones were something out of a vitamin bottle. Chenza didn't care if the woman was a diesel dyke or cross-dresser—May was a top Hollywood casting director and she was lucky to get an interview with her.

The woman wore a manly looking business suit, Italian cut, with wide padded shoulders. She reminded Chenza of someone and decided it was the villainous Russian female colonel in the James Bond movie *From Russia with Love*.

May tossed Chenza's resume in the trash can behind her. "You have no high school drama credits, no college drama credits, no equity waiver credits. In fact, the only acting credit you seem to have is the snow job—or should I say blow job—you did on my assistant to get this interview."

"I've won beauty contests—"

"Being 'Little Miss Schwartz's Department Store' at twelve and a runner up for Miss Wisconsin at eighteen hardly qualifies you for movie roles. Miss America doesn't get movie offers. Every one of you blondes who've had a few modeling gigs and won a Miss Dime-Stores contest think you're ready for the big screen. Doesn't it occur to any of you that it takes more than wiggling your ass to get a part?"

Chenza stood up, her face hot. "I'm sorry I took up your time."

"No you're not. You're sorry I didn't fall over backward when you walked in. Sit down. Movie roles require charisma and there is something about you that might do it." May looked at the pictures attached to Chenza's resume. "Take off your blouse."

"I don't do porn—"

"Neither do I. Take off your blouse. And brassiere."

Chenza unbuttoned her blouse and slipped it off, then removed her bra. She was proud of her breasts. They stood tall, as one male admirer, a sailor, described them.

May got up and came around to her, half-sitting against the side of her desk.

"You might do for the part."

"What kind of part is it?"

"One of our top box-office actresses just had her second kid and she let her breasts sag."

"You think my acting would be good enough to take her place?"

"Acting? Honey, I'm not going to cast your face. They need a body double, a pair of boobs for a scene. That's where all your charisma is, right in the tits."

May leaned closer and put her hand on the side of Chenza's breast. Chenza flinched. Her hand slowly moved around the breast and cupped the nipple.

"It's five thousand for a day's work," May said. She squeezed the nipple. "If I cast you."

Chenza had always known what the score was when it came to men— and the May Epsteins of this world. Born in Brooklyn the same year the war ended, she grew up in an atmosphere of quiet desperation. Her mother had been a frustrated actress who never made it beyond a vaudeville sister song-and-dance act that lasted two years and never got out of the sticks and into the big time. She married a salesman who worked for a furniture manufacturer and settled down to spend the rest of her life a martyr, regretting her lost "opportunities." She passed her own frustrations about stardom onto her daughter like a genetic defect.

Her mother, Faye Zimmerman nee Green, tried to mold Chenza into the star she had never been. At an early age, Chenza got rid of her Brooklyn accent. It was either speak "like other people" or get soap in her mouth. She also had to get rid of her ethnic name. Her mother chose "Berlin" as her surname because her favorite movie was the 1954 classic *White Christmas*, from the song written by Irving Berlin.

After braces straightened her teeth, she started making the rounds of beauty contests, starting with the one run by Schwartz's Department Store. Her first-place prize had been one hundred dollars' worth of new dresses.

Watching her mother act around her father and other men taught her the power a woman holds over a man—sex. She watched how her mother got her way with her father—the body language, feigned anger, "headaches"—all designed to keep her father from getting what he wanted—before her mother got what she wanted. When she was thirteen, her breasts already small mounds and pubic hair growing, she had her first experience at using her "power" to get what she wanted.

"Hi, Uncle Art." Chenza gave her mother's brother a kiss on the lips. She'd only kissed boys twice before and she had more opportunity to kiss her uncle who came to visit than boys her own age. Uncle Art was her favorite uncle—better looking than the others although at forty he was already losing his hair and gaining love handles.

Art, with beer in hand, sat on the stuffed chair in their living room and watched the Yankees play the Los Angeles Dodgers while her mother fluttered around the kitchen. It was the first year the Dodgers were playing without the word *Brooklyn* on their uniforms and her dad said he'd never watch those bums again, but Art was more tolerant of the team's move to L.A. As for her mother, she always fluttered when she was in the kitchen, never really comfortable with household duties even after fifteen years of marriage.

Chenza came into the living room. She wore a white dress with white panties underneath and a white bra. She wasn't wearing a slip and knew her mother would make her put one on if she caught her. She didn't like slips because they helped hide her body shape. She was blossoming as a young woman and very much aware of her shape. And proud of it.

"Uncle Art, can you lend me ten dollars?"

Art took his eyes off the game long enough to give Chenza a look that asked whether she had fallen out of a tree onto her head. Ten dollars was more than a day's wages for most men. "Do I look like John D. Rockefeller to you?"

Chenza slipped onto his lap. She'd been doing this since she could remember, but recently as she felt the warmth of his body against hers, she got sensations she'd never felt before.

"I need a new coat. I saw it at Macy's. It's white rabbit fur. My friend Nancy says it looks just like the fur coat Doris Day wore to the premier of *The Pajama Game*."

Art kept his beer from spilling and looked around her at the TV as leftie pitcher Sandy Koufax cut the outside corner of home plate, low and away. "Sorry, kid, I don't spend that kind of money even on grown women."

Chenza snuggled in closer to him. For the first time Art noticed that she was wearing perfume. He sniffed her neck. "Does your mother know you're wearing that stuff?"

"You like it? It's musk-scented. A boy in high school gave it to me."

"You didn't answer my question. Does your mother know?"

She tapped his chest with her finger.

"No . . . my . . . mother . . . doesn't . . . know. You're not going to tell her, are you, Uncle Art?"

Art shifted uncomfortably and turned his head to take a sip of his beer. He was getting warm. Her body heat radiated through her cotton dress. Man, he hadn't realized the kid was growing up so fast. He could see the imprint of her nipples against her thin dress. What was the matter with his sister and brother-in-law? Were they blind?

Chenza's mother would lecture her that men wanted things from women. "Give them what they want, but always get what you want in return."

Right now she wanted a white rabbit fur coat being worn by a mannequin in the girl's department of Macy's. She cuddled closer to her uncle. She felt her uncle's smooth shaven face with her hand. "Please, Uncle Art," as she ran her fingers through his hair. "It's just ten dollars. Don't you like me?" His face was turning red and she was starting to feel a hard bulge against the inside of her thigh. He took his wallet out and gave her the money. She bounced off his lap and smiled. "Thanks, Uncle Art."

Her breasts turned out to be a big success in the movie, but the unofficial screen credit didn't get her any parts except modeling for girlie magazines and offers from porn producers. She found out there really was a Hollywood casting couch, but it didn't get her far because there was always someone who had more talent—or who slept with someone higher up—who got the part. But she understood the attraction that Hollywood and Broadway had for her mother. The lure of wealth and fame was more addictive than Karl Marx ever imagined religion to be. She was twenty-one with a pretty face and dynamite looks when she answered to her true calling in Vegas.

She came to Sin City with Sam Tarkoff, a small-time producer of B horror films that were one step above porn and one step beneath even the garbage that drive-ins played from dawn to dusk. She had a small part in one of the films, another starring role for her breasts, although there was actually one scene in which she ran half-naked in a dark forest before a maniac lumberjack caught up and sawed her up with a chain saw.

They went to a casino theater with two other couples to watch a Parisian dance revue, which consisted mostly of women walking—not dancing—on stage wearing Busby Berkeley costumes. Some of the headdresses were almost as tall as the chorus girls. Every woman was bare-chested, something Berkeley never managed in Hollywood. One of the couples at their table was the show's choreographer and his wife.

"These babes are really talented," Tarkoff said.

"Talented, my ass," Chenza said, "What's so talented about them, they're not dancing. You men are just ogling their naked breasts like you've never seen a pair before."

"Retract the talons, kid," the choreographer said. "Everyone of my girls has perfect breasts."

"Perfect, hell, most of those boobs are implants. You want to see a perfect pair?"

She stood up at the table and pulled down the front of her dress. "Tell me if any pair on that stage can match these."

Cheers, whistles, and wolf howls erupted throughout the theater.

The next day she was walking the stage with a two-foot-high pineapple-shaped hat à la Carmen Miranda! Bar none, or perhaps bare none, Chenza had the best tits on the stage.

She gave new meaning to the phrase "just another pretty face."

Part 8

★ ★ ★ ★ ★ ★

"WHOSE DOG?"

"Low class."

I didn't know if Morgan Halliday was referring to me personally or to Halliday's. We were in Con's office. Morgan had blown in with her fiancé from back East. Years of Swiss finishing school and Ivy League college had turned her from a spoiled brat into a sophisticated business woman. I had to give her some credit because she was raised by a father who thought women were only good for jumping on in bed and having them serve him food in a restaurant—with a pat on the ass for a tip. For Morgan to have broken his "waitress" mentality about a woman, Morgan had to prove she had something on the ball.

Furthermore, she was now a woman in all respects. I always thought Vassar women had more between the ears than on their chests, but now I had to change my opinion. To be perfectly honest, she looked damn good, very professional, acted very businesslike. She wasn't a statuesque beauty like Chenza, but she was no longer Con's freckled-faced little cowgirl, either.

The only problem was that she still hated my guts for whatever real or imagined slight I gave her when she was a kid.

"Dad, this place needs an overhaul."

Resisting the impulse to bust her chops, I gave her a toothy smile. "This isn't Monte Carlo. James Bond doesn't play baccarat here. Our clientele is the little guy, the husband and wife who, once the kids are grown, get more excitement from pulling the handle of a slot machine than each other."

She didn't bother looking in my direction. "Gambling palaces do not have to be the size of football stadiums. Arthur," pointing to her fiancé, "has done a study on the gambling industry."

Arthur looked like a tennis jock—sandy hair, light blue eyes, sun-bronzed skin, good build, not too tough. Guys who played basketball, football, hardball, were tough. Guys who played tennis and racketball were soft-shelled crabs—they may look good on the outside, but you could crush them with your teeth.

You didn't learn about casinos from a book. That was like wearing a condom during sex—you feel something but you're not experiencing the flesh. But I kept my mouth shut. Like I was once told, blood is thicker than water.

"Arthur sees Halliday's as a boutique."

I groaned aloud. It was impossible to keep my mouth shut. "Jesus, what the hell is that? A fancy flower shop?"

Morgan had been ignoring me and I finally had her attention. Pure animosity was beamed my way.

"Sorry, I forgot you have a limited education."

"Why don't you give me the benefit of what an expensive education paid by your old man got you."

"Com'on now boys and girls, let's not play dirty," Con said, "But, honey, I'm so damn stupid, what exactly is a boutique?"

"A boutique is a small establishment with class. The word is usually associated with fashion. Macy's is a big department store; Haverville's is a small store, a boutique that sells to the rich. The word refers to a small, classy operation. Nowadays stock brokers leave big firms to open boutique investment firms; lawyers jump ship to open boutique law firms."

"Halliday's isn't a boutique?" he asked.

"Surprisingly, Dad, when you ran it and gave it that Old Wild West ambience, it was like a boutique. Now it's more like a cattle pen." She indicated I was the culprit for the fall of the Halliday Empire with a tilt of her head.

Boy, did she tube me. And gall me. Worse, Con was showing his age—and his booze, cigarettes, and screwing. He usually pulled on his cowboy boots and rolled up his pants legs when the bullshit got deep, but the old bastard was eating it up. Sure, I'd made a big change in the casino—*made it profitable*. We had gone from one foot in IRS prison and bankruptcy court to the busiest club downtown. We did it by loosening the payoff on the slots and comping Mom and Dad to beers and hot dogs when they came to Vegas in their camper and cashed in a few hundred in chips over the weekend. I also ran championship poker, blackjack, and even slot machine tournaments.

"Dad, you need an atmosphere that encourages people to spend money," Arthur said.

The guy should have knocked off that "Dad" crap until they were married. And maybe can it even then. Never having had a father, I found hearing him use the word grated on me.

"Studies show that people don't buy big-ticket items in supermarkets," Arthur said. "Despite the heavy foot traffic in store aisles, supermarket shoppers won't buy a fifty-dollar radio because they're not conditioned to spending that kind of money grocery shopping. The problem with Halliday's is customer conditioning. Like Pavlov's dog—"

"Whose dog?" I asked.

Arthur's mouth dropped. "Pavlov, the—"

"Go on, darling. We'll give Zack a book to read." Morgan's facial expression implied some doubt as to whether I could read.

Arthur went on. "Our studies show that a Halliday player spends only about $107 per visit to the casino. That sort of money wouldn't last an hour up on the Strip but could last several hours of play here. Why? Because Halliday's is not a big-ticket operation."

"We're not the Strip," I said. "We don't have the floor space, the hotel rooms, the foot traffic, the restaurants, the shows. We're down and dirty in Glitter Gulch and—"

"That's it," Wonder Boy said, "you just used the 'G' words—*'Glitter Gulch.'* People don't spend money in Halliday's because people don't spend money in Glitter Gulch—that's the conditioning. They're not on the Strip. Now if we put in deep carpets, Oriental rugs, chandeliers, an elegant restaurant—"

"Marcel Dubrey," Morgan said, "the second chef at the Four Seasons, is interested in running a gourmet grill in our casino. Think about it, Dad, Monte Carlo right here in downtown Vegas."

Fifteen minutes later I got on the elevator behind Morgan and pushed the emergency stop button as soon as the doors closed, pulling the button out enough to keep the alarm bell from ringing but the elevator stopped.

"What the hell do you think you're pulling," I said. "I spent three years as casino manager getting your old man out of hock. Halliday's is making money and you come in with a harebrain scheme—"

"Harebrained."

"What?"

"Harebrain*ed*. You mispronounced the word." She released the stop button and the elevator lurched upward.

"Fuck your English lesson. You and Wonder Boy are full of crap. I don't blame him. He's just a spoiled rich kid who hasn't gotten knocked on his ass enough, but you were raised in Glitter Gulch. You should know better."

"You're right. I do know better. That's why I like the boutique idea."

"The boutique idea is garbage."

"My father didn't think so."

We left the elevator.

"It appeals to your father's ego, not his good sense. It won't work. Downtown is for serious gamblers, even the little ones who lose a few hundred and brag that they come to Vegas to visit their money. Finger food to them is peanuts and potato chips. I finally got the club on a good footing and you want to take the money I saved for a new wing on the hotel—"

"I? I? That's all I hear from you, is 'I.' It must have been awfully lonely out there all by yourself running this place. Where was my father who built this place over the past thirty or forty years? Isn't he the guy who took you off the street and put you in a suit?"

"Yeah, and it was lonely work keeping your old man in business so you could go to fancy schools and your druggie brother could get his fixes."

She got in my face. I braced myself, expecting to be punched.

"You son of a bitch, you won't have to worry about that anymore. You've kept my brother out of his family's club. When I'm through with you, you'll be back on the street where my father found you."

I leered at her. "You're wrong about that. Your old man never found me on the street; he caught me stealing at a blackjack table. I'm lower than you even thought, but you know something, I can run a better casino standing on my head, than you and Wonder Boy."

"You won't be running this one!"

I was at the stairway and she was angrily fumbling with the key to her suite when a suitable rebuttal came to me that I couldn't resist.

"Nice boob job," I said.

42

"I want out," I told Chenza.

We were sitting beside her pool, drinking margaritas. I thought they were a sissy drink, but frozen tequila and lime went with the nachos her housekeeper had whipped up. Loaded with jalapeños, onions, cheese, and salsa, Josie's nachos were hot as lava.

"I've been wanting out for a long time."

She licked salt from the margarita glass. "You want to be on the Strip."

"Yeah, I want the Strip. I've outgrown Halliday's. I've been there for over six years. It's been good for me, but I've felt hemmed in for a long time. I wouldn't leave as long as Con needed me, but he's buying into Morgan's renovation plan. It's going to be a disaster, but that'll be their heartburn. I've put enough of my time and blood in."

"You don't just walk in and start running a Strip casino, it's not like getting a manager's job in a supermarket chain with a thousand stores. How many clubs are there, eight or ten?"

"I don't want to run one; I want to own one."

"Ahhh." She licked more salt. As I watched her lick the rim of the glass, I understood where she got the practice for the amazing things she did in bed with her tongue. "You must have been skimming more at Halliday's than I thought."

Paying myself "bonuses" for twenty-four/seven and increasing it in other casinos had gotten me a nice nest stake, but it would be chump change on the Strip.

"I was thinking about your pal Mr. Wan. You told me he was interested in buying a casino in the Caribbean. I've got a couple bucks, enough to buy in for a few points, but not what you'd need for a place on the Strip. I could help him put a deal together and run it for him. If I got the place going good, who knows, maybe the Strip will be next."

"That's interesting."

"Why?"

"Wan's coming into town and he asked about you."

"Is he being cheated again?"

"I don't know. But he wants to meet with you. Knowing Mr. Wan, it has something to do with money."

Trouble was brewing at Halliday's, and it wasn't just the interior decorator with the pink leisure suit and gold earring Morgan brought in from Manhattan to walk around the place and say, "Oh dear, that simply has to go."

The revenues from the table games had been coming up about twenty grand a month short for the past couple of months. That wasn't much of a deviation, even for Halliday's. A good run of luck could create it, but it was a consistent thousand bucks a day for twenty-some days of each month. What bothered me was the consistency. My nose told me that a dealer or croupier was skimming or giving away the store. I had a security manager, but Con and me still had the best noses for cheating in the business.

People always find ways to cheat casinos, and it was a full-time job keeping up with the schemes. Scam artists like Windell cheated slots with slugs, wires to trip payoffs, magnets to tilt the reels. But the biggest losses were in the gaming games—blackjack, roulette, craps. Sometimes it was just skillful players, but we made little distinction between cheats and skilled players—both took our money. When someone got too lucky, even if we didn't see a gimmick, we quietly told them their play was too rich for the house and asked them to take it elsewhere.

The biggest problem was dealers conspiring with players. A good dealer can shuffle a deck to create a "slug" of cold cards, cards that haven't been shuffled. A slug is a set of unshuffled cards arranged for the player to win. The dealer buries the slug in with the other decks and when the cards start coming out of the shoe, the player in on the scam knows what cards will be dealt and when to increase bets.

It is impossible for a pit boss to spot this sort of thing. It can only be done by studying the surveillance tapes and even then it is often hard. I caught one dealer using a slug by standing back and watching his hands as he shuffled. He was good, Embers would have been proud of him, a real card mechanic, but what threw him off was the bull's tail didn't wag: Halliday's cards have a bucking bull on the back; as the cards are shuffled, the tails fly in a blur. Watching the deck through the dealer's fingers, I could see a stationary tail—the top card on the slug that wasn't being shuffled.

Another scam was the dealer signaling to a player the value of the hole card in blackjack. Sometimes dealers do this by accident. We called it "spooking." A team of card sharps would spot a careless dealer. One player positions himself at a spot behind the dealer where he gets a peek at the hold card and then signals the player at the dealer's table. People even try "peeping" at the hole card with a miniature camera.

Skilled dice mechanics used crooked dice—beveled, loaded, shaved, or otherwise gaffed—in a dozen different ways to cheat. You even had people who try to cant a roulette wheel. We got hit by a group of astrophysicists, the Einstein mafia we called them, who used physics to determine the area a roulette ball would drop into. They used hidden cameras that transmitted to a van in the parking lot, where a computer used the data to predict the winning numbers. They busted their bankroll trying it.

Most cheaters had one thing in common: They gave themselves away by changing their bets, suddenly upping their bet when the gaff comes into play. And that's what made the current situation so frustrating—the security people hadn't spotted any suspicious betting patterns.

I was in the security room viewing surveillance tapes when Morgan came in breathing fire.

"I need to talk to you, now!"

"Wait just a minute." I was concentrating on the tape of a roulette croupier. I couldn't put my finger on what was wrong, but my Geiger counter alarm was working again.

"No, I can't wait. How dare you bar me from the counting room? Who the hell do you think you are?"

I jerked my head back at her and told my security manager, "Tell her why she's barred from the counting room."

Rod cleared his throat. The employees were all terrified of her. "Owners and their families aren't allowed in the counting room."

"And when did Mr. Riordan make that rule?"

He cleared his throat again. "I think it's a regulation made by the

IRS or the state people, ma'am. It's to keep them from skimming."

"That's it. Look," I said to Rod, "the croupier's using a false cup."

The roulette croupier had a small round tube that looked like a stack of five-dollar chips. When he pulled in bets, he would bend over his chip pile and fill the cup with four hundred-dollar chips. He would eventually pay off a bettor who was playing odd and even with what appeared to be four five-dollar chips, with four hundred-dollar chips in the false stack—not a bad racket.

"Bust them," I told Rod.

Morgan had her arms folded and was still fuming, ready to explode at me, as soon as she figured a way to blame me for the antiskimming rules. I took a firm grip on her arm and pulled her toward the conference room we use for private interrogations.

"Take your damn hands off me!"

I shut the door and pushed her against the wall. She started to step around me but I took her hands and pinned them behind her back so she couldn't move.

"Don't you ever talk to me like that again in front of the help."

"Let me go. I'm going to tell Arthur—"

She was breathing heavily, her breasts moving up and down with each breath. I looked at the fire in her eyes. "Fuck Arthur! Tell him this." I kissed her long and hard on the mouth. She resisted like a trapped animal grappling to get free but then I felt her body relax and she stopped struggling. I kissed her again but this time she didn't resist. I was so tight against her body I could feel her jutting nipples on my chest.

"Let go of my arms."

I released my grip on her and we both stared at each other for a moment.

"How dare you!" she said.

"You've been hot for me from the first time you saw me."

"Well, I'm not anymore, you bastard. I've changed." She walked toward the door, straightening her dress. "I've had better."

Like hell she had.

"Bitch," I yelled after her as she slammed the door.

43

"Wan is a gangster, is that what you're telling me?" I asked Chenza, as I sat behind the wheel of my new car, a Jaguar XJ12.

We were on our way to meet with Wan at Caesar's Palace. Big shots in town drove Cadillacs and Lincoln Continentals. I chose the Jag because it was exotic and different. Like Chenza's Aston-Martin. It was another element in making me a class act.

"Just as Hong Kong's owned by the British, Macao's a Portuguese colony the size of a postage stamp on the Chinese mainland. It's been Portuguese for four or five hundred years but remains predominantly Chinese."

"How come the Reds haven't taken it over?"

She shrugged. "Ask Wan. I suppose they will someday. Anyway, the place is overrun by triad gangs. Italy has the Mafia, the Japs have their Yakuza, and the Chinese have the triads. They're like the others, but more dangerous and aggressive. After the Chinese Communists won the mainland, fleeing criminals and Nationalist soldiers formed triads in Hong Kong, Macao, and Formosa. Before the fall, Wan was important in Chiang Kai-shek's army—he ran some sort of Gestapo. He called his group the Dongchang, or Eastern Depot, after an old-time Chinese Imperial secret police unit. He escaped to Macao and set up a triad there and later expanded to Hong Kong."

"How do you know all this stuff? Does Wan talk in his sleep?"

She burned the back of my hand that was on the center gear shift knob with her cigarette.

"Don't be crude. Wan used to bring along a dancer that worked at one of his clubs. She told me all about Wan."

I didn't risk more burned skin by asking if the dancer had talked in *her* sleep. Chenza's taste in sex was eclectic, to say the least. She recently fired her housekeeper and hired a brother-sister team to replace her—they both looked like Jackie Chan in a wig. I always had a fascination for feminine faces of the Orient, women with golden skin and almond eyes that conveyed the mystery of temple doors. Of course, I immediately gave the sister the once-over and got a chewing out by Chenza that left me with the impression she was more concerned about the girl's unfaithfulness than mine. Sure as hell, she was doubling her pleasure and balling both of them.

"There's a war going on in Macao for control of the gambling. Like Vegas, the place is a tourist area, with the main industry being gambling, hotels, and organized crime. Only the Jewish and Italian thugs in Vegas are pussies compared to triads who were cutting each other's throats back when Europeans carried stone axes."

"So does Wan have an interest in any Vegas casinos?" I asked.

"I don't think so."

"I can see why he has to use someone else's casino to wash his money. The feds and state gaming people would gut him like a stuck pig if he tried to buy into this town. Not to mention the hard boys from Chicago and Jersey who consider Vegas their private turf."

"Whatever he wants to see you about, you can be sure there's money in it for us," she said.

I didn't miss the "us" bit. "Don't you ever think about anything besides money?"

"I'm dominated by the same two things you are. What's in my pocket and what's between my legs."

Mr. Wan was waiting for us in his lavish VIP suite. I found out from Chenza that his full name was Wan Kin Yung, and that the way the Chinese do it, Wan was his last name. When I was a kid, Betty's boyfriend Hop told me everything was backward in China because they were upside down from us. I guess he had it right.

Ling, the dark-suited sumi-soldier who clung to Mr. Wan like a shadow, was seated next to him. I didn't bother saying hello to Ling—I never heard him speak one word.

"For my new casino in Macao, I want to introduce some Las Vegas features, perhaps similar to what you did for Halliday's. This casino is for tourists and low-end gamblers from Hong Kong."

We discussed comps, contests, and other things I had done to make Halliday's friendly to the average Joe. Wan struck me as a man of secrets, layers of them, like one of those Russian dolls you opened up to find one after another hidden inside. I had the impression that he wanted something more out of me than just giving his casino a Vegas feel. I asked him about it but didn't get a straight answer.

"I do have a problem in Macao," Wan said. "A matter of small importance but annoying nonetheless."

He survived Mao, the fall of China, the triad wars, and had the annual income of a small country. That meant he didn't have any "small" problems. Any problem that couldn't be solved with a bullet probably needed the United Nations.

"So much skimming goes on by employees in Macao casinos, it is the equivalent of an organized-crime syndicate. To control the thievery, I had a computerized system installed. The system monitors our slot machines and table games, keeping a running total of our wins and losses."

"I'm not familiar with the system," I said. "We don't have anything like it in Halliday's."

"Yes, I know. It is a British system. The team who set it up in a London club are in Macao running the system and working out what they call 'bugs'."

"What are the bugs?" Bugs had a double meaning for me. A "bug" in gambling was a gimmick that aided cheating. A "bugged" slot did not pay off fairly.

"Technical problems with the system. I have no interest in them. My concern right now is that my revenues have dropped millions since the system was installed, a system that was intended to reduce thefts."

"You have any suspects for the thefts?"

"Hundreds of them. Naturally, Mr. Riordan, I will make it well worth your while to come to Macao and give my casino a Vegas ambience. In a few months you could earn more than you would in several years at your present employment. Have you ever been to the Far East, Mr. Riordan?"

"Does eating at Lo Fat's Shanghai Café count?"

When I got back to Halliday's, Moe, a casino security guard, was waiting for me.

Con had turned Morgan's wedding into a Glitter Gulch parade and
celebration, with the wedding at a local church, then a parade to the
club, where a private reception was taking place on the top floor of
the hotel wing. The outside of the club looked like a wedding cake.
Con even had "souvenir" silver dollars made with the happy couple's
pictures minted on them and gave them out as comps—naturally expecting the suckers to lose another hundred for every dollar he gave
them. I hadn't received an invitation to the wedding. Or the reception.

Moe had been around a long time. He was pretty embarrassed when
he stopped me as I entered. "I'm sorry, Mr. Riordan, but my orders
are to escort you to your room to pick up your personal effects and
then out of the building. You're not to go anywhere else in the place,
especially the count room."

I paused for a moment, not knowing if I was going to laugh or
explode. Poor old Moe wiped the sweat off the back of his neck with
a soiled handkerchief. He had been around plenty of times when he
saw me get physical with grifters and troublemakers.

"What's happened, Moe, has there been a palace coup?"

"Miss Halliday's been named president of the casino."

"I kind of suspected that. Go tell Morgan I need to see her in my
room."

"She's at her wedding reception."

"Then you know where to find her. Tell her I need to give her the
codes."

I was happy he didn't ask me about the codes. I didn't know any
codes. What I planned to give Morgan was a piece of my mind. And
Con, too, for pissing on my years of work.

When I got to my room, my bags were already packed and lined up, ready to be taken out. Very efficient of Morgan. No doubt she searched my stuff before she had a maid pack me. But she would have come up with snake eyes. The moment I saw Con was buying into her act, I moved my loose change from the couch to a safe-deposit box.

She came in without knocking and slammed the door behind her. "How dare you interrupt my wedding with a command? What are these codes you're talking about?"

"Which question did you want me to answer first, your majesty?"

Brides always look radiant on their wedding day, but Morgan was a knockout in her wedding dress. Since she had come back from school, I kept asking myself why I had brushed her off years ago.

"I want you off of the premises. You're fired, in case you haven't noticed. And that comes from my father, too."

"No problem. I just need to collect my severance pay."

I pulled her toward me and she immediately began to squirm out of my arms, ready to slap my face, but I caught her hand just in time. "Why are you fighting me? I know you want it." She bit my hand.

"You want to play rough, I can play rough, too." I pushed her up against the wall and pinned one of her arms behind her. She beat at me with her fist until my lips connected with hers and I shoved my tongue against her teeth. She opened them long enough to clench down and bite. I managed to pull her dress up with my other hand and was surprised to find she wore nothing underneath her dress. Her nakedness excited me even more. My hand lingered on her smooth and silky bare thighs until I found her bushy pubic hair.

She bit my tongue again so hard, I tasted blood.

"Don't fight me, Morgan," I groaned. "I know you want my cock inside you. I can see it in your eyes."

"No, I hate you."

I knew deep down she didn't mean those words and wanted me just as much as I wanted her.

I clamped my mouth back on her lips while my hand found her clit and I rubbed it slowly. She was dry at first until I put my finger in her hole and her fluids came and made her slippery wet with excitement. She let out a loud moan and her body shuddered against me. Her tongue now shoved past my lips and her arms came around my neck as I unzipped my pants and took out my throbbing organ. I was ready to come any minute and I plunged my cock into her cunt. She let out a gasp. My hands were on her firm baby-smooth buttocks, and I lifted her up and down on my hard shaft.

I exploded into her, our bodies pressed together, both of us breathless in the throws of ecstasy. I looked at her face. Her eyes were clear. The wildness and anger were gone but I noticed a sort of taunting triumph in them. The sexual pleasure she experienced in her body a few moments ago was gone. Her arms and legs relaxed. I slowly lowered her, still holding her close to me.

"Morgan," I started, and was about to apologize for my animal behavior, when she suddenly twisted away from me and hit me so hard I rocked back on my heels.

She triumphantly adjusted her dress and opened the door. Moe and another security guard were standing in the hallway.

"Escort Mr. Riordan off the premises." She glared back at me with those powerful eyes. "Through the back door, the way he originally came to Halliday's."

This woman wasn't satisfied with having me drawn and quartered; she wanted me chopped into eighths.

MACAO, 1982

Mr. Wan's private jet was waiting for us at the airport. Leaving Chenza in Vegas was not an option. Hong Kong and Macao were notorious money pits.

She brought along a video of the 1952 movie *Macao*, starring Robert Mitchum and Jane Russell, for us to watch on the plane. My mind wasn't exactly all there. I still had Morgan in the back of my mind. She had some magnetic clamp on me that affected me in the worst way. But it just wasn't in the cards for the two of us to be together.

I tried to focus on the film. I liked Mitchum. He was my kind of guy. In this movie he played a down-at-the-heels soldier of fortune and Russell was a torch singer with a big heart. They get tangled up in murder and intrigue with an unscrupulous Macao casino owner. There was also a great performance by William Bendix as a traveling salesman with more up his sleeve than contraband nylons. They sure didn't make movies like that anymore, especially with those kinds of movie stars.

"Howard Hughes made the movie," Chenza said, "back when he owned RKO. He made Jane Russell and Mitchum into major stars."

I didn't tell her Hughes was my father. I didn't want that part of me exposed. The only one who knew that was Embers, and he was dead now. I had arranged a high-stakes poker game for the old man, the first he'd played in decades. He died at the table, quietly, just heaving a sigh as his life oozed out. The other players with him gave me the last cards he was holding in his hand when he died: aces and eights—a pair he wouldn't bet on.

Howard Hughes was a part of my life that I didn't want opened or revealed. When Betty and I had moved to Vegas, one day she got scared when she thought she recognized two men who entered a restaurant where we were grabbing a hamburger. It was a false alarm, but that was the day she told me why her little finger was crooked. It killed any feeling I had for him.

Before leaving Vegas, I hired a private eye who did background checks for Halliday's to run down Windell. The last I heard of Windell, he had left the state of Nevada and gone to work for a computer company in Silicon Valley after doing a year in a Nevada pen. I hadn't seen Janelle, either, since she walked out of a Vegas bank after depositing a bag of stolen quarters. She did six months in county jail after copping a plea to an accessory charge, then disappeared from Vegas as soon as she was released.

I had no hard feelings for Windell. He tried to screw me and got his nuts in a nutcracker. But I needed him in Macao to look over the computer system at Wan's casino. Would Windell work with me if there was a buck involved? Do chickens have lips? I spoke to him on the phone and told him I'd arrange a plane ticket for a flight a week after mine. I wanted time to look over the operation before I brought Windell in.

Chenza and I landed in Hong Kong and stayed overnight at the classy hotel she selected. Nothing but the best, she said. The town was a cultural volcano for someone like me who had spent his whole life in the desert. The place vomited people, cars, noise, and pollution. We left the next morning on a private jetfoil that skipped like a water bug across the forty miles to Macao in less than an hour.

The wet-hot heat immediately pummeled us as we stepped off the jetfoil. You could fry eggs on Nevada rocks in July; in Macao, you could drown on a lungful of air. A large cockroach the size of my hand scurried near Chenza. She stepped on it—*snap-crackle-pop*.

"Welcome to the tropics," Chenza smiled. She wore white, the color of innocence, a deceptive color for her.

Waiting for us at the bottom of the ramp was a woman. "Mr. Wan is waiting at a restaurant," she said. A rickshaw driver was standing nearby and he muttered something to her in Chinese. She smiled at us. "He says the roach you killed would have made a champion. We have cockroach fighting matches. When a champion dies, the little creature is laid to rest in a handsomely carved wood coffin."

We climbed aboard the rickshaw, which took us down a line of sidewalk cafés along the wharf. Being pulled in a rickshaw down a street in exotic Macao almost made me feel like Robert Mitchum, but Chenza was no torch singer with a heart of gold—she had a heart of diamond with facets sharp enough to slice a pimp's conscience.

My first impression of the city was that it reminded me of a cheap whore. Everything Vegas hid, Macao flaunted: high-heeled prostitutes in red, yellow, and green silks; triad gangsters with black suits and fedoras; pimps and panhandlers putting on the hustle; blurry-eyed, cheerless gamblers heading for the boats back to Hong Kong after spending the night at smoky fan-tan tables.

We stepped out of the rickshaw in front of umbrella-covered tables and walked past plates of pungent *linguiça* and *chouriço* sausages atop white rice and steamy bowels of *cozido*, a heavy stew of chicken, meats, and vegetables. All the tables had bottles of *vinho verde*, the green Portuguese wine, on them. Two guys who never went to Sunday school eyed us as we went in.

"Wan's bodyguards?" I whispered. Chenza shrugged.

The restaurant inside was dark and cool with groaning ceiling fans and waiters shrieking orders in Chinese. Wan was at a corner table with his ever-present henchman, Ling, and another man.

We took a seat at the table after a round of introductions. Luís Kang, the third man, was a startlingly handsome Chinese-Portuguese. Kang had movie-star looks and dressed like a roaring twenties gangster. Wan told me back in Vegas that the dress code came from dubbed American movies and Hong Kong rehashes of gangster film noir.

"Luis has an interest in our gambling industry," Wan said.

I took notice of the strange description—not that Kang owned a piece of a casino but that he had an "interest" in the industry at large. The word that struck my mind was *protection*. The two Sunday school dropouts outside were probably his boys.

Chenza ordered grilled shrimp with lemon-cognac butter, and I opted for the roast chicken with garlic sauce and a cold beer with no glass, since pouring it in a glass killed the fizz.

"Good choice for the tropics," Wan told me. "Spicy food that equalizes your body temperature and beer to replenish your body fluids."

The discussion was all small talk around the table. I had the distinct impression that Wan had met us at the restaurant to show me off to Kang. Something about the body language between the two . . . polite as hell, as the Chinese do so well, but nevertheless an undercurrent, as if neither man would ever turn his back on the other.

"I have heard much about your abilities," Luís said to me. "Perhaps you will be able to give me lessons that will prove useful."

"Which abilities are those?"

He tapped his nose. "Smelling out crooks."

I could have told him that I smelled a couple right now, but instead saluted him with my beer bottle. "I've been lucky uncovering some scams in Vegas, but I don't pretend to know anything about how scams are run in a place like Macao." I asked him a question burning in my mind. "How does this postage-stamp place survive against Red China? Couldn't their army just march in and take over any time they wanted?"

I was told it was because Macao and Hong Kong were doors to the West through which technology and money could pass to the mainland. I changed the conversation to get out of the spotlight. I wanted to observe the dynamics between Luís Kang and Wan. If politeness could be canned, these two would have enough for an assembly line. Chenza's attraction to Luís wasn't lost on me, either. She was literally cooing as she asked him questions about Macao. Not that I blamed her. A Chinese babe on the other side of the room had caught my eye. If Chenza hadn't been there, I would have tried to see what the fortune cookies had to say about the two of us.

As we talked, a rider on a motor scooter stopped outside the restaurant and dismounted. He wore black biker pants and jacket, the kind of cheap imitation leather a real biker would never wear. For some reason, my eye was drawn to the figure in black. Maybe it was the deliberate way he got off his scooter, the slow, methodical removal of his gloves and helmet, adjusting a biker hat so it had a rakish tilt. He walked unhurriedly to the door, slow and cocky, like Marlon Brando in *The Wild Ones*, confident, arrogant, indifferent. After he stepped inside the restaurant, I watched him from the corner of my eye. The other people in the restaurant were either too busy eating or talking to pay attention to him.

With a singular stride, he walked straight up to a table that was occupied by a heavyset Chinese man with large gem-studded rings on all of his fingers. The man was sitting alone, savoring the sticky orange duckling he was eating with his fingers. He looked up, licking his fingers, as the scooter rider approached his table. The rider paused in front of the large man and nonchalantly pulled out a pistol.

Boom-boom-boom! Three shots in the chest. Deafening, paralyzing.

The hubbub of voices and dishes rattling suddenly stopped. No one moved, no one spoke. Everyone of us stared, frozen in place, at the black figure and the dead man. The Chinese man still sat upright in his chair, red stains creeping through his cream-colored jacket, his eyes wide open. A trickle of blood ran down the side of his chin.

The bored killer calmly leaned across the table and shot him between the eyes. The man's head snapped back for a second before he fell facedown in his plate of orange sauce.

It all happened in a matter of seconds. I sat fixed in my chair, unable to move.

Without even looking around the restaurant, the black figure walked out, in no particular hurry, leaving behind a haze of acrid smoke and stunned silence. As soon as he closed the door, the restaurant reverberated back to its noise and activity level, as if nothing had happened.

A waiter threw a tablecloth over the body.

My face unlocked its shock and I met Wan's eyes across the table. He giggled like a queer getting goosed.

"Welcome to Macao, Mr. Riordan."

Besides witnessing a cold-blooded murder, something else bothered me.

When the gunman had walked in, I was almost certain he was headed for our table because he had glanced in our direction.

Was he just saying hello to Wan or Luís?

"Who's the stiff?" I asked, keeping my voice from betraying my shock.

Kang smiled. "A man who runs high-roller rooms in some of the casinos. He has committed the sin of not appreciating a friend's financial assistance."

Chenza stared at Kang, her eyes glazed over with undisguised lust.

Who says the female is not the cruelest of the species?

46

"Welcome to Indiana Jones's den of iniquity."

The greeting came from Bert Regent, Wan's London gambling consultant. Regent was a white-fleshed, corpulent Britisher with thin, slicked-back hair. He reminded me of one of those James Bond villains who carry white cats and use cigarette holders to smoke.

Wan's casino definitely had a taste of the exotic East. A huge atrium enclosed a tropical jungle. The screams of monkeys and jungle birds punctuated the hum and chatter of slot machines. A crocodile pond was in the center, no doubt convenient for gamblers who lost their shirts and decided to end it all—or who were caught cheating.

Other than the jungle sounds, the casino was surprisingly quiet. Vegas gambling, especially craps and blackjack, rang with shouts and groans. The Chinese in Macao gambled with somber intensity, not unlike what you'd observe at a chess match. Old World Asians were always the most serious gamblers who came into Halliday's, whether they were betting one dollar or a thousand.

The setup was modern, but Wan had some special stuff for the Asian crowd. One was fan-tan, in which the croupier dumped an unspecified number of cubes on the table and then divided the pile into four parts until four or fewer were left. Before dividing the pile into four parts, the players bet on how many cubes would be left in the original pile when it got down to four or less cubes. There were only four possible bets: one, two, three, or four cubes.

There was also a card game called *dai siu*, which involved whether certain cards added up to a large or small number. The odds were roughly even for either configuration, so the betting system was like playing odd-even, red-black in roulette. Hong Kong dollars and Macao patacas were the coins of the realm.

"Quite a joint," I said, trying to imitate Robert Mitchum.

"Joint is right. I'm sure you have surveillance cameras and skywalks in Vegas, but have you ever seen a casino with gun ports? That should tell you something about the tenor of Macao's gambling industry."

I already knew that arguments were settled here the same way Al Capone settled his differences with Bugs Moran in that Chicago garage on St. Valentine's Day.

"They're jockeying for position—the triads and everyone else in town. The Portuguese have literally abandoned the colony because they know Macao's nothing more than a pimple on a gorilla's arse. The Chinese Communists can march in and take over Macao any time they like. When it goes down, the Reds will line up the crooks and shoot them. The fight is over who's going to control gambling because the Reds won't shut it down—it brings in too much money."

He began the casino tour by explaining the computer system. I listened to him but all I knew about computers was how to flip the on-and-off button. Finding the "bug" in the computer would be Windell's job. And I was sure there was one, not a computer virus, but a bug similar to a mechanical gaff to rig slot machines and clips to hold cards under a table. Bert Regent smelled like a crook to me. Unlike Windell, who punched out quarter slugs, he seemed like a slick operator who'd steal millions with the stroke of a pen or the keyboard of a computer. I looked at the revenue printouts for the club and they stunk. However, why Wan didn't come clean and admit he brought me in to find the bug was the big question. Last time I played this game with him I discovered he had more up his sleeves than a Rolex.

Looking for exotic bargains, Chenza headed for the shops off the side streets of San Ma Lo, Macao's main drive. We had some heated words about Luis Kang. I told her she did everything but bend down and give him a blow job at the table. Her reply was that whatever she did was none of my business. That was true. I wasn't in love with her, but as long as we presented ourselves as a number in public, I expected her to act straight.

I had lunch with Regent on the restaurant's balcony outside the casino.

"That's Wan's house up the hill," he said. "Qianqinggong. Wan calls it Palace of Heavenly Purity, after the old imperial palace in Peking's Forbidden City."

The "house" was almost as big as the hill it sat on. With peaked tile roofs that fanned down on four sides and lush gardens with bushes and trees carved into foreign shapes, the compound conveyed the magic of the exotic East to the Western eye. One thing I had developed a particular fondness for in the Far East, besides the women, was the architecture. It was a sharp contrast to the Vegas-style square towers of concrete and glass downtown and ranch-style tract houses in the suburbs. Other than Wan's and Kang's skullduggery, I was finding the Orient a feast to my eye—the buildings, the dress, and especially the beautiful women.

As we ate, I couldn't help but notice we were being watched by someone using a spyglass. It looked like a young woman, maybe in her teens, was watching us from a pavilion jutting out from Wan's Heavenly Palace.

"Wan's daughter?" I asked.

"A-Ma, one of Wan's whores. His favorite one."

I squinted at the figure in the distance. "She couldn't be more than fourteen or fifteen."

"Sixteen and he's had her for several years."

"The dirty old prick."

"You're in the Far East, old man: Life's cheap here, and the sex is even cheaper. There are places in Asia where baby girls are buried alive or thrown into rivers to get rid of them. From what I've heard, A-Ma would have ended up a floater in the Pearl River Estuary if Wan hadn't taken her in."

"I've heard the name A-Ma before."

"You'll see it around the city. It's the name of a goddess. I don't know the whole story, something about fishermen and how Macao got its name."

After lunch, I wandered around the casino, just checking out the action and getting a feel for the style of laying down bets. I went up to a balcony overlooking the casino floor. The balcony, which wrapped around the entire interior of the main room, was covered with tropical plants. I didn't know if its purpose was to display the monkeys and birds scattered around it, or to get a better aim if there was trouble below.

I sat on a folding chair with my arms on the banister and watched the action below. I soon realized that I was being watched again. On the other side of the atrium a beautiful Chinese face was poking out of the dense vegetation, the same face that had been spying on me with a telescope from Wan's house.

She was truly beautiful, not in the glamorous sense of a modern movie star or magazine cover model, but in a mysterious, erotic sense, the sort of languid sensuality of Marlene Dietrich and Greta Garbo. Her warm sex appeal radiated down to my groin. My phallus was immediately thinking about making love to this goddess.

"Hungry for some yellow cunt?"

I almost jumped out of my skin.

Chenza had come up behind me. She had a woman with her who looked like a product of Chinese-Portuguese mating. In fact, she looked a little like a gorgeous version of Luís the gangster.

"Maria is Luís's sister. Come upstairs, I want to show you something."

Once we were inside our suite in Wan's hotel wing, Chenza set down her shopping bags and walked up to Maria and kissed her on the mouth, a long, wet kiss. She reached down and pulled Maria's dress off over her head. She wore nothing underneath except black bikini panties that accentuated her hips. Her breasts were much fuller than Chenza's, her thighs and hips generous but lush.

I watched as Chenza caressed each breast with her hand, then bent down to suck the rose-colored nipples with her wet mouth. I was getting totally aroused watching them. Maria slowly began to take off Chenza's clothes and ran her hands down the sinuous body. They both stood stark naked in front of me. I couldn't hide the bulge in my pants.

"Fuck us," Chenza ordered.

"It's called the Dance of the Phoenix Birds," Maria said.

She lay naked on her back with Chenza spread on top of her. They were positioned so both their naked buttocks were at the edge of the bed. She paused as they kissed each other. "You enter Chenza's secret garden with your jade peak."

My "jade peak" was red and throbbing. Chenza was pressed breast to breast with Maria and had her buttocks up in the air with the secret garden between her legs already watered by Maria's tongue. It was the Tao Way of lovemaking. For sure, Maria hadn't learned it from a book.

Standing next to the bed, I slowly put my penis in Chenza's opening, feeling her wet hole suck me in.

"Now thrust slowly," Maria cooed. A few moments later she said, "Remove your jade peak and put it into my secret garden."

I went back and forth between the two of them, taking turns fucking Chenza doggy style and then Maria.

I had a rhythm going when I got that feeling again that someone was watching us. I looked up at the ceiling and saw the unmistakable small round lens of a video camera.

Good old Mr. Wan.

I laughed and gave the camera the finger.

THE GOLDEN
GODDESS

The storm came like a crouching tiger, suddenly springing.

47

A fisherman untangling a net in his sampan looked up as a young voice addressed him.

"There," a little girl about nine said. "There" was the peninsula and two islands that formed the Portuguese enclave of Macao eighteen miles across the Canton delta. The little girl was a mudlark, one of the hundreds that hung around the wharf—the lucky ones helping their parents handle fish, the others surviving on garbage until they're swept away by disease.

"Go away," he said.

"There," she pointed again.

He had seen her earlier, coming down the line of boats, using the same word and gesture. He hadn't heard her speak another word and wondered if *there* was the only word she knew. Her meaning was clear enough. She wanted a ride across the water to Macao. She had been turned away by all of the boats. His was the last in the line. He was a poor man and his boat was also the smallest and least seaworthy of the sampans and junks along the waterfront.

He went into the sampan's tiny hut formed by mats and put on a slicker.

Like all the fishing people, his whole being was in tune with the weather, especially in the bay during August, when sudden storms could erupt with the mindless fury of a rabid dog. When that happened, his poor boat was the least likely to survive. He had been swamped before and nearly drowned. Now he could taste rain. He had to get back to Macao with his catch or it would rot on him, but he feared the crossing.

When he came out, she hadn't moved. She stood on the dock and looked up at him with liquid almond eyes. Her eyes were unusual, he thought; large and round, intense, as if she saw things that others didn't.

He squinted at the clouds. The sky was darkening. He had to hurry. On impulse he said, "Come."

She scrambled aboard and sat in the V formed by the bow as he rolled with a scull from the stern, working the oar from side to side to move the boat forward. Into open water, he raised the sampan's small sail and went back to rowing. Other boats, some even with small outboard motors, passed him as he rowed and kept an eye out on the darkening sky and freshening wind.

The little girl took well to the action of the boat, hardly moving when waves burst over the bow as the boat rode the choppy water. He wondered if her parents had been fishermen, drowned in a sudden storm or struck down by an epidemic. She didn't fear the sea—children often don't—but she seemed to embrace it as did the children of fishermen.

The storm came like a crouching tiger, suddenly springing. An angry wind roiled off the hills and blew across the top of the water, carrying rain and sea. The fisherman quickly took down his sail and got back behind the helm, rowing faster.

"Come here, come back here," he yelled to the little girl.

She gave no indication that she heard him. Standing at the bow, she laughed as wind and water lashed the boat. He was a good man and he would have crawled forward to grab her but it was all he could do to hold onto the helm.

The storm tore at the small boat, ripping the sail loose and tearing the roof off the small hut. Other boats around him were also in trouble, keeling over from the force of the storm. A larger and sturdier boat near him keeled over until water swamped it and it sank. No one could help the people who were thrown into the water; the storm had command of the sea.

Gripped by fear, the fisherman held onto the helm with all his might and prayed. The rain and sea lashed the boat. He could barely see the bow of his boat, but the little girl was still there, as if glued to the bow, a dark silhouette in the storm. He was sure he could hear her laughter over the fury of the storm.

The storm died almost as suddenly as it had risen. Rowing toward the wharf at Macao, he heard from the other boatmen that in its fury, eight boats had been lost, the most at one time in anyone's memory. Other fishermen shook their head with amazement that his boat had survived the storm when so many more seaworthy boats had been torn asunder.

He yelled back to them that A-Ma had protected him and he pointed to the little girl, still riding the bow. A-Ma, the goddess of the sea, protector of sailors. Macao's name was derived from that of the goddess.

When they reached the shore the little girl disappeared as he was unloading his catch. He paused for a moment, looking around for her. He had little but he would have shared it with the child, who he was sure had brought him luck.

Wu-hou was a procurer. As a girl of ten, she had been sold by her parents to a man who trained young girls and boys for roles as "jewels" to wealthy men who could afford such trinkets. The man carefully chose children who would grow up to be pleasing to the eye and who had the intelligence to master music and poetry, which their culture esteemed.

Wu-hou had been an orphan and he gave her the name of a famous Chinese empress, a woman of intrigue and utter ruthlessness. He had sold her to a man who admired more practical qualities in a woman than the liberal arts.

Wu-hou's own benefactor died when she was thirty. Only modestly attractive and far beyond the desirable age for jewels, she avoided life in a house of prostitution by her business acumen, eventually entering the "jewel" trade herself. Success had awarded her many luxuries and she found life pleasing.

Walking with a servant along a Macao wharf, selecting fish for her table, she saw the little girl. A nine- or ten-year-old in a ragged dress rummaging for food in a trash can would not have caught the eye of most people but Wu-hou had an eye for high art. She saw in the little girl's dirty face valuable grace and rare beauty.

When she asked the girl's name, she said, "A-Ma."

"Take her home and wash her," she told her servant, "and delouse her good. Take her to my doctor for shots. Who knows what she picked up in garbage cans."

Three years of training polished the jewel to a fine sheen.

"Please play a song for me," Wu-hou told A-Ma. She lay on her bed in a silk robe. The room was heavy with the poppy incense that Wu-hou preferred and cloaked in darkness except for candles. Hearing the soft melody played by A-Ma on the lute until Wu-hou closed her eyes had become a bedtime ritual for the older woman.

The girl sat on a stool next to the bed and began to play. A-Ma had been on her mind for some time. She was the quintessential jewel; the quietest of her trainees but the one that glistened the most. She rarely talked yet when she did her voice was musical. She studied in silence and absorbed everything. At thirteen she was proficient in English, French, and three Chinese dialects, including Hakka, which Wu-hou believed to be her native tongue.

Like all of her students, A-Ma was taught to walk and talk with grace and poise, learning business and scientific terms besides the arts, and even more important to *listen* to a man's woes, rubbing the man's neck and murmuring condolences when he had troubles, clapping with enthusiasm at his victories. It was the way of the Chinese concubines of an earlier age. In the days when concubines were common, her feet would have been bound from childhood to create the tiny crippled feet Chinese men found so sensuous.

A-Ma was the first jewel that Wu-hou had wanted to keep for herself, the first that she was willing to give up a fat commission to keep. But the client who asked for her was not someone she could refuse.

She held up her hand to signal A-Ma to stop playing. The time for her had come.

"You are the best of my students, little one. Now it is time for you to learn the most important things that a man desires. In a moment I will have Kao come in," she said, referring to a young male servant. "You will learn with him the places a man is to be touched to please him and the places he will want to touch you. But before you learn to please a man, you must know all about a woman's body."

Wu-hou slipped out of her robe and lay back, naked. She was forty years old and although her face showed her years and more, her body was still firm and lush.

"Come here, my child."

A-Ma sat beside her. She took the girl's hand and placed it on her breast. "A body is like the lute. You must learn how to play it."

Deception and deceit are the tools of a wise general.

—Sun Tzu, *The Art of War*

When Windell's plane landed at Hong Kong, he took his time getting off so he could follow two flight attendants. The two women tried to ignore the character leering behind them, but Windell was hard to ignore.

"Can I buy you girls a drink?"

They both shook their heads at the same time and gave him a professional smile. Anyone watching them would easily have realized that the only thing the two women wanted was to get rid of the creep trying to pick them up.

Windell's ticket, courtesy of Zack, had been in coach, but Windell bumped himself up to first class by hacking into the airline's computer system. During the long flight, he had made himself the caliber of jerk to the flight attendants that only he was capable of achieving. He identified himself as the CEO of a major, but unnamed, Silicon Valley computer company. Had he shut his mouth after that he might gotten a half-blind, developmentally challenged flight attendant to give him the time of day, but after several hours of hearing him trip over his own boasts, the general consensus of the flight crew was that he had won his first-class seat in a McDonald's fast-food contest.

"Windell?"

Windell turned to the only two attractive women who had voluntarily initiated public contact with him in his life.

"I'm Zack's friend, Chenza. And this is Maria."

"Hey, is Maria for me?"

"Do chickens have lips?"

"Hey, you do know Zack. I don't know about chickens, but I've got the hottest lips in town."

A limousine awaited them outside. The two women sat on either side of him and smiled. Other than Janelle's purposeful seduction, this was more attention than Windell had gotten from women since he had had his diapers changed. The limo took them into the heart of the teeming city to a down-at-the-heels hotel in a narrow alley crowded with butcher shops with naked chickens and ducks hanging from hooks in the windows.

"I thought we were taking a boat to Macao?"

"Later," Chenza said. "You need to relax before making the trip."

"Relax?"

Chenza put her hand on his thigh and squeezed. "I think you could do with a nice hot shower and a massage."

Windell was speechless for the first time in his life.

The inside of the hotel smelled like sweaty feet, but Windell was too mesmerized to notice the smell or the undesirables hanging around the lobby. Chenza entered the room on the fifth floor first. When Windell stepped inside, he found Luís Kang and two other men waiting for him.

"What the fuck—"

Kang punched him in the stomach. Before he could catch his breath, they grabbed his arms and taped his mouth. They dragged him to a window and shoved him halfway out. Windell stared wide-eyed at the street five stories below. He couldn't scream but the terror came through in his frantic eyes. They pulled him back in by his belt and let him lie on the floor as he tried to get air through his nose.

"Take off the tape," Luís said.

Chenza and Maria sat on the bed and sniffed in a line of coke while Luís stood over Windell who was still gasping for breath. He threw a computer disk in Windell's lap.

"There are instructions on the disk. When you work on Wan's computer, you will follow those instructions. Understand?"

Windell nodded.

Luís knelt beside him. "You see those ducks and pigs dripping fat in the shops below? You fail to obey my instructions and I'm going to have you skinned alive and hung by the hooks over a slow fire. Understand?"

Windell nodded again. He couldn't control his trembling. As soon as Luis and the two thugs left the room, Chenza and Maria helped him to the bed. They peeled off his jacket and lay him back on the pillow. While Maria took off his shoes and rubbed his feet, Chenza sat down on the bed beside him and unbuttoned his shirt and pants. Her hand slipped inside his underwear and began to massage the limp penis.

"Poor baby," Chenza said. Her cool lips caressed his. "We're going to make it up to you."

I got Windell working on Wan's computer system. The British had their own nerd, a guy as geeky as Windell. I informed him that Windell was there to test the system's defenses against outside hackers. That story settled well with him because the British nerd had heard of Windell, or at least the handle he used in the world of hacking— The Stud.

Meanwhile, I studied the casino operation and worked out ways to attract more business. Wan's story that he wanted me to introduce Vegas-type player comps and contests at his casino had another big flaw besides my suspicious nature—the place was packed every night. He couldn't have handled any more business. I figured I was the pawn in some intrigue between him and Luís. That gave me two choices: turn tail and run or ride it out and see what I could make of it. It was a tough town, tougher than Vegas, but I didn't have it in me to return to Vegas with my tail between my legs.

To honor Windell's arrival, Wan threw a dinner party for his British and American crews. Chenza said she had "other plans" and I didn't bother asking what they were—we hadn't drifted, we raced apart since arriving in Macao. At the party, Wan had the girlie crew that services the casino's high rollers. One of them had even been told to be nice to Windell. I hoped she got a bonus.

The women didn't do anything for me. They reminded me of Chinese dolls—very pretty but pure porcelain underneath.

A-Ma was not at the party and I hadn't seen her since spotting her at the casino. Nobody at the casino seemed to know much about her. I couldn't find anyone that had actually spoken to her. "She's a *jinni*," a croupier from Malaysia told me. "A ghost-spirit who can take human form."

After the meal I slipped out the patio door to get some air. A full moon lit Wan's incredible garden. With dozens of bushes in the shape of people and animals, he must have spent a fortune keeping the place trimmed. I had nothing else to do, so I tried to find a method in the madness, looking for a common theme in his design. Some of the bush-statues struck me as warriors in battle. I was looking over a warrior slaying a two-headed monster when a voice behind me said, "Gesar of Ling."

I had never heard her speak, but I was sure that the voice belonged to the enigmatic A-Ma.

"Good evening," I said, turning to the young woman. She wore a pale pink silk robe that glowed in the moonlight. It was hard to believe that she was sixteen. There was a timeless quality to her features. "What did you say?"

"Gesar of Ling, that is the theme of Mr. Wan's garden," she said, as if she had read my mind.

"Some kind of Chinese myth?"

"Somewhat Chinese, but mostly central Asian. Gesar is a hero to Tibetans, Mongolians, Manchu, and the Khams in Szechwan. In the West you have the *Iliad* and the *Odyssey*. In central Asia, Gesar was a warrior-hero much like Odysseus and other Greek heroes."

"Really." I couldn't come up with anything more brilliant. I never heard of this guy Odysseus.

"As a young shepherd boy, Gesar won the right to a kingdom and a beautiful princess in a horse race, but he had to go on a journey to find treasures to finally claim the kingdom. He had to defeat terrifying monsters to claim the treasures of Magyalpumra. Those are the treasures there." She pointed at a row of carved bushes. "The knots of life that protect the wearer: a magic helmet, a thunderbolt scepter, arrows tipped with iron from the gods, a whip with a magic charm inset in its handle, and a spear called 'the conqueror of three worlds.'"

I followed her as she pointed out the shapes. No question about it, I was sexually attracted to her. But I kept a lid on it, not only because she was Wan's property, but I figured she'd had enough older men on her tail.

"That's King Lutzen." She pointed at the tallest of the carved bushes, one three times my height. "He was an evil giant whose tongue was a bolt of lightning. His subjects were all demons, except for his wife, who was beautiful. Gesar seduced the giant's wife and persuaded her to reveal his vital spot, a round white mark on his forehead. Gesar slew him by shooting an arrow into the spot. It was his Achilles' heel, you see."

"Clever," I said.

"Yes, but Gesar didn't understand the wiles of women. After he slew her husband, the giant's wife drugged Gesar to keep him in her bed and her in control."

She fascinated me. I followed her around as she explained other shapes—his horse Karkar, a terrible monster named Machig, the three demon kings in the land of Hor.

She finally stopped and looked at me appraisingly. "I am boring you."

"Conversations with beautiful women never bore me. I was just thinking how unlikely it was that a man like Wan would have a fantasy garden." Actually what I was thinking was that if it truly was Wan's garden, he would have beasts coupling with humans.

"You've guessed a secret. Yes, the garden is mine. Gesar is an all-but-forgotten hero and I wanted to bring him back to life."

"Does Wan give you everything you want?"

"Mr. Wan is very generous."

She looked meaningfully at one of the leafy statues. I took a closer look and saw the wire to a sound bug. That was no surprise to me. Wan trusted no one. People who were untrustworthy themselves tended to be overly suspicious of everyone else.

"Would you like to see more of the garden?"

"Sure. Give me the whole tour."

She led me down the hillside of the garden to a waterfall and pond with large iridescent fish.

"There are no ears here."

I leaned against a rock wall and watched her as she knelt by the pond. She murmured something in Chinese as she put her hand in the water and a fish swam to her hand. It didn't surprise me that she could call a fish. I wouldn't doubt this bewitching young woman could call birds from the sky.

"What do you think of Macao, Mr. Riordan?"

"It reminds me of a wet towel that's been used too often at a school gym. Damp, moldy and smelly."

She laughed, a musical sound. "Macao is a Portuguese city of Chinese run by gangsters. We live under the shadow of the Red Dragon and know that someday the Reds will march in. Like the people in the movie *Casablanca*, Macao is a city of refugees. When the Reds come, men like Mr. Wan expect to be shot."

"If I was Mr. Wan, I wouldn't stick around for the firing squad. What about you, A-Ma, what do you want?"

She remained silent for so long, I asked, "Tough question?"

"More than you realize. No one has ever asked me that and I am puzzling over the answer. Your question betrays a difference in cultures. You grew up expecting to have choices in life, decisions about where you will live, work, whom you would marry. My life follows a path put out before I was born. My feet will walk the way set out for me. I cannot take the detours that you do."

I started to tell her that she could do anything she wanted, but I knew that wasn't true. She wasn't Wan's prisoner, but a lovely bird in a gilded cage. She would be helpless outside the cage because she knew so little about the practical matters of life—working a job, paying rent, lights, and gas. I would have loved to take her with me when I left Macao, but she was too young. And Wan would get revenge for his loss of face wherever I took her.

"I'll make you a promise, A-Ma. I'll be your friend from now on. If you ever need anything that I can give you, call me, no matter where I am. If I can help you, I will."

She looked at me, puzzled. "Why would you do this for me?"

"I don't know." That was the truth. I really didn't know. "Maybe because I'm a gambler. We're a screwy breed, all with lucky charms. Something tells me that you'll bring me luck someday."

She was silent again for a moment. "You know that there is a war going on?"

"You mean here in Macao? I figured that on my first day on the job."

"It reminds me of the warring states period."

I gave her a puzzled look.

"You don't study Chinese history in America, do you, Mr. Riordan?"

"I don't know what they study. I never hung around school enough to study anything."

"It's a time when many small states fought to gain control of all of China. Have you ever read Sun Tzu's *Art of War*?" She pronounced the name *Sun-sue*.

"I must have missed that one on the comic book racks."

"I apologize, Mr. Riordan."

"Call me Zack."

"All right, Zack. I was not trying to be condescending. The treatise was written over two thousand years ago, but is well read today by many Japanese and American businessmen, who practice its teachings. Napoleon, the German high command, and even the great Mao Zedong read Sun Tzu. Mao used the tactics to fight the Japanese and defeat the Nationalists."

"What's the guy's pitch?"

"Sun Tzu was a Chinese general for one of the kings in the warring states period. His theory is that one must avoid combat until one is certain to win. He advocated using speed and surprise against enemy forces."

"Sounds logical." I didn't have the faintest idea where the conversation was headed, but A-Ma appeared so sincere about this guy Sun Tzu, I listened politely.

"He taught that a good general plans in secret, never letting his own officers know his plans. He must maintain complete self-control and his face to the world must be unfathomable. And a good general is patient, which is a trait cultivated by my people."

"Patience is a virtue only to those who already have what they want," I said.

"Deceit and deception is an art of war, Sun Tzu wrote. The clever general must spread false rumors, create false appearances, employ trickery and deceit. Everyone around him must be expendable, especially the agents he uses to gain information or confuse the enemy. He called them 'doomed men.' "

She let a fish nibble her fingers for a moment before looking up at me.

"Mr. Wan has studied Sun Tzu carefully."

I left the party early, keeping a happy face on for Wan when I said good-bye. Rather than returning to my room, I headed for a nightclub I'd gone to before with Chenza and Luís's sister María. The torch singer at the club reminded me of a Chinese Jane Russell, give or take a few bra sizes. I needed to think out what to do about Wan. A-Ma's message was clear: I was expendable, one of the "doomed men" in the

Macao war of the triads. Deception and trickery, that fit nicely with my own appraisal of the devious Mr. Wan. My deep-down suspicion was that Wan had brought me in to throw his triad opponents off while he planned something else.

I was even more sure now that I could get one of those 9mm café coronaries they served in Macao restaurants.

The maître d' was showing me to a table in the nightclub when I saw Chenza with Luís at a table across the smoke-filled room. She stared across the room at me with drug-glazed eyes, wide and excited. Grinning, she ducked her head into Luís's crotch. I left as she was fumbling with his zipper.

All in all, I was beginning to dislike Macao a little more every day. And the town was definitely not liking me. But what the hell, maybe it wasn't my fault. Maybe it was what A-Ma said: Our lives were set out for us and we had to walk a set path. Maybe that was it.

Maybe it wasn't Macao that stunk, but my karma.

I decided to get drunk in the casino bar when I got back to my hotel. I managed to stagger into my own bed and slept until early afternoon the next day. A message had been pushed under my door and I retrieved it as I was leaving.

LUCKY,
MEET ME AT KUAN'S. I FOUND OUT SOMETHING REALLY IMPORTANT.

No signature, but it was Windell's almost illegible scrawl and he was the only one who knew my nickname. I had warned him not to use it because I didn't like it, but that didn't stop him. He confused being clever with being obnoxious.

Kuan's was a waterfront joint one step above fast food with half a dozen outside tables. The place was cheap, the fish was fresh, and the beer cold. Windell and I went there to talk because it was the least likely place to run into any of Wan's entourage. The restaurant was in a warehouse area no one with money in their pockets frequented and that gave us some privacy to talk. To date, I had done most of the talking, questioning Windell about why he hadn't come up with anything with the computers. What I got from him was a lot of whining and a lot of computer nerd jargon that no one with an IQ below 230 could understand. The gist of it was that he hadn't found anything. I didn't have a good feeling about Windell's work on the computer system, but laid it down to my growing paranoia about becoming a crime statistic.

I left the hotel in good spirits, thinking maybe Windell had found the bug in the system.

It was late afternoon and the humidity could be spooned if anyone had any reason for collecting hot, wet air. There was no one at Kuan's except a drunk sleeping at one of the tables. Using hand signals and facial expressions, I inquired about Windell from a cook with a dirty apron who I assumed was Mr. Kuan and got a bunch of sing-song and head shakes for my pains.

Just as I was walking away from the greasy spoon, I saw A-Ma in the entrance to a dock ahead. At first glance I thought it was just another Chinese girl but then she pulled back a scarf covering her head far enough for me to see her face. She turned and hurried down the dock. I took the hint and followed after her when I noticed the motor scooter. At the same time the scooter came around a corner behind me, revving after it made the turn. When I looked back my blood ran cold. The rider was wearing black biker leathers. It might have been just another one of the thousands of motor scooters on the streets of Macao, but the hair on the back of my neck told me my number had just come up.

I ran, not walked, to the dock that the girl had just gone down. As I came whipping around the corner of the dock, I glanced back and saw a gun in the biker's hand. When I raced onto the dock, I came face to face with a bunch of fishermen who charged at me like the front line of the Green Bay Packers. I twisted sideways giving them the shoulder and stumbled through them as they flew around me. The motor scooter rammed down the dock at breakneck speed and went crashing down with screeching metal as it swerved to avoid the crowd.

A-Ma was three-quarters of the way down the dock, standing by one of the dozens of sampans that were crowded together gunwale to gunwale. I ran like a bat out of hell and followed her aboard. The fisherman at the helm quickly backed the boat up with a small electric motor and turned it toward open water. My breathing came about as fast as the little gas motor pushing the boat along as I lay out of breath on top of fish nets.

"I think I've been around this town too long," I gasped.

"There is an old Chinese expression, Zack Riordan. If you sit by the river long enough, the body of your enemy will come flowing by. Someone has been sitting by the river waiting for you."

"You knew they were gunning for me. That someone has to be Mr. Wan."

Her face was inscrutable. I looked back at the fisherman manning the helm. "Can he be trusted?"

"He is an old friend. We once shared a ride across the bay together, when he was a poor fisherman and I was a homeless orphan. He would not do anything to betray me. The men who delayed the killer know nothing, just that a woman paid them to stop the motor scooter."

"I owe you my life."

"Only if you leave Macao now. We can take you directly to the Hong Kong ferry. I don't have to listen at keyholes to know that your life line will be very short if you don't get out of the city."

"You're right, of course, getting out of town is the only thing I can do. But wouldn't you know it, I left my toothbrush back at Wan's. I have to go back and get it."

"That's insane. Wan brought you to Macao to intimidate Luís. He knows Luís bribed the British experts to cheat him with their computer."

"Wan couldn't accuse Luís of stealing from him, that wouldn't go with the way honorable Chinese treat each other. So he brought me in to let Luís know not too subtly that he was on to his scheme," I said.

"You have served his purpose."

"And now I'm expendable, so it's okay for Luís to save face by rubbing me out. There's only one thing wrong with the whole damn picture."

She raised her eyebrows.

"No one asked me if I wanted to play the game. Can your friend here keep this boat afloat until after dark?"

"Of course."

"When it's dark, I want him to drop me off onshore as close to the casino as he can get me. I'm going to pay an old friend a visit."

"You'll be dead in an hour."

I pulled a jagged-edged fisherman's knife from a leather holder. "Ask him if he'll sell this to me."

"What are you going to do?"

"Skin a skunk."

I went into the casino along with a busload of tourists who sounded like Germans and made my way up to the computer room. I still had my passkey to the place with me and used it to open the door to a room that was off-limits for most of the employees.

Windell was in front of a computer playing a porno serial rapist game he claimed to have invented himself and sold in adults-only stores back in the States. He and the British nerd Jerry were updating it in their spare times. They were both sick minds.

"Jerry, I—" He started to turn around when I grabbed his hair and put the fish knife to his throat.

"Hi, Windell, old buddy."

His response was a gurgle. Anything more would cut his throat.

"I got your message. I came by to get that really important information you uncovered." I let up the pressure on the knife. It came away from his neck with blood on it. I showed him the blood. "I'm going to cut off your fucking head if you don't unload everything you know."

"Zack—"

The knife went back to his throat and cut in a little further. "Next time you miss a beat, your head's gone. Tell me what's going on with the computer system. Now." I eased the knife back so he could talk.

"It's bugged. Remember how I did the weigh scales at Halliday's where I programmed false weight? That's what those limeys are doing. The computer's programmed to give false results from the gambling take. It's really clever, it mixes up the numbers in such a way that doing a random check would never reveal it."

"I'm glad it meets your high expectations of cheating. So why doesn't Wan just knock off the limeys and trash the system?"

"Luís is protecting them. Some kind of territorial thing with these Chinese. Wan knows the stealing is going on but can't do anything without starting a war with Luís. And even if he buys out Luís, he's got another problem—everything is tied into the system. The limeys destroyed the hard copies of all Wan's records when they fed the data into the computer and threw in a poison pill. They're pulling half a mil a month from the club."

"What's a poison pill?"

"A timed computer virus. They have to put the antidote code in every twenty-four hours or there's a complete wipeout." Windell stared up at him, his face glowing with pride, his neck wet from blood. "I uncovered it all myself—Jerry never told me anything. Now they need me around here. I changed the antidote code and blocked it so it would take 'em a year to figure it out."

"How do you block it?"

"With another code."

The knife went back to his throat. "We're going to play a game, Windell. You're going to access the codes and we're going to change them. Only I'm going to use my own codes, something only known to me."

"They'll kill me."

"I don't think so. I'll give you a head start to the Hong Kong ferry— which is more than you gave me. If you run fast enough, you'll have a fifty-fifty chance of making it. If you don't help me change the codes, you'll be throwing snake eyes."

I watched him access the antidote code and poison pill. His first code was Pussy. The second Galore. I had forgotten he was a James Bond fan.

51

Wan was in his office and didn't flick an eyelash when I walked in, but his shadow, Ling, pulled a gun. Wan waved him away. "I can see from Mr. Riordan's face that he has news for me. Let's listen to him . . . first." He leaned back and put his hands up the wide sleeves of his robe.

I sat down and stretched my legs out. "You know, Mr. Wan, I thought the Jews and Italians in Vegas had a wrap on crime, but your style of Oriental skullduggery makes them look like chippies."

"Thank you." He gave me a little bow. "I imagine it's because we Chinese are a culture more ancient than yours in the West. While you have surpassed us admirably in technology, we are still richer in things of the spirit. We first experienced the West with their gunboat diplomacy, taking Macao and Hong Kong, forcing the sale of opium to our people. Now we are being invaded by computer technology. One has to fight with the weapons in hand when faced with superior weapons of destruction."

I shook my head. "I hate to tell you this, but you're up against another case of gunboat diplomacy." I told him about changing the codes.

"Has it occurred to you, Mr. Riordan, how simple it would be for us to get the codes from you? I could turn you over to my friend Ling," who smiled widely, "or Luís Kang. I can assure you that you would be disclosing the codes after they apply their persuasive techniques."

"Yeah, I thought about that. That's why I also had the time frame changed. Instead of applying the antidote code every twenty-four hours, I have to do it every hour." I pulled a small black device from my pocket. "Windell planned to use this to keep your system for ransom no matter where he was in the world." I grinned. "He also planned to get out of Macao. With this, he could dial up the computer from any phone and tap in the code."

Mr. Wan nodded. "Very ingenious. Your friend, of course, is a genius with gimmicks and toys but he has the personality of a worm."

"I'm also offering you something else. Once you have the codes and get rid of the bug in your system, you can send the British packing . . . or wherever else you plan to send them. Luís will lose his leverage—and face. Right now you're losing five or six million a year to the computer scheme. Luís is taking much more than that controlling the VIP room in your casino. From what I've seen in this town, the minute Luís shows a weakness and loses face, the junkyard dogs will jump him and rip out his liver."

"I see, I see." Wan stroked his chin. "Naturally, I must impose upon you a financial reward. Shall we say that I double your salary?"

"Shall we say you wire-transfer five million to my Vegas bank? That's about a third of what Luís and his pals take from you every year."

Wan's eyes turned to black ice. "I will cut out your eyes, cut off your nose, chop off your arms and legs, before I will pay you five million dollars."

"I thought you might feel that way, so I had Windell fill some disks with your financial records. The ones you turn into the governments here and in Hong Kong—and the ones you don't. I don't know what the British would do to you in Hong Kong for tax fraud, other than seizing all your assets, but I've heard that when someone's a particular problem in Macao, the police have been known to take him to the city limits and hand 'em over to the Red Chinese. If that should happen, I guess you can renew some of your old civil-war acquaintances."

Wan suddenly smiled and clapped his hands. "Mr. Riordan, you have the mind of a Chinese. I salute you."

I took the public jetfoil to Hong Kong and went directly to the airport. Wan had wanted Ling to accompany me to the airport and have me give him the codes as I boarded the plane. I told him no way. Instead I insisted on one of his good-looking croupiers, a Chinese-Portuguese babe whose dress was so tight she couldn't have hidden a butter knife under it least of all a gun. I would have asked for A-Ma's company, but that would have clued Wan in on who helped me get away from the wharf gunman.

At the airport, I purchased a ticket for Paris. Chenza had reminded me on our flight to Hong Kong of what an uneducated clod I was, referring to herself as a "globetrotter" because she had traveled around the world. I decided I that I was going to check out Europe, especially the casinos in London and Monte Carlo, then hit the Caribbean venues, getting some culture and new ideas about the gambling business at the same time. Macao had been a real education for me, not just about skullduggery but about their way of gambling and the layout of a casino.

I didn't bother saying good-bye to Chenza. I found out from Windell that she had helped Luís rough him up so he wouldn't reveal the bug in the computer system to me. Not that it took that much to turn Windell. A buck or a fuck would do it.

Chenza knew siding with Luís against me was a death warrant for me. She could rot in hell as far as I was concerned, which was probably where the triads would send her if she stood too close to Luís when they came after him.

Getting in line at the boarding gate for the flight to Paris, I told the croupier the two words used to decode the computer system.

"Sun Tzu."

Part 9

★ ★ ★ ★ ★

MR. ZACK HALLIDAY

LAS VEGAS, 1983

It felt good stepping off the plane at McCarran Airport. I had left Vegas for Macao over a year ago. The route home had taken me to the world's premier gambling venues. I drank Champagne with a bona fide countess in her Louis XIV four-poster bed after playing baccarat in Monte Carlo, and bedded a croupier wearing a tuxedo—and skirt— after dropping a bundle at a casino in London. I even picked up some culture. I knew that taxis in London were all black—except for a few maroon ones—and cockney speakers dropped their h's. Ell, I even stuck me 'ead in the Louvre to get a peek at the *Mona Lisa*. I couldn't figure out what was so special about her; I've had better-looking dames. At the Guggenheim museum in New York I took one look at the screwy art on the walls and asked the guard where the dinosaurs were. After I hit Atlantic City, I had had enough "culture" for a while and was getting homesick.

As I left the plane, I grinned at the cute flight attendant who I'd been flirting with for nearly three thousand miles.

"Happy to be home, Mr. Riordan?"

"We globetrotters are always ready to return to home and hearth." Yeah, that's what I was officially: I went around the world, so I was a globetrotter. Her flight was continuing on to L.A., so I didn't bother wasting anymore of my charm.

I took a taxi to the Sands. I decided to stay there because the assistant security manager had once worked for me at Halliday's and would be a good source to update me since I had been away.

I was feeling real good—and real rich. I had five million dollars burning a hole in my bank account—and that ain't no yen. It was a big bundle, not enough to finagle my way into a piece of the Strip, but maybe enough to buy into a club on Glitter Gulch and use it as a stepping stone to the Strip. There was one club I wouldn't be visiting. I had run into a croupier on the Cayman Islands who used to work

Vegas and he said that Halliday's was in trouble. The "boutique" look, with high prices for food and jacking up the slot return percentages to pay for it, had driven away the weekenders. The club looked great, a polished diamond in the mud of Glitter Gulch, but not doing enough business to keep the crystal chandeliers dusted.

"That son-in-law of Con's is a real prick," the croupier said. "He walks around with his nose in the air. What really pisses off everyone is when he tries to act like one of the boys—and speaks to you like he was talking to an old family retainer. The employees who end up staying do it out of loyalty to Con and Morgan."

He had more dirt. Bic was bringing undesirables into the club, and rumors about Con losing—big time—playing poker and craps in other clubs. Con had lost his license and Morgan had gotten herself licensed.

I ate up the dirt because I was a vindictive bastard by nature. As far as I was concerned, the croupier could have told me the earth opened up and swallowed the club and I wouldn't have shed a tear.

That night I went downstairs dressed in a tuxedo that I had bought in Paris and sat down at the baccarat table. A crowd had gathered because Rock Hudson was at the table. His assistant, a young guy who looked like an Adonis, stood by as half a dozen of us played. I made thousand-dollar bets and was down more than fifty thousand in a couple hours. Hudson, his assistant, and the crowd had long since evaporated when I stretched and yawned and mentioned that I'd had a long flight from London. It was a white lie—I'd left London weeks ago—but what the hell, I wanted the Sands management to know that Zack Riordan had class, culture, and money, remembering what Chenza had told me. Vegas was a small town with big ears. By morning the phone in my suite—now comped—would be ringing off the hook with opportunities to invest my mysterious bankroll. I hoped one of the calls would be from a club owner with money troubles.

A shill, a pretty ex-showgirl who had been at the table, gave me the signal she was available but she reminded me too much of Chenza. And I was too tired. I must be getting old, I thought, when my pecker is too tired to get it up. I went upstairs and crashed in bed.

The next sound I heard was an ill wind at my door.

I crawled out of bed and staggered to the door to relieve the pounding that the door and my head were taking. When I opened the door, I came face to face with Con Halliday. His big fist was a blur, coming from out of nowhere. He hit me in the jaw and knocked me across the room. I stumbled and went down on my back. For a moment I saw and felt nothing. When the fog cleared and feeling returned, I felt like I'd kissed a sledgehammer and that an elephant was on my chest. The elephant was Con's knee. He was kneeling on my chest and had his long-barrel .44 pointed between my eyes.

"Kiss your ass good-bye, you sidewinder bastard."

The most I could manage was a gasp for breath. He let up the pressure on my chest, probably so I would have the wind to beg for mercy.

"Where do you want it, boy? I consider this a mercy killing, meaning I'm gonna let you choose where you take the slug."

I took a few deep breaths and tried pushing his knee off but it didn't go anywhere. I tried a little flattery instead. "You're too fat and old and red in the face to kill me. You crazy bastard, get the fuck off me before that thing goes off while you're having a heart attack."

He stood up and I crawled over to the bed. Sitting on the edge, I rubbed my jaw and thought about what I'd like to do to him if he put away the cannon. He might have looked like he was ready to bite the dust, but he still had a fist that delivered the message.

"What's your beef, Con? The last time I was in Halliday's you were hiding your head while your bitch daughter ran me out of the place."

The gun exploded in his hand and a bullet hit the bedpost, shattering it.

"Jesus Christ, you crazy sonofabitch, you'll bring security and a goddamn SWAT team."

"Naw, these rooms are soundproof."

"Not for that cannon, they're not. What's eating you?"

"Call Morgan a name again and the next one's taking off your dick. I may be old, but I can still hit something that small. You raped my daughter, boy."

That one almost stopped me. There was nothing like the truth to shut me up. "If it's true—and it isn't—why isn't Mr. Blue Blood here? He need you to protect his wife's honor?"

"He's gone, left for back East. They're getting a divorce."

"Yeah, I heard that things aren't going too well at the club. You've had your license pulled and Morgan's about to get her's jerked because your dickhead son has been frequenting the place with undesirables.

Not that he doesn't meet that qualification just walking into the place alone."

"The club's knee-deep in cowshit, and it's all your fault. Because of you, Morgan had to turn over running the place to that worthless shit of a husband of hers, and he ran the place into the ground."

"Look, all I did was knock off a piece of ass before I left town. I figured I had that coming."

He cocked the big pistol.

"Okay, okay, I apologize for the comment, but I had nothing to do with the club taking a dive. That's Morgan's fault."

He walked toward the door. "Yeah, well, whose fault is this?" When he opened the door, Nadine, Morgan's old nanny, was standing outside. She had a child in her arms. Noticing the blue blanket, I assumed the kid in her arms was a boy.

"Meet Zack Jr.," Con said.

"Nice-looking kid."

It wasn't the cleverest thing I could say to Morgan about our son, but that's what came out between the *anchovis à la grecque* and the *palais de boeuf en salade*. We were having dinner at the fancy French restaurant that Morgan's Four Seasons chef launched. It was called a "grill" because that made it more chic. Like boutique, chic did not translate into money. As with the rest of the casino, "Le Grill" was hemorrhaging money worse than the national debt. I wanted to tell her that serving salty little fish and ox tongue to low-budget week-enders wasn't the brightest marketing plan in the universe, but I was on my good behavior.

Con had made me an offer I couldn't refuse: I invest my five big ones in the club and take over complete management, with one-third interest. For me it was a hell of a bargain because a third was prob-ably worth twice that much. If the club survived. Halliday's wasn't the Strip, but when I was running it, no one in Glitter Gulch could beat its revenues. There was only one kicker in the deal—I had to marry Morgan.

Neither one of us was making any pretense about the deal. Part of it was simply family business: Con wanted Halliday's to remain in the family—*his* family. And part of it was saving face. Morgan and Won-der Boy had a knockdown, drag-out fight in which about a hundred people heard his accusation that the baby was mine and she admitted it. Con wasn't quite as liberal about having a bastard in the family as my mother had been. I had some serious suspicion that he would shoot me if I didn't make an honest woman out of his daughter.

Marrying Morgan meant she and I would own two-thirds of the club when Con passed away. The other third would belong to Bic. Person-ally, I hoped he'd die soon from a drug overdose. The big problem was getting Morgan to marry me. Con was threatening to shoot me if I didn't marry her and she was threatening to shoot me *and* herself if I did.

"The only reason why I would consider marrying you is that I don't want my son to grow up like you," she admitted.

"I can understand that. The men in your own family are such terrific role models for a child. You know, the grandfather who's drinking himself into an early grave—if he doesn't blow a gasket porking every woman he can get his hands on. And there's the uncle—"

"Leave Bic out of this."

"Why are you always defending him?"

"Why are you always bad-mouthing him?"

"Because he's treated me like crap since the first day I met him."

"And have you ever wondered why? Let me tell you, it's a lot easier being Con Halliday's daughter than his son. Bic has never lived up to being the mustang stud that my father expected his son to be. Con took a liking to you. He bragged about you. He introduced you to people in front of Bic like you were his son. How do you think it made Bic feel?"

"Poor little rich boy."

She threw her napkin down and started out of her chair. "I knew this wouldn't work."

"How were the starters, Madame?" The frog who ran the place, Marcel, was at our table.

"The food—"

"Was wonderful," Morgan said, finishing my sentence. She kissed the tips of her fingers. "As usual, you are a culinary master."

He floated away, ecstatic.

"We need to get down to basics, Morgan. I'm very fond of you."

"How romantic."

"This isn't about romance. You don't exactly make me feel welcome."

"Maybe you've forgotten how crude and rude you were to me when I was a kid."

"Look, can't we just put aside the past and all the recriminations? You want to save Halliday's. I have the money and maybe the desire. We put up a front for your old man and the world until the club's back on its feet. It'll be strictly business."

"I will marry you on two conditions: that you never touch me and you treat Bic with respect."

"Okay. You got a deal. But when your brother's conduct threatens the club, I have to address it." I planned to ignore the first condition and lied about the second. I thought that part about having to "address it" was a nice, businesslike touch. It even sounded sincere.

I drove her home to her faux Tudor-style house beside the ninth hole of a golf course at a private country club. She asked if I wanted to come in and see "William." William Conway Halliday-Duvale was his full name. I said sure, why not. I had to admit I was a little apprehensive about the kid. I hadn't thought about being a father before and it was hard to concentrate on being one now. My life was unsettled and I needed to get it into order.

In William's room, I said all the nice things. He actually was a cute kid. Maybe that was how all kids looked before they grew up. We tiptoed out to the hallway.

"How about a nightcap?" I asked.

"No."

"Morgan—"

"Absolutely not. No sex. We have a deal."

"I had my fingers crossed." I came closer to her and she backed up.

"You've got to leave. If you don't, I'm going to call Nadine."

"If Nadine was a little younger, I'd say go ahead, we could make it a threesome."

"You haven't changed, have you."

She was about to swing at me but I grabbed her wrist and pulled her to me. This time she hardly put up a struggle. She smelled good. Her red lips were moist and inviting. Someone once told me that a man's attracted to a woman's lips because her sex organs are entered through the pink lips between her legs. Whatever the reason, I've always been a lip man. And Morgan had lips I wanted to kiss. In both places. I wanted to make love to her this time, wanted her to love me back.

Morgan tried to push him away, but not with any real effort. The moment he got close to her, a ripple of heat ran through her and her nipples swelled with desire. *Damn him!* It had been that way the first time she saw him when she was a teenager and he was a young hustler fresh off the streets. She had loved him from the first moment she saw him. He had always been insensitive to her feelings and she had tried to hate him for it, but couldn't keep up the pretense.

He was a maniac and his intense passion lighted fires in her. He had her clothes off, scattered down the hallway and on the bedroom floor, by the time he laid her on the bed. He knelt beside the bed and pushed her legs apart. He started with his tongue on her belly, caressing her with its hot tip around her belly button and moving up the bare skin to her chest. His hot tongue teased her swollen nipples, dipped between her breasts, moved up to her neck. She quivered as his warm lips nibbled her neck. Then he moved back down, slowly, touching and tasting every part of her body, down to the soles of her feet before moving back up to where her hot-moist womanhood waited for him.

She wanted him, wanted his tongue inside her, wanted his maleness to fill her and join with her in the rhythm of love, but his lips caressed the inside of her thighs instead, working their way slowly closer, inch by inch, to the swollen lips between her legs.

Finally she couldn't stand it. Her legs widened involuntarily and her back arched as she reached down and pulled his head deep between her legs.

"Come inside me," she whispered.

54

The wedding was no big deal—literally. Con had made Morgan's last wedding a Vegas event. This time there would be just family and a few friends with a quiet dinner after tying the knot in a private ceremony. I had no family and no friends, so that made my guest list real simple.

Dinner was at Le Grill, of course. I had to admit that having been raised on hamburgers, getting into frog food was not easy for me. The French stuff tasted good, but there was never enough to get a man full. My plans for the restaurant were to close it ASAP and convert it into an all-you-can-eat buffet with lots of fatty ham, greasy burger patties, mashed potatoes and gravy that tasted like wallpaper paste, a salad bar, and other good old American delicacies that the weekenders loved.

Marcel, le Chef, knew my feelings toward him. As soon as I sat down, he was at our table with a bottle of champagne. He poured himself a glass and toasted us as he stood by the table. "Á Monsieur et Madame *Halliday*."

I took the slam without batting an eye.

"Good champagne," I told Marcel. As Morgan spoke to a pit boss who offered her congratulations, I gestured at Marcel to lean down so I could whisper something to him. As he leaned close, I reached over and got a handful of his cajones and squeezed. He gaped at me with wide eyes.

"Be out of here by tomorrow morning. You're fired," I whispered.

He hurried away and I toasted Morgan with my champagne glass.

"Isn't that sweet," she said, "Marcel looked teary eyed. I didn't realize he's so emotionally connected to us."

"He obviously had a lot of feeling deep down."

Bic came over to kiss Morgan and shake hands with me. He was only a couple years older than me but looked much older. He was

Morgan's half-brother and there was little family resemblance be-tween them. Bic looked like a pasty-faced, shallow reflection of his father. He had Con's raw-boned frame, but lacked Con's hardness.

"Welcome to the family," Bic said, not meaning a word of it.

"Thanks, Bic," I said, wishing he'd drop dead.

He introduced the two people with him. "This is Sugar Kelly and my pal Bronco."

Sugar had "slut" written all over her body. She was a stripper at a Glitter Gulch joint that was tacky even by downtown standards. Her tits were vast plastic mounds, her lips collagen balloons. Morgan rarely said anything bad about anyone, except me, but she hated Sugar.

Sugar and Bic both looked airborne.

His other friend I had never seen before but I knew exactly who and what he was. In the days when I was a bagman for Morty Lardino, I had to collect a cut from drug dealers. Bronco fit the mold perfectly: pale, acne-scarred face, straggly dirty hair. He was the kind of street trash who'd sell crank to kids with diseased needles as a bonus give-away.

Morgan smiled radiantly when they left. "I'm so glad you and Bic finally will have a chance to get to know each other. I know you'll like him when you know him better."

I smiled politely and watched Bronco out of the corner of my eye. He had turned back and looked at me as they were walking away. It fanned the short hairs on the back of my neck. He spelled trouble with a capital T.

Our honeymoon was to bury myself in work at the club to reverse everything Morgan and Wonder Boy had done. First thing I did was get on the phone and call dozens of employees who had left, asking them to come back and help make the club a success. I ran ads in the L.A. and San Diego papers announcing that Halliday's was back being the best bargain with the loosest slots in town. I offered comps for just spitting on the sidewalk in front of the place. I ran a million-dollar slot machine tournament, a million-dollar poker championship that was carried on national TV, and offered single-deck blackjack.

"Great buffet," Con told me, walking back to his table with a plate heaped high with ham, potatoes, and corn bread. We also had a ninety-nine-cent breakfast buffet and had free coffee and donuts any-time.

It wasn't a class act, but mama and papa started coming back to the club, parking out back in their campers or staying in one of our bargain rooms. The smartest thing I did was get to the tour operators and bribe them to bring junkets in by the busload.

In a month I had the place humming. Morgan worked with me, keeping Con out of my way, getting him to wander around the club entertaining the gamblers with his stories of the old days and country-fried charm.

Morgan went home to the kid every night, but I often hung around the club, watching it twenty-four hours a day, getting shut-eye in one of our hotel rooms, but waking up every couple of hours and checking out the action to make sure everything was okay.

I was shooting the bull with a pit boss when Bic, Sugar, Bronco, and a woman I recognized as a prostitute came in. They went directly to the lounge. They were loud and high, and not on life. Now they were going to add booze.

"Take some deep breaths, count to ten, and then go take a nap," the pit boss told me. She was one of the returnees who left the Stardust to come back to work at Halliday's.

A burst of coarse laugher and "Take it off!" came from the lounge. An elderly couple came out, shaking their heads.

"That's it. They're driving out my customers," I said.

In the lounge, Sugar was grinding and bumping to the music. Her blouse was unbuttoned and pulled down off her shoulders so her naked breasts jiggled openly. "You move like this—and this—and this—" People were staring open-mouthed at the stripping lesson she was giving the whore.

"Pull your blouse up and get your ass out of here," I said. I met Bic's eye. "All of you. And don't come back in here again. You're eighty-sixed."

Bronco grabbed my left arm. "Hey, pal, you don't know who you're dealing with."

That's when I lost it. From pure reflex action, my right elbow came around and smashed his nose. I felt the sickening crunch of cartilage under my forearm. He flew backward, blood spattering everywhere.

"It wasn't my fault," I told Morgan.

I sighed and stared out at the ninth hole. I had stayed the night at the club and came over to have breakfast with her and the kid and confess my sins.

"Do you think he'll sue?"

"Sue? I'm not worrying about him suing. This is Vegas, the system's stacked in our favor. I'm worried about your reaction."

"My reaction? I'm sorry that Bic brought his friends to the club and caused trouble. He knows better. Or maybe he doesn't. I'm worried about him. He's losing weight and looks like roadkill. I can't talk to him anymore. He needs to be in rehab, but he won't listen to anyone. I asked Dad to cut off his money but I think he's squirreled away a load of money that he skimmed from the club. It's probably the only smart thing he ever did."

I was relieved that Morgan was getting more insight into Bic's problems.

"I have some other news," Morgan said.

"Yeah?"

"I missed my period."

"You did? Think you should see a doctor?"

"You're not getting it."

"Getting what?"

"You're trying to avoid it."

"How the hell could you be pregnant?" I groaned.

"We've been married two months."

"Aren't you on the pill?"

"I wasn't the night you raped me."

"Morgan—"

"Don't even think about it. I'm having the baby."

Jesus. For a guy who never had a family, I was making up for it quick. I had a father-in-law who thought he was Wyatt Earp, a brother-in-law who was a crackhead, a wife who had threatened to kill herself at the thought of marrying me, and a kid who had another man's name. Now I was going to be a father again. It scared the hell out of me.

My karma had more twists than a licorice stick.

A hectic week passed at the club while I worked day and night to make a success of a million-dollar poker playoff. It was late, after midnight: I was dead tired and heading for my room to sack out when a cocktail waitress stopped me.

"Zack," she whispered, "a guy just told me that he knows someone who's cheating in the tournament."

That's all I needed, a cheating scandal just when I had the club back on its feet.

"He said he'd wait for you out back."

"Call Cross," I told her, referring to the shift supervisor for security. "Tell him to meet me out back."

Things like this were bound to pop up. Probably just someone with an axe to grind, but better he informed me than calling the news people or the gaming board. I was so tired and rummy, not even the adrenaline pumped out by the allegation perked me up.

I went out the back door and looked for the man who wanted to ruin a good night. He had his back to me.

"What's the deal, guy?" I asked, coming up behind him.

If I hadn't been so rummy, I never would have walked out the back by myself—it wasn't something I even permitted my security people to do.

As he turned around, I saw the gun jump in the man's hand and a powerful blow struck my chest. Then there was nothing.

Part 10

★ ★ ★ ★ ★ ★

"HERE'S CHEVY!"

Lin Piao stood in a circle of people watching Jackie Chan direct himself as he performed a stunt on the back lot of a Hong Kong studio compound. Chan defied the laws of gravity as he crawled up a wall like a spider.

"Amazing," Lin said to a script supervisor of the Chinese-language film. Lin was not producing this movie, but his mouth watered at the idea of casting a major star like Jackie Chan in the low-budget action films his company was cranking out.

During a break in the shooting, Mr. Wan entered the studio. The crew had been informed that he would be visiting the set and several of them took covert looks at the man who was notorious in the British and Portuguese colonies. In the Far East, a figure like Wan received the same cautious respect that a Mafia don received in America. His shadow, Ling, and companion, A-Ma, trailed behind him.

"Mr. Wan, so good to see you," Lin said. It had taken a great deal of manipulation to get the famous man to the set. Now that he was there, Lin was a little nervous. He was playing the game of puffing up his small production company with potential backers, but one could not sell too much "air" to Wan. "Is this one of your movies?" Wan asked.

"No, not this one, I just dropped by to talk to Jackie about another project I have under development." He had deliberately set up this meeting with Wan to leave the impression he used actors of Chan's caliber. Actually he was struggling to put together his third low-budget film. Neither of his first two films had received any critical acclaim or captured any significant box office reward. But making movies was like a treasure hunt—you never knew what would happen when you turned over the next rock.

Lin noticed A-Ma for the first time. "Who is this beautiful woman?"

"My secretary," Wan said.

Lin immediately understood that Wan's "secretary" performed more than dictation. He was so busy staring at her, he didn't hear Wan speaking to him. "Sorry, I am captivated by your secretary. She should have a screen test."

Wan raised his eyebrows to A-Ma. "Are you interested in becoming an actress?"

"I have no talent for acting."

Wan shrugged. "You see? Young people today think they have to be born with talent. In my day we knew that talent came from hard work."

Wan was considered a potential "angel" who could finance movies and A-Ma was obviously one of his stable of women, so the idea of a screen test was not taken seriously by anyone but Lin himself. He was struck by an essence emanating from the young woman, different from the raw sex portrayed so often it became shopworn from overuse and abuse. A-Ma radiated something more sensuous and exotic. But people often appeared different on film than in person. The camera had a love affair with a truly charismatic movie star, reproducing not just a naked reflection of the person on the screen but also some of the essence that made them charismatic.

During their break, Lin escorted Wan over to meet Jackie Chan. While Wan talked to the always smiling, amiable actor, Lin slipped over to a cameraman who had the job of shooting the production on video so the director had an instant replay of filmed scenes.

"See the young woman over there," he indicated A-Ma, "shoot her for me."

"Doing what?"

"Just shoot her as she's standing there. It's an impromptu screen test."

That night Lin played the video to an up-and-coming director and a Hong Kong rep for an international film distributor.

"Look at this girl, she's only about eighteen or nineteen, but she has an ageless quality to her. And she has a great screen presence. The moment I saw her I realized she was something special."

"She's looks wonderful," the director said. "At least on video. But we'll have to shoot her in 35mm to get a true reflection of her camera quality. She has that agonizingly unattainable look. It's something the great stars have, a mystery about them that you can't grasp. Charismatic women aren't just pretty objects. They've got something that we can feel but just can't define."

"This is Wan's girlie?" the distributor asked.

"Yes," Lin said.

"What makes you think he'd let her star in a movie?" the director asked. "I'm not so sure he wants to share her with the world. Wan is not a person you want to antagonize by taking away his girlfriend."

Lin rubbed his fingers together in the universal gesture indicating money. "He'll not only let her play, he'll *pay*. Wan's heart ticks with the same rhythm as the money press at the government mint. With the Reds breathing down our necks, he's always looking for ways to get money out of Hong Kong and Macao. A movie brings in money all over the world and his share can stay in the countries where it's earned."

"But can she act?" the distributor asked.

"She has to pretend to like that old lizard, doesn't she? That has to be worth an Academy Award all by itself."

57

A-Ma sat at the dressing room table and examined her reflection in the mirror while the makeup artist put the finishing touches on her face.

"You have to rub the body oil all over," the artist said. "*All* over. We want water to bead up on you when you come out of the river. The director wants to see not only wetness but drops of water on your skin."

As soon as the makeup artist left, A-Ma took off all of her clothes and applied the oily lotion to her body. The reality that she was actually acting in a movie finally struck her. She had seen hardly any movies in her life, reinforcing the fact that her acting seemed even more fanciful than anything she had ever imagined. Mr. Wan not only had given his blessing, he had insisted she take the opportunity. She knew nothing about the financial arrangements, had no interest in money or money matters, but knew that Mr. Wan did very little that was not related to increasing his wealth.

Wang Su, the director, came in without knocking.

She pulled on a robe. "Please knock before you enter."

"Sorry. But you'll find that there isn't much time or need for modesty on a movie set."

He knew when he hired her if she hadn't been Mr. Wan's property, he would have insisted she audition for the role on the casting room couch. During their first rehearsal session alone, he had tested the waters by touching her buttocks. She had stopped him cold from any further familiarities with her body. Besides her "guardian" there was something else that kept him from trying again, an almost elusive quality about her that made her untouchable.

"I just want to go over some things. I want you to be yourself," he said. "You are very lucky because you have not been hired to play a role. In a sense, the part has been written expressly for you. We are so impressed with your natural style that we want to film you as you are rather than having you assume a role."

"Since I can't act, that works out nicely for all of us."

He grinned. "Your lack of acting experience had occurred to us when we rewrote the script to add a small part for you." He sat on the makeup artist's stool and leaned forward with his elbows on his knees. "To give a convincing performance, an actress must walk in the shoes of her character. She must think, feel, and act as the character would. That means not just putting on a mask and pretending you are the person in the role, but living the part. It's like a spirit enters your body and takes it over, and it's the soul of the spirit that the audience experiences. Am I making any sense?"

"Yes."

"In your case, though, we want you to be yourself. It's your own soul we want to expose to the audience. The woman you are playing has been wronged. Her soul has been bruised. Ask yourself how *you* would react. Don't think about how the character in a movie would act. The harm was done to you, *you personally*."

She closed her eyes for a moment. "We have been over this many times."

"And we'll do it again and again. Movies are very expensive products. Millions of dollars go into what ends up on a roll of film. I'm sure you are as anxious as I am to ensure that Mr. Wan gets a fair return on his money. Do you understand the scene?"

"What is there to understand? I take off my clothes and walk into a river to wash. I have washed many times in rivers, so that much will come naturally to me. But I never did it to entice the men who watch the movie. Or move the hearts of women who might sympathize with my predicament. If you want me to twist myself into a sex symbol or an object of pity, my performance will not satisfy you. I am nothing more, nor nothing less, than what you see before you. I am not an actress. You say you want me to be myself, but each time you say it, I hear doubt in your voice."

"This movie is important to me and many other people. The producer was so eager to get Mr. Wan's financing, he would have cast Godzilla in a role. Not that I'm not happy to give you a chance—your screen test was excellent. I just want to make sure you are comfortable with your part. You must relax completely. And have confidence in yourself."

"As you have told me many times. I will be myself, Mr. Wang. Is there anything else we need to discuss? I have to finish my preparation."

"No. I can see you're shy by the way you covered up when I came in. Remember you'll be exposing your breasts today to the whole cast, crew, and bystanders?"

"I am not shy, just particular."

Heaven's Warrior was a film about a young warrior's odyssey through China's countryside at the time when the Manchu armies broke through the Great Wall and were at the gates of Beijing in the seventeenth century. A-Ma only had a few minutes of screen time as a woman brutalized by bandits. The hero-warrior single-handedly takes on a dozen bandits with his bare fists and feet, kills the bandits, and makes love to her before moving on. Her pivotal scene was to go into a river and cleanse her body and soul, washing off the filth of her attackers. The scene was difficult because there was no dialogue—like a star of the silent movies, she had to capture and hold the audience's attention without speaking a word.

She was naked up to her waist in the river scene. When the makeup artist tried to stimulate her nipples with a piece of ice, A-Ma pushed away her hands. "I am already cold and shivering."

"Let's get some angles on her breasts," the director told the cameraman. "They're not very large, we need to increase the impression of their size. A-Ma, can you arch your back a little to make your breasts strut out more?"

"No, I am sick and tired of the focus on my breasts. Breasts, breasts, breasts. What is it about a woman's breasts that so fascinates you men? I am not a side of beef to be touched and poked and examined."

"All right, let's shoot the scene. Our actress is getting antsy."

She went into the river wearing nothing but a ragged piece of cloth around her waist. Her breasts were bare, nipples tense, and her body shivering. She stood in knee-deep water and instead of thinking what was supposed to happen to her by make-believe bandits, she thought about the first time she had been alone with Mr. Wan.

She was thirteen years old and new in his house when she was instructed by a servant to present herself at his bedside late one winter night. As she came up to his bed, he instructed her to take off her robe. She let her robe slip down to her feet and stood shivering in the cold room. Her body had not completely filled out yet and it was still girlish and bony. When he threw open the blankets, he was naked as well, skinny and ill-formed, his small penis buried in a burr of black hair. "Get on the bed, child. Not next to me, down at my feet." He had her sit with her back to the end of the bed and then spread her thighs open. Her recent growth of pubic hair had been shaved by a servant before she was called to Wan's room.

He put his icy cold feet between her opened legs, pressing them against her naked crotch.

"Ahhh," he purred, "that feels good."

She came out of the cold water in a trance, oblivious to the cameras, the cast, and crew. She stood shivering on the riverbank, the oil on her skin faithfully beading the water. For a moment she froze as she came out of her trance, suddenly realizing that she was being watched by a hundred eyes. She felt that they had experienced her shame, the humiliation of having her female part being used as a foot warmer for an old man, and tears came down her eyes. She stared defiantly at the people and pulled back her shoulders, refusing to surrender to the emotional pain. She walked straight ahead and went directly to her dressing room. No one said a word or stepped in her way. She felt defeated. *I've failed*, she thought. She wanted to crawl the last few feet to the dressing room door. As she opened the door she heard her name called and turned around.

They all began to clap and she stared at them, confused. Then they began to whistle and cheer.

The director told her later, "You were magnificent. You could see those bastard bandits bruised your body but never touched your soul."

58

I sat in the club's lounge and sipped a Jack Coke while I watched the Academy Awards. You didn't find TVs in the bars of most casinos, but Halliday's was never a typical gambling joint. We had locals who dropped in for a drink and a cheap lunch or used it as a watering hole for grabbing a couple beers after work. Few of them got away without paying their dues on the casino floor.

"Who's winning?" Manny Stuber asked. Manny was the casino manager, a gal who went to UNLV during the day while working nights, going from a Halliday cocktail waitress to dealer and then pit boss. I made her casino manager two years ago and I never regretted the choice.

"The Yankees," I joked. But the name of a few sports teams I heard thrown around was about all I knew of who played. And I hadn't seen many movies since I groped Nadine in the backseat of my car at a drive-in theater a zillion years ago.

"Know why the man crossed the road?" Manny asked.

"Uh-huh."

"He heard the chicken was a slut."

Manny moved on, her eye catching everything. Sometimes she reminded me of myself, though no one in Vegas had an eye to catch a cold deck or a dealer-player going for the money like I did. Con Halliday could have done it, but we buried him over three years ago, a year after I took a .38 slug in my chest. I spent most of the first year after the shooting in bed, in therapy, or both. I was nearly thirty-four now, still young in an age where sixty-year-olds kicked up their heels and grandparents bragged about their sex lives, but I felt old. And looked it. I had some gray in my hair and lines on my face. People still said I could have doubled for Lee Marvin, but they no longer said a "young Lee Marvin."

I had the casino off to a running start before I took the hit in the alley and Morgan had been smart enough to keep the ball rolling, though it had to be pushed uphill sometimes during that first year when I was recuperating. She had to deal with a tough pregnancy and the birth of our daughter while worrying about how much of me would recover.

Not all of me left that alley that day, but I was the only one who knew it. Besides the blood I left there, some part of me had spilled onto the pavement. I don't know what it was, but Morgan said I lost some of my tolerance for the world after that, that I became more ruthless and single-minded. I died in that alley, got revived by paramedics, and died again in the emergency ward. What I learned most of all was how capricious the gods were, especially the Dark Sisters who determine our fate and cackle when it suits them to cut the thread of a life.

I had a list of things I needed to accomplish before I died. Getting shot brought home the fact that there was only so much time on earth allotted to each of us. So did seeing small children growing before my eyes. The kids brought home to me my own mortality. They were the future, but I wasn't willing to give up my own wish list.

The only thing that mattered to me was to have the biggest casino in Vegas. Whatever got into my blood when I was twelve years old and saw the Strip for the first time was still there, an urgent need unsatisfied.

For me, Halliday's was just a prick teaser rather than a good piece of ass.

"Here's Chevy," from someone imitating Ed McMahon, brought a laugh from the awards audience as Chevy Chase, hosting the program instead of the ubiquitous Johnny Carson, came back onstage to introduce the actor and actress who would announce the Best Actress winner.

It was unusual that one of the nominees was an actress in a foreign film with subtitles. A-Ma's performance in *White Flower*, her third movie, had gotten universal acclaim. I wasn't even aware she was an actress until I saw a newspaper article about *White Flower*. I was struck by her screen presence when I watched the movie. Every man in the audience that night could feel her body heat, her lush sensuality.

The most amazing part was that although she barely spoke in the movie, she was able to play her character with the sheer strength of her physical presence. Someone told me that when Alan Ladd came into the studio commissary for lunch and was asked how the morning shooting went, he said, "I got in one good look." I guess he managed once that morning to get himself deep enough into the character to have an audience suspend disbelief that he was only "acting." But Ladd lived during the golden age of movies, when actors were required to get deep into their character. Most actors today turn me off because they put on a thin façade and you know they're acting. A-Ma's role of a woman avenging her husband's murder was amazing because her sorrow and quiet hate seemed to emanate from someplace deep within. She didn't have to speak to the audience; she made you feel her pain and anger as if you were sharing her emotions.

Wan had been listed as executive producer in the credits, so I knew the yellow spider was still in her life. As I watched the movie, I realized that Wan could hold her prisoner but would never dominate her. She was too ethereal, too other-worldly for anyone to own.

She wasn't at the awards. The director of the movie was there to accept the award in case she won. She didn't. Cher took the Best Actress award for *Moonstruck*. It was just too much of a stretch for the American Academy members to give the Oscar to a woman who barely spoke in a Chinese movie shown only in art houses and with subtitles. I read in the papers A-Ma wouldn't attend the awards because she said she didn't speak English. That was a lie, of course; her English was excellent.

I hadn't seen either Wan or A-Ma since I left Macao over four years ago and took off to become a "globetrotter" and checked out other gambling venues. Wan had been indicted in absentia in New York for illegal money transactions in the States. The long arm of the feds didn't reach to the Far East, so it was a standoff: He stayed away and they left him alone.

A security officer appeared at my side. "Mrs. Halliday and Bic are ready for you." Morgan had kept her last name. I didn't mind that except when people inadvertently called me Mr. Halliday. Like Ben Siegel, I was touchy about what people called me.

I left the lounge for my office upstairs. Making an appointment to see my wife is what our married life had come down to. I couldn't get back into the domestic shoe after dying twice in an alley from a gunshot wound. I moved into the room I kept at the club and led a life separate from Morgan's. The distemper in our relationship was entirely due to me. After the shooting occurred, in addition to running the casino during her pregnancy, when the police failed to find the shooter, she hired a former L.A. homicide dick to track him down, but nothing came of it. My suspicion was that Bic's buddy Bronco had a dirty hand in it. I would have gone after Bronco myself when I was back on my feet, but he apparently ran for Tijuana soon after the shooting. Morgan's detective believed he was MIA when a drug purchase down there went bad. Hopefully he was lying on his back in a shallow grave with a mouthful of dirt somewhere under the Baja desert. I figured Bic was too stupid and indecisive to have engineered the shooting, but I wouldn't have put it past him to have financed a hit on me. That brooding suspicion about her brother, and my physical retreat from her following the shooting, terminated anything left in our marriage. Of late, Morgan had been quietly seeing a UNLV history professor who was leaving a teaching career to write. Her plans were to take the kids and move to Martha's Vineyard with him. I said nothing about the move. There was only one thing I wanted—the Strip. And that's what our meeting today was about.

I walked into my office and my past hit me with a shock. Janelle was there.

"What are you doing in here? You're banned from Halliday's." I hadn't seen her since she did time for the quarter scam.

"Janelle's with me," Bic said. "She's allowed where I go and I own a third of this club—an honest third."

"What is—" Morgan started.

"She's a thief whose been barred by the gaming board. Your rocket scientist brother is still trying to get our license pulled."

Bic jumped out of his chair. "Janelle was set up by you and your pal."

I laughed. "I heard about her act in court. Don't forget, I know her. Get her ass out of here or I'll call security."

"Fuck you, you asshole."

Bic came at me ready to swing but Morgan put herself between us. "Stop it! Bic, is it true, is she barred from here?"

He didn't bother answering her but grabbed Janelle's arm. "Let's get out of here! I'll sell my goddamn interest in the club and get my own place."

Janelle gave me a smirk as she went out the door. But her eyes weren't smiling. There was a hardness to her, like the look a woman gets when she's been knocked around too much.

"What is going on here?" Morgan was near tears.

"Sit down and I'll explain."

I told her about Janelle, starting with how I met her, leaving out the intimate parts. She bent over and buried her head in her hands and cried. I couldn't move three feet to comfort her. I didn't have that sort of feeling anymore for anyone. Not even myself.

"I just don't understand," she said. "If she's barred, why would Bic bring her in here?"

"He's been trying to sabotage the place for years."

"Does he hate you that much? And what about me? Would he hurt himself and me to harm you?"

"I've been getting a bum rap from you about Bic almost from the day we met. Bic was a grown man when I came on the scene. He was fucked up then. He's a creature of your old man, not me. He's self-destructive and a loser and he directs his hate at me so he doesn't have to face himself."

I thought for a moment about Bic's threat to sell his share of the club. The threat was meaningless. His share went into a family trust that Con set up, and Morgan controlled the trust.

She blew her nose. "I've got to get away from here, out of Vegas. I can't stand it anymore. It's affected my father, my brother, and now you. I'm moving back East, you know that."

I didn't say anything.

"I'm taking the kids, of course."

That went without saying, but she said it anyway, to get a response from me, some sort of fatherly comment, like "I'll miss them." But there was no emotion in me and I couldn't cross the gap between us to make a polite listening response about losing my son and daughter.

"You've changed, Zack." She had said that a hundred times ever since the day I stared at her from a recuperation bed. And each time she looked at me it was as if she was trying to find the man she used to know.

"Maybe I haven't changed. Maybe this has been me all the time and the only thing that has changed is taking off the mask I wore."

"You're so damn grim. There isn't an ounce of humor in you. You used to be funny. But you don't smile anymore. And your eyes are as dead as that girl that just left."

I shook my head. "I can't give you whatever it is that you want from me. It's not in me."

"No, but you want something from me, don't you."

"I'm not asking you for charity. We still have Halliday's, thanks to me, and something worth almost as much as the club."

The valuable "something" was linked back to Windell. Yeah, Windell, the nerd who could hack his way into the Pentagon or the Soviet Command Center but couldn't figure out how to get laid. The clever bastard had finally come up with a good one. He had contacted me two years ago with a new electronic concept for random-number generation. The random generation of numbers was what made a slot machine tick. If it worked right, a casino was guaranteed the exact return it programmed its slots for. The problem was it never worked exactly right—until Windell figured out a way to do it. I bought the rights, gave Windell a good financial package that guaranteed him a return for the next twenty years, and started a company that provided the technology to casinos all over the world. Windell "retired" to Grand Cayman and the only connection with Nevada, other than a monthly check, was a chicken ranch near Reno that sent him a prostitute each month.

"Between what I can raise mortgaging Halliday's and selling the random-generator company, there'll be enough to exercise the option on the Condor."

The Condor was an enormous, rundown budget motel complex on the Strip. It was an eyesore that needed to be torn down. Jack Evans had built it back in the early fifties. Somewhere along the line Con had acquired an option to buy the place, most likely during a poker game between the two Vegas old-timers. He never exercised the option, probably because he had to pay "current market value," the value of Strip property being too rich for his blood. The option had laid dormant until Evans died and a property title search found it during probate. The option was in the name of the Halliday Corporation and could still be exercised. Since Morgan and I each owned a third interest in the corporation, as long as she sided with me, Bic was powerless to stop me from using the club to raise the money to exercise the option.

"Even with the club and your company," she said, "you're not going to have enough money to build a Strip club. You'd have to raise two or three times more money."

"Try ten times more."

"Excuse me?"

"I'm not going to build just an ordinary casino. There's already enough competition out there for the weekend crowd and people from back East. I'm going to build a casino that draws people from all over the country, like Disneyland and the Universal Studio tour."

"Are you serious? Zack, those are family places, for mom and dad and the kids. Vegas is for adult gamblers. The only place that even comes close to being user friendly to families are the circus acts at Circus-Circus."

"Why can't mom and dad come here and gamble while the kids are enjoying a theme park with rides and games? Don't you see, by not opening the door to families, we're turning away most people. There's no reason Vegas can't be a family vacation spot. I'm going to build a theme casino that the whole family can enjoy. You don't remember, but Circus-Circus was not designed for family entertainment. When it first opened, kids weren't allowed. You played slots with an elephant walking around but it was all for adults. It was the right idea to open the doors to children but the circus acts are not enough. Kids need something to do while their parents are making their contribution at the slots and tables. I'm going to build a super casino that has something for everyone."

"Zack, you're asking me to risk everything we have—and Bic has—to give you a shot at the Strip."

"I'm going to make you and that jerk richer than you've ever dreamed."

"I don't care about the money. What I care about is that I just told you I'm taking our kids three thousand miles away and you don't give a damn." She got up and started for the door. "All right, I'll sign for your dream. If you'll do one thing."

"Which is?"

"Give away all parental rights to the children. I'm going to marry Todd after we get settled back East. He'll adopt the children and they'll bear his last name. You'll never see the children again."

I didn't hesitate for even a moment.

She shook her head. "I should hate you, but I don't. I feel sorry for you. You never had a mother, father, brother, sister. You're worse than an only child who doesn't know how to share—you don't know how a family functions. You don't know what you're supposed to do with a home and kids." She stared at me for a moment, hoping for some answer from me. "You're going to end up like the father you never knew. I'm taking our children out of this town so they won't have to see a sick stranger carried out of the back of a hotel someday and realize that it was their father."

Bic Halliday was fifteen years old when Con took him out to a chicken ranch to get "the velvet rubbed off his cock," Con said. The night Con decreed the boy was to lose his virginity, two of Con's old friends from Texas had shown up in Vegas for "a little shit kicking and pussy poking."

After several hours of hard drinking and carousing, Con loaded his buddies and his son into his 1942 Packard and headed down the road for Sally's Ranch across the county line. Clarke County, where Vegas was located, didn't have legalized prostitution, but the county next door did.

Bic sat in the front seat dreading the ordeal ahead of him. He had done heavy petting with girls and heavy "petting" on himself in his own bed at night, but he had never gone all the way with a girl. His fear was that he would fail and be humiliated.

"You're not going to be in there with me?" he anxiously asked Con when his old man told him he was taking him and his pals out to a chicken ranch.

"Hell, no, I'm not gonna be watching your little prick. I'm going to be sticking my own in Wanda."

Wanda, Bic had been told, was a big redhead from Tallahassee who Con claimed wrestled him to the floor and mounted him the last time he went out to Sally's.

"Stomp that goddamn pedal to the floor, Con, my dick's yelling that it needs to be milked!" one of the Texas friends yelled from the backseat. The other one leaned out the window and threw a bottle at a parked car. It missed the car and shattered in front of it.

Con took a swig of whiskey and nudged Bic. "Take a shot, boy, it'll calm your nerves. You look like you're going to be the guest of honor at a cannibal's feast rather than finally knocking off a piece. By the time I was your age, I had every woman in the county lining up to get theirs, like a goddamn bull in a corral full of milk cows."

The big Packard came across the dividing line at a curve in the road and almost rocketed into a big truck coming from the opposite direction. Bic gripped the dashboard as Con whipped the car back across the line before a head on.

They went by a sheriff's patrol car parked on the other side of the road and Con stuck his head out the window and *yippeed!* He waved with the whiskey bottle. Bic tensed with hope that the deputies would pull them over, but they only waved back. He knew they'd drop around Halliday's tomorrow and pick up drink, meal, and slot comps.

Out on the highway, one of the cowboys in the back leaned way out the left passenger side and threw a bottle high over the car. His buddy on the right side fired out the window at the bottle but missed. He cursed, then emptied his six-shooter at a road sign.

Con nudged Bic with the whiskey bottle and Bic took it reluctantly. He didn't like hard liquor, but he took a swig to please his father. It exploded in his mouth and went down his throat like burning aviation fuel. He started coughing and Con leaned over and hit him in the back so hard he went forward and hit his head on the window.

"Goddamnit, boy, I've told you a man swallows whiskey without tasting it. Just shoot it down. You just can't get it right, can you?"

Bic couldn't get it right. And drinking whiskey "like a man" was just one of a long list of things he couldn't get right. He was big, like his father, but where Con had the backbone of a grizzly, Bic had the spine of a rabbit. He grew up without the tough-skinned, barroom-brawler, ride-the-river cowboy tenacity of his father. The truth was Bic was scared of a lot of things. In school smaller kids beat him up. "It's not the dog in the fight," Con told him when he came home with his tail between his legs after a fight with a kid physically smaller than him, "but the fight in the dog. Get some fight in you, boy, and go back there and kick ass." He spun Bic around and gave him a kick in the butt in front of people. "Don't come back without the scalp of that kid who hit you."

He came home from school with a red nose and a cut on his forehead after being whipped again by a smaller boy in his high school class. He went into the casino and to the corner table of Halliday's restaurant where Con held court. Con looked up from a discussion with two of his pit bosses and stared coldly at Bic as the boy stood next to the table. Defeat was written all over the boy's face. "You cunt," Con said, and turned his back on him.

His reaction to his father's disapproval was always the same—he screwed up worse. When he was little, if he got slapped for dripping mustard on his shirt while eating a hot dog, he ended up with mustard all over him.

"You're like a goddamn steer that keeps butting a fence post because he ain't got the brains to move to the side," Con had told him over and over. "You fuck up and fuck up and fuck up."

Con made the turn onto the side road to Sally's Ranch, running into a ditch before getting the car centered on the road. The "ranch" was half a mile ahead, several "modular home" units linked together. Bic began trembling. His friends at school who had lost their virginity had almost always got their first piece at a drive-in theater. None of them had been taken to a chicken ranch by their father. He had seen the whores who hung around Halliday's bar. Hard women with coarse voices and clothes that struck him as trashy rather than sexy. He didn't want to have sex with any of them. There were plenty of girls at school he could've had sex with. One time he boasted to his dad that he had made love to a girl he had dated, Janey Wayne, and when Con had picked up the phone to call and ask her if it was true, Bic panicked and confessed his lie. That got him hit across the side of the head.

"That's for letting me call your bluff—with a bluff. Don't play cards you can't handle."

Sally was a surprise. Bic had expected a "madam" but Sally was a barrel-shaped man with big ears and a round face.

"Get the crew out here," Con told Sally. "My boy's gonna pick the filly he'll ride."

The four "girls" lined up next to each other. Bic was shocked when he recognized one of them. She was the mother of a boy he knew. He avoided looking at her.

"Go ahead, boy, pick one." Con slapped Bic on the back. "Hell, pick two or three if you think you can ride 'em all."

"I—I don't know—"

Con grabbed his arm and steered him to a Latino woman. She was a little younger than most of the other women. Bic guessed she was in her early twenties.

"What's your name, honey?" Con asked.

"They call me Tijuana Rose."

"Well, T-Rose, you think you can fix up my boy here? He's been pumping his Long Tom by hand so often, you'd think he was milking it to fill baby bottles."

Con's pals howled with laughter and Bic turned redder than he already was.

Rose took Bic's hand and winked at Con. "When I'm finished with him, the girls at school will drop their panties every time he walks down the hallway."

The dimly lit corridor was lined on both sides with room doors. Bic heard noises coming through the thin walls; a squeal of female laughter, a man grunting like he was lifting heavy weights. His mouth was dry and his stomach knotted. She held his hand as they ventured down the hallway, a wet, sweaty hand full of fear and panic.

They went inside a room that had tacky budget motel furniture, the smell of perfume from Woolworth's, and another odor that couldn't be hidden, a scent more primeval than perfume, his first smell of cheap sex.

Rose closed the door behind them and stood only inches away from him, her breasts jutting against the restraints of the sheer silky blouse. She took his hands and put them flat on the bare skin below her neckline and slowly moved them down, squeezing his hands tight over her breasts.

"These don't feel like the girl's at school, do they?"

"Uh-huh," came out as a dry mouth mumble.

"Why don't you take off my blouse?"

His hands fumbled with the buttons and she helped him, unable to suppress a grin. "Don't be nervous, I'm not going to bite you—except where it'll feel good."

She laughed lewdly and it increased his nervousness. When they left the room, Con would cross-examine her about how he performed and he'd be humiliated again. His dread of what would be said later panicked him and he did what he always did in those moments, he tried harder and failed worse. Unable to get a button undone, he jerked at the blouse.

"Take it easy, honey, don't damage the merchandise."

She undid the last button and slipped off the blouse. Her brown

breasts were barely restrained by the size thirty-eight bra. She un-
hooked the brassiere and let it fall on the floor. Taking his hands, she
put them under her breasts and had him hold them. "Like 'em,
honey?"

Not waiting for a reply, she pushed him back to the bed. He sat on
the edge and she pulled his shirt off over his head. "Stand up, sweetie."
She undid his pants and dropped them and his underwear, then had
him sit back down and pulled them off his legs. She slipped out of her
skirt and stood in front of him wearing only bikini panties. "Like me?"
She did a little tiptoe dance step in a circle, then moved in closer,
putting her large breasts in his face. The breasts had the same cheap
perfume scent of the rest of the room. Instead of turning him on, his
stomach turned and he felt nauseated. He pushed her back so he could
breathe.

Shaking her head, she stepped into the bathroom and came out a
moment later with a bowl of warm soapy water and a wash cloth. "Lay
back for me." She spread his legs and gently washed his penis and
testicles, massaging them as she did. His organ stayed limp.

"Lay the other way on the bed, honey."

Rose hit the on switch of an eight-track player next to the bed and
a Spanish disco beat started blaring. With Bic lengthwise on the bed,
she stood on the bed with his prone body between her legs, her legs
spread wide enough so he could see the pink between her legs. She
swayed and moved her body seductively to the beat of the music, fon-
dling her own breasts and smiling at him. She slowly came down on
him, and spread her soft moist pink zone across his virile part, rubbing
against him as she slipped down his body until her head was in his
groin area.

He still hadn't gotten hard yet. She ran her hands up his naked
abdomen and felt his tension. She teased his virile parts with her
tongue, starting below his belly button and moving down and under,
tickling his balls and taking his limp shaft in her mouth and sucking.
She sucked off and fucked hundreds of men a year, so many that the
only sexual response in her was artificial, but she found herself getting
a little turned on by the boy's limp cock, her mouth getting hotter and
warmer. Most men's cocks were hard red stems. The softness and pli-
ability of his was refreshing. But no erection came.

She shook her head in disbelief as she glanced at a black curtain that covered one wall of the room.

"I'm sorry," Bic said. "I'm really sorry." His voice quivered embarrassingly. "Can I pay you just to talk for a while?"

He heard giggling come from the curtained area, not a girlish sound but that of a drunk man. Con Halliday jerked open the curtain. Standing next to him was one of his Texas buddies bending over with mirth.

"You'd fuck up a wet dream, boy."

"Do you know why I've always hated that bastard Riordan?" Bic said. "He reminds me of my father. He's an arrogant bastard who thinks he is king shit. My father said he hired him because he walked tall. The guy was nothing but street trash, a cheap hustler, and a crook. Know what my old man caught him doing?"

Janelle grinned as he talked. She knew only too well what Con Halliday caught Zack doing.

They were in the living room of the house that was on the ranch Bic inherited from Con. Like everything else he touched, the ranch had gone from a money-making spread with two employees to a dry hole Bic retreated to when things got too hot for him in town, which was most of the time.

"Dad always favored Riordan, liked him better than his own son. And Riordan played him, sure as hell, he knew how to ingratiate himself with my father, kiss his ass."

Janelle let him blow off steam. She had her own opinion of why Con and Zack had clicked and it had nothing to do with ass kissing. Bic was almost dead right when he said that the two were cut from the same mold. But they weren't twins.

She never thought of Con as particularly smart; instead of real smarts he had an ability to read people, along with a bravado that mowed them down. She thought of Zack as having real smarts. She had smarts, too, and she was finally going to use them to get what she wanted. Zack owed her. She felt that Zack had cheated her. Yeah, she had played that creep Windell, manipulating him into scamming Halliday's, but in her own mind she had been driven to it by Zack. He had treated her like dirt, drawing away from her after he got his break at Halliday's, acting like a lap dancer wasn't good enough for him, wanting her to give up the dancing and constantly slamming her because she needed a fix once in a while to face the dirty world around her. She hated Zack, hated him for his arrogance, for his strength, for getting her busted.

She met Bic purely by accident. After getting out of jail, she left Nevada with her probation officer's permission and knocked around L.A. and San Diego for a while, serving cocktails in lounges and doing tricks out in the parking lot. She made a connection with a small-time drug pusher who supplied her and moved in with him and was soon introduced to the "business" of selling drugs.

When a friend who hauled the products to Vegas got busted, she drove a kilo herself across the state line and delivered it to a man in a bar on the west side of town. Bic was with the buyer, financing the deal for a piece of the kilo at wholesale prices. He recognized her as a former Halliday's dealer and Zack's girlfriend, and as soon as she bad-mouthed Zack, she and Bic became old friends.

"He turned my father against me, turned Morgan against me, and stole the club. I should own half of it, but I've only got a third and I don't really own that. Morgan controls it and he controls her. Now that bastard is going to lose even that to make himself a big shot on the Strip. My father knew better than to mess with the Strip. It's nothing but an ego trip."

Janelle's eye caught a picture of a woman on the end table next to the couch. "Who's that?"

"My mother. She was beautiful, a Follies dancer, a real star."

To Janelle the woman in the picture was just another Vegas show-girl, a product cranked out by the town by the thousands, but if Bic wanted to think of her as something special, that was okay with her. She usually wasn't submissive to a man, but in this case she had her reasons. Bic needed a woman he could dominate and she needed what he had—an inheritance worth millions.

"She killed herself when I was seven, walked in front of a train. She couldn't stand my old man. She killed herself because she couldn't take his abuse anymore. He doesn't care about anyone but himself. He used to tell people she greased the railroad tracks. I heard him say that a dozen times. He's not capable of loving anyone."

"What about Morgan?"

"He treats her okay because she knows how to handle him. If she had ever got in his way, he would have treated her like shit, too. But I was never tough enough, smart enough, or fast enough for him. The old man said the only thing I succeeded at was failure. Real encouraging words, huh."

Janelle listened and stroked him. She cooked heroin in a teaspoon over a candle and soaked a cigarillo in it. Bic smoked the dope and soon was relaxed. She learned how to manipulate his drugs, sometimes giving him cocaine to elevate him and heroin to bring him back down. Right now she was expecting company and wanted him out of the way. As he was slipping into sleep, she stroked him and rubbed his groin. She knew he was impotent from wasting his body with drugs, but she kept up the pretense with him.

She waited outside and smoked a joint until sunset, when the yellow Camaro she was expecting drove down the road. The man who stepped out of the car was big, over six-foot-two and weighing in at two hundred twenty. He wore sunglasses, thousand-dollar cowboy boots, a Stetson, and five-hundred-dollar silk shirts. His tight black jeans bulged in the crotch.

"Hello, lover." She gave him a wet kiss.

Diego Gomez squeezed her buttocks. "Missed me, baby?"

"Yeah, I missed your cock and your dream powders."

"I can fix that real quick."

He retrieved a gym bag from the trunk and followed her into the house.

"Where's your friend?"

"Sleeping, but keep the noise down. He might wake up."

"Nice place," he said, throwing the gym bag on a couch. "But not exactly a millionaire's ranch."

"It *is* a millionaire's ranch, but Bic doesn't spend much time out here. Neither did his dad. He said his father bought the place for old times' sake, so he could keep up the pretense of being a Texas rancher. They own Halliday's in town."

Diego whistled. "And the guy's a drugged-out slug?"

"He's getting there. You bring me the stuff?"

"In the bag."

She opened the bag and pulled out a kilo of cocaine, a metropolitan telephone book–sized package wrapped in plastic and aluminum foil. "I'll need more heroine, too," she said.

"I'll get it, but you should get your contacts into crank and away from coke. It's the drug of choice for the future. Crank can be made anywhere; people mix the meth and other shit in their kitchens, it's dirt cheap, and gives a better kick than cocaine."

He sat down on the couch and pulled her onto his lap. He kissed her as he put his hand between her legs.

"So what's the scam, baby?"

"You mean what's in it for you."

"What's in it for us?"

"I'll bet you if we swept the property with a metal detector, we'd find millions in gold and silver buried. That's how these casino owners are. Con Halliday used to fill a suitcase with money from the counting room before the feds put a stop to it."

"So let's do it. I'll buy a metal detector."

"No, he'd have the sheriff after us in five minutes. Besides, there's more involved than that. Bic's sister is married to a guy I used to know, Zack Riordan. Zack's building a five-hundred-million-dollar casino with money from Bic and his sister."

"You're shitting me. Five hundred million bucks?"

"And Bic owns a third of the club. Can you imagine what life would be like if we controlled a third of the biggest club in Vegas?"

"Christo, it would be like being a king. The goddamn president would kiss your ass."

"That's why we forget about the buried crap. This is my opportunity to connect big time, as big as it can get. And to exact some revenge on a bastard who has it coming. When I'm—"

"Don't forget it's we, baby, we."

"I keep asking, you greaser bastard, what do I get out of it from you?"

Diego grabbed his crotch. "This baby, you get to suck me. That's good enough for any woman."

Diego had her bent over the arm of the couch and was pumping her doggie style when Bic staggered into the darkened living room. "Janelle? Where are you?" His words were slurred.

She pulled down her dress as she walked across the room.

"Right here, hon."

"I thought I heard somebody else."

"It's my delivery man, hon, bringing the candy I ordered for you."

Macao still smelled like sweaty gym clothes.

I called Wan to talk about old times before I left Las Vegas. He told me Luís had had a 9mm café coronary, taking a shot between the eyes as he ate a plate of *chouriço* sausages. Not one to cry over spilled blood, Chenza had jumped into bed with a Japanese computer tycoon and moved on to Tokyo.

Wan now controlled most of the gambling of Macao and a big chunk of Hong Kong. It sounded like he was rolling in dough. I never mentioned A-Ma on the phone because I wasn't sure if she was still with him. I did mention I needed an angel for my project. The price tag on my super casino was running over five hundred million. To complete the financial package, I needed a hundred million to go with what I had already raised. Once I had it, a commitment by the banks for the balance would kick in. That kind of money was chicken feed to the Hong Kong–Macao crowd, and the clock was ticking for Wan and his triad buddies. When the Chinese Communists marched in, they knew better than to hang around waving a red flag. And before they got out, they needed to pad their nests with investments in safe locales.

Wan couldn't directly loan me anything—neither the feds nor the state gaming people would approve a license if he did. What I wanted from him was clean money from people he had juice with. As long as the third parties could show an honest source for the money, I wouldn't have a problem. What went on between them and Wan was their business. Bottom line, I would not get a dime from Wan and would owe him nothing—except my life, if I fucked up.

I was delightfully surprised when I found A-Ma waiting for me in the 1930ish Rolls Royce limo parked outside the wharf reception area.

A-Ma looked exquisite. She wore a dark silky red dress that came down to her ankles. A seductive slit went up to her thighs. Her hat was small and round, with a mesh veil that fell over her face. A single string of priceless pink Indian pearls showed between the high collars of the dress. She looked like the model of a 1936 issue of *Vogue*. Her perfume attacked my senses, but I didn't need an aphrodisiac. One look at her and I forgot about the hundred million dollars I wanted from Wan.

"I wore the dress especially for you."

I raised my eyebrows. "Then take it off."

"No, the color. Red is the color of luck. You will need it in dealing with Mr. Wan."

"What color will he be wearing?"

"Hopefully not white. White is the color of death and mourning." Her eyes appraised me. "You look different," she said.

"So do you."

"You look older . . . more manly."

I didn't know what she meant by that, but she could have told me I looked like the woman on the Aunt Jemina box and I wouldn't have disagreed.

"You look like a Popsicle," I said.

"A what?"

"A cool, sweet juice bar that tastes heavenly on hot days."

"Mr. Riordan, I'm not sure that's a compliment."

"You smell like Eve in the garden. Chanel No. 5?"

"Ylang-ylang, from what we call the perfume tree."

"Marilyn Monroe had the best way of wearing perfume."

"Which is?"

"She said it was the *only thing* she wore to bed." I leaned across the seat, pulled up her veil, and brushed her lips with mine. "I thought so. Cool and sweet. For a man who's been crossing a scorching desert, you are an oasis."

"You don't look very deprived, Mr. Riordan."

"You haven't looked at my love-famished soul. And if you call me Mr. Riordan again, I'm going to rape you."

"Is that a promise . . . Mr. Riordan?"

"A-Ma has become a problem to me," Wan said. "Now that she is a movie star, she attracts too much attention for an old man seeking the peaceful anonymity he has earned for his many years."

There was one thing I had learned in working with Wan: You could always tell when he was lying. It happened every time his lips moved. He hated the attention created by escorting a beautiful woman as much as lions hated red meat. He had a reason for priming the pump about his "problem" with A-Ma and it had nothing to do with his sudden penchant for privacy. Whatever it was, at the moment it appeared to be tipping the scales in my favor.

As soon as we reached Wan's "palace," Wan and I got down to business after the preliminaries of hello and an offer of tea. I passed on the tea and went for a Jack Coke. "A bottle of Jack Daniels was left over from your last visit," he said, too polite to mention I was almost murdered during my last visit to Macao.

He wore a black robe for our meeting. I didn't know what black meant.

"We heard about the unfortunate attack on you in Las Vegas, and your narrow survival." He clicked his tongue. "America is such a violent country."

I choked on my drink. "Mr. Wan, I'm going to have to bend the laws of politeness to a host and tell you that you are the most amazing bastard I have ever met."

He shook a bony yellow finger at me. "A-Ma tells me you are different but I suspect that you have still not learned the art of patience. Instead of waiting for your enemies to float by, you go out and bludgeon them."

"Let's get down to brass tacks before I end up floating facedown in some goddamn Chinese river. I need a hundred million dollars in clean money. The person who puts it up will have a foothold in the biggest money machine in Vegas. What can you do for me?"

He shook his head with true Chinese regret. "Nothing, I'm afraid. As you pointed out during our telephone conversation, a single dollar from me in the pile and you would never get a license."

I sipped my Jack Coke and waited. Wan didn't have me fly halfway around the world for a simple answer—he could have said no on the phone. But I needed to exercise some patience and let him expose what he had up his sleeve at his own pace.

"Hear any news of Chenza since the last time we talked?" I asked.

"An interesting and provocative woman. You know, there was a dark rumor that she lured Luís to that restaurant the day he was killed because another woman was displacing her in his affections. But of course, one should not believe everything one hears, should one, Mr. Riordan?"

It was hard to keep a straight face. Wan no doubt was behind Luís's murder and convinced Chenza—for love or money—to assist in taking him out. What tangled webs this yellow spider wove.

Wan stroked his short beard. "It has occurred to me that perhaps you are approaching the wrong person with your need for financing. Have you spoken to A-Ma about the matter?"

He said it so casually that I almost bought into it as an innocent remark. I cleared my throat. So A-Ma was the game.

"No, uh, I haven't. I wasn't aware acting in Hong Kong movies was so profitable."

"A-Ma does not just star in movies, Mr. Riordan; she owns the production company that makes her movies and many others. Because of the international nature of the business she has many financial contacts, even in your country."

"I see," said the blind mouse. But there was light at the end of the tunnel. Wan was a known Asian gangster and was probably monitored by the FBI, Interpol, and other police agencies. A-Ma was a young woman without a police record. It didn't take much imagination to realize that Wan not only owned the movie company, but probably didn't give a damn if any of his movies made a profit. He could pump money into accounts all over the world for production costs, publicity, and every other front he could think of . . . and leave every dollar earned in foreign bank accounts.

"Do I have your permission to speak to A-Ma concerning the matter?" I asked.

"Of course, of course," he cackled, "it is no affair of mine what she does with her money. But as her guardian, I do offer the young woman some small advice in financial matters. Perhaps you will let me help you arrange an agreement in which A-Ma assists you in financing your 'super' casino?"

I bowed my head and saluted him with my drink. "Nothing would please me more, Mr. Wan. I'm sure A-Ma values your advice over all others."

I always loved street carnivals. A-Ma said this one was called "Feast of the Drunken Dragon," as we walked along the happy crowds in the wharf area.

"Why did the dragon get drunk?" I asked as a fifty-foot-long paper dragon flowed by. I had to admit that he definitely looked a little cock-eyed.

"Because he's happy. The fishing season has been good and the fishermen's and their families' bellies are full."

"Sounds like an excuse for a bunch of fishermen to take time off work and drink it up."

"Exactly. It's the only vacation these poor people have."

We walked around a string of firecrackers going off. "What is it about you people and firecrackers?" I asked.

"Don't you know that we Chinese invented gunpowder? It's one of the paradoxes of China's relationship with the West. We invented gunpowder, but used it mostly for celebrations. The Europeans refined it, stuck it in cannons, and used the cannons to force us to let them sell our people opium."

"Come again?"

"It happened in the middle of the last century. The British and French were selling opium to the people of China. The emperor tried to put a stop to the evil practice, and the countries sent warships and armies to make China open its door to the trade." She smiled. "You see, Mr. Riordan, my people learned many bad things from yours."

"Oh, I'm sure, *Miss* A-Ma, that your buddy Wan is an original number who learned nothing from nobody—he was born crooked."

We detoured onto the dock that I once ran down with a motorcycle gunman hot on my heels. The old fisherman who had taken me from harm's way was still there. But he had a new boat, a larger sampan with a modern motor and helm.

"I wanted to buy him a big cabin cruiser, but he would not have felt comfortable with it," A-Ma said. "This was all he would let me do."

I followed her aboard his boat and we drank wine as we leisurely sailed toward a small island. She told me the fisherman's name, but I found it unpronounceable and ended up calling him Sam.

"I don't understand your life with Wan," I said. "You're not a naive teenager anymore; you're an international movie star. You can walk out any time you want."

"Choices, you are always talking about choices, Zack. I told you that I don't have the same choices as you do."

"Yes, you do. You just don't want to use them."

"Perhaps you're right. Perhaps my choice is to not make one."

"I don't blame you if you're afraid of Wan. But if you left behind his money, he'd probably leave you alone."

She laughed. "You do not know Mr. Wan. He discards people, but no one discards him. You call him a spider. You should know by now that nothing leaves his web. Look what he did to you when you took his money."

"Did to me? Wan—he had me . . . ?"

"I didn't think you knew; otherwise you would never have come back."

"How do you know?"

"I heard talk after news came that you had been shot."

"Jesus. I thought someone else did it. And I came right back into his lair."

"You have nothing to fear. Mr. Wan saved face by having you shot, even if you did not die. And now you have something he wants—a place to put his money."

For a moment I faltered, wondering if I could handle what I was getting myself into. Wan's tentacles reached a long way. "I can handle it," I said, as much to myself as to her. "Our deal will be strictly business. He'll have someplace to stick his money and get a nice return also."

"Do you see what I mean about choices?" she asked. "You have a choice to leave Macao and return to your already successful casino in downtown Las Vegas. That is the rational choice. But you choose to remain in Macao and make a deal with a dangerous spider who tried to kill you once."

"You know something, A-Ma, I'm beginning to believe that you're right, that we all walk a path that's been set out for us. What the hell else could explain the dumb things I do? I have shitty karma."

She found that funny and laughed and spilled her wine. She found that funny too and laughed some more.

"That's the first time I've heard you laugh."

She wiped the wine off her dress. "You are good for me. The other women in Wan's household say I was born an old woman and am living my life in reverse. Being around you, I am just learning how to laugh."

"I need a favor from you."

"I know. A hundred million dollars. I do not have that much in my name, but Mr. Wan will get you the balance from a man in America named Tommy Chow."

I chuckled. "I should have known."

"You know Mr. Chow."

"We're old friends. I'll tell you about it sometime, but that's not the favor I need. In your movie *White Flower* there were scenes of a Chinese palace complex called the Forbidden City—"

"The palaces of the emperors of China in Beijing."

"And the Great Wall. I want to see them."

She clapped her hands. "Oh, do you want me to take you to see them?"

"That's what I had in mind. Do you think we can get it by the old spider?" It was a rhetorical question; I already suspected the answer. I was pretty sure that Wan not only knew I was going sailing with A-Ma, but encouraged my personal contact with her. I had read the complete *Art of War* by Sun Tzu before getting on the plane for Hong Kong. One of Sun Tzu's teachings was to use deception and deceit. I intuitively knew that Wan was dangling A-Ma before me and would jerk her back at will once I was hooked. What he didn't know was how helpless I was. A-Ma didn't just steal my heart—and my gonads—she took my soul, too.

"Perhaps. I would love to go. I've never been a tourist and I've always wanted to see the Forbidden City and Great Wall."

"But you were there in the movie."

She laughed. "Movie magic. We never left Hong Kong."

Sam anchored the boat when we were a hundred yards off the island. A few minutes later I heard a splash. Sam had jumped in the water and started swimming toward the island.

"Why has he abandoned ship?"

"He knows we want some privacy."

"Why would he think that?"

"Because I told him."

She led me down to the interior of the boat, which was surprisingly cozy and warm. It was still light out, but the heavy curtains were drawn and white candles that gave off a pleasant rose scent were burning. On the floor was a flowered quilted mattress with several dozen small pillows.

Standing in the center of the snug room, I felt the warmth of her body and smelled her scent next to mine and the heat began to run through my body. I stared into her eyes for a moment, then lifted her head and kissed her on the mouth, softly at first, then with ardent passion. We moved over to the mattress and our clothes came off quickly, neither one of us ashamed of our nakedness.

"I want to give you a massage. Lay on your stomach," she said.

She spread the warm oil on my back and began kneading my flesh with her hands, then massaging my buttocks and legs. The smooth kneading almost put me to sleep. She made me turn on my back and started again with my feet and worked up to my scrotum, gently massaging my testicles. I felt myself growing hard. After her silken hand stroked my throbbing cock, a voracious hunger consumed me and I lowered her onto my hardened phallus. She moved rhythmically back and forth, up and down, keeping in motion with the rocking swells of the boat. Then she began to move feverishly as the climatic shudders shook her body. The explosion came from my body a moment later. We pressed our bodies together and closed our eyes and let the swaying of the boat rock us to sleep.

A-Ma was instructed to see Mr. Wan in the dining room when she arrived home that evening. Wan was at the table eating a late meal. Laid out before him were rice, noodles, and six different catches from the sea. He wore a large white bib and was sucking noisily on a crab leg as she walked in.

"Did you enjoy your day with our American friend?" he asked.

She took a seat at the table. "You told me to entertain him."

"Of course, of course, but I didn't tell you to enjoy being with him, which, from the satisfied look on your face, I suspect was the case. Did you think you could get away from my spying by taking him out onto the water? I had your lovemaking filmed."

She didn't know if he was lying, but would not have put it past him to have spied on her. Wan trusted no one, took nothing for granted. He believed nothing he couldn't see with his own eyes, and doubted much of what he witnessed.

As they talked, she realized Ling was standing against the wall in the shadows. Ling made her skin crawl. She had never met anyone so totally devoid of any human emotions. He reminded her of a windup toy, only active when Wan wanted him to be.

Wan cracked another crab leg with his teeth. Juice dripped down his chin as he talked and sucked on the leg.

"Riordan is going to China to see the Forbidden City and Great Wall," he said.

"I know. He's looking for ideas for his casino."

"You are to go with him."

"Go with him?"

He sucked air through his teeth and used a gold toothpick to loosen a morsel. "You want to please me, don't you, my dear?"

"Of course." Her personal preference was that he be reborn a worm in hell, but that wish she wisely kept to herself.

"You are to go to China with Riordan. Satisfy him in all aspects. I am sure you have already ascertained his pleasure points. Make sure that you make yourself indispensable to him in all ways."

She shrugged. "I don't see what good that will do you. He will only be in China a week or two and then will return to America."

"And you will return with him."

She gaped at him. "To America?"

"I know how hard it would be for you to leave me." Wan cackled so hard he started choking. A servant girl brought him a napkin and he used it to smother his cough. The girl was new but looked vaguely familiar to her.

She was always taken in by him, but his coughing spasm gave her mind a chance to catch up with her emotions. Wan gave nothing away. Nothing that he did not expect a much greater return from.

He wiped his mouth and got his breathing under control. She stared at him blank faced, waiting for the other shoe to drop.

"I am giving Mr. Riordan everything he wants," Wan said. "But it is only a loan. Someday I will take it all back, along with everything else he has."

So that was it—a trap. And she was part of the cheese.

"I can't accompany him to America, you know that. He's married—"

"My sources in Vegas tell me that the marriage is, as the Americans put it, on the rocks. Besides, his marital status has nothing to do with his relationship with you."

"What is it you want me to do?"

"Nothing, my child, nothing but enjoy yourself. And obey my instructions. All financial matters will be put into your name; you will be my surrogate. Naturally, your stay in America will be limited by how long I need to have my plan succeed. Then you will return here, to your home, your family. As your benefactor, your guardian, the master of your soul, you will pine until I send for you, but send for you I will." He slurped noodles and then looked up at her, juice dribbling down his chin again. "I would be greatly disappointed if you failed to follow my instructions while you are away from me. You understand that I expect all my sons and daughters to be absolutely loyal to me. You have such loyalty, don't you?"

"Of course."

"Good, good." He wiped his chin. "Ah, yes, Ming, please give me another napkin."

A-Ma recognized the name. The young woman nicknamed "Ming" was a dealer at Mr. Wan's casino. A-Ma gasped as Ming used her left hand to hand Wan a napkin. Her right hand was missing. The stump was nearly covered by her long sleeves, but A-Ma could see that it was still bandaged.

Wan padded his lips with the napkin and locked eyes with A-Ma.

"As you can see, Ming can no longer deal cards at the casino. I have taken pity on her and permit her to serve me in the household. Is that not the case, Ming?"

Ming lowered her eyes. "Yes."

"It's unfortunate," Wan said, "some of my money had found its way into her hand while she worked in the casino. The hand that offended is now gone."

A brain syndrome developed when someone took too many drugs. During her time in L.A., Janelle had gotten down and dirty with users and saw the effect of long-term use on them. After years of use, more and more brain connections ceased to work. People didn't just stop thinking straight, they developed a skewed view of the world. The drugs did a frontal lobotomy on their emotions. People who normally wouldn't harm the proverbial flea stared blank-faced at convenience store clerks as they fired .38 rounds into them for the price of a fix. She called the syndrome "fried brains."

Bic Halliday wasn't down to the 7-Eleven till-tap mentality, but he definitely was experiencing fried brains. Having an in-house drug supplier had sped up the deterioration. Janelle had taken Bic out of the mainstream, keeping him coddled in her arms with bigger and purer doses of heroin.

"Know where heroin comes from?" she asked Diego, when he arrived at the ranch with a preacher and a supply of the drug.

"Yeah, I got a contact—"

"No, not how you sneak it into the country, how they grow the stuff."

"They grow heroin? No shit?"

"No shit. It comes from the poppy flower. They make morphine from the flower and make heroin from morphine. I read it in the encyclopedia. I've been stuck out on this goddamn godforsaken ranch for so long, I got desperate enough to read something."

"You'll be out of here soon, babe. I brought preacher man here to do his thing with you and Bic. He can notarize documents, too."

Bic was in the bedroom asleep. He spent much of his time sleeping now. She no longer gave him cocaine or crank—he was now strictly a heroin addict, the big leagues. Bic was isolated now at the ranch, and she kept him drugged and under her control. Life for him had now come down to long periods of sleep with short periods of ecstatic moments awake. After he would come out of a deep sleep, she would give him an intravenous injection of heroin that spread a warm, glowing sensation over his body. He'd grin like the Cheshire cat when the rush hit him. Then he'd go into a drowsy state of relaxation before falling into a deep sleep.

His tolerance for the drug quickly built up and she had to give him more and more injections to keep him in the revolving state of quiet ecstasy and sleep. Heroin was usually diluted from two to five percent purity and she had avoided increasing the purity of the drug, preferring to give him more injections. She had her own reasons for not building up his tolerance for higher purity.

She was using more and more drugs herself. Having a big supply available and preparing the drugs for Bic helped feed her own habit. Down deep she knew that the drugs were affecting her judgment, but all that mattered was the glorious kick she got when she took a hit.

"Did you get the papers signed?" Diego asked.

"Right here." Janelle handed him a marriage form and a will. "We need to finish off the will with witnesses and a notary."

"Preacher here is a notary. He can also witness the will. I'll witness it, too."

"Preacher" was a typical Hollywood Boulevard scumbag, Janelle decided. He had a soiled look—not physical dirt, but the type of veneer people get when they've spent most of their adult lives as trash hanging out with trash. She didn't doubt he had some sort of real credential as a preacher man; Diego was a smart businessman—he wouldn't screw up by using a phony, not with so much at stake.

Preacher stood at the door to the bedroom and stared at Bic. Bic was sleeping soundly.

"This is highly unusual," Preacher said.

"That's why you're getting paid plenty," Diego said.

"Well, I've thought about that. I agreed to perform the marriage and apply my notary stamp. Now you want me to witness the will. I'm going to need another ten thousand dollars."

"Fuck you," Janelle said.

"Now, let's not get excited," Diego said. "Preacher's performing some real deep shit here and there's plenty to go around. I don't see anything wrong with kicking it up a notch. I agreed on ten and now we'll make it twenty. It's as simple as that."

Diego pulled Janelle aside as she started cussing again.

"You're going to let that pig take us—"

"Quiet, babe. You think I'd trust that turd with millions of dollars at stake? There's a couple hundred miles of desert back to L.A. He's going to disappear somewhere along the way. Ever heard that old American expression 'Loose lips sink ships?' Babe, dead lips don't say nothing."

She kissed Diego. "You're a genius."

"Yeah, that's why I get the big dinero. Don't forget who set this up. There's plenty of room in the desert for one more."

She grabbed his crotch. "If you kill me, bury me with this in my mouth."

"You have any problems getting your friend's signatures on the will?"

"None. I told him he was signing a letter to his lawyer to sue Zack Riordan for his interest in the casino. He'd sign the Declaration of Independence if I told him it would screw Zack."

"This is the royal palace, encased by the Great Wall of China, and mounted on the Great Wall is a Red Dragon roller coaster. It will be the fastest and scariest roller coaster in the world," I told the fifteen bankers and state and federal officials assembled in my Strip conference room. As I spoke, I pointed out the features on a five-by-five-foot model of Forbidden City.

We were in a fifth-floor conference room of my temporary headquarters, which was an old casino-hotel I had bought next door to where my super casino was being built. I needed a place to train the employees of the new casino, and having a real operation for the staff of thousands, from chefs and dealers to maids and security, worked out great.

When the super casino was finished, I planned to knock the old club down and make it part of the parking lot. A-Ma and I had taken up residence in a suite on the tenth floor of the old building. Like the conference room, the suite overlooked the building project.

There was caviar, goose pâté, hundred-dollar bottles of champagne, and thousand-dollar a night "show" girls on hand to sweeten the presentation. I imported the girls from Hong Kong to "entertain" backers and critics of the project. I introduced them as one of the Oriental acts that would play after the casino opened, but never got specific about what their routine would be. Naturally, these particular girls did their best moves in bed.

A hundred yards from where we stood in my temporary headquarters, the actual casino was rising in the desert. I was overbudget, but that was inevitable for a project this size. But I had to keep the bankers onboard and the regulatory people off my back to stay afloat.

"As you might have read, I got the inspiration for the casino's Chinese imperial theme from a visit I made to China with Ms. A-Ma." I told myself they better have read it; it cost me plenty to have the most expensive PR agency in the country plant that and a dozen other stories about the project. "I visited Beijing with Ms. A-Ma six months ago when she was filming in the Far East, and I marveled at the artistic beauty of the former imperial complex called the Forbidden City and the summer palace outside the city. I trekked on the Great Wall, the over four-thousand-mile-long fortification the Chinese called *Wanli changcheng*, the Ten Thousand Li Wall. Li is an ancient Chinese measurement like miles and meters."

Hot damn, was I full of culture and knowledge. I almost was tempted to tell them about the Gesar of Ling and the Opium Wars, but reined in my enthusiasm to show off. One thing I learned the hard way in my hustling days, never talk past the close—when you've hooked a sucker and you're reaching for his wallet, you stop selling and shut your mouth because you might say something that quenches the sale.

The casino model showed a tall, central building with pagoda roofs scaled after the imperial palace. The Great Wall, with periodic "forts," completely wrapped around the building. The elevated red dragon roller coaster used the wall as a track. It was a nice, compact design. When finished, it would be the size of a square block—Manhattan style. Stretching out from the backside of the casino were the carnival games and rides. On each side of the amusement park were parking lots.

The interior was laid out in paintings and smaller structures around the conference room. Exotic Chinese statues, works of art, and animals in a rain forest–like setting would be scattered throughout the exterior and interior of the casino. There were slot machines in Chinese themes; ceramic elephants; the emperor's terra-cotta army; a zoo with tigers, lions, elephants; the irresistible pandas as well as dragons; Chinese dancers; firecrackers; kites; and lots of lakes and ponds, with real Chinese junks and tough-looking pirates holding tourists for ransom. I wanted it to look authentic.

"Despite a couple of half-hearted previous attempts at a family-oriented casino, Forbidden City will be the first casino where parents can enjoy gambling while their children of all ages can have wholesome entertainment. We'll even have a daycare center for employees and guests." I beamed with social consciousness. "We have a three-thousand-room hotel, and for those guests who get tired of dumping their money into the casino, we have a complete retail shopping center they can make deposits at."

"That's what worries us most," an investment banker from New York said. "There's a lot of doubt that you can fill a three-thousand-room hotel in Vegas. That's a convention hotel scale, not a tourist venue."

"Nobody's done it because no one's tried it," I said, smiling to dull the sharp edge I was accused of using on idiots. "People said Bugsy Siegel was wrong when he wanted to put a two-hundred-room hotel on the Strip, that Walt Disney was crazy because no one would bring their kids thousands of miles to see Mickey and Donald, when the Mexicans started putting high-rise hotels along a sandbar called Cancún. Hey, come on, people, the fact that it's never been done only means that we'll make more money than anyone else ever did."

"You give people something they want, and they'll come," Betsy Meyers, my PR person said.

"What about all of the cost overruns—"

"You know, you get what you pay for. I've been criticized—"

"Zack, you've bought a solid-gold throne that once belonged to an emperor, a treasure that the Chinese government says was stolen during the Japanese invasion of China. And you've hauled in real Chinese junks, acquired a private passenger jet, and literally bought a zoo to rob their pandas—"

"Yeah, and I've got some five-thousand-square-foot VIP suites with Italian marble and gold fixtures. Every one knows what the Great Wall is, but did you know that some parts of it were built with such perfection that a single inch was a day's labor for several men? That's part of the perfection that will make Forbidden City the most talked about casino in the world."

"Wasn't that what got Bugsy Siegel a bullet in his eye?" a banker from Chicago asked. "Perfectionism?"

"Is that a hint about what you people are going to do to me if we're not in the black pretty soon?" I asked.

I was pretty proud of the way I had spent tens of millions of dollars to get real antiques and fixtures. My looting of Oriental art and antiquities had been compared to the rape of European works done by William Randolph Hearst nearly a century ago.

Betsy slipped beside me. "You're starting to show your irritation.

Back away while I work the room. You're like a man with a chip on his shoulder who's been threading a sewing machine—while the machine's running."

Bill Peel, managing partner of Vegas's biggest law firm, the one I hired to represent the project, edged up to me.

"Those Oriental babes and the booze should do more to grease your relationship with the male bankers than your dog-and-pony show."

"I wish someone would grease my relationship with the governor. He refused to attend."

"He had a church meeting to attend. But I gave him your invitation for golf, dinner, and an overnight at your country club home. He's a funny guy, you know: the governor of the most corrupt state in the nation, if you don't count New Jersey as part of America, and the man acts like he's one of the Puritan fathers."

"If you ask me, he acts like a guy who hasn't gotten laid enough. Men get real mean when they've been horny for so long their dicks have shriveled."

"I wouldn't blame him," Peel whispered, "his wife makes Phyllis Diller look like a beauty queen. Not to change the subject, but have you given thought about the finance committee the bankers are asking for?"

"Yes and no. Yes I've given it thought and no they're not going to get it. They want to control the purse strings and choke me with them. Committees don't do things; they're designed not to make decisions until everything goes to hell. Haven't you heard that a giraffe is a horse made by a committee?"

"Wasn't that a camel?"

"Whatever it is, I'm not letting them turn Forbidden City into sushi. No committee."

"They're threatening—"

"Fuck their threats. I'm in so deep into their pocketbooks that they have to keep me afloat. It's bad enough I have to fight the unions, the building contractors, architects, engineers, inspectors—Jesus Christ, every day I have to wade in and punch it out—"

"I wish you'd make more of your fights verbal and less physical. That guy you hit and threw down a flight of stairs last week is hollering lawsuit."

"Let him. He was trying to extort money from me, telling me I'd have 'union troubles' if I didn't pay him off."

"Next time send him to me."

I let Peel intercept a guest who wanted reassurance about the project while I floated to the back wall with a drink. Betsy's remark about me threading a sewing machine that was running was right on the nose. That's how I felt since the project started. When I wasn't moving fast enough to thread the machine, I was stamping out fires with my bare feet. Deep down I had a sense of panic I had to keep smothered. Sometimes I'd wake up in the middle of the night and think, Christ, what a fool I was, to think that I could really pull this thing off, to go from a street kid running a Glitter Gulch grind joint to the biggest casino in the world. I realized I had some of Betty's fatalism in me—trying for the jackpot but knowing I'd never really get it. I had never realized that deep down I had some of that attitude. I had to fight it; I was running with wolves and if you showed any weakness, they turned and devoured you.

Watching Betsy and Peel work the room, I started to relax a little until a piece of ugly memory from my past strolled over—Charles Ricketts, the dump-truck deputy DA at the Kupka proceeding, who was now in charge of investigations for the state gaming control board. He was thrown out of the district attorney's office a few years after he dumped Betty's case because he blew a murder case. He was so bad at doing his job, he let a guy who chopped up his girlfriend's body and put her in a trash bag in the trunk of his car go free. Ricketts couldn't make it in private practice as a lawyer, even with a rich father-in-law, and ended up with the state job because his wife's father got elected to the state legislature.

I hadn't seen him since he sent me off to juvie after dumping my mother's case, but I was occasionally reminded of his existence in the local papers, though the only thing I wanted to read about him was his obituary.

Ricketts contacted me for an investigative interview after I applied for my gaming license for the super casino. I met with him in my attorney's office and let my attorney do all the talking. Last thing I wanted now was to talk to the guy, but Peel was too far across the room for me to shout for him to run interference. I had to be nice to the weasel because my gaming permit was hanging in the balance—but only on the surface. I knew he would try to tube me.

"Good to see you again, Zack."

"How ya been, Charles?"

"Fine, fine. We didn't get to talk about it last time, but did you know that that guy Kupka, the one who killed your mother, dropped out of sight some years ago?"

"No kidding."

"Yeah, must be ten, fifteen years ago, about the time I left the DA's office. Hell of a coincidence, you working at Halliday's, but Kupka had been last seen at Halliday's and probably headed back for his hotel room on the Strip, but never showed up. I heard he was drunk when he left Halliday's. My theory is that he grabbed a cab and the guy took him out into the desert and robbed and murdered him. But I was gone from the DA's office when he disappeared and no one asked for my opinion."

"Really." I hid my feeling behind a blank face and a glass of Jack Coke I rubbed my lower lip with to keep from sneering at the guy.

"You were working for Halliday's, weren't you, when Kupka disappeared?"

"I don't know, Charles. When exactly did the guy take a powder?"

"I'll have to check on the exact date. You know, of course, that I'm in charge of the investigation into your licensing application for the casino. I have to tell you, Zack, I have some real doubt about the viability of your financing."

"Ms. A-Ma has no criminal record. Period."

He shook his head. "The people she's associated with sound like the Chinese version of the FBI's Ten Most Wanted. I am afraid this application may need serious alteration before it will be approved."

I had two major hurdles to jump. The FBI investigation and the state gaming board investigation. I had spread "campaign contributions" to every state, congressional, and senatorial member who could apply juice. Only twenty percent of the total package for the casino came through A-Ma and Mr. Wan's other sources, and not a dime of that had dirt on it. And if it did, it was buried so deep in international corporate transactions that it would take years to uncover it. My problem was that Mr. Wan was in the state's black book as prohibited from entering a Nevada casino. The gaming board had the authority to proscribe anyone who even breathed close to someone in the black book.

In other words, a weasel like Ricketts could put in a bad report on A-Ma based upon guilt by association and my license could be denied without an iota of hard evidence. If not denied outright, the proceedings could keep me tied up fighting a legal battle until my banks and investment angels took a hike. Ricketts was also making a not so subtle threat about Kupka. I knew he wouldn't be able to piece together anything after all these years, but if it was a close call on my license, the gaming board could be influenced by rumor and innuendo. So could the herd of sheep in the other room. If the going really got tough, there was a contractual clause that allowed the bankers and investors to form an "advisory committee" I had managed to sidestep up to now.

I grinned at Ricketts. "I don't know where you're getting information that A-Ma has criminals hanging around her. My understanding is that around Hong Kong and Macao, they compare her to Mother Teresa."

"I want that bastard burned. I don't care what it costs," I said.

Jack Moody, an investigator on my payroll, nodded. "So you've told me."

I tapped Moody on the chest. "I want Ricketts destroyed. I want his house burned down and salt sowed into the earth where it stood, his car blown up . . . I want him robbed of every cent he owns. I want his wife turned out onto the streets to hook, his kids sent to an orphanage, his arms and legs cut off . . . I want him castrated, his tongue ripped out. You get the idea?"

"You don't like this guy big time?"

"You're getting the idea."

Moody was a former Vegas police detective, the best they ever had, a cop who worked both homicide and vice. I was lucky he was never assigned the Kupka disappearance. He knew every bad actor in the town and had put a lot of them away. After he retired, he set up his own detective agency and I used him for lightweight stuff at Halliday's, mostly doing background checks on employees or investigating thefts. I liked him and kept him on retainer when I became Halliday's manager because I knew I'd need him for a big one someday. From the moment I started the Forbidden City project, I put Moody to work doing background checks on everyone who could affect the project, from investment bankers and architects to FBI agents involved in investigating my background and sources. Information from the brand of booze they drank to who was cheating on their spouse came in handy. The worst people I had to deal with were the county building inspectors, and Moody had done a terrific profile on each of them, letting me know which ones could be had—for love or money.

When Charles Ricketts came back into my life, Moody was the first person I turned to. He also had a bone to pick with Ricketts—he was the investigating officer on the body-in-the-trunk case Ricketts blew.

After he blew the trial, Ricketts lied to the news media about why the case went to hell in the courtroom, claiming that Moody and his partner hadn't put together a viable case. The accusation came at a critical time for a promotion and someone else got the job Moody wanted.

"The goddamn body was found chopped up into pieces, stuffed into a plastic garbage bag, and then into the trunk of the defendant's car. Did Ricketts need a video of the creep swinging the ax to get a conviction?" Moody growled, the first time I met him.

I met with Moody the same evening Ricketts bragged he was going to take me down through A-Ma. We were in my penthouse office overlooking the construction site. I got up from my desk and walked to the window, looking down at the work being done by the night crew on the project.

"I told you about Betty, how the jerk dumped her case. I know Ricketts gave you grief, too. Now he's as good as told me that he's going to keep me from getting my license. If this gets out to the bankers, they'll pull the plug and let me wash down the drain."

"You really want to see Ricketts completely ruined? I mean, so bad nobody would talk to the guy or listen to him?"

"Do chickens have lips?"

"I don't know. Do they?"

"There's a couple Chinese expressions that pop into my mind when I think about Ricketts. One is that with a single monkey in the way, ten thousand men cannot pass. I want the monkey out of the way. What do you have in mind?"

"Well, when I ran a check on him for you, I came across an allegation dating back to the time when he was a deputy DA. Back in those days he ran a youth program at the church he and his wife attended, taking fatherless boys out fishing and camping, that sort of thing. One of the mothers made a stink about Ricketts sharing a bed with her teenage son during a camp-out."

"He molested the kid?"

"The kid said Ricketts's hand fell on his groin area while Ricketts was supposed to be asleep. The kid was mature enough to remove the hand. Nothing really came from the allegation; dirt can get swept under the rug pretty easy in this town if you have any juice. His father-in-law has run interference for Ricketts for years, but now that

Ricketts is on the outs with the man's daughter, you can bet he might join a parade to tube Ricketts."

"Let's find the kid and make it public."

"It's ancient history. I have a different idea. Before I retired, I busted a male prostitute known as Sonny Boy on a morals charge. You might not remember him, he worked the Strip after you took that slug in the back of Halliday's. After I busted him every time he spit on the sidewalk, he finally left town and set up shop on Sunset Strip in Los Angeles, got discovered by a blue movie producer, and became a top porn star because of a unique trait."

"Which is?"

"He has the longest pecker in the world. Twelve, fourteen inches, something incredible. He couldn't act worth a damn, but who has to act in a porn flick? He's out of work because word's spread that he has a particularly virulent social disease."

"So what's all this got to do with Ricketts?"

"Sonny Boy was once a jock, the horse-racing variety. He's small built, kind of delicate looking, can pass for a teenager when he dresses right. I spent a couple decades dealing with chicken hawks; I know how they think and operate. I'm sure Ricketts is one. If he hasn't already gone over the line, he's primed for it. His marriage is breaking up, his wife's filed divorce papers and gotten a restraining order kicking him out of the house, and being a screwup, if it wasn't for his father-in-law, he would have been shit-canned from his state job a long time ago."

It never occurred to me that Ricketts could be a chicken hawk, an older man who preys on young boys. I thought back to when he was handling my mother's murder case. He hadn't tried to put the make on me, but we were never alone, either.

"Sonny has an innocent, boyish, Boy Scout look that turns on chicken hawks," Moody said. "And he's got a trained penis that snaps to attention on command."

"Spare me the details. Just nail the bastard."

Moody paused at the door. "You didn't tell me what that second old Chinese saying was."

"It's good to execute some people as an example for others."

A-Ma had imported a slut from Hong Kong who looked so young and innocent, I immediately nicknamed her "Sonny Girl."

"Where did you find her?" I asked A-Ma.

"Hong Kong is a small place. Every woman of beauty in the colony is being paid for sex, sometimes in marriage, but usually not."

"She's perfect. I wouldn't mind molesting her myself."

"If you do, I will make sure you have a new nickname, too."

"Which is?"

"Eunuch."

The governor was spending the night at the country club house that Morgan and I once shared. His wife was back in Atlanta at a church convention. It took a fat campaign contribution to get the governor to come down and spend the evening talking about the Forbidden City project. The man was noted for being Mr. Clean, a churchgoing, loving husband and father without a spot on his record. But Moody had an instinct for perverts.

"Remember those bumper stickers that said an orderly desk is the sign of a disorderly mind? Truer words were never spoken. The moral is, never trust someone who looks too clean. All this good churchgoer stuff is pure corn. You can't make it in politics without being a glad-handing phony. We know what the governor is—the question is, how do we get him to reveal it."

I had just the bait—Sonny Girl.

I had to turn the governor around. Ricketts was trying to blacken my name with the gaming board in Carson City, describing me as a former street hustler and A-Ma as a gangster's moll. A joke was going around that "Bugsy and Virginia" were back in town. I had to turn off the heat from Ricketts and get the governor on my side, or turn over control to the investors. If I aced out, the project would fall flat on its face. The owners of one of the other clubs would buy in and end up building my casino.

"So good to see you, Governor." I welcomed him at the front door of the country club house. I had the house opened so we could hit balls after dinner. His driver carried an overnight bag for him. "I've arranged a room at Ceasar's for your driver, if that's all right."

"Fine. Joseph, I'll call you when I need you."

Inside, A-Ma and Sonny Girl were lined up as the reception committee. The governor was short, about five-six, and heavy built but not plump. He wore a conservative gray suit with an American flag pin in his lapel and a plain black tie that would be perfect for funerals.

"May I present A-Ma, and her cousin, Kim."

Sonny Girl's name was unpronounceable to an Occidental. After hearing the unpronounceable gibberish, I gave her a new name—Kim. I didn't care if it was Chinese, male or female. I just figured the governor would be able to pronounce it. And I gave her a family relationship: she was A-Ma's cousin, a college girl supporting her younger siblings while she went to school. A-Ma thought there was too much b.s. in the description, but I liked it.

"I have heard many things about you, A-Ma."

There was no clue in the governor's words as to what he had heard, but I didn't need a lie detector attached to the guy to know that some of those "many things" were dirt from Ricketts and the feds. As I introduced him to the two women, I watched his eyes, looking for the telltale widening of his pupils that signaled his interest in the two women, but he just squinted at them. I figured he must be nearsighted and too vain to wear glasses. Or probably took a poll and found out that 51.5 percent of the people liked him better without glasses.

The most expensive restaurant planned for Forbidden City, to be located at the top of the complex, was going to be a gourmet joint that would please an emperor of China. I imported the chef from Hong Kong and set him up with an experimental kitchen in the old casino-hotel we were using for training so he could refine his magic until the casino opened.

I had the Chinese gourmet genius prepare our dinner meal and brought him out from the kitchen to meet the governor, who graciously stood up and did a lot of bowing and muttered some greeting in Chinese. It didn't surprise me that a seasoned politician knew enough Chinese to say hello—he could probably speak the devil's language if the need arose.

Dinner began with all of us holding hands while the governor said a prayer of thanks. It was the first dinner prayer I had ever participated in, ditto I'm sure for A-Ma and cousin Kim. When the meal was finished, we took our after-dinner drinks out to the balcony that overlooked the golf course. He asked for lemonade, to which I added gin.

"My cousin is attending college in Hong Kong," A-Ma said.

"What are you majoring in, Kim?"

"Massage."

I almost croaked.

"She means physical therapy," A-Ma said. She rattled off something in Chinese to her "cousin."

"Yes," Kim said, with her broken English, "physical therapy. I work with people injured in accidents or have strokes."

"That's a very public-spirited occupation, my dear. You should be very proud."

After dinner I had floodlights turned on to the ninth hole and accompanied the governor out to hit balls. I was a lousy golfer, actually I hated playing golf, but letting the governor show his stuff was good politicking.

"I have to confess, Zack, I am one of your big fans."

"Thank you, Governor."

Cagy bastard. What he really meant was that there were people who didn't like me.

"My concern, as governor, is that the project you've launched will be managed in a way that will benefit the state and not create any black marks." He hit a ball down the fairway. "You know, of course, that the focus of the inquiry is A-Ma's background. It took decades for us to remove the stranglehold organized crime had on the state. We don't want to stick our heads in a noose again, this time with undesirables from the Far East."

"I share the same concern. That's why eighty percent of the money for the project comes from good old USA bankers and investors."

"But those people are just money managers. You and I both know it's the person who controls that other twenty percent that will run the operation."

"I control it. A-Ma only provided loans."

"I don't really want to get into the particulars, Zack, that's for the gaming board. But I have heard that A-Ma has been associated with one of the most notorious triad mobsters."

"Macao and Hong Kong are small places. Together they aren't the physical size of most Nevada counties. There's no question A-Ma knows and has associated with people at all levels of society there. But A-Ma has no criminal record—she's kept her nose clean. Frankly, governor, the way I see it, a small group of jealous casino owners are going after me and A-Ma because I'm taking Vegas into a whole new era." I dropped my voice, even though the only other creature I saw on the golf course was a coyote moseying by. "To be honest with you, I think there's racial prejudice and gender prejudice involved in the attacks on A-Ma."

I could see that one got to him. We lived in a time in which people of color were demanding equal rights and women were slugging it out with the Old Boys' network.

Back inside the house, he drank another "hard" lemonade before his eyes started drooping and he announced he needed to hit the bed.

"It didn't work," I told A-Ma after she escorted the governor to his room. "He hardly looked at Kim all night. And there's another problem. Moody got a peek at his medical history. He's had a problem with being impotent."

"Don't give up hope yet. He is a smart politician with one face for the public and another in private. Perhaps Kim is exactly the therapy he needs to cure his impotency."

Governor King heard a noise coming from his bathroom as he started to get into bed. Wearing his pajamas, he padded across the deep carpeting in his bare feet to the bathroom. He had been given the master suite and the bathroom was one of several doors leading from the bedroom. Set in white marble with black trim and solid-gold fixtures, the pièce de résistance in the room was a sunken circular spa tub.

The governor followed the splashing noise to the spa tub around the corner.

Kim looked up from the tub. "Ohhh."

"Young lady, what are you doing in here?"

"I am so sorry, I must have come into the wrong room."

"No, I don't think so. I think you know exactly what you're doing, sneaking into my bathroom like this. You can tell Riordan that he's washed his casino license down the drain." He stamped back into the bedroom and started dressing.

As he dressed he heard soft sobbing in the bathroom. His pants were open to put in his shirt when Kim came out of the bathroom. She stopped at the door, her eyes full of tears.

"I am sorry. You don't understand." She pointed back at the bathroom. "My room is next door; this is the bathroom for it."

He stood in the middle of the room and stared at one of the other doors. He rushed to it and opened it. Another bathroom. There were two bathrooms in the large bedroom.

She went back into the bathroom and sat down with her legs in the tub and continued to cry softly.

The governor came in behind her and checked out the room. She was right: There was a door to another bedroom. The second bathroom could be used by the master suite or by the second bedroom. And a couple with separate bedrooms could gain access to each bedroom through the connecting bathroom. He and his wife had a similar arrangement because they had separate bedrooms.

The girl would not look him in the face. She had a towel wrapped around her shoulders that modestly draped down and covered the top of her legs.

"I am in trouble," Kim said. "I made a mistake and now my cousin will not help me and my family. I have dishonored my family."

"Oh, of course you haven't. Anyone could make the mistake."

"No, it is my fault. I am a terrible person." As she lifted the towel to wipe her eyes, the dark hair between her legs was exposed. He experienced a jolt in his mid area when he saw it.

"It's not your fault," he said.

"No, I have dishonored my cousin and my family." She turned her head from him. The towel slipped away from one of her breasts. He stared at it like a thirsty man stumbling onto an oasis. It had been more years than he could count since he had seen a woman's breasts. He and his wife had had separate bedrooms for a decade and years before that since they had their last marital relations.

"I should kill myself."

She threw herself into the water and went under.

"No, Christ!" He slipped into the water still wearing his pants and grabbed her. She came up naked in his arms, struggling against him. In the struggle his pants slipped down and his penis slipped out of the opening in his boxer shorts.

She leaned her head against his chest and put one arm around him. Taking his penis in her other hand, she gently stroked it. Smiling to herself, she thought about the bonus Zack had promised her if she did her job well. The governor's penis was hard. While Zack had been spicing his lemonade with liquor, she and A-Ma had poured in enough Chinese herbal remedy for impotence to get a horse aroused.

I awoke in the middle of the night to find A-Ma gone from bed. She was curled up on a window seat, naked underneath the robe over her shoulders. A full moon lit up the golf course. Hopefully the governor was asleep in the master bedroom—with Kim in his arms.

I went to her. "Can't sleep?"

"No," she said, "I awoke when I heard a dog barking. I saw two dogs out the window, skinny yellow ones."

"Coyotes, wild dogs. They come around at night looking to make a cat their meal. You probably heard a neighbor's dog who smelled them."

"Dog eat dog, isn't that what you Americans say about the world?"

I kissed her on the cheek, the nose, and slipped down to brush her lips with mine. "What's the matter?"

She pulled her robe tighter. "I saw my own death."

"What do you mean, you saw your own death?"

"I dreamt that I had died and was in a coffin."

"Oh, Jesus. Look, forget that crap. We all do that sometimes. It's probably something you ate."

"A messenger came when you were playing golf with the governor. He delivered financial papers, transferring more money for the project. I signed the papers and sent them on to the bank."

I stroked her hair. "You own me body and soul."

She pushed my hand away. "I own nothing, not even my own soul; it belongs to the devil. You were a fool to get involved with Wan, I told you that. He knows how to twist things to suit himself."

"I'm not afraid of Wan."

"You should be. He tried to kill you once; he will do it again."

"Maybe it was my death you dreamt about."

She turned her head away and stared out at the golf course lit up by moonlight. "Promise me that if I die, you will not let them bury me during ghost month."

"What are you talking about?"

"The time of year you call August is ghost month, when the ghosts from hell walk the earth. It's a dangerous time to be outside, to travel, or even get married or buy a house. To keep the ghosts in hell from taking my soul, you cannot bury me during August." She grabbed my arm. "When I die, I want to return to the water, to the place were we made love the first time."

"Christ, A-Ma, don't talk like that, you're going to outlive me. Hell, I'm the one everyone hates. Come on, let's go back to bed."

John Bevard stared at his son-in-law across the conference room table and wondered what it would be like to sink his fist into the man's mouth. John was the old-fashioned kind: The owner of the state's biggest fleet of long-distance eighteen wheelers, he had to use his fists more than once on a driver—or a competitor—who treaded on his toes. When he went into politics, he carried the same pugilistic philosophy into the state legislature.

Why his daughter married Charles Ricketts had been one of the great mysteries of his life. But Ginger had never been a rocket scientist when it came to men. Ricketts knocked her up and John spent the last twenty years making sure Ginger and his grandchildren had a roof over their head and putting up with a son-in-law that he frankly disliked. As a man who worked for everything he got, he didn't respect a man like Ricketts who coasted through life on someone else's coattails. But the worse sin Ricketts had committed was hitting Ginger. Every time he looked at his daughter and saw the swelling around her right eye he had to resist the urge to punch out Ricketts.

Everything about Ricketts annoyed him. Over the years, his son-in-law had become more and more compulsive about his behavior, driving his wife and kids nuts with demands that everything be neat and in precise order. Crazy bastard went wacko because one of the children had moved a lamp while playing a game. Dishes could not be stacked on the kitchen sink for two minutes without him going into convulsions. Ginger told him that there was something sexual about Ricketts's compulsions, that she thought that whenever he got excited about something being out of place, he'd run into the bathroom and jack off.

"Dad, I want you to know that in ordinary circumstances, I'd want everything to go to Ginger and the kids," Ricketts said. "But I do need a little of the family assets to help me get a fresh start."

John scoffed. "What you call the 'family assets' came out of my wallet. I bought the house you live in, your Tahoe cabin, the trust funds for the kids, the whole shebang. You've blown your salary for years on gambling and fucking around behind my daughter's back."

"Dad, I really don't think—"

"If that isn't the truth."

Ricketts's lawyer cleared his throat. "Mr. Bevard, we should keep this on a professional level. We're here to work out a property division so the divorce can go through without a hitch and these two wonderful people can get on with their lives."

"There is no goddamn property to divide because all they have is what I gave them. You're here to extort money from me to keep my daughter's loser husband from harassing her."

Ginger started crying.

"Stop that goddamn sniveling. I'm going to buy you a divorce just like I bought you a marriage. Only next time you get married, find a man who can keep a job without me running interference."

Charles Ricketts came out of the Fremont Street office building that housed his father-in-law's office. Outside the building, he parted with his lawyer, who headed back to his office down the street while Ricketts went around the corner to the parking lot where he had left his car.

He thought about the meeting with his wife and father-in-law. The old man's barbed remarks didn't bother him; he was more interested in getting a chunk of money than he was in saving his pride. And he'd be damn happy to get away from that whining bitch. Bevard thought he knew everything; yeah, he could run him into the ground, but the man never said a word about the fact his daughter was an alky— except to claim that Ricketts drove her to it.

The big beef with his father-in-law was that he made his wife's life hell. So what, she deserved it. The woman claimed to have had a headache every day since their wedding. Chopping off her head would have cured that. Along with that self-righteous prick of a father. Neither his wife, kids, nor father-in-law understood him or realized what he had gone through in life. His parents had gotten divorced when he was fifteen and neither one wanted him. He ended up being raised by a grandmother who was too old and too regimented in her ways to be raising a teenager.

When he came around the corner, a kid in shorts and a tank top was sitting on the hood of his car.

"Get off my car, goddamnit."

The kid hopped off. "Jeez, I'm really sorry, mister, I didn't mean no harm."

Ricketts examined the hood to see if it was scratched. He was very particular about keeping his two-year-old car in showroom conditions. Just last week he sued the gardener who cut his front lawn for turning on the sprinklers and getting water stains on the car on a hot day.

"Is it okay, sir?" the boy asked.

"You should have more respect for people's property."

"You're right, sir, I should have. And it's a really nice car. It's just that I've had things on my mind. Troubles."

Ricketts took a good look at the kid for the first time. He was small built, almost delicate and feminine. Lazy blond hair fell down his forehead to just about blue eyes. His skin was pale and smooth, without the acne that young people tend to get ravaged by. The boy had a helpless look.

"What kind of trouble do you have? Are you a runaway?"

"No, but my parents broke up and things are tough."

"What'd you mean by tough?"

"Aw, it's nothing. I have to live with my grandmother. She's okay, but now she's off visiting my aunt in Frisco and I'm all alone."

Ricketts shook his head. "That's weird."

"Weird?"

"Same thing happened to me when I was a kid. And I hated the old lady who raised me. She took me in so I could wait on her and take care of her house."

"Hey, man, that's the scoop with my grandmother. She's gonna be gone for three days and she gave me a list of things to do that'll keep me busy for a month. Say, you're not going toward Decatur, are you? I need a ride home."

"As a matter of fact, I am. Hop in."

The boy picked his gym bag off the ground and went around to the other side of the car to get in. As Ricketts got the car started, he asked, "What's your name?"

"They call me Sonny."

When they were half a block from Mel's Drive-in, Sonny said, "I've got five dollars. Can I buy you a hamburger for the ride?"

"I'll buy."

While Ricketts was giving their order to the car hop, Sonny secretly turned on a tape recorder in his gym bag.

"What kind of work do you do?" he asked Ricketts. "I'll bet you're a lawyer?"

"How'd you know?"

"You got that distinguished look lawyers have. I knew a lawyer once, a big criminal lawyer in L.A., a friend of my dad's, and he had that same look."

"I used to be a criminal lawyer, but right now I'm in charge of investigations for the state gaming board."

"Wow, that sounds cool. Who do you investigate?"

As they spoke, Ricketts noticed that a bulge had appeared in the crotch of Sonny's tight shorts and was slowly spreading down his thigh.

"Who? Uh, well, just about everyone. Any accusation about cheating or organized crime or other undesirables." His mouth had suddenly turned dry. He wanted to take his eyes off of the phenomenon, but was drawn to it.

"No kidding. If someone wanted a license to run a casino, they'd have to ask you?"

"Well, not really ask me, but they'd have to get my approval."

"How does that work?"

"You know about the new casino that's going up, the biggest one in the world?"

"Yeah, I think so. My grandmother said a big one was being built."

"Before that casino can operate, the person or entity licensed to run it has to pass my investigation."

"No kidding, you're that important?"

The sausage-shape on the inside of Sonny's thigh had to be a foot long, Ricketts thought. He took a drink of the Coke he had ordered and tried again not to stare at it, but keep glancing back at it. "I guess I'm important," he said.

"Give me an example, like how do you decide whether to grant a license or not."

"I investigate the people involved, their backgrounds, sources of their money, their associates and family. I have investigators and we get reports from the FBI, DEA, and even the IRS."

"I guess that guy asking for the license for the big casino is a shoo-in, huh? My grandmother says he's the most important guy in Vegas."

"Your grandmother's wrong on two counts; I'm the most important person in Vegas, and Riordan's not getting a license."

Sonny gave out a girlish giggle and reached over and squeezed Ricketts's thigh. A jolt went through Ricketts at the touch. He was getting warm and he squirmed uncomfortably on the seat. He had the urge to get out of the car and run into the restroom to masturbate.

"Can you really keep this guy named Riordan from getting a license?"

"I sure as hell can and I'm going to."

"I suppose it's really just a matter of him qualifying, huh. You don't really make the decision yourself?"

"You damn right I make the decision. Riordan and me go back a long ways. He pissed me off once, but I keep a professional attitude about it." His grin told Sonny that the "professional attitude" is poison for Riordan.

"What'd the guy do? Cheat you?"

"He insulted me twenty years ago. He was just a kid at the time, about your age, so I couldn't do anything about it, but I don't forget and don't forgive." He got cautious again. "But like I said, I won't let it affect my decision about the license."

"I'm getting excited being here with you," Sonny Boy said. His voice was low and husky. He took Ricketts's hand and put it on his erection, squeezing the hand against his cock.

Ricketts froze with the dick in his hand. He couldn't speak.

"Could we just go to my grandmother's house and talk?" Sonny asked. "I have to be alone with you or I'll die."

"Turn it off," Zack said.

Moody stopped the audiotape of Ricketts and Sonny in the car. Zack refused to view them naked in "Grandma's" house.

"Hell," Moody said, "we're just getting to the good parts. By the time he's fucking Sonny in the ass, he's bragging how he's going to deny your license just to spite you. He just couldn't help bragging."

"Disgusting bastard," Zack said.

"Which one?"

"Both. I have no pity for Ricketts; he's a cocksucker—literally—but I don't like handling the dirt."

"That's why I get the big bucks. You'll understand the true meaning of that phrase when you get my bill for this. There's nothing cheap about Sonny but his morals."

Whatever the price was, it was cheap. Ricketts would have cost him control of the casino. And it was the closing bell on the betrayal of Betty by the justice system.

"Send the tapes to the gaming board—anonymously, of course. They wouldn't dare refuse me a license after hearing that their chief investigator had set out to shaft me. And, hey, didn't you tell me Ricketts was involved in a nasty divorce? Send it to his wife. No, to Bevard, his father-in-law. The old man will know how to use it."

"Jesus, Zack, you are a vindictive bastard, aren't you."

"Ricketts is paying for his sins. I'm just God's messenger."

"You still have a problem with Dirkson."

Dirkson was the agent-in-charge of the local FBI office and supervised the federal investigation into Zack's and A-Ma's backgrounds. He was less dangerous than Ricketts because his recommendations didn't carry the weight of an in-house probe. The gaming board was chafing under recent criticism from Dirkson and wasn't in a mood to tow the line with the feds. But Dirkson was critically important in linking A-Ma with organized crime figures in the Far East.

"I got to know Dirkson well when I was working homicide. He's never won any popularity contests at the agency. More than one agent left the agency to get away from the guy. I had a couple of his old 'buddies' come into town last week, a man and woman who left to take high-paying jobs with a Wall Street firm that investigates billion-dollar mergers. They got Dirkson on tape using the 'C' word, 'N' word, and 'K' word."

"Which are?"

"Dirkson said he'd rather see 'chinks' with a big club in Vegas than 'niggers,' who'd call their club Uncle Tom's Cabin. And either would be better than the kike mafia that runs the town."

"How'd you do it? How did you know that Dirkson has a racist streak?"

"You know, Zack, sizing up people is no different than sizing up a crime scene. You collect *everything* and put it all under a microscope. FBI agents are uptight jerks in love with their own press-kit image. But they're human, right? In Dirkson's case, he served in Vietnam. When we worked together on a Vietnamese version of Murder, Inc., he called the suspects 'gooks' when he had a couple drinks in him. Booze, loose lips, racial slurs—when I called the two Wall Street operatives they both confirmed Dirkson was a closet racist."

Moody tapped on the surveillance evidence against Ricketts. "I want a bonus for this work."

"You'll get it."

"A million."

"Excuse me?"

"I saved your whole project."

"Moody, you saved nothing. I would have gotten Ricketts one way or another, with or without you." I slapped him on the shoulder. "Hey, look, pal, you did a great job, you'll get a fat bonus, but I'm not making you one of the family."

After Moody left, I gave some thought to him. I liked Moody; he was good. But he jacked me up for money every time he sneezed. He had a greedy streak in him. I wondered if I would have trouble with him someday.

71

Morgan examined her nude body in front of the mirror at her Martha's Vineyard home. Not bad, she thought, for a thirty-something-old woman with two young children. Her breasts were not the store-bought variety. They had miraculously sprouted toward the end of her adolescence when she also added an inch to her height and mellowed out the girlish curves down her side and rear profiles. She didn't have the exotic sensuality of A-Ma, but "My body is better than yours, you little slut," she told the mirror in the absence of the movie star. Still damp from her bath, she toweled off and began the process of creams and powders that are such an aphrodisiac to the male of the species.

She was preparing herself for making love.

Propping a leg up on a low stool, she rubbed it with cream, working it in firmly, moving up from her ankles to her knee and inner and outer thighs, squeezing the softness of the thigh flesh in a manner her masseur said would help fight cellulite, the bane of women over thirty.

She had taken special care with her bathing because she wanted to make the night a special one for Todd. They lived together on the island, in a Cape Cod–style beach house she had purchased. He had a cottage that gave him privacy and she refused his help with family expenses, telling him to keep the small income he was making from his books that got good reviews but sold poorly. He had everything going for him but her love. She had been faking her orgasms since the day they met and she wasn't a good actress. He worked long and hard at their lovemaking, giving of himself, holding his own reward back to give her pleasure.

"You bastard," she told the mirror, talking this time to Zack. Todd was better looking, better mannered, a better husband and father. In fact, lined up against Zack Riordan, he looked like Mother Teresa compared to Jack the Ripper.

But she was still faking her orgasms.

"Bastard," she snarled. It was his fault. She had loved Zack since the first time she saw him, a cocky, rude, pushy street kid who walked around Halliday's like he owned the place and was ready to use his fists on anyone who gave him lip. "No sane woman would love you," she told the mirror. But she did. Loved him when he humiliated her after she threw herself at him when she was a teenager, when he impregnated her on her wedding day to another man, when he was lying helpless, breathing through a tube, after he'd been shot.

She had twice chosen men who were kinder, gentler, more sophisticated, and educated. And had to fake her orgasms because the only man who ever made her cream her pants was the bastard who used her as a doormat, cheated on her, married her for her money, and abandoned his children.

"What a fool." This time she spoke to her own reflection in the mirror.

How do you learn to hate someone who richly deserved it? Unconditional love was just psychobabble. Anyone who gives unconditional love without getting the same in return needs his or her head examined, which is exactly what she did—have her head examined. By her third session she was giving advice to her psychoanalyst, who was going through a messy divorce and child-custody battle and didn't know if she should go back and try again with her husband. "People don't change unless they want to," she told the analyst, mouthing a buzz phrase of the day. "You either have to accept him or find someone else with the qualities you want," she advised the woman. When the woman sent her a bill for the session, she scribbled *Physician heal thyself* across it and returned it without a check enclosed.

The hardest thing for her to accept was that she could feel so much for a man who didn't return her feelings. Love was a strange phenomenon. She had no idea why she loved Zack from the moment she saw him. But she had made one discovery about love: You didn't choose who you loved. Choosing implied rational behavior, and there was nothing rational about love. Logic and reason had nothing to do with love. Ask any one of the thousands of women whose husbands used them as punching bags, or the men whose wives took the gold mine and they got the shaft.

The only conclusion to reach from her behavior toward a man who used and abused her was that there was something wrong with her.

How else could it be explained? There was nothing wrong with Zack: He had everything he ever wanted, slept with whom he wanted, made babies he didn't plan to raise, and used her family's money to climb the dung heap. "He's one smart hombre," she said, "and you're one dumb bitch."

Todd fit his name, she decided. The only other Todd she ever heard of was a blond actor from the 1950s she saw in a beach movie video, and he fit the mode of the actor—tall and willowy, deceptively broad-shouldered, thin but muscular, hair like the tarnished gilt on the frames of old oil paintings, eyes cornflower blue. She relaxed him with three glasses of Chardonnay, thick juicy salmon steaks, grilled asparagus, scalloped potatoes, and a spinach–goat cheese salad.

She sent the kids off with their nanny on an overnight trip to a special showing of the circus in Boston so they would have the house entirely to themselves.

He sat back on the couch while she sat on the floor and slipped off his shoes. She put his feet in her lap and massaged them.

"God, that feels wonderful. Where did you learn how to do it?"

"My masseur does my feet better than the rest of my body. He claims that even though our feet occupy only a small part of our frames, they're packed with more bones and nerves than the rest of our body."

He leaned back and shut his eyes. "Hmmm, your masseur is right, I can feel it all the way up my body."

Morgan slowly worked her fingers up from the soles of his feet to his groin.

He was already getting aroused. "All you have to do is touch me and I get hard."

She unzipped his pants and pulled out his warm phallus. She bent over and licked it all over, then shoved it in her mouth and began sucking. He stopped her after a few minutes. "I want to be inside you," he said.

Todd picked her up and carried her into the bedroom and lay her on the bed. He undressed her, savoring the removal of each item of clothing, kissing each part of her body until she was completely naked. He buried his head in the bushy mound between her legs, teasing the folds of her vulva and her clit with his tongue and moving deep into her pink area. She drew his head from between her legs. "Put your cock in me," she said, and spread her legs until he was deep within her. Gripping his buttocks with her hands, she forced him harder and harder into her, moaning with pretended pleasure every time he made contact.

As he was making love to her, she thought about Zack. She fantasized that it was Zack who was inside her, remembering the first time they made love, almost giggling aloud that she let him take her like a bitch in heat on her wedding day. Thinking about Zack's hot tongue violating her mouth, caressing her breasts, his hard penis inside her, suddenly got her into rhythm with the man on top of her and she began to flow with his lovemaking. Electrified pleasure gripped her and her body grew excited without any pretense. Her mouth devoured his hungrily, her tongue frantically violating his mouth. Arching back her legs, she pulled him in deeper, her hard nipples rubbing against his chest. She screamed out his name when the orgasm came and raked his back with her nails as he pumped her body with a frenzy.

When it was over she lay quietly, soaking in the pleasure, in the relief and sheer delight. She had never experienced sex like that before. She reached over to touch him, to whisper words of endearment, but he rolled onto his side and turned his back to her. His skin was cold and tense to her touch.

"What's the matter?"

His was the cold voice from the grave, sending goose bumps crawling over her.

"My name is not Zack."

72

I came out of a dead sleep to the jarring ring of the phone next to my bed.

"Zack . . . it's Moody."

"Yeah."

"Bic's dead."

I heard the words but they didn't penetrate right away. A-Ma turned over in bed and asked me who it was, and I waved away the question. Finally I said, "How?"

"Overdose. I got a call from my former LVPD partner. He knew I was working for you. Nine-one-one got a call about two hours ago from his wife saying that he had taken a hit of heroin and was overdosing. He was DOA in the med center."

"What did you say?"

"DOA at—"

"No, no, you said 'his wife.' Bic's not married."

Moody was quiet for a moment. "I'm sure Nick said 'wife.' But he could be using the word generically, you know, that significant-other thing."

"Find out. Fast."

"Could be trouble?"

"With a capital 'T'. He had a drug slut named Janelle Troy hanging out with him. If she's Bic's wife, I can see trouble down the line."

"I thought I heard you say once that Morgan controls Bic's money."

"Morgan controls the trust, but if Bic dies leaving an heir, the money goes to the heir. It still has to remain in the trust, but when Bic threatened to break the trust, my lawyer told me he wouldn't be able to do it because of his history of being a spendthrift drug addict. But that wouldn't apply to his heir."

"Well, if he got hitched and ditched, you'll just have to live with it."

"Moody, listen to me carefully. I'm not living with it. Get your ass out to that crime scene and find something to hang the wife on."

"Hang her? You think she killed Bic?"

"The woman's got the temperament of a black widow spider. I guarantee you she aced Bic. Get her. I don't care how, just take her down."

"You're the boss. And, Zack . . ."

"Yeah?"

"Sorry about your brother-in-law."

"Yeah."

I hung up and cursed.

"Bic's dead?"

"Dead. Janelle's alive. If I had to choose between the two, I'd rather have him. I must have really pissed off someone big time in a past life. Everything I ever did comes back to haunt me."

"Can she really cause that much trouble?"

"Do chickens have lips? Janelle's like a thousand other Vegas losers, people who spend their whole lives going for the money but coming up with a handful of dirt. This time she's gone all the way."

"Has anyone told his sister?"

"Morgan? No, I don't think so. I guess it's up to me."

Jack Moody pulled up a chair at a table in Black's Beer & Pizza, where two plainclothes detectives were seated.

"Nick, Paul, how'ya guys doing?"

"Oh, good," Nick told his partner, "the rich retired cop's here to pick up the tab. One pepperoni pizza split two ways, four beers, we know how you rich dicks on expense accounts like to spend money."

"Here, take the wife on a special night to Caesar's, on my boss. Dinner, 'gamboling,' the whole nine yards." Moody passed comp certificates across the tables.

"Is this a bribe?" Nick asked.

"Do chickens have lips?"

"What?"

"Never mind, a dumb reply I picked up. Of course it's a bribe. Why the hell would I give you two dumb dicks anything if I didn't want something in return? I want the dope on Bic Halliday."

"Good," Nick said, "I just wanted to make sure I wasn't compromising my professional duties for nothing. In answer to your question, Bic Halliday's death is accidental, plain and simple. You might call it an accidental suicide. Guys who have been shooting up half their lives are not only bound to make a mistake and suck in more than they can handle sometime, they're just as likely to get their hands on pure shit and blow their lid. That's what happened to Bic boy. One day he goes from a five- or ten-percent solution to a hundred-percent solution and bingo, he's dead. Case open and shut."

"What if someone slipped him the pure stuff?"

"You think maybe the butler did it?" Nick nudged his partner. "Did you get that, Paul, the butler did it."

"You're a funny sonofabitch."

"I was thinking more like the wife," Moody said.

"Good candidate. Janelle Troy was probably ready, willing, and able. Now how do you prove it? Bic's fingerprints are on the syringe."

"You checked fingerprints? I'm impressed. You used to just do everything by the seat of your pants—large-sized pants, at that."

"Yeah, you'd be surprised at how high-tech we've gotten since you left for the big bucks with Riordan. We even take pictures of bodies before we turn them over to a mortician."

Moody ate a piece of pizza as he talked. "I called an old friend of mine with the LAPD and he ran Janelle Troy's California rap sheet and did some checking. She's an up-and-coming small-business woman with her own franchise selling cocaine and heroin. Kinda funny that a pro like her would let her husband OD on pure stuff. Unless she had a reason. Does Bic have a will?"

"We found it in his desk. His wife okayed a search of his papers to see if he left a suicide note."

"And?"

"What'd you expect? They got married, he made a will, his wife's the natural beneficiary."

"That marriage is real interesting," Moody said. "The scion of the most prominent family in Vegas gets hitched and no one knows it. They get an out-of-town license and use an out-of-town preacher no one ever heard of. And no one's seen the preacher since the marriage. My L.A. contact tells me the preacher's sister filed a missing persons report because she hasn't seen him since about the time of the wedding."

"You've been busy," Nick said.

"That's why I get the big bucks."

"So you think the wife iced him."

"If it walks like a duck, quacks like a duck . . ."

"Okay, big shot, you tell us. How do we take her down? In case you haven't met Janelle Troy, this is not a woman who spills her guts when tough guys like us sneer at her. She'd hold her guts in and scream for her lawyer."

Moody ordered another round. "We put her and the situation under a microscope. We do things you never see in an OD case. You haven't done Super Glue fuming on the body, have you?"

"No use," Paul said. "If her prints showed up on his skin in the injection area, she'd just claim she examined his arm. Paramedics would have handled the body, too."

"Do it anyway, the angle of her prints compared to the angle of the body when she found him could make her a liar. Get in a handwriting expert to examine the will and marriage certificate. Do a background check on everyone even remotely connected to Janelle Troy. Question the neighbors, find out who's been visiting the ranch. Maybe someone saw the missing preacher man. Get a search warrant and let's take that entire place apart, piece by piece. Sweep it with a vacuum and look for traces of anyone who's been out at the ranch. Get a chemist to do further analysis of the heroin residue in the syringe. We know it's pure stuff, but I want to be able to identify the batch it came from. His wife's obviously his supplier; if we can bust her on a trafficking charge she may roll over on an accomplice. And we need to find the other man."

Nick nudged Paul. "Didn't I tell you he was smart? Already figured out that there had to be another man. I bet he learned that watching movies."

Paul said, "I have just one question of Mr. Deep Pockets Moody. Who's gonna get this gig approved by the chief? There's going to be a big bill for the kind of case work-up he wants."

"Don't worry about it. Zack Riordan's calling the chief, and so is Morgan Halliday. The chief knows what side his bread is buttered on."

74

I met Morgan and the children at McCarran Airport. I sent Forbidden City's private jet for them and was waiting with a limo on the tarmac when the plane taxied to a stop. Bic's funeral was tomorrow. Bic's friends could be counted on one hand, and they were all scumbags who were either in jail or rehab, so I had to do something about giving him a funeral because he was Morgan's brother. As far as I was concerned, Bic's remains could have been ground in a meat grinder and poured down a sewer, but I had to think about Morgan. We were closing Halliday's for two hours so the employees could attend the funeral. That would be the first time the club had had its doors locked since it came into existence. I put the word out that any employee who didn't attend the funeral wouldn't have to bother reporting back to work—ever. The same thing went for anyone who wanted to work at Forbidden City. With that kind of arm-twisting, I expected to get the sort of turnout Con got on his sendoff.

I greeted Morgan and gave her a peck on the cheek. Her features were impassive. She was really aging well. Women complain that they lose a little of their looks for every day past thirty. I don't know if that's true or not, but Morgan sure made the statement a lie. She looked like the proverbial million dollars. I had seen her three times in my life after long absences and for the third time I found myself amazed at what a good-looking woman she was. Not only good looking, but Morgan had something else—class, that Vassar look I used to kid her about.

The kids stared at me shyly. I was a stranger to them and they were strangers to me. I realized I didn't even know their ages. William—aka Zack, Jr.—I guessed to be about seven and the girl, Monica, a couple years younger. I didn't dare expose my ignorance by asking their ages.

Morgan asked, "Trying to figure out their names? How old they are? Whether they're yours?"

I grinned as I opened the limo door for her. "All of the above. Monica's as gorgeous as her mother and William is a chip off the old block."

I instructed the driver to take us to the country club house.

"Is there any more word from your detective or the police?"

"Janelle hasn't been arrested yet, but it's just a matter of time. Moody's put together a pretty good circumstantial-evidence case against Janelle and a guy who supplies her drugs. The DA is reviewing the evidence to see if there's enough to bring a murder charge. Moody says that when the case gets to court, the DA will waver between murder and manslaughter because Janelle's pretty whacked out on drugs."

"Why manslaughter? She killed him."

"They're afraid she might prove it was an accident and that her brains are so fried, she didn't know what she was doing. A manslaughter rap would get her put away for years, but I'm pushing for a murder charge."

"Will she be at the funeral? I don't think I could stomach that."

"There's nothing we can do about it. She was his wife, although we've got a handwriting expert to question how the signature was obtained."

"Forgery?"

"No, it's Bic's signature, but the expert thinks it was made under the influence of drugs and while Bic was lying down. Gives us an argument that he didn't know what he was signing. She's made a demand for a hundred million dollars."

"My brother's been dead for a few days and she's already demanding money?"

"Moody tells me she's high twenty-four hours a day. He says she's been running around the ranch with a metal detector looking for buried treasure and acting nuts. Look, it's not all as bad as it sounds. Moody thinks the minister who did the marriage and notaries may not have even been licensed in Nevada. That alone would blow her out of the water."

"How could she be that stupid?"

"Janelle's not stupid, but she's been on drugs for so long she doesn't know what side is up. People who push drugs and use them have their own sense of reality. A little thing like being properly licensed doesn't enter into their worldview when their brains are baked."

"This is all insane." Her look told me that she blamed me and I got hot fast.

"Look, I hadn't seen Janelle in a million years before she hooked up with Bic. And your brother was deep into drugs and trouble before I showed up at Halliday's."

"I'm not blaming you for anything."

Like hell she wasn't, but I kept my mouth shut.

"I saw your casino from the air."

"Our casino."

"Your casino. Very impressive, more than twice the size of anything else on the Strip. You finally got what you always wanted."

"Not yet, the doors aren't open yet. As we get closer to opening day, the fires I have to spend my day stamping out get bigger. When the doors open, I want the kids there."

The statement surprised me as much as it did her. Seeing William and Monica had affected me. They weren't babies anymore, but little people, with inquiring eyes and personalities.

"It's going to be an historic event," I said. "Every major player in town has plans for super casinos being drawn up. They're not even going to wait to see if I draw a Bugsy bad-luck hand and it rains on my parade. They know the super casino is the thing of the future."

I didn't verbalize it, but suddenly I had a fear that my kids might someday see me being carried on a stretcher out the back of the casino as Morgan predicted. I realized Morgan had been right when she said I had no role model for being in a family. Betty hadn't been a family, nor were the trailer-court trash who raised her.

"Congratulations. No, I'm not being sarcastic," she said. "I didn't comprehend the size of your accomplishment until I saw it from the air and realized there was nothing that could come anywhere near matching your club, either in size or style. My father was a great man in his own way, the King of Glitter Gulch and a real Vegas gem and character, but he never had your ambitions. Neither did I. I think I wanted to run Halliday's more to step on your toes than any other reason."

I thought about her confession for a minute. "I really got you that mad at me?"

"You really got under my skin. I loved you from the first moment I saw you, a cocky punk straight off the streets."

"Morgan—"

"It's okay, I'm long over it. Loving you has been my addiction. I finally went through withdrawals and shook the habit."

"I was that bad?"

"Worse. You used me as a stepping stone. And kicked me aside when you didn't need me anymore. And you cast aside your own children to make your own dream come true. Look at them, Zack, can you see yourself in their faces? You have a habit of pulling your ear when you're thinking—William does the same thing. They're your blood and flesh, too. You're an unfaithful husband, no father at all, and a ruthless bastard in general." She paused. "By the way—great suit."

I grinned. "Maybe you can bury me in it someday."

"I used to think I would have to hire professional mourners to attend your funeral, Zack. From what I've heard about the savage way you've handled yourself building your dream, I don't have that fear anymore. People are going to come to your funeral just to make sure you're dead."

Bic was carried to his grave on a horse-drawn wagon escorted by the sheriff's posse—nice touch. Really a hell of a turnout. My arm-twisting got results. I saw wet-eyed people who didn't even know who the hell Bic was, some of them straight from the Salvation Army soup line who would pick up a bottle of Wild Irish Rose after the funeral.

"I didn't know so many people liked Bic," Morgan said as we pulled up in the limo.

"Life's a mystery," I murmured.

"I hope that bitch has enough sense to have stayed home."

"Don't count on it. I called the DA this morning. He said he'd be here today and talk to me about the case they're building against Janelle.

I was sure Janelle would be there. Moody and his cop friends had been dogging her heels, letting her know they knew she was guilty and she was going to be busted. "Try to get her to run," Moody said. "There's an instruction that juries get when they're deciding criminal cases, it literally says flight is a confession of guilt." Moody said Janelle was really whacked out. Police surveillants have seen her wandering around the property with a metal detector. "Acting strange, muttering, and cursing," Moody said. "I saw the surveillance films: She's acting real nuts, talking to herself, and to some guy named Diego, who we think was her drug supplier."

Moody's opinion was that she had sampled some of the pure stuff she had knocked off Bic with. "Pure stuff is irresistible to an addict. They use a little more and more and inevitably cross the line and either ice themselves or fry some of their brain connectors. You see them down at the skid-row missions, people you went to high school with are now wide-eyed zombies. The worse ones are the paranoid schizos, the kind who see snakes crawling up their legs and who chop up mama and papa when the folks won't hand over the money for another hit."

When her lawyer made a demand for millions, I sent back a message that I'd buy her cigarettes when she was in jail. But so far, so good. I hadn't spotted Janelle.

As a sheriff's honor guard carried the coffin up to the grave site, a Bourbon Street jazz band played "Summertime."

"That was Bic's favorite song," Morgan said.

"And his favorite group. They insisted upon coming all the way from New Orleans to attend the funeral."

Teary-eyed, Morgan squeezed my hand. "Thanks."

I got kind of teary-eyed myself. Sending Bic off in style had cost plenty, including the jazz band.

Hearing the preacher talk about Bic's golden path to heaven, Bic's old high school phys ed teacher talk about what a great sportsman Bic was, almost put me to sleep on my feet.

My mind roamed and I thought about A-Ma. I didn't introduce her to Morgan; neither woman seemed eager for an introduction. A-Ma had been unusually quiet since I told her Morgan was coming. Considering that she was normally private to the point of sub rosa, more silence was hard to notice. "You are busy with your family," she said, when I asked her why she seemed to be avoiding me. *My family*. The phrase had a strange ring to my ear ever since Morgan and the kids stepped off the plane. I was really puzzled by my feelings. There was no doubt that I loved A-Ma. But like the woman herself, my love for her had an almost unreal feel to it, like loving a ghost. A-Ma was lushly sensual, but sometimes she seemed illusive, as if she wasn't of this world.

Forbidden City was nearly complete. The grand opening was in a few weeks and I had the finishing-touches crews working twenty-four hours a day. Everything went to hell in a hand basket on a daily basis, of course. Everybody who had anything to do with the project said I was crazy. There was no longer any pretense of love between me and the bankers—my lawyer and PR people kept them away from me because I was in no mood to deal gently with them. The standing joke was that they were looking for the guy who punched Bugsy's ticket after Bugsy went overbudget on the Flamingo—to give the shooter a contract on me. I didn't give a damn. They had too much money in the project to bail out and it was late in the game for them to fight me for control. Their leverage went out the door when the gaming board granted me a license. They had to after reviewing the Ricketts tapes. Ricketts fled the state for parts unknown, so he wasn't available even to defend himself. Besides, the casino hotel was booked solid for opening day and the next three months, and that helped the bankers justify the overages.

I was running through everything I had to do as soon as the funeral was over, when Morgan gasped beside me. Janelle came into the clearing created around the grave site, pushing her way through the crowd. "Get the fuck out of the way," she told someone.

It wasn't the Janelle I had known. My first thought was that Morgan was right. She was crazy. She had that mission-house hollowed-eye look. Her clothes were disheveled; her hair unkempt and stringy. She looked like she had just crawled out of bed after a serious drinking bout. She stood in the clearing in front of the grave, her hands in the pockets of a scroungy black leather motorcycle jacket.

"Get her out of here," Morgan whispered.

For Morgan's sake, the last thing I wanted was to turn her brother's funeral into a can of worms. If the cops tried to take her away, she was going to get nasty, so I stepped in to try to convince her to leave quietly. As soon as she saw me, something stirred in her dull eyes. For a moment I thought it was simply recognition. As soon as she saw me, her face twisted into an ugly grimace. I realized it was pure hate. Moody and his cop buddy Nick were moving through the crowd toward her. I stopped, figuring it was best to let them handle her; all I would do was cause a bigger scene.

I saw the gun when her hand came out of her pocket. Déjà vu. It was the second time in my life I had faced a gun. Nothing about having taken a slug in my chest once before had made me any better prepared to be murdered. I watched the action, as if in slow motion, and saw the gun come out of the pocket and point at me. It was a small gun, a woman's purse gun, probably .25 caliber. My feet turned to cement and froze in place. The grimace on Janelle's face twisted into a sneer as her arm extended out and she pointed the gun point blank at my face. Her hand tightened on the trigger and I heard the telltale click of the gun's slide coming forward, carrying the firing pin to the bullet. And then a dull click.

A moment frozen in time passed. Then Moody's cop buddy grabbed Janelle and jerked the gun out of her hand. She was on the ground being cuffed in a flash.

Moody came up to me, a quizzical look on his face.

"You are the luckiest guy alive."

Alive—a nice word. Morgan was at my side. William and Monica were there, too, Monica crying and holding on to me. Morgan felt me like she wondered if I was real.

"Are you okay?"

My knees were water, but I was too macho to show it. "Sure. Nothing like a gun jamming to make my day."

"Congratulations. You have fallen in love with your wife."

"A-Ma—"

"No, Zack, there is no need to apologize. I am the other woman. If my friend Wang Su was directing our scenes, he would insist that I cry. Do you see my tears, Zack? Am I not a good actress to be able to produce tears on command?"

"You're overreacting, A-Ma. I told you I wanted to go to Disneyland weeks ago, to feel the magic and reassure myself that Forbidden City had the same touch."

"Now you are taking your wife and children. How . . . middle class."

That one got me laughing. "Christ, now you sound like Chenza. Look, I'm taking the kids because they've never been there, but this is a business trip."

"Look me in the eye, Zack, and tell me that you don't love your wife."

I took her face in my hands and pulled her to me, looking her in the eye without flinching. I studied her eyes, deep pools of mystery and sensuality. "I love you, A-Ma. From the first moment I saw you, when you were just a twerpy, flat-chested little monkey hiding in the bushes and spying on me." I kissed her. I hadn't lied. But I hadn't told her the whole truth, either.

She put her head against my chest and her arms around me and squeezed tight. "I believe you. But you never answered my question, did you? You are a tricky bastard."

I took Morgan and the kids to Disneyland in Anaheim. We flew in the corporate jet and I had a limo pick us up at the airport. It felt great to be really rich—or at least to act that way.

I didn't know what to expect, taking Morgan and the kids to a place like Disneyland. I had made a trip there by myself when I first started the project, to get the feel of the most magical place on earth. Forbidden City wasn't an amusement park, but I wanted not only the best that gambling had to offer on the Strip, but also the best family entertainment I could provide. And there was nothing better than Disneyland on the face of the earth. The place was packed with eye-pleasing things everywhere one turned. What was really fascinating was how so many things in Disneyland were in *motion*. Walt didn't just paint characters onto walls or create plastic models of them. Every time you turned around, Mickey was prancing around, Donald wisecracking with his nasal voice, Goofy playing dumb, Tinker Bell flying overhead, and a riverboat sounding its horn while bears on the bank waved at the boat.

Morgan asked me why I was so fascinated with Disneyland and I gave her the bottom line: You can't knock success.

"Disney was a builder. Nowadays you hear about corporate raiders and junk-bond kings who take over companies and make a fortune firing thousands of employees and cheating them out of their retirement. Those people are nothing but scabs on the face of the earth. It's the people who built dams and pyramids and the Great Wall who count, not the new corporate types who are destroyers."

Every inch of Disneyland was thought out and planned by a man with talent, drive, and a dream. That's what it took.

"It's got to be the real McCoy," I told Morgan, as we walked behind the kids. "You can't foist off an imitation on people; they'll see through it. It's like your old man. Con was genuine, a real cowboy who got transplanted to Vegas. I'd be laughable if I put on a cowboy hat and tried to act like a cowboy. Con acted like a man who was used to manure on his cowboy boots and people instinctively knew it. Walt Disney had that kind of innate shtick. He knew how to get your attention and keep it. Everywhere you turn in this place, there is something you could stop and stare at, but you don't. Everything is so well designed, so cleverly presented, you don't see a bunch of parts; instead you always see the whole.

"That's what I want to happen when people walk into Forbidden City. I don't want something to attract their attention; I want them to feel like they're welcome guests in the emperor's palace."

Morgan gave me a look and shook her head. "That sounds like something from a press release."

"It is. Pretty good, huh?"

"Wonderful. What did your cop friend tell you about Janelle? You got a call this morning when I was getting the kids ready."

"She confessed that she killed Bic. And the friend who helped her, a guy named Diego." I didn't tell her the cops found Diego in a shallow grave on the ranch with his penis stuffed in his mouth.

"Is she going to get out of it because she's crazy?"

"I asked that question. I think she's nuts, but the law has a different definition. Moody says she isn't legally crazy and wasn't crazy when she killed Bic."

"I know she killed my brother, but, I don't know, I kind of feel sorry for her. From what you told me, she never had a chance in life."

I let that one slide.

"You're getting bored being here with the kids."

It was an accusation, not a statement.

"That's not true."

"Yes it is, I can see it on your face. You needed to come to Disneyland and spend ten minutes walking down Main Street, USA, to get the feel again. Now you're ready to get back to work."

"I want the kids to enjoy themselves."

"Go back to the hotel and get on the phone and drive everyone in Vegas nuts. I'll give the kids another couple of hours and we can return to Vegas."

"Thanks." I gave her a kiss on the cheek.

"Do me a favor, will you, Zack?"

"What?"

"Don't make me love you again."

"I thought you might invite me to your next wedding. As your groom."

"Are you kidding? You came to two of my weddings and spoiled both of them."

77

A-Ma sat at a desk in the suite she shared with Zack near Forbidden City. Ling stood on the other side of the desk. Two things were on the desk: a telephone and a document drawn up by a lawyer. She had been at the desk waiting for the past ten minutes, after Ling arrived with the papers and informed her that Wan was going to call her and give her instructions. She waited stoically, showing no emotion, her face and body expressing only the quiet patience for which the women of her country were noted.

Ling also appeared impassive, but his countenance was more forced. She found Zack's characterization of Ling as a ticking bomb true. She sensed he was a bundle of bottled-up nerves. The only overt clue he gave was his hands. He continuously made a noose with his hands and "strangled" one of his fingers with it. She found the nervous habit unsettling and sinister, but never revealed that it bothered her. Helplessness and fear fed the egos of men like Ling and Wan.

She had a premonition about what the phone call would be about. It was to be the call she dreaded, the one she knew would come someday from Wan.

The phone rang and she involuntarily flinched. Her reaction brought something resembling a smile to Ling's face. He reached down, pressed the speakerphone button, and gave Wan a traditional Chinese greeting.

"How are you, my child?" Wan asked her.

"Very good." It was a game they played, the pretense that he actually cared about whether she lived or died.

"You used to call me 'Uncle.' Is there a reason the word would not come today? Have I fallen in your esteem?"

"No—no, of course not, Uncle."

"You have to be careful in the West, my child—it can be a very seductive place. One can get so caught up with all its technology and gadgets, you forget about the traditions that have made the Chinese people great."

"Yes, Uncle."

"Remember, they are nothing more than barbarians with guns." He laughed at his own joke so hard he started coughing.

A-Ma folded her hands in her lap and sat quietly during the spasm, wishing that he drop dead during the attack.

"My apology, A-Ma. As you can see, I am getting old and weak and will soon join my ancestors."

She had to stop herself from laughing aloud. Zack claimed that Wan would piss on all their graves and she was certain he was right.

"You recall, my dear, that when I sent you to Las Vegas, you were to be a two-edged sword, first clearing the way for Mr. Riordan's casino . . . now it is time to use the other blade. The corporation is fully licensed to run the casino. Mr. Riordan controls the corporation only because I have permitted it. I control the corporation, in your name, of course. Sadly, I no longer am able to trust you to do my bidding. The papers before you assign your entire interest to Mr. Chow. The papers also replace Mr. Riordan as President and CEO of Forbidden City. In his stead is an associate of Mr. Chow's, who at this very moment is on his way to Las Vegas. Neither have criminal records and should qualify to run the casino."

"What will happen to Zack?"

"Why, he will get on his horse and ride off into the sunset, as in those Western movies." More insane laughter came over the phone before Wan came back on, smothering a cough. His voice turned harsh. "What happens to him is none of your concern. Ling reports that you have become infatuated with Mr. Riordan. I will forgive your foolishness, this time. But understand that I am not pleased with you. Ling, show her the photograph that was faxed to us an hour ago from the man who is following Mr. Riordan."

The whisper of a smile on Ling's face grew into a real smile, the first she had ever seen him make. He pulled a piece of paper from his inside coat pocket, unfolded it and spread it on the desk. Zack kissing Morgan. Mickey Mouse in the background.

"After you sign the papers, begin packing. You will be returning to Macao immediately."

"Why?"

"My feet are cold."

Wan hung up and dial tone returned to the line. She ignored the buzz. Ling reached over and hung the line up.

"Sign," he said, gesturing at the papers before her.

She looked down at the papers, but the print was blurry as tears invaded her eyes.

"Sign."

"I have to read them." She pressed a button under the desktop.

He took a step back, shaking his head like he was trying to clean out his ears. "You do not need to read them."

"I have to see what I am signing."

"I will call Mr. Wan."

"Go ahead, but do it in your own room."

"No, sign the papers now."

Her maid came into the room, answering the signal sent from the button under the desk.

"Show Mr. Ling out."

"I will call Mr. Wan," he repeated, as he walked out.

When the door to her room closed, she locked it. Back at her desk, she tore up the faxed picture and threw it in the wastebasket. She stared down at the papers for a long moment. Scratching out the names of Tommy Chow and his associate, she wrote in Zack's name and signed the paper.

She stared down at the paper for a long moment. Pushing back the chair, she got up. She felt both heavy and tired—burdened. Dealing with Mr. Wan was a burden. Everything about life was complicated. In the bedroom, she selected a white dress. After slipping it on, she opened the sliding glass doors and went out on the tenth-floor balcony. Forbidden City was lit up, being prepared for the opening, but already the brightest thing on the Strip. Light from God, Zack's perception of the Strip, and now he had added the most brilliant beacon.

Sitting on the small balcony, she swung her legs over the low railing and put her head back, letting the warm August breeze stir her hair. Her mind floated with different thoughts, some for only a fleeting moment—crossing the Pearl River delta with the wind and rain in her face, a woman who turned children into "jewels," seeing Zack for the first time. She wondered what her fisherman friend in Macao would think if he saw the Strip. Probably the same thing Zack thought when he first saw it as a child—that it was God's lair. But the fisherman would not understand the passions and greed behind the bright lights. To him, life was simple, struggling each day against the sea, simple pain, and pleasures until one day he passed beyond sorrow. That was how he thought of life, as a time of sorrow that he would someday pass. And it was how she thought of it now.

For a moment she frowned down at the pavement, over a hundred feet below. Then she smiled and leaned forward. The fall was exhilarating.

She realized that for the first time in her life she was completely free and in charge of her own destiny.

Part II

★ ★ ★ ★ ★ ★

FORBIDDEN CITY

August was the ghost month.

Waking up at three or four o'clock in the morning had become a habit for me. Sometimes I would just lay in bed, running everything about building Forbidden City through my head; other times I got up and went over piles of paperwork. We were getting down to the wire—the club would either open soon or blow up in my face. The quiet and isolation in the wee hours when others were sleeping had become my thinking time.

It was the middle of August. A-Ma had died over a week ago, and each night since then I awoke to think about her. This night was no different. August was the ghost month. I couldn't lay A-Ma to rest in August, so I had the body preserved until I could fly it to Hong Kong. I had no doubt Wan would try to kill me, but regardless of the risk, I was going to take A-Ma to her fisherman friend on the Pearl River tributary where together we would return the sea goddess to her rightful resting place in the waters she came from, in a red dress to bring her luck in the afterworld.

Since A-Ma had died, I had become sensitive about everything. I felt like someone had sand-blasted away my outer shell and left my nerves raw and exposed. Tears streamed down my face when I saw her on a slab. I don't remember crying before, at least not since I was old enough to remember. I couldn't even remember crying for Betty. Tough guys don't cry, ever—that's what Con always said. Maybe I wasn't as tough as I thought. I had been torn between A-Ma and Morgan. And feeling guilty about the kids. Now the choice was gone and all I had left of A-Ma was the memory of a woman I loved but who never seemed quite real to me, not even when we were naked in each other's arms.

Morgan stirred beside me. "Can't sleep again?"

"Just thinking. Go back to sleep."

Morgan had been good about giving me space to get my emotions under control about the loss of A-Ma. This was the first night we slept in the same bed since we got back in town with the kids. And we hadn't touched each other. She said she wasn't ready. I had been staying alone in the suite I once shared with A-Ma, in a strange way sensing that she was still there. Last night I wanted to have dinner with Morgan and the kids at the country club house and ended up staying the night. I felt lonely for the first time since Betty died and being around Morgan and the kids helped. They felt like a natural part of my life.

The phone rang and broke the quietness in the room. "Fuck." Morgan sat up.

"Someone's died or the club's burned down," I said automatically.

"Who knows the number?"

"Nobody I want to hear from at three in the morning."

I let it ring three more times before I picked it up.

"How are you, Mr. Riordan?"

At the sound of Wan's voice, a shot of murderous anger spiked me. But I needed a clear head to deal with the devil. I closed my eyes and leaned back. "What do you want?"

Wan crackled like a goosed hen. "My money, Mr. Riordan, I want the money you have stolen from me."

"Your money? I don't recall getting any money from you. Maybe you have the wrong number."

"You do not seriously believe that I would let you steal a hundred million dollars from me." He clicked his tongue. "I have veered far from the Way that was set out for me at my birth if someone in this world believes he can take my property without forfeiting his life. Perhaps we are having a language problem; my English is not the best."

"How does 'fuck you' translate? You know, Wan, you screwed up royally when you took on A-Ma. She was too damn smart for you. Those footsteps you hear behind you are your pals like Tommy Chow coming to carve you up. I had one of my men meet your friend Chow at the airport and bring him to me. Before I kicked his balls up between his teeth, I let him know that you and I were partners in ripping off the triads."

A sudden gasp came from the other end of the line.

"Is that a death rattle I hear?"

The silence seeped over the phone like the chill of the dead. Finally

Wan's voice came back. "You have not read enough Sun Tzu, Mr. Riordan. He advised taking from the enemy that which he values the most."

Wan hung up. I listened to the dial tone in my ear for a moment before I put the receiver down.

"What's the matter?" Morgan asked.

"Wan."

"Isn't there some way we can deal with the man? Before he murders us all?"

Murders us all. I rolled the thought around in my head. I didn't think he'd harm my family, he was after me, but I didn't like getting anywhere near the idea, either. His threat about taking what I hold dearest was obviously the casino. He planned to take it away from me. But having Morgan and the kids around would complicate things when the going got tough.

"I want you and the kids to go back East in the morning. The corporate jet will fly you."

"No, I want the kids at the opening of Forbidden City. Do you really think there's any danger to us?"

"No, but I don't want to take any chances. I'll move you into a VIP suite I've set up in the hotel tower. Don't leave the complex without security people with you. Understand?" I threw off the blankets and got out of bed. "I need a shot of rot gut. I can't sleep."

"Tell me what Wan said."

"He said I didn't read enough Sun Tzu, that Sun Tzu defeated enemies by taking away what they held dearest."

I was to the bedroom door when she spoke again. "He's going after Forbidden City."

"Of course."

"You say that as if the most important thing to a man is his business."

"Morgan—" I started, not in any mood to argue.

"No, forget it, I always want you to be something, somebody, that you're not."

"Whatever happened to unconditional love?"

"Is that another way of saying unconditional surrender?" She quickly changed the subject. "Why do you think you can keep Wan's money?"

"A-Ma transferred her interest in the casino corporation to me by scratching out Tommy Chow's name and writing in mine. Okay, that locked me into a deadly game with Wan. She told me he had used not only his own money, but the money of triads stretching from Shanghai to Taipei. If he got rid of me, he might be able to stall the triads from killing him until he figured out a way to cover their losses. Or had them gunned down first. But since I'm living proof that he has lost their money, his days are numbered. The question is, which of us has the highest number?"

"Why don't you just give him back his interest in the casino?"

"It's not that simple. Wan has double-crossed me twice and tried to kill me. I earned the money, but I honestly don't give a damn about it. He was responsible for A-Ma's death, just the same as if he pushed her. I have to punish him for it."

"Zack, I'm afraid. I don't want anything to happen to you."

"Don't worry, I'm not stupid. I'm not going to die for money. If it comes down to it, I'll just sign back the interest to Wan."

I lied to calm her fears. Even if I signed back the interest to Wan, he would probably kill me anyway to save face. The only way to handle Wan in the long term was to play his game. He lived by the sword. He had to die by it. But I needed a bigger sword.

I chugged two shots of Jack Daniels and made three phone calls before I returned to the bedroom.

"Who did you call?"

"Moody, to tell him to round up some of his cop buddies who have retired. I'm going to beef up security at the casino. And I called the sheriff and told him to put a patrol car outside the house for the rest of the night." I didn't say anything about the third call, setting up a lunch date at the country club.

The lights were off and my mind was still buzzing when she spoke.

"No pain, no gain."

"What?"

"I was just thinking how tough life is."

"You were born with a silver spoon in your mouth. You don't have any idea of how tough life is."

"Why didn't you tell that to Bic, you arrogant bastard. You know, you always had an unfair advantage over him. You were born poor and had no place to go but up. Everything you ever did ended up successful. Bic choked on his silver spoon because he had to compete against a father who had pulled himself up by the bootstraps. Bic always had to walk in his tall shadow. He was never good enough for his father."

She turned her back to me and I rolled over and took her in my arms. She tried to push me away, but I held on to her tight.

"Hey, I'm sorry I started with nothing and got successful. In my next life, I'll try to make up for it by reversing the process."

"If you don't give Mr. Wan back his money, your next life may come sooner than you think."

Lunch at the country club was with Anthony DeCicco. DeCicco was a silver-haired, distinguished man in his mid-sixties, with pale gray eyes, a handsome face without a single wrinkle, and a manner more polished than a Cartier diamond. He was the kind of guy whose pictures appeared on society pages laughing with the mayor at charity fund-raisers. Everyone who was anyone in town knew Anthony—and that he didn't go by the name of "Tony." But no one knew for sure what kind of business he had. He looked like a million, dressed like it, drove a big Caddie, lived in a suite on the top floor of the Hilton, gambled modestly but frequently, but never really said what he did for a living.

I was aware of what he did for a living only because Con told me years ago. The feds knew what he did for a living. They probably had his line bugged. He was a professional go-between, a smooth guy who had connections—and some said was connected. He called himself a "business consultant" and his business relationship with Con concerned arrangements for occasional loans Con needed. The loans never involved any paperwork and the creditor was always someone that had their picture in the gaming board's black book.

I had never conducted any business with DeCicco and was surprised when he called me and wanted to set up a meeting last week. I had postponed the meeting because I was too busy, but called him in the wee hours last night to set up the luncheon. Assuming that his phone was bugged, and maybe even the table we sat at, we would have to tap dance around what we really wanted to talk about.

"I was surprised to get your call in the middle of the night, Zack. Are you a restless sleeper or were you catching up on work?"

"Sorry, I forgot about the time. I get wound up and forget what day it is sometimes."

"I don't blame you, Forbidden City is the biggest thing that ever hit this town. You have a lot going on, I'm sure. I hear you're opening the doors soon and the place is already fully booked."

"We're booked solid for the next three months. It's like the old saying, give people what they want and they'll come running."

"Who said that?"

"Hell, I don't know. Do I look like a philosopher to you?"

"You look like success to me. You probably don't remember it, but I was playing poker with Con years ago when you first started working for him. He introduced you to the guys at the table and after you left, he said, 'See that kid, he's going to run this town one day.' "

I didn't know if DeCicco was bullshitting or not. He was that kind of guy—smooth, made you feel important. Super Glue would slide off of him.

"What did you want to see me about, Zack?"

I looked at him, a little surprised. "Anthony, you called me. I was just returning the call."

He knew I called for a reason different from his, that something must have happened between the time of his call and mine, but I wanted to hear his proposition first.

"I hear you've been borrowing heavily because of building overruns. Bottom line question, Zack, do you need money?"

"Do chickens have lips?"

He laughed. "I understand you and Morgan have hocked Halliday's up to its gills. You may end up defaulting, could lose the old family spread."

"Halliday's was Con's dream, not mine."

"I know that. You could fit Halliday's and most of the rest of Glitter Gulch on Forbidden City's footprint. But I have a client, an investor, who's interested in the old club, not to run it himself, but to see his investment grow."

"Who's your client?"

"I'm not at liberty to say."

"I'd need to know; you can't just sell an interest in the club. Your client would have to be someone who could qualify with the gaming board."

"You'll just have to take my word that qualifications could be made. I'd get axed if I told you anymore."

He had already told me plenty. His "investor" would not qualify, thus someone else would front. And I got the hint about who his client was. Vinnie "the Ax" Farrara, the head of a New York Mafia family. The papers said he was the slick of slime that rose to the top in the aftermath of Gotti's fall. He got his name from an incident in which he chopped up a partner who double-crossed him and then mailed the pieces to the guy's brother.

That Vinnie the Ax wanted into Las Vegas came as no surprise. Organized crime and Vegas had always had an illicit affair. Vegas was the whore that crime lords lusted after because of all the loose money in town, baskets of it, trainloads of it. Where else in the world would businesses have to *weigh* their daily receipts because there was too much of the stuff to count?

It used to be guys like Vinnie the Ax wanted a piece of a casino because of the prestige, glamour, and tax evasion a casino offered, but now it was all laundering. The old mob, with its cut from prostitution, protection, hijackings, and fencing, dealt in millions. The new mob, with its drug connections, dealt in billions. And cleaning money became an art and science unto itself.

DeCicco and I looked at each other for a long moment. Finally I said, "You know, Anthony, it's a funny thing how great minds work alike sometimes. You called me. But I was going to call you, anyway. I've got a proposition your investor would be interested in."

"An offer he can't refuse?"

"Yeah, and no horse's head in the deal. But there is a horse's ass."

George chattered nonstop as he kneaded Morgan's naked buttocks. She had disobeyed Zack's instructions to stay around Forbidden City and had sneaked over to the gym because George was her favorite masseur.

"She's completely phony, manufactured," George said. "My friend Joey does her hair, and he would know."

"She" was the movie star on this week's issue of *People* magazine. Morgan was only half listening to his nonstop chatter. Her mind was on Zack. Forbidden City would open soon and she would no longer have an excuse to stay around Vegas. She told Zack she was staying until the opening because she wanted the children to experience the historic moment. That was true. But there was another half to the story—Zack. No man ever stirred her blood—or caused it to boil—like he did. What was she going to do when the casino doors opened and she no longer had an excuse to stay? How was she going to take the place of the memory of a movie star who was already being mourned as a legend?

"Joey has seen her 'before' pictures when she was Plain Jane," George said. "Then she went plastic and now look at her."

Morgan glanced down at the magazine where she had dropped it on the floor. Plastic or not, Morgan wished the hell she looked like the woman on the magazine cover. But she had to admit that the woman, who was British, lacked the sensuality that A-Ma had had. That's my problem, she thought, I'm not manufactured, I have all of my original parts. Maybe Zack would love me more if I added a little Chinese to my features.

It was tough enough competing with the woman when she was alive. Morgan wondered if it was going to be impossible to connect with Zack emotionally now that there was a ghost between them.

"Why don't men get cellulite?" Morgan asked, deliberately changing the subject George had been going on and on about. "Women are expected to stay attractive and desirable, regardless of their age or how many kids they've had, but a bald, toothless, beer-bellied man with a big bank account can get any woman. It's not fair, George; they should at least get cellulite."

On that note, she got up and went to the showers.

She stood under the hot water and let it flow down her body, from the top of her head down to her feet. She got the massage as much for her tight muscles as her real and imagined cellulite. Coming back into Zack's life had ripped open old wounds, hurts that had never healed.

Todd was gone, out of her life. She knew she could never love him, especially if she had to think of Zack during their lovemaking to get excited. He would have made a good father to the kids, but she didn't want to spend the rest of her life with him. And it wasn't fair to keep Todd dangling.

She didn't want to go back to Martha's Vineyard. The place was beautiful. She loved the different seasons, the harshness of the winters tempered by the surrounding water . . . but it wasn't for her. She missed the desert, missed the crisp mornings and warm sun in January, the fierce dry heat in summer. And most of all she missed Zack. She wanted to be a part of his life again. She only hoped Zack felt the same way.

"Damn, men," she said out loud.

A woman in the next shower stall overheard her.

"I know what you mean, honey. You can't live with them and you can't live without them," she said. "But you know what a girl's best friend is? Her vibrator. They don't make you cook for 'em, pick up after 'em, do their dirty laundry, and listen to their hard day at the office routine after you've worked your ass off all day. And you know the best part? It gives you all the foreplay you want—and never prematurely ejaculates!"

Betty was buried in the municipal graveyard. I toyed with the idea of moving her to a private graveyard, but it didn't seem right to disturb her. I wanted to make sure she had the best grave in the place so I had the interior decorator who was buying marble for my VIP suites send me a slab of the best rose marble money could buy in Italy. He tried to send me a freebie from our supplier and I said nuts to that, no comp crap. I wanted the best for her and only money exchanging hands could buy that.

I went out to the grave the day Forbidden City opened its doors. Yeah, there were a million things still to do at the casino, half the goddamn toilets in the place were backing up—what kind of engineering nerd would connect one thousand toilets together electronically?—a whole bank of slot machines had a nervous breakdown during the trial tests and paid nothing but thousand-dollar jackpots, a fire in the buffet kitchen cooked the goose of a chef, you name it. If it walked or talked, it threatened to quit, or was so butt-dumb it didn't know how to flush an electronic toilet. And if it was supposed to work mechanically, the ghost in the machine made sure it ran backward or not at all.

But when the doors opened, I wanted to be with Betty. I never thought I'd be standing in a graveyard on the day my dream came alive. You just couldn't plan everything in life. You had to live each day because you never knew if there was going to be a tomorrow.

I had so many plans for Betty, so many things I wanted for her. I used to lie awake in bed at night and think about the things I'd do for her. My favorite dream was to buy her a little greasy spoon to run so she could stand at the end of counter and drink coffee, smoke, and talk to the customers. But it didn't work out that way because you can't plan the way things turn out. There was always a surprise. Like the people who put their nickels and dimes away for their "golden

years," then found out one day they had the big "C" or met a drunk
driver head on. You just couldn't wait until tomorrow; you had to grab
what you could today and hoped tomorrow took care of itself.

"Hey, Betty, I did it. You would really be proud of me," I said out
loud.

I wanted to share the day with her. "I only wish you could be here.
I can just see you, walking into the casino like a queen, people calling
you 'Mrs. Riordan' and kissing your feet with every step you take . . ."

Betty was the real McCoy, nothing phony or pretentious about her.
I hoped that bastard Kupka was on his back in that cold water on the
other side of the dam, staring up at the bit of blue sky and not being
able to move an inch to feel its warmth.

I wished I could kill him again. Once was not enough.

I said good-bye to Betty and headed back into town to tell someone
else I loved—and lost—about the opening.

A-Ma was otherworldly even in death. Her beauty was so rare, so
unique, I often felt as if she was only a visitor to our world. Maybe
she came from the world of Gesar of Ling, with its heroes and monsters. Or fell to earth from another planet, like Venus, where all the
women were goddesses.

I kissed her cold lips.

"I wish I could breathe life into you," I whispered.

I wished she had loved life more.

Rolling down the Strip in my Jag, I could see where all the action was.
Forbidden City. A magic kingdom. And I was the king.

A line of limos were dropping off people in front of the club, not
ordinary people, but Hollywood people, a planeload of them, all
dressed like it was Academy Awards night. Camera crews from three
major networks were covering the opening, beaming the gala event
around the world. The stars and cameras had a symbiotic relationship.
The stars came for the big comps they pocketed. The cameras came
because of the stars.

Besides the Hollywood crowd, I made up a list that had to be filled
opening day: last year's Cy Young winner, who came from the Yankees; the heavyweight champ, fresh from another beef with the law
for smacking his wife; and tennis and football notables as well as the

court king of basketball. I didn't care about the cost—I figured most of them would be stupid enough to drop what I paid them and more at the tables before they left.

I wanted to play it cool, be Mr. Big Shot, act like opening the biggest casino in the world was just another turn of the cards for me, strut into the club with a cigar, surrounded by sycophants, cracking orders . . . instead I got a case of stage fright. I avoided the camera crews and celebrities out front and pulled up to the valet parking in back.

When the parking attendant ran up to get my car, I almost hit the gas and drove off. Jesus, this was it. My knees were weak and my underarms perspired when I got out of the car. And I was all choked up.

Tough guys don't cry.

Rather than enter through the back, I went back around front, but snuck in like the common folk as the lesbian star of a popular sitcom got out of a limo accompanied by her significant other.

As I went across the moat to the main "gate," the Red Dragon roller coaster rumbled overhead on the Great Wall, and I listened to the people shrieking and screaming as the serpent made a deep dive that took it under the club. Pirate junks plied the lake inside the gate. A pirate ran up to drag me aboard one of the vessels and hold me for "ransom," and I shook him off.

"Save that for the paying customers."

He didn't know who I was. Neither did I.

I had borrowed one of Walt Disney's most significant innovations— motion. The "palace" courtyard was alive with *life*. Besides the blood-thirsty pirates, I had characters from Chinese history running around making people smile and laugh—not Mickey and Donald, but all twelve animals of the Chinese calendar: rat, ox, tiger, hare, dragon, snake, horse, sheep, monkey, fowl, dog, and pig.

Overhead the Red Dragon roller coaster spit fire every few seconds as it roared around the Great Wall while another dragon, a fifty-foot Drunken Dragon, snaked through the crowd.

But this was no Disneyland. Hell, it looked more like a scene from *Guys and Dolls*: Mingling with ma and pa from L.A. and Philly were gamblers and hookers, guys with Stetsons and guys with tuxes, women letting it all hang out of tank tops and short-shorts as well as sequined gowns.

I moved through the casino in a daze. Forbidden City was a giant slot machine, all lit up, its reels spinning, lights flashing, bells ringing, money sliding in, pouring out the bottom.

Christ, the place swarmed with people, big and small, short and tall, all the colors of the human rainbow. They gambled, they drank, they ate, they laughed at the Chinese pirates trying to drag them into junks, and lined up by the hundreds to get comps, greedily dropping the Forbidden City "souvenir" silver dollar into a dollar slot. What a bunch of suckers! Had they just put the dollar in their pocket and walked out, they would have made a profit, but when that dollar went into a slot, another hundred followed it—which was exactly the idea. Always give a sucker a break, was my motto, just enough rope to hang himself.

Hot damn, but it wasn't raining on my parade. They were all here, young and old, from Glendale to New York, thousands of them. The casino was pressed with people, shoulder to shoulder at the slots, elbow to elbow at the gaming tables, knee to knee in the lounges. Happy people, excited people. A captive audience. Like all the other casinos in town, there were no clocks, no windows—and no place in the gaming area to sit. Keep 'em on their feet, pulling out their dough. Don't let them stop and think about what they're losing. Keep the booze flowing and that narcotic song of money singing.

I listened to the song of money as I floated through the casino in a daze, the same song that I heard when I was twelve years old and saw the Strip for the first time. This time it was playing for me, but it was the same music Bugsy Siegel must have thought he heard the day he drove down a black ribbon strip of highway and imagined a glittering casino rising from the sagebrush. The words to the song were the stickmen calling out the numbers at the dice tables; the one-armed bandits dropping silver; the dance of roulette balls; people screaming, laughing, shouting for joy, begging for divine intervention.

Back in the sixties, when the government was financing dime-story psychology studies of the sex life of gnats and how long a cockroach's dick is, one of those behaviorist rocket scientists figured out that if you played fast music in supermarkets, people would shop faster; with slower music, they'd take their time. The song of money was like that—it sent a subliminal message to people, manipulated them without their knowing. It was seductive, numbing, guaranteed to create a dream state and rob you of your senses—and your money. The more slot reels spun, the more sweaty hands dropped coins in, the louder the screams and shouts at the gaming tables for the throw of dice or the turning of a card, the more feverish people who could hear the song gambled. The law of physics in the gaming pit was simple: The more action in the area, the more hurried the tune sounded, the bigger the bets, the faster they went down.

All those sounds of money in the casino weren't accidental. If it didn't come naturally, I'd have a team of Hollywood sound-effects editors pipe it in. Hustlers who used shills to sound excited about winning could have told those supermarket people a long time ago that the best way to part people from their hard-earned dough is to show someone else winning. That's what the song of money was, the biggest shill in the world. It said, "Com'on down, you can be a winner, too!"

I soaked it all in, rolled in it, swam in it, listened to the slot reels singing, cards shuffling, a chorus of *yeahs!!!* at a craps table. I felt my own blood thickening as the seductive tune crept in, felt the rush of adrenaline as it shot through my veins. On impulse, I shot over and stuck a quarter in a slot. The reels rolled and came up one at a time: bell, cherry, red dragon. No win. But two more red dragons showed on the no-win line. That wasn't any accident. The slots were programmed to frequently show jackpot emblems on the no-win lines. Slots were prick teasers.

The place was like New Year's Eve in Times Square, the elephant parade when the circus came to town, Mardi Gras in New Orleans, the Kentucky Derby and Super Bowl. It was mine. I had created it. Every brick, every nail, every goddamn roll of toilet paper in the place.

I got down on my hands and knees and kissed the floor. Some of the pit people recognized me and caught the scene. They whistled and cheered. Strangers patted me on the back—some of them worked for me.

"Good going, Mr. Riordan."

"Terrific place, Lucky."

I don't know where the hell the guy got my nickname, but unlike Siegel, who kicked some poor bastard in the ass for calling him Bugsy, I wasn't *that* temperamental.

I just kept trucking through the casino, out the back to the biggest little amusement park in the world. Lights were everywhere; overhead, in front of me, to each side, blue, red, green, white, so many, they all became a blur to me. Chinese firecrackers going off, a series of bangs, one after another, sending off smoke and the smell of sulfur. A fire-breathing dragon chasing screaming kids. Motion, life, action. Everything was a feast for the eyes. Walt Disney would have loved my vision.

I felt as if I was back in Hawthorne, twelve years old, and at the carnival, the music of the merry-go-round spinning in my ears. Chant of the hustlers at the dime throw, guess-your-weight, knock-over the milk bottles. Yeah, sure, like Dizzy Dean could have pitched a ball just right to knock over those bottles. A Gypsy fortune teller giving me a dark look and gesturing for me to come to her tent. "What'd I tell you, lady, I wanted everything."

A cocktail waitress took a tip off her tray and put it in the pocket of her money apron. It reminded me of Betty: With that pocketful of tip money, we'd eat that night.

Someone grabbed my arm and I almost swung on him. It was one of my own security guards.

"Sorry, Mr. Riordan, I've been calling you, but you were preoccupied. Your wife's trying to get a hold of you. And the game is ready to start."

"The game?"

"The baccarat game. Mr. Wan is waiting for you."

The words slowly seeped in. Mr. Wan is waiting for me. Baccarat. I felt like someone had just pissed on my parade. Or maybe on my grave.

As I approached the roped-off baccarat area, Jay Guiness, my VIP coordinator, hurried over.

"Zack, we managed to get it all set up on short notice. You sure know how to surprise a guy. Hell, I didn't even know you had solicited his play for the opening, less more that you would be playing." He leaned close to whisper. "I heard Mr. Wan was persona non grata in this town. This is really a surprise."

"Yeah, I'm full of surprises."

They all gave me the eye as I talked to Guiness: Mr. Wan, big creepy Ling, Tommy Chow, and a couple of boys who looked like the type that gave 9mm café coronaries in Macao. Waiting for me like a pack of jackals ready to rip off pieces of flesh. What fucking nerve. I had to give Wan credit—the bastard had brass balls.

He was seated at Tommy Chow's lucky-for-him, unlucky-for-his-wife, chemin de fer table. He lifted himself out of the chair just enough to give me a small bow. I couldn't help it, I had to laugh. Fucking brass balls.

Moody appeared at my elbow. We exchanged looks and I said to Guiness, "Do me a favor, double-check and make sure the kitchen and wine cellar serve nothing but our best to our guests Mr. Wan and his companions."

As soon as Guiness left, I asked Moody, "How'd you find out?"

"Your wife called me as soon as they showed up. Your VIP man buzzed up to your suite looking for you. I hope you know what you're doing with these guys. A couple of them look like candidates for China's Most Wanted."

"I know as much as you do."

He shot a glance at the Macao mafia. "What d'you mean?"

"I mean they showed up unannounced. I thought Wan had a federal warrant."

"Not anymore. The minute Mrs. Riordan sent out an SOS, I called an old pal at the FBI office. Wan settled up by paying a seven-figure income tax problem. What's going on, Zack, how can these guys just pop in?"

I shrugged. "I guess Mr. Wan wants to play shimmy. With me."

"For what?"

"Everything you see."

I turned to go to the table and Moody stopped me.

"I can have them out of here in no time flat, just say the word. These guys are no joke. If you need them out of your life, it isn't beyond the realm of possibilities that they could end up in shallow graves pushing up sagebrush."

"It won't work. There's a funny thing about life, Moody, it's all a big circle. You head out in one direction, take all kinds of turns, but no matter if you go up or down or how many turns you make, one day you come face to face with yourself again. This is my day. But I do want your help. Get some protection for Morgan and the kids."

"Already taken care of. Two of your security people were outside the suite. I sent them away and put two of my best people there."

"Then let's play shimmy."

I stopped at the table and gave a bow to Wan and another to Chow. "Gentlemen. Mr. Wan, I see you are wearing your lucky red robe."

I wondered what the old bastard had up his sleeve.

"So good of you to consent to play with me, Mr. Riordan. Frankly, I am tired of losing to Mr. Chow. I hope you are not as lucky as he is."

I took a seat at the table. "I suspect I used up all my luck for a two-bit jackpot a long time ago. But maybe the fickle Lady will smile on me again tonight."

"For my sake, I hope she will not smile too broadly in your direction. Shall we say a million a hand?"

A gasp escaped from the group of people who had gathered to watch the game. I laughed out loud. A million dollars a hand was better than playing for fingers and toes—and meatier parts when you ran out of those.

"If you want to get it over with fast, let's just cut the cards. The loser throws himself from the top of the hotel tower."

Wan clicked his tongue. "Patience, Mr. Riordan, patience. Giving pleasure—and inflicting pain—are not to be hurried if they are to achieve their goals."

"And what is your goal this evening, Mr. Wan?"

He cackled. "Everything you have, Mr. Riordan."

We were going to play shimmy for Forbidden City, that was the bottom line. The rest of the message was subliminal: We do it this way or we do it the Macao way. It goes without saying that Wan planned on winning. He was too smart a cookie to rely on luck when he was playing with his own money. I was sitting on a hundred million dollars of his and he wanted it back. Plus a pound of my flesh.

So what was the gimmick? This time it wasn't going to be something as clumsy as a card up the sleeve—no one ever accused Wan of being stupid. The table was the obvious candidate for hiding the gaff. I had examined it a long time ago for Wan, now it was time to examine it for myself.

"Good of Tommy to let us use his lucky table." I started poring over the table, with hands and eyes. Moody got down with me and did his own check.

"How's Tommy's wife?" I asked, just making conversation to fill in the void while we checked out the table. "Still stuck in Saigon?"

That produced an ugly grunt from Tommy Chow.

I took Moody aside after we struck out examining the table. "Tell security I want two cameras on the table at all times, and beam the images onto the big-screen TV in my suite. Tell Morgan I need to know what the bug in the play is."

"How she can tell?"

"She's almost as good as her old man was."

Almost. But not quite. And the "not quite" covered a lot of territory. Whatever Wan had done to put a bug in the play, it had to be first class, something he was sure would get by even me. And if it got by me, Morgan catching it would be a real long shot.

If it wasn't the table, it had to be something—or someone—else. The croupier and ladderman were the only people besides me and Wan who participated in the play. And the ladderman didn't touch anything; he was just there to make sure the rigid rules were observed.

I went over and whispered to him.

"Nick, if you ever see me tug my ear, like this," I pulled on my earlobe, "you do it, too."

"You want me to tug my ear?"

"Only if you see me do it."

The croupier handling the paddle and shuffling was a long-time employee from Halliday's. I nodded at him.

"Everything okay, Zack?" he asked.

"Everything's cool. Just give me a good shuffle."

"You'll have to talk to the machine." He jerked his head at the automatic shuffler.

Like everything else in the club, the electronic shuffler was state of the art. I hoped it worked better than the goddamn electronic toilets. The purpose of mechanical shufflers was twofold: to save the time it took for a dealer to shuffle the six decks that went into the shoe and to ensure a random shuffle. The decks of cards came out of their original packaging in suit and numerical order, but using an automatic shuffler instead of a croupier to get a true random shuffle didn't mean we were trying to give the sucker a break. The odds in favor of the house were based upon a random shuffle, the more random the shuffle, the more predictable the return.

Only two people were in a position to cheat: the croupier and Wan. They were the only ones handling the cards besides myself. I trusted the croupier, but that didn't mean anything. The kind of money that was at stake meant that anyone's price could be met.

The croupier opened each of the six decks of cards and fanned them to show that the decks were true before loading them into the automatic shuffler.

"I'd like to check the shoe," I told the croupier. I wanted to make sure there was no secret pocket in it.

"La sabot," the croupier said, grinning at his use of the French name for the shoe.

Wan did a cursory inspection of the shoe and the croupier passed it to me on his paddle.

"Just making sure we have an even playing board," I told Wan, and passed the shoe back to the croupier.

"As the player immediately to the croupier's right, I shall act as banker-dealer first," Wan said.

Each of us were given a hundred one-dollar chips.

"Each dollar chip is worth a million dollars," Wan said. "I thought you would enjoy the irony that the highest-stakes game of chemin de fer ever played is being done with dollar chips. Each coup will be a minimum million-dollar bet from each of us."

A coup was a hand of play. The chips could have been potato chips—their value was meaningless. We were playing for the casino. The player that ended the game with all the chips stacked in front of him won the casino.

I had to think about the rules, get them straight in my head. Like the play I observed between Wan and Chow years ago, we would not be playing Las Vegas baccarat, but European-style chemin de fer, what we used to call shimmy in the States. Each player was dealt two cards, facedown, one at a time. Like blackjack, the player must always play before the dealer. You couldn't bust your hand, but you could end up with a score of zero to nine. The objective was to get nine or close to it. That much was played almost exactly like Vegas baccarat, but unlike baccarat, which had a rigid rule for every play, in shimmy the player and banker-dealer had some optional moves that could make or break them. The player had to take a hit on four or less, stay on six or more, but had the discretion to stay or take a hit on five. Because the player had to go first, whether he took a hit or not revealed a lot about his hand and affected the optional play the dealer had. Sometimes the dealer had an option to take a hit or stay.

Playing shimmy was actually a more interesting game than Vegas baccarat because there was some modicum of decision making involved.

After the shuffle, I inserted an indicator card for the cut. The croupier cut the cards and put another indicator card near the end of the deck, loaded the shoe, burned three cards, and passed the shoe to Wan.

Wan dealt me a card, one to himself, another card to me, then another to himself. I lifted my cards to take a peek. Four and a three, for a total of seven—a good hand.

His face lit up. *"La grande,"* Wan announced.

He had a natural nine.

I had a terrible feeling that things were not going to go well for me.

———

Morgan watched the game on the large-screen TV in the suite. The connection to the security center divided the screen into four parts: a global view of the chemin de fer table and the surrounding area, an overhead of just the table and players, and a view of each player. Cameras mounted to the side could focus in on players' hands when they lifted the cards to check their values. She had an open telephone line to the security room and a supervisor ready to follow her instructions.

"Mommy, what's Daddy doing?" William asked.

"Just playing cards, sweetie."

Her eye followed the action, recalling what Con had taught her. Few girls sat on their daddy's lap and were shown how to stack a deck, spot a false cut, or catch a card pulled from the bottom before they were old enough to ride a bike. "Look for the bum moves," Con told her, "anything that just doesn't jive." But a good card mechanic rarely revealed himself with a suspicious move. Con taught her to think backward about cards: "Ask yourself what had to be done to get the hand. Most cheaters telegraph their moves, even by appearing overrelaxed."

"How's he doing it?" she asked herself. Wan didn't shuffle; he had to deal from a shoe. So how was he cheating? He maintained an impassive, stoic presence as he played, revealing nothing she could spot in his body language that telegraphed he was cheating.

"When shuffling is done or Wan deals, give me the shoe with camera angles from every direction," she told the security room supervisor. The cheating had to be done when the cards went into the shoe or came out. There was no other way it could happen. And Wan's long, wide sleeves were perfect to cover cheating. But she saw no false move as the cards were dealt. Wan came up with an eight, so close to a perfect nine, it was also called a "natural."

He was beating the hell out of Zack, winning eight straight hands. Mathematically, something was rotten. But what? And she wondered if she had her heart in finding out. She told herself she wanted Zack to win . . . but a voice inside her wasn't sure that's what she really wanted. What she really wanted wasn't Zack the dreamer who built the world's biggest casino, but a husband, a lover, and a father who wanted her and their children.

She realized that they had similar emotional backgrounds. She'd been raised with a brother and a father, but neither constituted a family. Con had treated her more like a prized possession than a daughter. He bragged about her and bought her expensive things, but didn't nurture her in a wholesome family environment. Not having a mother meant no one to run to when she had the fright of her first period, no one to talk to when she needed a training bra, when her hormones started playing hell with her emotions as she went into puberty. Con had never come to a meeting with a teacher, never took them on a picnic, or on a trip to an amusement park. Blank checks and a succession of nannies had not filled the gap.

She stared at the screen. Another deal: two cards facedown.

"Let's see Wan's hand," she told the control room. "And Zack's."

When they lifted their hands, Wan had a five and a two—seven. Hard to beat. Zack pulled a king and a three. Thirteen points, which gave him three, because face cards and ten counted as zero. Wan dealt him an eight. That gave him eleven, and since only the second number counted, he had a total of one. He had lost again.

I asked for a five-minute break to stretch my legs. From the looks of the crowd that had gathered, the game was also as popular as the fire-breathing roller coaster. My name buzzed from ear to ear in whispers. I expected to be asked for my autograph at any moment. "Give 'em hell, Zack," someone yelled. I smiled and waved back. I didn't know the guy from Adam. But I guess calling a celebrity like me by his first name made the guy feel important.

I called Morgan on the house phone, chuckling over the idea that I was now a celebrity.

"See anything yet?" I asked.

"You losing your shirt."

"I'll be down to my shorts soon if I don't figure out how Wan's cheating." I got the sounds of silence from the other end.

"How are the kids?" I didn't know what else to say.

"They're fine. If you're going to lose, do it quickly. We'll be leaving as soon as you're cleaned out."

She hung up on me. There were two things I knew I could count on with Morgan. When she was mad at me, she'd let me know. And when the chips were down, she'd back me up. And then pound me when I was back on my feet. I knew she'd be up there looking for the gimmick until the game was over, of that I was sure.

I poured a Jack Coke and moseyed back to the table. Mr. Wan was leaning back and smoking a cigar. I sat down and gave him a stare.

"You know, don't you, that they'd never let you run a casino in this town. If you ever got a controlling interest in a club, the gaming board would pull its license, pronto."

He waved the cigar at me. "I have no intention of running this casino. My old friend, Mr. Chow, will represent me in any necessary dealings."

"Fat chance on Chow getting a gaming license."

"Those are small hills to be climbed, Mr. Riordan. Right now I have to scale a mountain."

I saluted him with my drink. "You'll never see the summit, Wan, the altitude will be too much for you."

I was dealt two sevens, fourteen, which gave me four. The hit was a three, making my total seven. Not bad. Wan turned over an ace and a five, for a total of six. I won. The shoe passed to me.

I dealt myself a natural eight. Things were beginning to look up. I kibitzed as we played. If Wan was cheating, maybe keeping up a conversation might break his concentration and cause him to inadvertently expose his gimmick. Cheating and talking were like rubbing your stomach and patting your head at the same time.

"Hear anything more about Chenza?" I asked.

"Miss Troy, I understand, met an Arab prince in Tokyo and is now cohabiting with him in a sheikdom somewhere in the Persian Gulf."

"You can't keep a good woman down. Have you murdered anyone since you had Luís bumped off?"

Wan didn't flicker an eye.

"No one that didn't have it coming." He spoke with an American gangster's accent. And cackled.

I was doing pretty good, getting back my losses. The deal shifted to Wan. He turned to speak to Chow and knocked the shoe off the table. For a split second, I froze. So did the croupier and ladderman. But people in the crowd were more vocal. I heard everything from gasps of surprise to four-letter words. The word *cheating* seemed to be a popular response to the move.

I looked back at the peanut gallery and got thumbs up and muttered sympathies. "Don't take that shit," someone yelled.

"So sorry," Mr. Wan said.

"Everyone get up and stand back from the table," the ladderman said. "The croupier will retrieve the shoe and cards."

I went and got another drink and Moody handed me the phone.

"If that was an accident, I'll kiss your feet," Morgan said.

"We'll have a new deck, new shoe, and I'll check them out."

"It doesn't make sense. I can hear Dad yelling at me from the grave."

I knew what she meant. My internal Geiger counter was screaming.

Back at the table I rejected the six decks of cards the croupier pulled out.

"Mr. Wan, to make sure we use clean decks, you can pick the decks from our supply cabinet in the gaming area. And a new shoe."

He cackled again. I hated that sound.

"No need. Choose any decks, any *sabot*."

I sent Moody for six fresh decks and a shoe and gave the cards to the croupier. While the automatic shuffler was going, I examined the new shoe and passed it to Wan. He brushed it aside. He seemed to be greatly amused at my precautions.

"Sorry to be so cautious, Mr. Wan, but I want to make sure you get a fair break. I know how important this match must be to you."

"Oh, no, no, Mr. Riordan, you are incorrect. This match is not of great import to me. You see, I am just here because of money. You have mine and I want it back. You are here because of pride. If you lose, your fall will be much greater than mine had I proved the loser."

"You know, ever since I met you, you've been giving me those cute little Oriental pearls of wisdom. How about if you shove the next one up your ass."

"Mr. Riordan, there is no necessity for you to be uncivilized."

"You're right, but I was just thinking about A-Ma. It's your deal. Hopefully, you'll get what's coming to you during this game and I won't have to wait for you to burn in hell."

"I did not cause the death of A-Ma. For some people, living is more painful than dying."

He won again. And again. What luck the bastard was having.

"You know, of course, that you will never really win," I said. "I don't give a damn how this game goes. I'd sooner burn the place down before I'd let you have it."

He won again. He never seemed to deal himself anything less than a six-point count.

Moody gave me a grim look. He bent down and whispered, "You can call this stupid match off anytime."

"Too late. I'm down millions."

My voice carried loud enough so Wan caught the gist of what I said. "Yes, it is too late."

"There's an old American expression you can add to your Eastern pearls: 'Don't count your chickens before they hatch'."

I finally won a hand. The tension was crawling up my back and tying the muscles in my neck. I leaned back and stretched, staring up at the mirrored ceiling. I froze in mid-stretch as I saw a familiar face in the group of onlookers behind the cordoned-off playing zone. It gave me a hell of a jolt.

Windell.

He grinned at me, exposing the gap between the front teeth my fist had left. He had false teeth there last time I saw him, and I got the hint—it was payback time for me busting his chops and sending him off to jail.

"Taking five." I got up from the table and went over to the drink table and poured myself another Jack Coke. Windell. Going for the money, of course, that's what Windell always did. And Forbidden City was the biggest jackpot in the world.

Windell. Wan. There had to be a connection. A gimmick. It all added up. But what it totaled was still beyond me.

The house phone rang. Moody answered it and gave it to me.

"What's going on?" Morgan asked.

"Windell's here."

"Windell? Your computer nerd buddy? Jesus, do you think he'd help Wan?"

"Do chickens have lips? Windell would sell his mother for a nickel jackpot. Besides, he doesn't cheat for the money. He cheats to cheat."

"But Wan wouldn't be stupid enough—"

"To let Windell parade through here? You're right, but Windell's dumb enough to do it. You can always trust Windell to screw you— and shoot himself in the foot doing it. Don't you remember how your old man caught on to my act?"

"What are you going to do?"

"Punt."

"Punt?"

"It's what you do when it's fourth down and your back is to the wall."

I returned to the table. As I sat down, it suddenly struck me. It was just a process of elimination. I had clued in on every possible way that the gimmick could be done, from the cards, croupier, shoe, and Wan. I left out just one thing, and so that had to be it.

The croupier passed me the deck. As I reached for it, I turned to say something to Moody and "accidentally" pushed the shoe off the table.

"Hell, sorry about that. We'll need new decks and a new shuffle."

Wan's eyes immediately went to the automatic shuffler and back to me. It was the first tipoff that he had given.

The shuffler had to be the gimmick, of course. Windell had bugged it so it stacked the deck—but only when fresh decks were used. Fresh decks came in a set order of suits and value. Windell would have bugged the shuffler based on that order, and maybe only for the first dozen or so hands, because that's how Wan was winning, hand after hand after shuffling fresh decks for about ten of fifteen hands, and then the play started evening out between us.

That's why he dropped the shoe, to force a new shuffle and new decks when it was his turn to deal. Now it was my deal—and I had fresh decks. I had no idea how Windell could bug a shuffler. But if it could be done, that perverted twerp would be the one who could do it. They say the good Lord acts in mysterious ways. So does electronics.

I dealt myself a natural nine first time out the gate. I grinned at Wan. "I guess Lady Luck is finally turning my way. Want to get this over quick? How about we play one hand for table stakes? Winner take all."

He nodded. "That will be satisfactory."

That surprised the hell out of me.

"You have miscalculated me, Mr. Riordan. To your detriment, you have failed to prepare yourself for the battle."

"Funny thing, Mr. Wan, I did get around to reading Sun Tzu, but I'm finding out that what I learned from a couple of old-time Nevada gambling men comes in more handy than your ancient general's advice."

"You may have read Sun Tzu, but like many of your culture, you have failed to understand what he is saying, even after I pointed you in the correct direction."

"Maybe I'm a little dense." I dealt the cards. Wan left his sitting untouched, as I did mine. "Maybe you can tell me how Sun Tzu is going to give you a winning hand."

He cackled, goddamn, just like a hen. The sound was like fingernails on a blackboard.

"You still do not understand, Mr. Riordan. I told you that Sun Tzu taught that one must take from the enemy that which the enemy holds dearest."

"And we'll know if you succeeded when we turn the cards over."

He shook his head and grinned, toothy, a little foolishly, like he was enjoying a private joke. Then the smile went off his face and I met those dark pools where his eyes belonged.

"You still do not comprehend, Mr. Riordan. I have already won. I have taken what you hold dearest."

I repeated his words in my mind: *I have taken what you hold dearest.* Hold dearest. The phrase vibrated between my ears. Forbidden City was everything I had. I closed my eyes. I suddenly realized what a fool I was. I had been wrong. My heart began racing.

Moody handed me the phone. I didn't even hear it ring.

"Zack. *Zack!*" Morgan screamed.

The line went dead. I held the phone to my ear, listening to the dial tone. I was unable to move, to even flinch, my spine was cold at the bone. I lifted my head to look up at Moody. A little twinge of guilt swept across his face. And shame. Then his features turned mean. I should have seen it coming. Moody always had his hand out. Everything he did for me cost an arm and a leg and he wanted more. He had not wanted to get paid for nailing Ricketts; he wanted to get rich. I turned him down and Wan had met his price. The two men he sent to guard Morgan and the kids had obviously kidnapped them.

I handed him back the phone. "You're dead," I whispered.

"Fuck you," Moody said.

I took a deep breath and let it out slowly. The croupier and ladderman both stared at me.

"Zack—" the croupier said. His hand was on the security call buzzer.

"Don't touch it," I said.

I looked up at the ladderman and pulled my right ear.

My cards were still facedown in front of me. I wondered where they had taken Morgan and the kids. They couldn't have had much time to get them out of the place. Most likely they were still in the casino. If they touched her or the kids . . .

I shook my head at Wan. "No, I'm afraid your Chinese general failed you on this one. I won't let you win this way. I'm going to play my cards the way I want to. When I get a call and know they're safely out on the street, I'll play my cards."

"And how will you play the cards?" Wan asked.

Before I could reply, four men shoved through the crowd and stepped into the baccarat area. Anthony DeCicco was right behind them.

The Chinese may have had thousands of years to refine the triads and tongs into killers, but the Mafia made up for it by being just plain innovatively brutal. Wan's two triad gangsters looked like rabbits to these four sheep-killing dogs.

"Like I said, I'll pay the cards the way I want to," I told Wan. My voice was low, not because I was trying to keep my voice down, but because I was so angry, I had to control myself from leaping across the table and ripping out Wan's throat.

Wan and I stared at each other. Yeah, he was one smart son of a bitch. I had to run to keep up with him and make up for some of it by being just plain stubborn. I kept up a tough front, but my heart was still pounding. The fuckers had my wife and kids. My anger was turning black and ugly. I gripped the table with both hands. I wanted to get up and kill these bastards.

Wan was no fool, he read the murder in my face. His death.

"You have a call to make," I said.

He nodded to Moody. Moody got back on the phone. I could see that the ex-homicide dick had shrunk a little at the sight of DeCicco and the thugs. He had been around the town long enough to know DeCicco was connected.

No clock was in sight and I didn't look at my watch. After Moody hung up, the seconds ticked off in my mind. The tension built up around the baccarat area. The croupier, the ladderman, no one knew what was going on, but they could feel the tension filling the area like a Miami heat wave. The people in the audience were quiet, too. I looked back to catch Windell's eye. He saw the rage in my eyes and ran, shoving his way through the crowd.

The phone rang. I didn't flinch but my heart nearly jumped out of my chest. Moody listened and handed the phone to me.

"Zack, we're on the street. We're safe. I'm not leaving, Zack. I want us to be a family, a real family, and I want the kids to know their father."

A sudden longing came into me, one that I never felt before.

"So do I," I said softly.

I handed Moody back the phone. He was looking at DeCicco's boys, and not liking the looks he got back. I grinned at him. With my lips, not my eyes.

"You look a little pale, Moody, something you ate?"

I lifted up my cards and took a peek. A queen and a nine—a natural nine. Moody was behind me. I knew he saw the cards when I heard the disappointed grunt. Like someone had punched him.

I met Wan's eyes again. His lids had come down, half shading the bottomless black pits. *Taking what you hold dearest.* The words kind of waltzed around my head, doing a little dance. Smart bastard. He had seen what I almost didn't see myself. What I had almost lost. I had been so preoccupied with the club, I lost sight of what was important in my life. I had lost Betty and A-Ma. I loved both of them, but it was Morgan and the kids that I wanted in my life. I wanted the same thing Morgan wanted—a family.

I threw the cards across the table, facedown.

"You win."

Wan gaped. I laughed. I had finally broken through that stoic mask.

"By the way, meet Mr. DeCicco, the club's new general manager. He represents some out-of-town interests who have bought the club."

"Bought the club?" Wan stared down at the shimmy table like the words had fallen there and he needed to examine them.

"Yeah, I sold my interest, Mr. Wan. You know how it is, casinos are so much trouble nowadays, so much paperwork, all those government regulations and snoops. I'm getting away from the business . . . for my health."

"My money—"

"Oh yeah, congratulations, you won whatever interest I still have in the casino. Mr. DeCicco will be discussing that situation with you."

I got up to walk away and brushed against Moody.

"Sorry, pal," Moody said.

I turned, cocking my fist, and went straight across his jaw, throwing my shoulder into it, giving it everything I had. I heard his teeth shatter as his mouth slammed shut. He went backward, spraying blood. I wasn't finished with him. I could've given him more, but my hand hurt like hell.

I left the club, walked out the front doors, out the gate beneath the Great Wall, and across the drawbridge. Behind me the Red Dragon roller coaster came around again, breathing fire.

I could never have won by myself with Wan because he was a one-hundred-percenter. He would go all the way to win, no matter what it took. In my own mind, I think I was tougher than Wan in most ways, maybe even smarter, but he was willing to go all the way. All the way meant doing anything to win. He would think nothing of sending back my wife and kids in pieces.

Sitting there at the shimmy table, my family in one hand, the club in the other, a casino didn't seem that important to me. Hell, there were lots of other casinos. I knew how to make money. Nothing was impossible. You just did it. You don't stop living. You go on to bigger and better things.

I walked outside to the Strip. A strange thought hit me and I started laughing. Maybe I had been wrong all this time. Maybe God didn't live on the Strip. Maybe the devil did.

A horn honked and a taxi pulled up to the curb alongside me. The back door opened and Morgan got out.

"I stopped a squad car to send them back to the club to get you. They told me you left. They said you walked away from a natural nine."

"I knew a rumor like that would start. Must be one of those urban legends, alien rape and that sort of thing. I had snake eyes."

Tears welled in her eyes. "You didn't have to do it. I told you we were safe."

"I did it because I wanted to do it. Besides, I'm tired of that place."

"What about Wan—"

"You might as well start using the past tense when referring to him. There's a guy name Vinnie the Ax who hates having partners. I suspect Mr. Wan will soon be coyote bait."

"You let gangsters take over your dream?"

"No, I just let them borrow it. I sold Vinnie the joint in return for him paying off the notes to Halliday's. We own the old club free and clear. The gaming commission and feds will turn DeCicco inside out and revoke the license in a year. By then, Vinnie will have laundered a billion bucks and be smiling. He'll sell me back the place if I want it, but I don't know, with the new place and all . . ."

"New place?"

"Didn't I tell you? I'm going to build a bigger and better club. I already know exactly how I'm going to do it, with volcanos exploding, lava pouring, and—and, hey, knights in shining armor, a medieval castle, maybe even a moat full of pirate ships—"

"How many places are you going to build?"

I looked up and down the Strip.

"How many do you think it will hold?"

Then she was in my arms and held me tight.

"Zack, promise me you won't ever leave me."

"I promise."

We held each other as lovers long apart. We must have put some real heat out because the cars up and down the Strip started honking their horns and yelling out cat calls. I didn't care.

I finally figured out what was important to me.